imperfect
ideal

SELECTED AND EDITED BY
Denise Ahlquist, Louise Galpine, and Donald H. Whitfield

CONTRIBUTORS
Nancy Carr
Steven Craig
Kelsey Crick
Mary Klein
Dylan Nelson
Tom Pilcher
Devin Ross
Audrey Schlofner
Josh Sniegowski
Jamie Spagnola
Samantha Stankowicz
Mary Williams

imperfect
ideal

utopian
and
dystopian
visions

THE GREAT BOOKS FOUNDATION

A nonprofit educational organization

Published and distributed by

THE GREAT BOOKS FOUNDATION
A nonprofit educational organization

35 E. Wacker Drive, Suite 400
Chicago, IL 60601
www.greatbooks.org

Shared Inquiry™ is a trademark of the Great Books Foundation. The contents of this publication include proprietary trademarks and original materials and may be used or quoted only with permission and appropriate credit to the Foundation.

First printing
9 8 7 6 5 4 3 2 1

Library of Congress Cataloging-in-Publication Data

Imperfect ideal : utopia and dystopian visions / selected and edited by Denise Ahlquist,
    Louise Galpine, and Donald H. Whitfield.
        pages cm
        ISBN 978-1-939014-20-7 (pbk. : alk. paper) — ISBN 978-1-939014-21-4 (ebook)
        1. Utopias. 2. Dystopias. I. Ahlquist, Denise. II. Galpine, Louise. III. Whitfield,
    Donald H.
        HX806.I57 2015
        335'.02—dc23
                                                                            2015002951

About the Great Books Foundation

The Great Books Foundation is an independent nonprofit educational organization that provides opportunities for people of all ages to become more reflective, critical thinkers and readers through Shared Inquiry™ discussion of written works and ideas of enduring value.

The Great Books Foundation was established in 1947 to promote liberal education for the general public. In 1962, the Foundation extended its mission to children with the introduction of Junior Great Books.® Since its inception, the Foundation has helped thousands of people throughout the United States and in other countries begin their own discussion groups in schools, libraries, and community centers. Today, Great Books instructors conduct hundreds of workshops each year, in which educators and parents learn to lead Shared Inquiry discussion.

Contents

Preface

Through the ages, people have looked at the communities in which they lived, with all their virtues and flaws, and dreamed of how they could be perfected. Their proposals have taken many forms but what they have in common is confidence in the ability of human beings to intervene in the headlong rush of history and implement plans to reorganize and reorient existing societies for the purpose of securing the well-being of all their citizens. In sixteenth-century England, Thomas More published his version of a plan for a perfect society and coined the term "Utopia." Ever since, this name has attached itself to the wide range of proposals, both those preceding and following More, that hold out visions of communities more just, more rational, and more perfect, according to the author's lights, than any of those that exist.

But a utopian solution to society's ills carries with it the risk that fallible human beings are limited in their ability to foresee the consequences of plans for the radical reorganization of society. Remedies for the perceived flaws of complex communities, no matter how benign in principle and well-intentioned, may result in horrific conditions that far exceed the abuses of the pre-utopian world. In recent years, many works of literature have portrayed these malign consequences and given rise to the term "dystopian" to describe such worlds.

The selections in *Imperfect Ideal* represent some of these utopian and dystopian visions and challenge readers to address many of the perennial questions regarding how human society should be structured and governed and what kinds of communities are most conducive to human fulfillment, both privately and in the civic arena. *Imperfect Ideal* is organized into six sections, each containing selections that are thematically related, as described in the introduction to each section. Individual readers and discussion groups will find that reading and talking about the selections in the sections in relation to each other will lead to a more stimulating and rewarding experience.

About Shared Inquiry

A Shared Inquiry™ discussion begins when the leader of the discussion group poses an interpretive question to participants about the meaning of a reading selection. The question is substantial enough that no single answer can resolve it. Instead, several answers—even answers that are in conflict—may be valid. In effect, the leader is telling the group: "Here is a problem of meaning that seems important. Let's try to resolve it."

From that moment on, participants are free to offer answers and opinions to the group, to request clarification of points, and to raise objections to the remarks of other participants. They also discuss specific passages in the selection that bear on the interpretive question and compare their differing ideas about what these passages mean. The leader, meanwhile, asks additional questions, clarifying and expanding the interpretive question and helping group members arrive at more cogent answers. All participants don't have to agree with all of the answers—each person can decide which answer seems most convincing. This process is called Shared Inquiry.

In Shared Inquiry discussion, three kinds of questions can be raised about a reading selection: factual questions, interpretative questions, and evaluative questions. Interpretation is central to a Shared Inquiry discussion but factual questions can bring to light evidence in support of interpretations and can clear up misunderstandings. On the other hand, evaluative questions invite participants to compare the experiences and opinions of an author with their own and can introduce a personal dimension into the discussion.

The following guidelines will help keep the conversation focused on the text and assure all the participants a voice:

1. **Read the selection carefully before participating in the discussion.** This ensures that all participants are equally prepared to talk about the ideas in the reading.

2. **Discuss the ideas in the selection, and try to understand them fully.** Reflecting as individuals and as a group on what the author says makes the exploration of both the selection and related issues that will come up in the discussion more rewarding.

3. **Support interpretations of what the author says with evidence from the reading, along with insights from personal experience.** This provides focus for the group on the selection that everyone has read and builds a strong foundation for discussing related issues.

4. **Listen to other participants and respond to them directly.** Shared Inquiry is about the give and take of ideas, the willingness to listen to others and talk with them respectfully. Directing your comments and questions to other group members, not always to the leader, will make the discussion livelier and more dynamic.

5. **Expect the leader to mainly ask questions.** Effective leaders help participants develop their own ideas, with everyone gaining a new understanding in the process. When participants hang back and wait for the leader to suggest answers, discussion tends to falter.

How to Use This Book

The twenty-three readings in *Imperfect Ideal: Utopian and Dystopian Visions* were chosen for their ability to raise questions and provoke stimulating discussion about the aims and results of planned societies around the world. In order for discussions to be most rewarding, it is strongly recommended that a significant amount of time be spent coming to an understanding of what the author is saying, by continually returning to the selection during the discussion. Doing so will provide a strong central focus for whatever personal accounts participants introduce into the conversation, as they evaluate the author's ideas in light of their own experiences.

To help prompt lively discussion, each small group of selections is preceded by an introduction giving brief background about the authors and introducing some of the topics explored. Following each selection is a set of discussion questions to encourage exploration of the author's ideas. "Questions for Discussion" address the meaning of the selection itself. They are organized into clusters containing a main question (in boldface) and some related questions below. "For Further Reflection" questions address general issues related to the selection; these questions are broader and invite discussion of personal insights and opinions. Addressing both kinds of questions during a discussion, without tipping the balance heavily toward one or the other, will make for a more satisfying experience that not only engages with each author's distinctive voice, but also allows for participants in the group to contribute their insights in their own individual way.

What Else Belongs?

From the first dreams of ideal communities to contemporary visions of perfected societies, utopian projections have consistently prompted dissent and challenge as well as enthusiastic support. A framework for an improved society has a different appeal to different people, and the conflicting responses to such plans suggest that no utopia may ever be universally welcomed. Is disagreement then inherent to utopian thought? Does every utopia contain within it the seeds of another's dystopia? The selections in this section consider some of the inner oppositions found in utopian thinking, from classical times to the modern day.

In "The Ones Who Walk Away from Omelas" (1973), American author **Ursula K. Le Guin** (1929–) depicts a perfectly functioning society, complete with festivals, games, and happy citizens, which is undermined by the revelation of the conditions necessary for its main-tenance. In this utilitarian construct, the comfort of many is predicated upon the misery of the few. How the people of Omelas respond to this ethical dilemma highlights a tension in other planned societies. Often the experience of social benefits is unequal. Where do those who reject this disparity go? To what alternative do they aspire?

Behind many utopian and dystopian narratives lies the work of the English statesman **Sir Thomas More** (1478–1535), a prominent figure at the court of Henry VIII. It was More who coined the term "utopia," punning on the Greek *eu-topos* meaning "good place" and *ou-topos* meaning "no place." The perfect place he describes, the island state of Utopia, is in fact no place at all—it cannot exist. Even in the text that gives its name to this entire genre, the author implies that utopia is unobtainable and glosses his proto-communist vision with a satirical deflating of the island state's attributes. Was More sincere in his depiction of a humanist, communal utopia, or does his narrator figure, who listens and responds to his interlocutor's description of Utopia, operate as a distancing strategy to throw into relief the author's skepticism?

The poem "Utopia" (1976), by the Polish poet **Wislawa Szymborska** (1923–2012), clearly references the island imagery More set out in his earlier text. Initially positive, Szymborska waits until the close of the poem to reveal an unpalatable reality—the island is empty and all footprints lead away from it and into "unfathomable life." What then is her view of utopia? Are people forced away or do they choose to leave? Is life without certainty and perfection ultimately more appealing? Does utopia, in its purest form, exist only in the abstract, before any human implementation?

In Book 18 of the *Iliad*, the ancient Greek poet **Homer** depicts the anguish of Thetis, who knows that her son, Achilles, will shortly be killed in battle. Thetis commissions Hephaestus to fashion a fine shield for Achilles, and the excerpt here describes the imagery with which the shield is adorned. The shield portrays different strata of an idealized and well-ordered society, although an element of conflict does prefigure the death of Achilles. Thousands of years later, British poet **W. H. Auden** (1907–1973) overturns the harmonious imagery of the shield in his poem "The Shield of Achilles" (1955). Writing shortly after World War II, with the Cold War gathering pace, Auden reimagines Achilles's shield to reflect the society around him—corrupt, violent, and inhumane. Again the duality of the utopian proposition is highlighted, as Auden probes beneath an ordered surface to uncover a more dubious vision of society.

Proposals of planned societies with utopian implications are often more complex than they first appear. Internal conflict, challenge, and contradiction are central issues in many utopian texts. To what extent does utopia contain within it the seeds of dystopia? And can utopia ever exist without also fostering dystopia?

The Ones Who Walk Away from Omelas

Ursula K. Le Guin

With a clamor of bells that set the swallows soaring, the Festival of Summer came to the city Omelas, bright-towered by the sea. The rigging of the boats in harbor sparkled with flags. In the streets between houses with red roofs and painted walls, between old moss-grown gardens and under avenues of trees, past great parks and public buildings, processions moved. Some were decorous: old people in long stiff robes of mauve and grey, grave master workmen, quiet, merry women carrying their babies and chatting as they walked. In other streets the music beat faster, a shimmering of gong and tambourine, and the people went dancing, the procession was a dance. Children dodged in and out, their high calls rising like the swallows' crossing flights over the music and the singing. All the processions wound toward the north side of the city, where on the great water-meadow called the Green Fields boys and girls, naked in the bright air, with mud-stained feet and ankles and long, lithe arms, exercised their restive horses before the race. The horses wore no gear at all but a halter without bit. Their manes were braided with streamers of silver, gold, and green. They flared their nostrils and pranced and boasted to one another; they were vastly excited, the horse being the only animal who has adopted our ceremonies as his own. Far off to the north and west the mountains stood up half encircling Omelas on her bay. The air of morning was so clear that the snow still crowning the Eighteen Peaks burned with white-gold fire across the miles of sunlit air, under the dark blue of the sky. There was just enough wind to make the banners that marked the racecourse snap and flutter now and then. In the silence of the broad green meadows one could hear the music winding through the city streets, farther and nearer and ever approaching, a cheerful faint sweetness of the air that from time to time trembled and gathered together and broke out into the great joyous clanging of the bells.

Joyous! How is one to tell about joy? How describe the citizens of Omelas?

They were not simple folk, you see, though they were happy. But we do not say the words of cheer much anymore. All smiles have become archaic. Given a description such as this one tends to make certain assumptions. Given a description such as this one tends to look next for the King, mounted on a splendid stallion and surrounded by his noble knights, or perhaps in a golden litter borne by great-muscled slaves. But there was no king. They did not use swords, or keep slaves. They were not barbarians. I do not know the rules and laws of their society, but I suspect that they were singularly few. As they did without monarchy and slavery, so they also got on without the stock exchange, the advertisement, the secret police, and the bomb. Yet I repeat that these were not simple folk, not dulcet shepherds, noble savages, bland utopians. They were not less complex than us. The trouble is that we have a bad habit, encouraged by pedants and sophisticates, of considering happiness as something rather stupid. Only pain is intellectual, only evil interesting. This is the treason of the artist: a refusal to admit the banality of evil and the terrible boredom of pain. If you can't lick 'em, join 'em. If it hurts, repeat it. But to praise despair is to condemn delight, to embrace violence is to lose hold of everything else. We have almost lost hold; we can no longer describe a happy man, nor make any celebration of joy. How can I tell you about the people of Omelas? They were not naive and happy children—though their children were, in fact, happy. They were mature, intelligent, passionate adults whose lives were not wretched. O miracle! But I wish I could describe it better. I wish I could convince you. Omelas sounds in my words like a city in a fairy tale, long ago and far away, once upon a time. Perhaps it would be best if you imagine it as your own fancy bids, assuming it will rise to the occasion, for certainly I cannot suit you all. For instance, how about technology? I think that there would be no cars or helicopters in and above the streets; this follows from the fact that the people of Omelas are happy people. Happiness is based on a just discrimination of what is necessary, what is neither necessary nor destructive, and what is destructive. In the middle category, however—that of the unnecessary but undestructive, that of comfort, luxury, exuberance, etc.—they could perfectly well have central heating, subway trains, washing machines, and all kinds of marvelous devices not yet invented here, floating light sources, fuelless power, a cure for the common cold. Or they could have none of that: it doesn't matter. As you like it. I incline to think that people from towns up and down the coast have been coming in to Omelas during the last days before the Festival on very fast little trains and double-decked trams, and that the train station of Omelas is actually the handsomest building in town, though plainer than the magnificent Farmers' Market. But even granted trains, I fear that Omelas so far strikes some of you as goody-goody. Smiles, bells, parades, horses, bleh. If so, please add an orgy. If an orgy would help, don't hesitate. Let us not, however, have temples from which issue beautiful nude priests and priestesses already half in ecstasy and ready to copulate with any man or woman, lover or stranger, who desires union with the deep godhead of the blood, although that was my first idea. But really it would be better not to have any temples in Omelas—at least, not manned temples. Religion yes, clergy no. Surely the beautiful nudes can just wander about, offering themselves like divine soufflés to the hunger of the needy and the rapture of the flesh. Let them join the processions. Let tambourines be struck above the copulations, and the glory of desire be proclaimed upon the gongs, and (a not unimportant point) let the offspring of these delightful rituals be beloved and looked after by all. One thing I know there is none of in Omelas is guilt. But what else should there be? I thought at first there were no drugs, but that is puritanical. For those who like it, the faint insistent sweetness of *drooz* may perfume the ways of the city, *drooz* which first brings a great lightness and brilliance to the mind and limbs, and then after some hours a dreamy languor, and wonderful visions at last of the very arcana and inmost secrets of the Universe, as well as exciting the pleasure of sex beyond all belief; and it is not habit forming. For more modest tastes I think there ought to be beer. What else, what else belongs in the joyous city? The sense of victory, surely, the celebration of courage. But as we did without clergy, let us do without soldiers. The joy built upon successful slaughter is not the right kind of joy; it will not do; it is fearful and it is trivial. A boundless and generous contentment, a magnanimous triumph felt not against some outer enemy but in communion with the finest and fairest in the souls of all men everywhere and the splendor of the world's summer: this is what swells the hearts of the people of Omelas, and the victory they celebrate is that of life. I really don't think many of them need to take *drooz*.

Most of the processions have reached the Green Fields by now. A marvelous smell of cooking goes forth from the red and blue tents of the provisioners. The faces of small children are amiably sticky; in the benign grey beard of a man a couple of crumbs of rich pastry are entangled. The youths and girls have mounted their horses and are beginning to group around the starting line of the course. An old woman, small, fat, and laughing, is passing out flowers from a basket, and tall young men wear her flowers in their shining hair. A child of nine or ten sits at the edge of the crowd, alone, playing on a wooden flute. People pause to listen, and they smile, but they do not speak to him, for he never ceases playing and never sees them, his dark eyes wholly rapt in the sweet, thin magic of the tune.

He finishes, and slowly lowers his hands holding the wooden flute.

As if that little private silence were the signal, all at once a trumpet sounds from the pavilion near the starting line: imperious, melancholy, piercing. The horses rear on their slender legs, and some of them neigh in answer. Sober-faced, the young riders stroke the horses' necks and soothe them, whispering, "Quiet, quiet, there my beauty, my hope. . . ." They begin to form in rank along the starting line. The crowds along the racecourse are like a field of grass and flowers in the wind. The Festival of Summer has begun.

Do you believe? Do you accept the festival, the city, the joy? No? Then let me describe one more thing.

In a basement under one of the beautiful public buildings of Omelas, or perhaps in the cellar of one of its spacious private homes, there is a room. It has one locked door, and no window. A little light seeps in dustily between cracks in the boards, secondhand from a cobwebbed window somewhere across the cellar. In one corner of the little room a couple of mops, with stiff, clotted, foul-smelling heads, stand near a rusty bucket. The floor is dirt, a little damp to the touch, as cellar dirt usually is. The room is about three paces long and two wide: a mere broom closet or disused tool room. In the room a child is sitting. It could be a boy or a girl. It looks about six, but actually is nearly ten. It is feeble-minded. Perhaps it was born defective, or perhaps it has become imbecile through fear, malnutrition, and neglect. It picks its nose and occasionally fumbles vaguely with its toes or genitals, as it sits hunched in the corner farthest from the bucket and the two mops. It is afraid of the mops. It finds them horrible. It shuts its eyes, but it knows the mops are still standing there; and the door is locked; and nobody will come. The door is always locked; and nobody ever comes, except that sometimes—the child has no understanding of time or interval—sometimes the door rattles terribly and opens, and a person, or several people, are there. One of them may come in and kick the child to make it stand up. The others never come close, but peer in at it with frightened, disgusted eyes. The food bowl and the water jug are hastily filled, the door is locked, the eyes disappear. The people at the door never say anything, but the child, who has not always lived in the tool room, and can remember sunlight and its mother's voice, sometimes speaks. "I will be good," it says. "Please let me out. I will be good!" They never answer. The child used to scream for help at night, and cry a good deal, but now it only makes a kind of whining, "eh-haa, eh-haa," and it speaks less and less often. It is so thin there are no calves to its legs; its belly protrudes; it lives on a half-bowl of corn meal and grease a day. It is naked. Its buttocks and thighs are a mass of festered sores, as it sits in its own excrement continually.

They all know it is there, all the people of Omelas. Some of them have come to see it, others are content merely to know it is there. They all know that it has to be there. Some of them understand why, and some do not, but they all know that their happiness, the beauty of their city, the tenderness of their friendships, the health of their children, the wisdom of their scholars, the skill of their makers, even the abundance of their harvest and the kindly weathers of their skies, depend wholly on this child's abominable misery.

This is usually explained to children when they are between eight and twelve, whenever they seem capable of understanding; and most of those who come to see the child are young people, though often enough an adult comes, or comes back, to see the child. No matter how well the matter has been explained to them, these young spectators are always shocked and sickened at the sight. They feel disgust, which they had thought themselves superior to. They feel anger, outrage, impotence, despite all the explanations. They would like to do something for the child. But there is nothing they can do. If the child were brought up into the sunlight out of that vile place, if it were cleaned and fed and comforted, that would be a good thing, indeed; but if it were done, in that day and hour all the prosperity and beauty and delight of Omelas would wither and be destroyed. Those are the terms. To exchange all the goodness and grace of every life in Omelas for that single, small improvement: to throw away the happiness of thousands for the chance of the happiness of one: that would be to let guilt within the walls indeed.

The terms are strict and absolute; there may not even be a kind word spoken to the child.

Often the young people go home in tears, or in a tearless rage, when they have seen the child and faced this terrible paradox. They may brood over it for weeks or years. But as time goes on they begin to realize that even if the child could be released, it would not get much good of its freedom: a little vague pleasure of warmth and food, no doubt, but little more. It is too degraded and imbecile to know any real joy. It has been afraid too long ever to be free of fear. Its habits are too uncouth for it to respond to humane treatment. Indeed, after so long it would probably be wretched without walls about it to protect it, and darkness for its eyes, and its own excrement to sit in. Their tears at the bitter injustice dry when they begin to perceive the terrible justice of reality, and to accept it. Yet it is their tears and anger, the trying of their generosity and the acceptance of their helplessness, which are perhaps the true source of the splendor of their lives. Theirs is no vapid, irresponsible happiness. They know that they, like the child, are not free. They know compassion. It is the existence of the child, and their knowledge of its existence, that makes possible the nobility of their architecture, the poignancy of their music, the profundity of their science. It is because of the child that they are so gentle with children. They know that if the wretched one were not there snivelling in the dark, the other one, the flute player, could make no joyful music as the young riders line up in their beauty for the race in the sunlight of the first morning of summer.

Now do you believe in them? Are they not more credible? But there is one more thing to tell, and this is quite incredible.

At times one of the adolescent girls or boys who go to see the child does not go home to weep or rage, does not, in fact, go home at all. Sometimes also a man or woman much older falls silent for a day or two, and then leaves home. These people go out into the street, and walk down the street alone. They keep walking, and walk straight out of the city of Omelas, through the beautiful gates. They keep walking across the farmlands of Omelas. Each one goes alone, youth or girl, man or woman. Night falls; the traveler must pass down village streets, between the houses with yellow-lit windows, and on out into the darkness of the fields. Each alone, they go west or north, toward the mountains. They go on. They leave Omelas, they walk ahead into the darkness, and they do not come back. The place they go toward is a place even less imaginable to most of us than the city of happiness. I cannot describe it at all. It is possible that it does not exist. But they seem to know where they are going, the ones who walk away from Omelas.

QUESTIONS FOR DISCUSSION

Why do the majority of people in Omelas stay, despite knowing of the child's continuing misery?

1. Why are we told the people of Omelas are not "bland utopians"? (6)

2. Why are the young people who go to see the child "always shocked and sickened at the sight," no matter how well things have been explained to them beforehand? (10)

3. Why do most young people over time accept the "terrible justice of reality" despite their initial outrage? (10)

4. Why is "the acceptance of their helplessness" the "true source of the splendor of their lives" for those who stay? (10)

Why does the narrator say it is "quite incredible" that some people walk away from Omelas? (11)

1. Why does the narrator tell us that the people of Omelas were "mature, intelligent, passionate adults whose lives were not wretched"? (6)

2. Why does the narrator say it would perhaps be best if each reader imagined Omelas "as your own fancy bids"? (6)

3. Why do the people who leave say nothing about why they are going, and walk away alone?

4. Why does the narrator tell us that the place those who leave are going toward may not exist? (11)

FOR FURTHER REFLECTION

1. Do you think the people who leave are acting in vain or making a difference?

2. What would a society better than "the city of happiness" look like?

3. If our society had a better sense of "what is necessary, what is neither necessary nor destructive, and what is destructive," what social structures or practices would change?

Utopia

(selection)

Thomas More

But let's get back to their social organization. Each household, as I said, comes under the authority of the oldest male. Wives are subordinate to their husbands, children to their parents, and younger people generally to their elders. Every town is divided into four districts of equal size, each with its own shopping center in the middle of it. There the products of every household are collected in warehouses, and then distributed according to type among various shops. When the head of a household needs anything for himself or his family, he just goes to one of these shops and asks for it. And whatever he asks for, he's allowed to take away without any sort of payment, either in money or in kind. After all, why shouldn't he? There's more than enough of everything to go round, so there's no risk of his asking for more than he needs—for why should anyone want to start hoarding, when he knows he'll never have to go short of anything? No living creature is naturally greedy, except from fear of want—or in the case of human beings, from vanity, the notion that you're better than people if you can display more superfluous property than they can. But there's no scope for that sort of thing in Utopia.

These shopping centers include provision markets, to which they take meat and fish, as well as bread, fruit, and vegetables. But there are special places outside the town where all blood and dirt are first washed off in running water. The slaughtering of livestock and cleaning of carcasses are done by slaves. They don't let ordinary people get used to cutting up animals, because they think it tends to destroy one's natural feelings of humanity. It's also forbidden to bring anything dirty or unhygienic inside the town, for fear of polluting the atmosphere and so causing disease.

Every so often, as you walk down a street, you come to a large building, which has a special name of its own. That's where the Styward lives, and where his thirty households—fifteen from one direction and fifteen from the other—have their meals. The caterers for such dining halls go off at a certain time each day to the provision market, where they report the number of people registered with them, and draw the appropriate rations.

But hospital patients get first priority—oh yes, there are four hospitals in the suburbs, just outside the walls. Each of them is about the size of a small town. The idea of this is to prevent overcrowding, and facilitate the isolation of infectious cases. These hospitals are so well run, and so well supplied with all types of medical equipment, the nurses are so sympathetic and conscientious, and there are so many experienced doctors constantly available, that, though nobody's forced to go there, practically everyone would rather be ill in hospital than at home.

However, once the caterers for the hospital have got what the doctors have ordered, all the best food that's left is divided equally among the dining halls—that is, in proportion to the number registered at each—except that certain people receive preferential treatment, such as the Mayor, the Bishop, Bencheaters, and diplomats. The same applies to foreigners—not that there often are any; but, when there are, they're provided with special furnished accommodation.

At lunch time and supper time a bugle is blown, and the whole Sty assembles in the dining hall—except for anyone who's in the hospital or ill at home. However, you're quite at liberty to take food home from the market, once the dining halls have been supplied, for everyone knows you wouldn't do it unless you had to. I mean, no one likes eating at home, although there's no rule against it. For one thing, it's considered rather bad form. For another, it seems silly to go to all the trouble of preparing an inferior meal, when there's an absolutely delicious one waiting for you at the dining hall just down the street.

In these dining halls all the rough and dirty work is done by slaves, but the actual business of preparing and cooking the food, and planning the menus, is left entirely to the women of the household on duty—for a different household is responsible for providing the meals every day. The rest of the adults sit at three tables or more, according to their numbers, with the men against the wall and the women on the outside—so that if they suddenly feel sick, as pregnant women do from time to time, they can get up without disturbing anyone else, and retire to the nursery.

By the nursery, I mean a room reserved for nursing mothers and their babies, where there's always a good fire and plenty of clean water. There are also plenty of cots, so that mothers can either put their babies to bed, or, if they like, undress them and let them play in front of the fire. Babies are always breast fed by their mothers, except when death or illness makes this impossible, in which case the Styward's wife takes immediate steps to find a wet-nurse. This presents no problem, for any woman who's in a position to do so will be only too glad to volunteer for the job. You see, such acts of mercy are universally admired, and the child itself will always regard her as its real mother.

The nursery is also the place where the under-fives have their meals. The other children, that is, all boys and girls who aren't old enough to be married, wait at table in the dining room, or if they're too young for that, just stand there and keep absolutely quiet. In neither case do they have a separate mealtime—they're fed from the tables of the grown-ups.

The place of honor is the center of the high table, which is a platform across the end of the hall, and so commands a view of the whole company. Here sit the Styward and his wife, with two of the oldest residents—for the seating is always arranged in groups of four. If there happens to be a church in the Sty, the priest and his wife automatically take precedence, and sit with the Styward. On either side of them are four younger people, then four more older ones, and so on right round the hall. In other words, you sit with your contemporaries, but you're also made to mix with a different age group. The theory of this, I'm told, is that respect for the older generation tends to discourage bad behavior among the younger ones—since everything they say or do is bound to be noticed by the people sitting just beside them.

When they're handing out food, they don't work straight along the table from one end to the other. They start by giving the best helpings to the older groups, whose places are clearly marked, and then serve equal portions to the others. However, if there's not enough of some particular delicacy to go round, the older ones share their helpings, as they think fit, with their neighbors. Thus the privilege of age is duly respected—but everyone gets just as much in the end.

Lunch and supper begin with a piece of improving literature read aloud—but they keep it quite short, so that nobody gets bored. Then the older people start discussing serious problems, but not in a humorless or depressing way. Nor do they monopolize the conversation throughout the meal. On the contrary, they enjoy listening to the young ones, and deliberately draw them out, so that they can gauge each person's character and intelligence, as they betray themselves in a relaxed, informal atmosphere.

Lunch is pretty short, because work comes after it, but over supper they rather spread themselves, since it's followed by a whole night's sleep, which they consider more conducive to sound digestion. During supper they always have music, and the meal ends with a great variety of sweets and fruit. They also burn incense, and spray the hall with scent. In fact, they do everything they can to make people enjoy themselves—for they're rather inclined to believe that all harmless pleasures are perfectly legitimate.

Well, that's what life is like in the towns. In the country, because of the greater distances involved, everyone eats at home. Of course, they have just as good food as they'd have in town—for they're the ones who produce what the town-dwellers eat. . . .

In ethics they discuss the same problems as we do. Having distinguished between three types of "good," psychological, physiological, and environmental, they proceed to ask whether the term is strictly applicable to all of them, or only to the first. They also argue about such things as virtue and pleasure. But their chief subject of dispute is the nature of human happiness—on what factor or factors does it depend? Here they seem rather too much inclined to take a hedonistic view, for according to them human happiness consists largely or wholly in pleasure. Surprisingly enough, they defend this self-indulgent doctrine with arguments drawn from religion—a thing normally associated with a more serious view of life, if not with gloomy asceticism. You see, in all their discussions of happiness they invoke certain religious principles to supplement the operations of reason, which they think otherwise ill equipped to identify true happiness.

The first principle is that every soul is immortal, and was created by a kind God, who meant it to be happy. The second is that we shall be rewarded or punished in the next world for our good or bad behavior in this one. Although these are religious principles, the Utopians find rational grounds for accepting them. For suppose you didn't accept them? In that case, they say, any fool could tell you what you ought to do. You should go all out for your own pleasure, irrespective of right and wrong. You'd merely have to make sure that minor pleasures didn't interfere with major ones, and avoid the type of pleasure that has painful aftereffects. For what's the sense of struggling to be virtuous, denying yourself the pleasant things of life, and deliberately making yourself uncomfortable, if there's nothing you hope to gain by it? And what *can* you hope to gain by it, if you receive no compensation after death for a thoroughly unpleasant, that is, a thoroughly miserable life?

Not that they identify happiness with every type of pleasure—only with the higher ones. Nor do they identify it with virtue—unless they belong to a quite different school of thought. According to the normal view, happiness is the *summum bonum* toward which we're naturally impelled by virtue—which in their definition means following one's natural impulses, as God meant us to do. But this includes the instinct to be reasonable in our likes and dislikes. And reason also teaches us, first to love and reverence Almighty God, to whom we owe our existence and our potentiality for happiness, and secondly to get through life as comfortably and cheerfully as we can, and help all other members of our species to do so too.

The fact is, even the sternest ascetic tends to be slightly inconsistent in his condemnation of pleasure. He may sentence *you* to a life of hard labor, inadequate sleep, and general discomfort, but he'll also tell you to do your best to ease the pains and privations of others. He'll regard all such attempts to improve the human situation as laudable acts of humanity—for obviously nothing could be more humane, or more natural for a human being, than to relieve other people's sufferings, put an end to their miseries, and restore their *joie de vivre*, that is, their capacity for pleasure. So why shouldn't it be equally natural to do the same thing for oneself?

Either it's a bad thing to enjoy life, in other words, to experience pleasure—in which case you shouldn't help anyone to do it, but should try to save the whole human race from such a frightful fate—or else, if it's good for other people, and you're not only allowed, but positively obliged to make it possible for them, why shouldn't charity begin at home? After all, you've a duty to yourself as well as to your neighbor, and, if Nature says you must be kind to others, she can't turn round the next moment and say you must be cruel to yourself. The Utopians therefore regard the enjoyment of life—that is, pleasure—as the natural object of all human efforts, and natural, as they define it, is synonymous with virtuous. However, Nature also wants us to help one another to enjoy life, for the very good reason that no human being has a monopoly of her affections. She's equally anxious for the welfare of every member of the species. So of course she tells us to make quite sure that we don't pursue our own interests at the expense of other people's.

On this principle they think it right to keep one's promises in private life, and also to obey public laws for regulating the distribution of "goods"—by which I mean the raw materials of pleasure—provided such laws have been properly made by a wise ruler, or passed by common consent of a whole population, which has not been subjected to any form of violence or deception. Within these limits they say it's sensible to consult one's own interests, and a moral duty to consult those of the community as well. It's wrong to deprive someone else of a pleasure so that you can enjoy one yourself, but to deprive yourself of a pleasure so that you can add to someone else's enjoyment is an act of humanity by which you always gain more than you lose. For one thing, such benefits are usually repaid in kind. For another, the mere sense of having done somebody a kindness, and so earned his affection and good will, produces a spiritual satisfaction which far outweighs the loss of a physical one. And lastly—a belief that comes easily to a religious mind—God will reward us for such small sacrifices of momentary pleasure, by giving us an eternity of perfect joy. Thus they argue that, in the final analysis, pleasure is the ultimate happiness which all human beings have in view, even when they're acting most virtuously.

Pleasure they define as any state or activity, physical or mental, which is naturally enjoyable. The operative word is *naturally*. According to them, we're impelled by reason as well as an instinct to enjoy ourselves in any natural way which doesn't hurt other people, interfere with greater pleasures, or cause unpleasant aftereffects. But human beings have entered into an idiotic conspiracy to call some things enjoyable which are naturally nothing of the kind—as though facts were as easily changed as definitions. Now the Utopians believe that, so far from contributing to happiness, this type of thing makes happiness impossible—because, once you get used to it, you lose all capacity for real pleasure, and are merely obsessed by illusory forms of it. Very often these have nothing pleasant about them at all—in fact, most of them are thoroughly disagreeable. But they appeal so strongly to perverted tastes that they come to be reckoned not only among the major pleasures of life, but even among the chief reasons for living.

In the category of illusory pleasure addicts they include the kind of person I mentioned before, who thinks himself better than other people because he's better dressed than they are. Actually he's just as wrong about his clothes as he is about himself. From a practical point of view, why is it better to be dressed in fine woolen thread than in coarse? But he's got it into his head that fine thread is naturally superior, and that wearing it somehow increases his own value. So he feels entitled to far more respect than he'd ever dare to hope for, if he were less expensively dressed, and is most indignant if he fails to get it.

Talking of respect, isn't it equally idiotic to attach such importance to a lot of empty gestures which do nobody any good? For what real pleasure can you get out of the sight of a bared head or a bent knee? Will it cure the rheumatism in your own knee, or make you any less weak in the head? Of course, the great believers in this type of artificial pleasure are those who pride themselves on their "nobility." Nowadays that merely means that they happen to belong to a family which has been rich for several generations, preferably in landed property. And yet they feel every bit as "noble" even if they've failed to inherit any of the said property, or if they have inherited it and then frittered it all away.

Then there's another type of person I mentioned before, who has a passion for jewels, and feels practically superhuman if he manages to get hold of a rare one, especially if it's a kind that's considered particularly precious in his country and period—for the value of such things varies according to where and when you live. But he's so terrified of being taken in by appearances that he refuses to buy any jewel until he's stripped off all the gold and inspected it in the nude. And even then he won't buy it without a solemn assurance and a written guarantee from the jeweler that the stone is genuine. But my dear sir, why shouldn't a fake give you just as much pleasure, if you can't, with your own eyes, distinguish it from a real one? It makes no difference to you whether it's genuine or not—any more than it would to a blind man!

And now, what about those people who accumulate superfluous wealth, for no better purpose than to enjoy looking at it? Is their pleasure a real one, or merely a form of delusion? The opposite type of psychopath buries his gold, so that he'll never be able to use it, and may never even see it again. In fact, he deliberately loses it in his anxiety not to lose it—for what can you call it but lost, when it's put back into the earth, where it's no good to him, or probably to anyone else? And yet he's tremendously happy when he's got it stowed away. Now, apparently, he can stop worrying. But suppose the money is stolen, and ten years later he dies without ever knowing it has gone. Then for a whole ten years he has managed to survive his loss, and during that period what difference has it made to him whether the money was there or not? It was just as little use to him either way.

Among stupid pleasures they include not only gambling—a form of idiocy that they've heard about but never practiced—but also hunting and hawking. What on earth is the fun, they ask, of throwing dice on a table? Besides, you've done it so often that, even if there was some fun in it at first, you must surely be sick of it by now. How can you possibly enjoy listening to anything so disagreeable as the barking and howling of dogs? And why is it more amusing to watch a dog chasing a hare than to watch one dog chasing another? In each case the essential activity is running—if running is what amuses you. But if it's really the thought of being in at the death, and seeing an animal torn to pieces before your eyes, wouldn't pity be a more appropriate reaction to the sight of a weak, timid, harmless little creature like a hare being devoured by something so much stronger and fiercer?

So the Utopians consider hunting below the dignity of free men, and leave it entirely to butchers, who are, as I told you, slaves. In their view hunting is the vilest department of butchery, compared with which all the others are relatively useful and more honorable. An ordinary butcher slaughters livestock far more sparingly, and only because he has to, whereas a hunter kills and mutilates poor little creatures purely for his own amusement. They say you won't find that type of blood lust even among animals, unless they're particularly savage by nature, or have become so by constantly being used for this cruel sport.

There are hundreds of things like that, which are generally regarded as pleasures, but everyone in Utopia is quite convinced that they've got nothing to do with real pleasure, because there's nothing naturally enjoyable about them. Nor is this conviction at all shaken by the argument that most people do actually enjoy them, which would seem to indicate an appreciable pleasure-content. They say this is a purely subjective reaction caused by bad habits, which can make a person prefer unpleasant things to pleasant ones, just as pregnant women sometimes lose their sense of taste, and find suet or turpentine more delicious than honey. But however much one's judgment may be impaired by habit or ill health, the nature of pleasure, as of everything else, remains unchanged.

Real pleasures they divide into two categories, mental and physical. Mental pleasures include the satisfaction that one gets from understanding something, or from contemplating truth. They also include the memory of a well-spent life, and the confident expectation of good things to come. Physical pleasures are subdivided into two types. First there are those which fill the whole organism with a conscious sense of enjoyment. This may be the result of replacing physical substances which have been burnt up by the natural heat of the body, as when we eat or drink. Or else it may be caused by the discharge of some excess, as in excretion, sexual intercourse, or any relief of irritation by rubbing or scratching. However, there are also pleasures which satisfy no organic need, and relieve no previous discomfort. They merely act, in a mysterious but quite unmistakable way, directly on our senses, and monopolize their reactions. Such is the pleasure of music.

The second type of physical pleasure arises from the calm and regular functioning of the body—that is, from a state of health undisturbed by any minor ailments. In the absence of mental discomfort, this gives one a good feeling, even without the help of external pleasures. Of course, it's less ostentatious, and forces itself less violently on one's attention than the cruder delights of eating and drinking, but even so it's often considered the greatest pleasure in life. Practically everyone in Utopia would agree that it's a very important one, because it's the basis of all the others. It's enough by itself to make you enjoy life, and unless you have it, no other pleasure is possible. However, mere freedom from pain, without positive health, they would call not pleasure but anaesthesia.

Some thinkers used to maintain that a uniformly tranquil state of health couldn't properly be termed a pleasure since its presence could only be detected by contrast with its opposite—oh yes, they went very thoroughly into the whole question. But that theory was exploded long ago, and nowadays nearly everybody subscribes to the view that health is most definitely a pleasure. The argument goes like this—illness involves pain, which is the direct opposite of pleasure, and illness is the direct opposite of health, therefore health involves pleasure. They don't think it matters whether you say that illness *is* or merely *involves* pain. Either way it comes to the same thing. Similarly, whether health *is* a pleasure, or merely *produces* pleasure as inevitably as fire produces heat, it's equally logical to assume that where you have an uninterrupted state of health you cannot fail to have pleasure.

Besides, they say, when we eat something, what really happens is this. Our failing health starts fighting off the attacks of hunger, using the food as an ally. Gradually it begins to prevail, and, in this very process of winning back its normal strength, experiences the sense of enjoyment which we find so refreshing. Now, if health enjoys the actual battle, why shouldn't it also enjoy the victory? Or are we to suppose that when it has finally managed to regain its former vigor—the one thing that it has been fighting for all this time—it promptly falls into a coma, and fails to notice or take advantage of its success? As for the idea that one isn't conscious of health except through its opposite, they say that's quite untrue. Everyone's perfectly aware of feeling well, unless he's asleep or actually feeling ill. Even the most insensitive and apathetic sort of person will admit that it's delightful to be healthy—and what is delight, but a synonym for pleasure?

They're particularly fond of mental pleasures, which they consider of primary importance, and attribute mostly to good behavior and a clear conscience. Their favorite physical pleasure is health. Of course, they believe in enjoying food, drink, and so forth, but purely in the interests of health, for they don't regard such things as very pleasant in themselves—only as methods of resisting the stealthy onset of disease. A sensible person, they say, prefers keeping well to taking medicine, and would rather feel cheerful than have people trying to comfort him, On the same principle it's better not to need this type of pleasure than to become addicted to it. For, if you think that sort of thing will make you happy, you'll have to admit that your idea of perfect felicity would be a life consisting entirely of hunger, thirst, itching, eating, drinking, rubbing, and scratching—which would obviously be most unpleasant as well as quite disgusting. Undoubtedly these pleasures should come in right at the bottom of the list, because they're so impure. For instance, the pleasure of eating is invariably diluted with the pain of hunger, and not in equal proportions either—for the pain is both more intense and more prolonged. It starts before the pleasure, and doesn't stop until the pleasure has stopped too.

So they don't think much of pleasures like that, except in so far as they're necessary. But they enjoy them all the same, and feel most grateful to Mother Nature for encouraging her children to do things that have to be done so often, by making them so attractive. For just think how dreary life would be, if those chronic ailments, hunger and thirst, could only be cured by foul-tasting medicines, like the rarer types of disease!

They attach great value to special natural gifts such as beauty, strength, and agility. They're also keen on the pleasures of sight, hearing, and smell, which are peculiar to human beings—for no other species admires the beauty of the world, enjoys any sort of scent, except as a method of locating food, or can tell the difference between a harmony and a discord. They say these things give a sort of relish to life.

However, in all such matters they observe the rule that minor pleasures mustn't interfere with major ones, and that pleasure mustn't cause pain—which they think is bound to happen, if the pleasure is immoral. But they'd never dream of despising their own beauty, overtaxing their strength, converting their agility into inertia, ruining their physique by going without food, damaging their health, or spurning any other of Nature's gifts, unless they were doing it for the benefit of other people or of society, in the hope of receiving some greater pleasure from God in return. For they think it's quite absurd to torment oneself in the name of an unreal virtue, which does nobody any good, or in order to steel oneself against disasters which may never occur. They say such behavior is merely self-destructive, and shows a most ungrateful attitude toward Nature—as if one refused all her favors, because one couldn't bear the thought of being indebted to her for anything. . . .

Well, that's the most accurate account I can give you of the Utopian Republic. To my mind, it's not only the best country in the world, but the only one that has any right to call itself a republic. Elsewhere, people are always talking about the public interest, but all they really care about is private property. In Utopia, where there's no private property, people take their duty to the public seriously. And both attitudes are perfectly reasonable. In other "republics" practically everyone knows that, if he doesn't look out for himself, he'll starve to death, however prosperous his country may be. He's therefore compelled to give his own interests priority over those of the public; that is, of other people. But in Utopia, where everything's under public ownership, no one has any fear of going short, as long as the public storehouses are full. Everyone gets a fair share, so there are never any poor men or beggars. Nobody owns anything, but everyone is rich—for what greater wealth can there be than cheerfulness, peace of mind, and freedom from anxiety? Instead of being worried about his food supply, upset by the plaintive demands of his wife, afraid of poverty for his son, and baffled by the problem of finding a dowry for his daughter, the Utopian can feel absolutely sure that he, his wife, his children, his grandchildren, his great-grandchildren, his great-great-grandchildren, and as long a line of descendants as the proudest peer could wish to look forward to, will always have enough to eat and enough to make them happy. There's also the further point that those who are too old to work are just as well provided for as those who are still working.

Now, will anyone venture to compare these fair arrangements in Utopia with the so-called justice of other countries?—in which I'm damned if I can see the slightest trace of justice or fairness. For what sort of justice do you call this? People like aristocrats, goldsmiths, or moneylenders, who either do no work at all, or do work that's really not essential, are rewarded for their laziness or their unnecessary activities by a splendid life of luxury. But laborers, coachmen, carpenters, and farmhands, who never stop working like carthorses, at jobs so essential that, if they *did* stop working, they'd bring any country to a standstill within twelve months—what happens to them? They get so little to eat, and have such a wretched time, that they'd be almost better off if they *were* cart horses. Then, at least, they wouldn't work quite such long hours, their food wouldn't be very much worse, they'd enjoy it more, and they'd have no fears for the future. As it is, they're not only ground down by unrewarding toil in the present, but also worried to death by the prospect of a poverty-stricken old age—since their daily wages aren't enough to support them for one day, let alone leave anything over to be saved up for when they're old.

Can you see any fairness or gratitude in a social system which lavishes such great rewards on so-called noblemen, goldsmiths, and people like that, who are either totally unproductive or merely employed in producing luxury goods or entertainment, but makes no such kind provision for farmhands, coal-heavers, laborers, carters, or carpenters, without whom society couldn't exist at all? And the climax of ingratitude comes when they're old and ill and completely destitute. Having taken advantage of them throughout the best years of their lives, society now forgets all the sleepless hours they've spent in its service, and repays them for all the vital work they've done, by letting them die in misery. What's more, the wretched earnings of the poor are daily whittled away by the rich, not only through private dishonesty, but through public legislation. As if it weren't unjust enough already that the man who contributes most to society should get the least in return, they make it even worse, and then arrange for injustice to be legally described as justice.

In fact, when I consider any social system that prevails in the modern world, I can't, so help me God, see it as anything but a conspiracy of the rich to advance their own interests under the pretext of organizing society. They think up all sorts of tricks and dodges, first for keeping safe their ill-gotten gains, and then for exploiting the poor by buying their labor as cheaply as possible. Once the rich have decided that these tricks and dodges shall be officially recognized by society—which includes the poor as well as the rich—they acquire the force of law. Thus an unscrupulous minority is led by its insatiable greed to monopolize what would have been enough to supply the needs of the whole population. And yet how much happier even these people would be in Utopia! There, with the simultaneous abolition of money and the passion for money, how many other social problems have been solved, how many crimes eradicated! For obviously the end of money means the end of all those types of criminal behavior which daily punishments are powerless to check: fraud, theft, burglary, brawls, riots, disputes, rebellion, murder, treason, and black magic. And the moment money goes, you can say goodbye to fear, tension, anxiety, overwork, and sleepless nights. Why, even poverty itself, the one problem that has always seemed to need money for its solution, would promptly disappear if money ceased to exist.

Let me try to make this point clearer. Just think back to one of the years when the harvest was bad, and thousands of people died of starvation. Well, I bet if you'd inspected every rich man's barn at the end of that lean period you'd have found enough corn to have saved all the lives that were lost through malnutrition and disease, and prevented anyone suffering any ill effects whatever from the meanness of the weather and the soil. Everyone could so easily get enough to eat, if it weren't for that blessed nuisance, money. There you have a brilliant invention which was designed to make food more readily available. Actually it's the only thing that makes it unobtainable.

I'm sure that even the rich are well aware of this, and realize how much better it would be to have everything one needed, than lots of things one didn't need—to be evacuated altogether from the danger area, than to dig oneself in behind a barricade of enormous wealth.

And I've no doubt that either self-interest, or the authority of our Savior Christ—who was far too wise not to know what was best for us, and far too kind to recommend anything else—would have led the whole world to adopt the Utopian system long ago, if it weren't for that beastly root of all evils, pride. For pride's criterion of prosperity is not what you've got yourself, but what other people haven't got. Pride would refuse to set foot in paradise, if she thought there'd be no underprivileged classes to gloat over and order about—nobody whose misery could serve as a foil to her own happiness, or whose poverty she could make harder to bear, by flaunting her own riches. Pride, like a hellish serpent gliding through human hearts—or, shall we say, like a sucking-fish that clings to the ship of state?—is always dragging us back, and obstructing our progress toward a better way of life.

But as this fault is too deeply ingrained in human nature to be easily eradicated, I'm glad that at least one country has managed to develop a system which I'd like to see universally adopted. The Utopian way of life provides not only the happiest basis for a civilized community, but also one which, in all human probability, will last forever. They've eliminated the root causes of ambition, political conflict, and everything like that. There's therefore no danger of internal dissension, the one thing that has destroyed so many impregnable towns. And as long as there's unity and sound administration at home, no matter how envious neighboring kings may feel, they'll never be able to shake, let alone to shatter, the power of Utopia. They've tried to do so often enough in the past, but have always been beaten back.

While Raphael was telling us all this, I kept thinking of various objections. The laws and customs of that country seemed to me in many cases perfectly ridiculous. Quite apart from such things as their military tactics, religions, and forms of worship, there was the grand absurdity on which their whole society was based, communism minus money. Now this in itself would mean the end of the aristocracy, and consequently of all dignity, splendor, and majesty, which are generally supposed to be the real glories of any nation.

However, I could see that he was tired after talking so much, and I was not quite sure how tolerant he would be of any opinion that contradicted his own—especially when I remembered his sarcastic reference to the sort of person who is afraid of looking a fool if he cannot pick holes in other people's ideas. So I just made some polite remarks about the Utopian system, and thanked him for his interesting talk—after which I took his arm and led him in to supper, saying:

"Well, I must think it over. Then perhaps we can meet again and discuss it at greater length."

I certainly hope we shall, some day. In the meantime I cannot agree with everything that he said, for all his undoubted learning and experience. But I freely admit that there are many features of the Utopian Republic which I should like—though I hardly expect—to see adopted in Europe.

QUESTIONS FOR DISCUSSION

Are we intended to agree with Raphael's endorsement of Utopia or with the narrator's more ambivalent view of it?

1. Why is Raphael convinced that Utopia is "not only the best country in the world, but the only one that has any right to call itself a republic"? (26)

2. Why does Raphael believe that the Utopians have succeeded in abolishing both money "and the passion for money"? (28)

3. Why doesn't the narrator express any of the "various objections" he thinks of while Raphael is talking? (29)

4. Why does the narrator conclude by saying that, despite his reservations, he would like to see "many features of the Utopian Republic . . . adopted in Europe"? (30)

Why is the Utopians' "chief subject of dispute" the "nature of human happiness"? (18)

1. Why do the Utopians believe that human happiness "consists largely or wholly in pleasure"? (18)

2. Why do the Utopians believe reason alone is "ill equipped to identify true happiness," and draw on religious principles to supplement it? (19)

3. Why do Utopians believe that if there is no afterlife, one should "go all out for your own pleasure, irrespective of right and wrong"? (19)

4. Why do the Utopians believe that people who claim to enjoy pleasures the Utopians consider illusory are having "a purely subjective reaction caused by bad habits"? (23)

FOR FURTHER REFLECTION

1. Does Raphael convince you that Utopia is "the best country in the world"?

2. Do you think it is possible to organize society in such a way that "the root causes of ambition, political conflict," and pride are eliminated?

3. Do you agree with Raphael that most modern social systems are "a conspiracy of the rich to advance their own interests under the pretext of organizing society"?

4. How does the Utopian idea of human happiness compare to the American "pursuit of happiness"?

Utopia

Wislawa Szymborska

Island where all becomes clear.

Solid ground beneath your feet.

The only roads are those that offer access.

Bushes bend beneath the weight of proofs.

The Tree of Valid Supposition grows here
with branches disentangled since time immemorial.

The Tree of Understanding, dazzlingly straight and simple,
sprouts by the spring called Now I Get It.

The thicker the woods, the vaster the vista:
the Valley of Obviously.

If any doubts arise, the wind dispels them instantly.

Echoes stir unsummoned
and eagerly explain all the secrets of the worlds.

On the right a cave where Meaning lies.

On the left the Lake of Deep Conviction.
Truth breaks from the bottom and bobs to the surface.

Unshakable Confidence towers over the valley.
Its peak offers an excellent view of the Essence of Things.

For all its charms, the island is uninhabited,
and the faint footprints scattered on its beaches
turn without exception to the sea.

As if all you can do here is leave
and plunge, never to return, into the depths.

Into unfathomable life.

QUESTIONS FOR DISCUSSION

Why does the island of Utopia remain uninhabited, despite "all its charms"?

1. Why do the bushes on Utopia "bend beneath the weight of proofs"?

2. Why do all footprints on the island lead to the sea, "as if all you can do here is leave"?

3. Why is the only alternative to staying on Utopia to "plunge, never to return, into the depths"?

4. Why are the landscape features of Utopia capitalized, while in the last line of the poem, the words "unfathomable life" are not?

FOR FURTHER REFLECTION

1. To what extent do you share the view of Utopia that Szymborska presents in this poem?

2. Is a life without doubts attractive?

3. Do you see life as "unfathomable," or do you think it is possible to get a clear view of the "essence of things"?

4. How do you typically respond to words spoken with "Unshakable Confidence"?

Iliad

(selection)

Homer

Thetis's silver feet took her to Hephaestus's house,
A mansion the lame god had built himself
Out of starlight and bronze, and beyond all time.
She found him at his bellows, glazed with sweat
As he hurried to complete his latest project,
Twenty cauldrons on tripods to line his hall,
With golden wheels at the base of each tripod
So they could move by themselves to the gods' parties
And return to his house—a wonder to see.
They were almost done. The intricate handles
Still had to be attached. He was getting these ready,
Forging the rivets with inspired artistry,
When the silver-footed goddess came up to him.
And Charis, Hephaestus's wife, lovely
In her shimmering veil, saw her, and running up,
She clasped her hand and said to her:

"My dear Thetis, so grave in your long robe,
What brings you here now? You almost never visit.
Do come inside so I can offer you something."

And the shining goddess led her along
And had her sit down in a graceful

Silver-studded chair with a footstool.
Then she called to Hephaestus, and said:

"Hephaestus, come here.
Thetis needs you for something."

And the renowned smith called back:

"Thetis? Then the dread goddess I revere
Is inside. She saved me when I lay suffering
From my long fall, after my shameless mother
Threw me out, wanting to hide my infirmity.
And I really would have suffered, had not Thetis
And Eurynome, a daughter of Ocean Stream,
Taken me into their bosom. I stayed with them
Nine years, forging all kinds of jewelry,
Brooches and bracelets and necklaces and pins,
In their hollow cave, while the Ocean's tides,
Murmuring with foam, flowed endlessly around.
No one knew I was there, neither god nor mortal,
Except my rescuers, Eurynome and Thetis.
Now the goddess has come to our house.
I owe her my life and would repay her in full.
Set out our finest for her, Charis,
While I put away my bellows and tools."

He spoke and raised his panting bulk
Up from his anvil, limping along quickly
On his spindly shanks. He set the bellows
Away from the fire, gathered up the tools
He had been using, and put them away
In a silver chest. Then he took a sponge
And wiped his face and hands, his thick neck,
And his shaggy chest. He put on a tunic,
Grabbed a stout staff, and as he went out
Limping, attendants rushed up to support him,
Attendants made of gold who looked like real girls,
With a mind within, and a voice, and strength,
And knowledge of crafts from the immortal gods.

These busily moved to support their lord,
And he came hobbling up to where Thetis was,
Sat himself down on a polished chair,
And clasping her hand in his, he said:

"My dear Thetis, so grave in your long robe,
What brings you here now? You almost never visit.
Tell me what you have in mind, and I will do it
If it is anything that is at all possible to do."

And Thetis, shedding tears as she spoke:

"Hephaestus, is there a goddess on Olympus
Who has suffered as I have? Zeus son of Cronus
Has given me suffering beyond all the others.
Of all the saltwater women he singled me out
To be subject to a man, Aeacus's son Peleus.
I endured a man's bed, much against my will.
He lies in his halls forspent with old age,
But I have other griefs now. He gave me a son
To bear and to rear, the finest of heroes.
He grew like a sapling, and I nursed him
As I would nurse a plant in my hillside garden,
And I sent him to Ilion on a sailing ship
To fight the Trojans. And now I will never
Welcome him home again to Peleus's house.
As long as he lives and sees the sunlight
He will be in pain, and I cannot help him.
The girl that the army chose as his prize
Lord Agamemnon took out of his arms.
He was wasting his heart out of grief for her,
But now the Trojans have penned the Greeks
In their beachhead camp, and the Argive elders
Have petitioned him with a long list of gifts.
He refused to beat off the enemy himself,
But he let Patroclus wear his armor,
And sent him into battle with many men.
All day long they fought by the Scaean Gates

And would have sacked the city that very day,
But after Menoetius's valiant son
Had done much harm, Apollo killed him
In the front ranks and gave Hector the glory.
So I have come to your knees, to see if you
Will give my son, doomed to die young,
A shield and helmet, a fine set of greaves,
And a corselet too. His old armor was lost
When the Trojans killed his faithful companion,
And now he lies on the ground in anguish."

And the renowned smith answered her:

"Take heart, Thetis, and do not be distressed.
I only regret I do not have the power
To hide your son from death when it comes.
But armor he will have, forged to a wonder,
And its terrible beauty will be a marvel to men."

Hephaestus left her there and went to his bellows,
Turned them toward the fire and ordered them to work.
And the bellows, all twenty, blew on the crucibles,
Blasting out waves of heat in whatever direction
Hephaestus wanted as he hustled here and there
Around his forge and the work progressed.
He cast durable bronze onto the fire, and tin,
Precious gold and silver. Then he positioned
His enormous anvil up on its block
And grasped his mighty hammer
In one hand, and in the other his tongs.

He made a shield first, heavy and huge,
Every inch of it intricately designed.
He threw a triple rim around it, glittering
Like lightning, and he made the strap silver.
The shield itself was five layers thick, and he
Crafted its surface with all of his genius.

On it he made the earth, the sky, the sea,
The unwearied sun, and the moon near full,

And all the signs that garland the sky,
Pleiades, Hyades, mighty Orion,
And the Bear they also called the Wagon,
Which pivots in place and looks back at Orion
And alone is aloof from the wash of Ocean.

On it he made two cities, peopled
And beautiful. Weddings in one, festivals,
Brides led from their rooms by torchlight
Up through the town, bridal song rising,
Young men reeling in dance to the tune
Of lyres and flutes, and the women
Standing in their doorways admiring them.
There was a crowd in the marketplace
And a quarrel arising between two men
Over blood money for a murder,
One claiming the right to make restitution,
The other refusing to accept any terms.
They were heading for an arbitrator
And the people were shouting, taking sides,
But heralds restrained them. The elders sat
On polished stone seats in the sacred circle
And held in their hands the staves of heralds.
The pair rushed up and pleaded their cases,
And between them lay two ingots of gold
For whoever spoke straightest in judgment.

Around the other city two armies
Of glittering soldiery were encamped.
Their leaders were at odds—should they
Move in for the kill or settle for a division
Of all the lovely wealth the citadel held fast?
The citizens wouldn't surrender, and armed
For an ambush. Their wives and little children
Were stationed on the wall, and with the old men
Held it against attack. The citizens moved out,
Led by Ares and Pallas Athena,
Both of them gold, and their clothing was gold,

Beautiful and larger than life in their armor, as befits
Gods in their glory, and all the people were smaller.
They came to a position perfect for an ambush,
A spot on the river where stock came to water,
And took their places, concealed by fiery bronze.
Farther up they had two lookouts posted
Waiting to sight shambling cattle and sheep,
Which soon came along, trailed by two herdsmen
Playing their panpipes, completely unsuspecting.
When the townsmen lying in ambush saw this
They ran up, cut off the herds of cattle and fleecy
Silver sheep, and killed the two herdsmen.
When the armies sitting in council got wind
Of the ruckus with the cattle, they mounted
Their high-stepping horses and galloped to the scene.
They took their stand and fought along the river banks,
Throwing bronze-tipped javelins against each other.
Among them were Hate and Din and the Angel of Death,
Holding a man just wounded, another unwounded,
And dragging one dead by his heels from the fray,
And the cloak on her shoulders was red with human blood.
They swayed in battle and fought like living men,
And each side salvaged the bodies of their dead.

On it he put a soft field, rich farmland
Wide and thrice-tilled, with many plowmen
Driving their teams up and down rows.
Whenever they came to the end of the field
And turned, a man would run up and hand them
A cup of sweet wine. Then they turned again
Back up the furrow pushing on through deep soil
To reach the other end. The field was black
Behind them, just as if plowed, and yet
It was gold, all gold, forged to a wonder.

On it he put land sectioned off for a king,
Where reapers with sharp sickles were working.
Cut grain lay deep where it fell in the furrow,

And binders made sheaves bound with straw bands.
Three sheaf-binders stood by, and behind them children
Gathered up armfuls and kept passing them on.
The king stood in silence near the line of reapers,
Holding his staff, and his heart was happy.
Under an oak tree nearby heralds were busy
Preparing a feast from an ox they had slaughtered
In sacrifice, and women were sprinkling it
With abundant white barley for the reapers' dinner.

On it he put a vineyard loaded with grapes,
Beautiful in gold. The clusters were dark,
And the vines were set everywhere on silver poles.
Around it he inlaid a blue enamel ditch
And a fence of tin. A solitary path led to it,
And vintagers filed along it to harvest the grapes.
Girls, all grown up, and light-hearted boys
Carried the honey-sweet fruit in wicker baskets.
Among them a boy picked out on a lyre
A beguiling tune and sang the Linos song
In a low, light voice, and the harvesters
Skipped in time and shouted the refrain.

On it he made a herd of straight horn cattle.
The cows were wrought of gold and tin
And rushed out mooing from the farmyard dung
To a pasture by the banks of a roaring river,
Making their way through swaying reeds.
Four golden herdsmen tended the cattle,
And nine nimble dogs followed along.
Two terrifying lions at the front of the herd
Were pulling down an ox. Its long bellows alerted
The dogs and the lads, who were running on up,
But the two lions had ripped the bull's hide apart
And were gulping down the guts and black blood.
The shepherds kept trying to set on the dogs,
But they shied away from biting the lions
And stood there barking just out of harm's way.

On it the renowned lame god made a pasture
In a lovely valley, wide, with silvery sheep in it,
And stables, roofed huts, and stone animal pens.

On it the renowned lame god embellished
A dancing ground, like the one Daedalus
Made for ringleted Ariadne in wide Cnossus.
Young men and girls in the prime of their beauty
Were dancing there, hands clasped around wrists.
The girls wore delicate linens, and the men
Finespun tunics glistening softly with oil.
Flowers crowned the girls' heads, and the men
Had golden knives hung from silver straps.
They ran on feet that knew how to run
With the greatest ease, like a potter's wheel
When he stoops to cup it in the palms of his hands
And gives it a spin to see how it runs. Then they
Would run in lines that weaved in and out.
A large crowd stood round the beguiling dance,
Enjoying themselves, and two acrobats
Somersaulted among them on cue to the music.

On it he put the great strength of the River Ocean,
Lapping the outermost rim of the massive shield.

And when he had wrought the shield, huge and heavy,
He made a breastplate gleaming brighter than fire
And a durable helmet that fit close at the temples,
Lovely and intricate, and crested with gold.
And he wrought leg armor out of pliant tin.
And when the renowned lame god had finished this gear,
He set it down before Achilles' mother,
And she took off like a hawk from snow-capped Olympus,
Carrying armor through the sky like summer lightning.

The Shield of Achilles

W. H. Auden

She looked over his shoulder
   For vines and olive trees,
Marble well-governed cities,
   And ships upon untamed seas,
But there on the shining metal
   His hands had put instead
An artificial wilderness
   And a sky like lead.

A plain without a feature, bare and brown,
   No blade of grass, no sign of neighborhood,
Nothing to eat and nowhere to sit down,
   Yet, congregated on its blankness, stood
   An unintelligible multitude,
A million eyes, a million boots in line,
Without expression, waiting for a sign.

Out of the air a voice without a face
   Proved by statistics that some cause was just
In tones as dry and level as the place:
   No one was cheered and nothing was discussed;
   Column by column in a cloud of dust
They marched away enduring a belief
Whose logic brought them, somewhere else, to grief.

She looked over his shoulder
   For ritual pieties,
White flower-garlanded heifers,
   Libation and sacrifice,
But there on the shining metal
   Where the altar should have been,
She saw by his flickering forge-light
   Quite another scene.

Barbed wire enclosed an arbitrary spot
   Where bored officials lounged (one cracked a joke)
And sentries sweated, for the day was hot:
   A crowd of ordinary decent folk
   Watched from without and neither moved nor spoke
As three pale figures were led forth and bound
To three posts driven upright in the ground.

The mass and majesty of this world, all
   That carries weight and always weighs the same,
Lay in the hands of others; they were small
   And could not hope for help and no help came:
   What their foes liked to do was done, their shame
Was all the worst could wish; they lost their pride
And died as men before their bodies died.

She looked over his shoulder
   For athletes at their games,
Men and women in a dance
   Moving their sweet limbs
Quick, quick, to music,
   But there on the shining shield
His hands had set no dancing-floor
   But a weed-choked field.

A ragged urchin, aimless and alone,
  Loitered about that vacancy; a bird
Flew up to safety from his well-aimed stone:
  That girls are raped, that two boys knife a third,
  Were axioms to him, who'd never heard
Of any world where promises were kept
Or one could weep because another wept.

    The thin-lipped armorer,
      Hephaestus, hobbled away;
    Thetis of the shining breasts
      Cried out in dismay
    At what the god had wrought
      To please her son, the strong
    Iron-hearted man-slaying Achilles
      Who would not live long.

QUESTIONS FOR DISCUSSION

In Homer's poem, why does Hephaestus include on Achilles' shield both scenes of people peacefully enjoying life and scenes of violence?

1. Why does Hephaestus include the earth, sky, sea, and sun on the shield, as well as scenes with people in them?

2. In the scene of war, why does Hephaestus show the progress of hostility, from two armies taking their positions through salvaging the bodies of the dead?

3. Within the scene of cows going to pasture, why does Hephaestus also include lions tearing apart a bull?

4. Why is the last scene described on Achilles' shield that of young men and girls dancing?

At the end of Auden's poem, why does Thetis cry "in dismay" at what she sees on Achilles' shield?

1. Why does Auden alternate describing the scenes on the shield with what Thetis expects to see on it?

2. Why does Hephaestus create a featureless plain on the shield, on which an "unintelligible multitude" waits for the order to go to war?

3. Why does the shield include victims of violence who "lost their pride / And died as men before their bodies died"?

4. Why is the last scene described on the shield that of "a ragged urchin" who had "never heard / Of any world where promises were kept"?

FOR FURTHER REFLECTION

1. Which shield do you think is a more accurate reflection of war and its place in society today?

2. Is Auden's poem criticizing warfare in general, or warfare as it is practiced in modern times?

3. Is the ability to "weep because another wept" a necessary foundation of a just society?

4. Do you think modern society has lost a harmony or order characteristic of earlier times?

The Yearning Remains

A fundamental problem that arises in utopian thinking is how to build a perfect society composed of individual human beings, all of whom possess complex and conflicting personalities, preferences, and ambitions. This problem crops up in any society, utopian or otherwise, as citizens must have a set of common behaviors and assumptions that assure a degree of stability for a society to function. In the case of utopian proposals, however, this problem is sharpened and magnified. A utopia is intended to remedy all social ills that a thinker believes a rational reordering of society can achieve, so all of society's members must fit into that reordering. But do humans possess an essential nature—angelic, demonic, or something in between—that remains intractable in even the most thoroughly organized society? Or, on the other hand, can imposed ideal conditions fundamentally modify individual behavior and ensure that a utopian society will flourish? The four selections in this section explore these issues under the overarching question of whether human nature, however defined, is conducive or detrimental to the realization of a utopian society.

In the excerpt from her book *A Paradise Built in Hell: The Extraordinary Communities That Arise in Disaster* (2009), American historian and activist **Rebecca Solnit** (1961–) reflects on how the altruism and mutual support that emerges following disasters fosters improvised social arrangements with many of the characteristics of utopian communities. Solnit wonders whether this temporary flourishing of something resembling a more just society is merely an aberration in human behavior under extreme conditions or a revelation of the untapped, obscured better nature of most individuals. She asks us to consider whether these transient communities can provide us with a lasting vision of "a transformed human nature and society" and point the way toward the realization of more lasting utopian plans.

"Time" (1931), a short story by the Japanese avant-garde author **Riichi Yokomitsu** (1898–1947), depicts a quarrelsome band of traveling performers as they struggle to survive an arduous and potentially disastrous journey. Yokomitsu explores how the performers, almost in spite of their ongoing conflicts of character, come to form a kind of utopian community that will sustain all and sacrifice none. He asks us to consider why they finally are able to do so, even in the face of powerful motivations to break their mutual bonds and disintegrate into a collection of self-serving individuals.

In "On the Cannibals" (1578–1580), French writer **Michel de Montaigne** (1533–1592) reflects on what he has learned about the native population of the New World from travelers' accounts and from his own contact with visiting tribe members from Brazil. Montaigne asks us to consider how we view so-called primitive cultures that contrast sharply with our own, especially since these cultures may utilize other forms of social organization that could solve some of our most entrenched dilemmas, particularly those having to do with the relations of individuals to each other and to society.

"The Dream of a Ridiculous Man" (1877) by Russian novelist **Fyodor Dostoevsky** (1821–1881) raises searching questions about the possibility and the desirability of perfected human nature that some utopian thinking proposes. In the story's titular dream, the narrator himself corrupts the ideal world and its inhabitants, and in doing so, comes to realize that "heaven on earth" is something very different from idealized utopian visions. Are such visions in fact detrimental to the fulfillment of the highest happiness for human beings that utopian plans often claim to provide?

A Paradise Built in Hell

(selection)

Rebecca Solnit

Prelude: Falling Together

Who are you? Who are we? In times of crisis, these are life-and-death questions. Thousands of people survived Hurricane Katrina because grandsons or aunts or neighbors or complete strangers reached out to those in need all through the Gulf Coast and because an armada of boat owners from the surrounding communities and as far away as Texas went into New Orleans to pull stranded people to safety. Hundreds of people died in the aftermath of Katrina because others, including police, vigilantes, high government officials, and the media, decided that the people of New Orleans were too dangerous to allow them to evacuate the septic, drowned city or to rescue them, even from hospitals. Some who attempted to flee were turned back at gunpoint or shot down. Rumors proliferated about mass rapes, mass murders, and mayhem that turned out later to be untrue, though the national media and New Orleans's police chief believed and perpetuated those rumors during the crucial days when people were dying on rooftops and elevated highways and in crowded shelters and hospitals in the unbearable heat, without adequate water, without food, without medicine and medical attention. Those rumors led soldiers and others dispatched as rescuers to regard victims as enemies. Beliefs matter—though as many people act generously despite their beliefs as the reverse.

Katrina was an extreme version of what goes on in many disasters, wherein how you behave depends on whether you think your neighbors or fellow citizens are a greater threat than the havoc wrought by a disaster or a greater good than the property in houses and stores around you. (*Citizen*, in this book, means members of a city or community, not people in possession of legal citizenship in a nation.) What you believe shapes how you act. How you act results in life or death, for yourself or others, as in everyday life, only more so. Katrina was, like most disasters, also marked by altruism: of young men who took it upon themselves to supply water, food, diapers, and protection to the strangers stranded with them; of people who rescued or sheltered neighbors; of the uncounted hundreds or thousands who set out in boats—armed, often, but also armed with compassion—to find those who were stranded in the stagnant waters and bring them to safety; of the two hundred thousand or more who (via the Internet site HurricaneHousing.org in the weeks after) volunteered to house complete strangers, mostly in their own homes, persuaded more by the pictures of suffering than the rumors of monstrosity; of the uncounted tens of thousands of volunteers who came to the Gulf Coast to rebuild and restore.

In the wake of an earthquake, a bombing, or a major storm, most people are altruistic, urgently engaged in caring for themselves and those around them, strangers and neighbors as well as friends and loved ones. The image of the selfish, panicky, or regressively savage human being in times of disaster has little truth to it. Decades of meticulous sociological research on behavior in disasters, from the bombings of World War II to floods, tornadoes, earthquakes, and storms across the continent and around the world, have demonstrated this. But belief lags behind, and often the worst behavior in the wake of a calamity is on the part of those who believe that others will behave savagely and that they themselves are taking defensive measures against barbarism. From earthquake-shattered San Francisco in 1906 to flooded New Orleans in 2005, innocents have been killed by people who believed or asserted that their victims were the criminals and they themselves were the protectors of the shaken order. Beliefs matter.

"Today Cain is still killing his brother" proclaims a faded church mural in the Lower Ninth Ward of New Orleans, which was so devastated by the failure of the government levees. In quick succession, the Book of Genesis gives us the creation of the universe, the illicit acquisition of knowledge, the expulsion from Paradise, and the slaying of Abel by Cain, a second fall from grace into jealousy, competition, alienation, and violence. When God asks Cain where his brother is, Cain asks back, "Am I my brother's keeper?" He is refusing to say what God already knows: that the spilled blood of Abel cries out from the ground that has absorbed it. He is also raising one of the perennial social questions: are we beholden to each other, must we take care of each other, or is it every man for himself?

Most traditional societies have deeply entrenched commitments and connections between individuals, families, and groups. The very concept of society rests on the idea of networks of affinity and affection, and the freestanding individual exists largely as an outcast or exile. Mobile and individualistic modern societies shed some of these old ties and vacillate about taking on others, especially those expressed through economic arrangements—including provisions for the aged and vulnerable, the mitigation of poverty and desperation— the keeping of one's brothers and sisters. The argument against such keeping is often framed as an argument about human nature: we are essentially selfish, and because you will not care for me, I cannot care for you. I will not feed you because I must hoard against starvation, since I too cannot count on others. Better yet, I will take your wealth and add it to mine—if I believe that my well-being is independent of yours or pitted against yours—and justify my conduct as natural law. If I am not my brother's keeper, then we have been expelled from paradise, a paradise of unbroken solidarities.

Thus does everyday life become a social disaster. Sometimes disaster intensifies this; sometimes it provides a remarkable reprieve from it, a view into another world for our other selves. When all the ordinary divides and patterns are shattered, people step up—not all, but the great preponderance—to become their brothers' keepers. And that purposefulness and connectedness bring joy even amid death, chaos, fear, and loss. Were we to know and believe this, our sense of what is possible at any time might change. We speak of self-fulfilling prophesies, but any belief that is acted on makes the world in its image. Beliefs matter. And so do the facts behind them. The astonishing gap between common beliefs and actualities about disaster behavior limits the possibilities, and changing beliefs could fundamentally change much more. Horrible in itself, disaster is sometimes a door back into paradise, the paradise at least in which we are who we hope to be, do the work we desire, and are each our sister's and brother's keeper.

I landed in Halifax, Nova Scotia, shortly after a big hurricane tore up the city in October of 2003. The man in charge of taking me around told me about the hurricane—not about the winds that roared at more than a hundred miles an hour and tore up trees, roofs, and telephone poles or about the seas that rose nearly ten feet, but about the neighbors. He spoke of the few days when everything was disrupted, and he lit up with happiness as he did so. In his neighborhood all the people had come out of their houses to speak with each other, aid each other, improvise a community kitchen, make sure the elders were okay, and spend time together, no longer strangers. "Everybody woke up the next morning and everything was different," he mused. "There was no electricity, all the stores were closed, no one had access to media. The consequence was that everyone poured out into the street to bear witness. Not quite a street party, but everyone out at once—it was a sense of happiness to see everybody even though we didn't know each other." His joy struck me powerfully.

A friend told me of being trapped in a terrible fog, one of the dense tule fogs that overtakes California's Central Valley periodically. On this occasion the fog mixed with dust from the cotton fields created a shroud so perilous that the highway patrol stopped all traffic on the highway. For two days she was stranded with many others in a small diner. She and her husband slept upright, shoulder to shoulder with strangers, in the banquettes of the diner's booths. Although food and water began to run short, they had a marvelous time. The people gathered there had little in common, but they all opened up, began to tell each other the stories of their lives, and by the time the road was safe, my friend and her husband were reluctant to leave. But they went onward, home to New Mexico for the holidays, where everyone looked at them perplexedly as they told the story of their stranding with such ebullience. That time in the diner was the first time ever her partner, a Native American, had felt a sense of belonging in society at large. Such redemption amid disruption is common.

It reminded me of how many of us in the San Francisco Bay Area had loved the Loma Prieta earthquake that took place three weeks before the Berlin Wall fell in 1989. Or loved not the earthquake but the way communities had responded to it. It was alarming for most of us as well, devastating for some, and fatal for sixty people (a very low death count for a major earthquake in an area inhabited by millions). When the subject of the quake came up with a new acquaintance, she too glowed with recollection about how her San Francisco neighborhood had, during the days the power was off, cooked up all its thawing frozen food and held barbecues on the street; how gregarious everyone had been, how people from all walks of life had mixed in candlelit bars that became community centers. Another friend recently remembered with unextinguished amazement that when he traveled the several miles from the World Series baseball game at Candlestick Park in the city's southeast to his home in the central city, someone was at every blacked-out intersection, directing traffic. Without orders or centralized organization, people had stepped up to meet the needs of the moment, suddenly in charge of their communities and streets.

When that earthquake shook the central California coast on October 17, 1989, I was surprised to find that the person I was angry at no longer mattered. The anger had evaporated along with everything else abstract and remote, and I was thrown into an intensely absorbing present. I was more surprised to realize that most of the people I knew and met in the Bay Area were also enjoying immensely the disaster that shut down much of the region for several days, the Bay Bridge for months, and certain unloved elevated freeways forever—if *enjoyment* is the right word for that sense of immersion in the moment and solidarity with others caused by the rupture in everyday life, an emotion graver than happiness but deeply positive. We don't even have a language for this emotion, in which the wonderful comes wrapped in the terrible, joy in sorrow, courage in fear. We cannot welcome disaster, but we can value the responses, both practical and psychological.

For weeks after the big earthquake of 1989, friendship and love counted for a lot, long-term plans and old anxieties for very little. Life was situated in the here and now, and many inessentials had been pared away. The earthquake was unnerving, as were the aftershocks that continued for months. Most of us were at least a little on edge, but many of us were enriched rather than impoverished, overall, at least emotionally. A more somber version of that strange pleasure in disaster emerged after September 11, 2001, when many Americans seemed stirred, moved, and motivated by the newfound sense of urgency, purpose, solidarity, and danger they had encountered. They abhorred what had happened, but they clearly relished who they briefly became.

What is this feeling that crops up during so many disasters? After the Loma Prieta quake, I began to wonder about it. After 9/11, I began to see how strange a phenomenon it was and how deeply it mattered. After I met the man in Halifax who lit up with joy when he talked about the great hurricane there, I began to study it. After I began to write about the 1906 earthquake as its centennial approached, I started to see how often this peculiar feeling arose and how much it remade the world of disaster. After Hurricane Katrina tore up the Gulf Coast, I began to understand the limits and possibilities of disasters. This book is about that emotion, as important as it is surprising, and the circumstances that arouse it and those that it generates. These things count as we enter an era of increasing and intensifying disaster. And more than that, they matter as we enter an era when questions about everyday social possibilities and human nature arise again, as they often have in turbulent times.

When I ask people about the disasters they have lived through, I find on many faces that retrospective basking as they recount tales of Canadian ice storms, midwestern snow days, New York City blackouts, oppressive heat in southern India, fire in New Mexico, the great earthquake in Mexico City, earlier hurricanes in Louisiana, the economic collapse in Argentina, earthquakes in California and Mexico, and a strange pleasure overall. It was the joy on their faces that surprised me. And with those whom I read rather than spoke to, it was the joy in their words that surprised me. It should not be so, is not so, in the familiar version of what disaster brings, and yet it is there, arising from rubble, from ice, from fire, from storms and floods. The joy matters as a measure of otherwise neglected desires, desires for public life and civil society, for inclusion, purpose, and power.

Disasters are, most basically, terrible, tragic, grievous, and no matter what positive side effects and possibilities they produce, they are not to be desired. But by the same measure, those side effects should not be ignored because they arise amid devastation. The desires and possibilities awakened are so powerful they shine even from wreckage, carnage, and ashes. What happens here is relevant elsewhere. And the point is not to welcome disasters. They do not create these gifts, but they are one avenue through which the gifts arrive. Disasters provide an extraordinary window into social desire and possibility, and what manifests there matters elsewhere, in ordinary times and in other extraordinary times.

Most social change is chosen—you want to belong to a co-op, you believe in social safety nets or community-supported agriculture. But disaster doesn't sort us out by preferences; it drags us into emergencies that require we act, and act altruistically, bravely, and with initiative in order to survive or save the neighbors, no matter how we vote or what we do for a living. The positive emotions that arise in those unpromising circumstances demonstrate that social ties and meaningful work are deeply desired, readily improvised, and intensely rewarding. The very structure of our economy and society prevents these goals from being achieved. The structure is also ideological, a philosophy that best serves the wealthy and powerful but shapes all of our lives, reinforced as the conventional wisdom disseminated by the media, from news hours to disaster movies. The facets of that ideology have been called individualism, capitalism, and Social Darwinism and have appeared in the political philosophies of Thomas Hobbes and Thomas Malthus, as well as the work of most conventional contemporary economists, who presume we seek personal gain for rational reasons and refrain from looking at the ways a system skewed to that end damages much else we need for our survival and desire for our well-being. Disaster demonstrates this, since among the factors determining whether you will live or die are the health of your immediate community and the justness of your society. We need ties, but they along with purposefulness, immediacy, and agency also give us joy— the startling, sharp joy I found in accounts of disaster survivors. These accounts demonstrate that the citizens any paradise would need— the people who are brave enough, resourceful enough, and generous enough—already exist. The possibility of paradise hovers on the cusp of coming into being, so much so that it takes powerful forces to keep such a paradise at bay. If paradise now arises in hell, it's because in the suspension of the usual order and the failure of most systems, we are free to live and act another way.

This book investigates five disasters in depth, from the 1906 earthquake in San Francisco to the hurricane and flood in New Orleans ninety-nine years later. In between come the Halifax explosion of 1917, the extraordinary Mexico City earthquake that killed so many and changed so much, and the neglected tales of how ordinary New Yorkers responded to the calamity that struck their city on September 11, 2001. In and around these principal examples come stories of the London Blitz; of earthquakes in China and Argentina; of the Chernobyl nuclear accident; the Chicago heat wave of 1995; the Managua, Nicaragua, earthquake that helped topple a regime; a smallpox epidemic in New York; and a volcanic eruption in Iceland. Though the worst natural disasters in recent years have been in Asia—the 2004 tsunami in the Indian Ocean, the 2005 earthquake in Pakistan, the 2008 earthquake in China and typhoon in Burma—I have not written about them. They matter immensely, but language and distance as well as culture kept these disasters out of reach for me.

Since postmodernism reshaped the intellectual landscape, it has been problematic to even use the term *human nature*, with its implication of a stable and universal human essence. The study of disasters makes it clear that there are plural and contingent natures—but the prevalent human nature in disaster is resilient, resourceful, generous, empathic, and brave. The language of therapy speaks almost exclusively of the consequence of disaster as trauma, suggesting a humanity that is unbearably fragile, a self that does not act but is acted upon, the most basic recipe of the victim. Disaster movies and the media continue to portray ordinary people as hysterical or vicious in the face of calamity. We believe these sources telling us we are victims or brutes more than we trust our own experience. Most people know this other human nature from experience, though almost nothing official or mainstream confirms it. This book is an account of that rising from the ruins that is the ordinary human response to disaster and of what that rising can mean in other arenas—a subject that slips between the languages we have been given to talk about who we are when everything goes wrong.

But to understand both that rising and what hinders and hides it, there are two other important subjects to consider. One is the behavior of the minority in power, who often act savagely in a disaster. The other is the beliefs and representations of the media, the people who hold up a distorting mirror to us in which it is almost impossible to recognize these paradises and our possibilities. Beliefs matter, and the overlapping beliefs of the media and the elites can become a second wave of disaster—as they did most dramatically in the aftermath of Hurricane Katrina. These three subjects are woven together in almost every disaster, and finding the one that matters most—this glimpse of paradise—means understanding the forces that obscure, oppose, and sometimes rub out that possibility.

This social desire and social possibility go against the grain of the dominant stories of recent decades. You can read recent history as a history of privatization not just of the economy but also of society, as marketing and media shove imagination more and more toward private life and private satisfaction, as citizens are redefined as consumers, as public participation falters and with it any sense of collective or individual political power, as even the language for public emotions and satisfactions withers. There is no money in what is aptly called free association: we are instead encouraged by media and advertising to fear each other and regard public life as a danger and a nuisance, to live in secured spaces, communicate by electronic means, and acquire our information from media rather than each other. But in disaster people come together, and though some fear this gathering as a mob, many cherish it as an experience of a civil society that is close enough to paradise. In contemporary terms, *privatization* is largely an economic term, for the consignment of jurisdictions, goods, services, and powers—railways, water rights, policing, education—to the private sector and the vagaries of the marketplace. But this economic privatization is impossible without the privatization of desire and imagination that tells us we are not each other's keeper. Disasters, in returning their sufferers to public and collective life, undo some of this privatization, which is a slower, subtler disaster all its own. In a society in which participation, agency, purposefulness, and freedom are all adequately present, a disaster would be only a disaster.

Few speak of paradise now, except as something remote enough to be impossible. The ideal societies we hear of are mostly far away or long ago or both, situated in some primordial society before the Fall or a spiritual kingdom in a remote Himalayan vastness. The implication is that we here and now are far from capable of living such ideals. But what if paradise flashed up among us from time to time—at the worst of times? What if we glimpsed it in the jaws of hell? These flashes give us, as the long ago and far away do not, a glimpse of who else we ourselves may be and what else our society could become. This is a paradise of rising to the occasion that points out by contrast how the rest of the time most of us fall down from the heights of possibility, down into diminished selves and dismal societies. Many now do not even hope for a better society, but they recognize it when they encounter it, and that discovery shines out even through the namelessness of their experience. Others recognize it, grasp it, and make something of it, and long-term social and political transformations, both good and bad, arise from the wreckage. The door to this era's potential paradises is in hell.

The word *emergency* comes from *emerge*, to rise out of, the opposite of merge, which comes from *mergere*, to be within or under a liquid, immersed, submerged. An emergency is a separation from the familiar, a sudden emergence into a new atmosphere, one that often demands we ourselves rise to the occasion. *Catastrophe* comes from the Greek *kata*, or down, and *streiphen*, or turning over. It means an upset of what is expected and was originally used to mean a plot twist. To emerge into the unexpected is not always terrible, though these words have evolved to imply ill fortune. The word *disaster* comes from the Latin compound of *dis-*, or away, without, and *astro*, star or planet; literally, without a star. It originally suggested misfortune due to astrologically generated trouble, as in the blues musician Albert King's classic "Born Under a Bad Sign."

In some of the disasters of the twentieth century—the big northeastern blackouts in 1965 and 2003, the 1989 Loma Prieta earthquake in the San Francisco Bay Area, 2005's Hurricane Katrina on the Gulf Coast—the loss of electrical power meant that the light pollution blotting out the night sky vanished. In these disaster-struck cities, people suddenly found themselves under the canopy of stars still visible in small and remote places. On the warm night of August 15, 2003, the Milky Way could be seen in New York City, a heavenly realm long lost to view until the blackout that hit the Northeast late that afternoon. You can think of the current social order as something akin to this artificial light: another kind of power that fails in disaster. In its place appears a reversion to improvised, collaborative, cooperative, and local society. However beautiful the stars of a suddenly visible night sky, few nowadays could find their way by them. But the constellations of solidarity, altruism, and improvisation are within most of us and reappear at these times. People know what to do in a disaster. The loss of power, the disaster in the modern sense, is an affliction, but the reappearance of these old heavens is its opposite. This is the paradise entered through hell.

The Mizpah Café

THE GATHERING PLACE

The outlines of this particular disaster are familiar. At 5:12 in the morning on April 18, 1906, about a minute of seismic shaking tore up San Francisco, toppling buildings, particularly those on landfill and swampy ground, cracking and shifting others, collapsing chimneys, breaking water mains and gas lines, twisting streetcar tracks, even tipping headstones in the cemeteries. It was a major earthquake, centered right off the coast of the peninsular city, and the damage it did was considerable. Afterward came the fires, both those caused by broken gas mains and chimneys and those caused and augmented by the misguided policy of trying to blast firebreaks ahead of the flames and preventing citizens from firefighting in their own homes and neighborhoods. The way the authorities handled the fires was a major reason why so much of the city—nearly five square miles, more than twenty-eight thousand structures—was incinerated in one of history's biggest urban infernos before aerial warfare. Nearly every municipal building was destroyed, and so were many of the downtown businesses, along with mansions, slums, middle-class neighborhoods, the dense residential-commercial district of Chinatown, newspaper offices, and warehouses.

The response of the citizens is less familiar. Here is one. Mrs. Anna Amelia Holshouser, whom a local newspaper described as a "woman of middle age, buxom and comely," woke up on the floor of her bedroom on Sacramento Street, where the earthquake had thrown her. She took time to dress herself while the ground and her home were still shaking, in that era when getting dressed was no simple matter of throwing on clothes. "Powder, paint, jewelry, hair switch, all were on when I started my flight down one hundred twenty stairs to the street," she recalled. The house in western San Francisco was slightly damaged, her downtown place of business—she was a beautician and masseuse—was "a total wreck," and so she salvaged what she could and moved on with a friend, Mr. Paulson. They camped out in Union Square downtown until the fires came close and soldiers drove them onward. Like thousands of others, they ended up trudging with their bundles to Golden Gate Park, the thousand-acre park that runs all the way west to the Pacific Ocean. There they spread an old quilt "and lay down . . . not to sleep, but to shiver with cold from fog and mist and watch the flames of the burning city, whose blaze shone far above the trees." On their third day in the park, she stitched together blankets, carpets, and sheets to make a tent that sheltered twenty-two people, including thirteen children. And Holshouser started a tiny soup kitchen with one tin can to drink from and one pie plate to eat from. All over the city stoves were hauled out of damaged buildings—fire was forbidden indoors, since many standing homes had gas leaks or damaged flues or chimneys—or primitive stoves were built out of rubble, and people commenced to cook for each other, for strangers, for anyone in need. Her generosity was typical, even if her initiative was exceptional.

Holshouser got funds to buy eating utensils across the bay in Oakland. The kitchen began to grow, and she was soon feeding two to three hundred people a day, not a victim of the disaster but a victor over it and the hostess of a popular social center—her brothers' and sisters' keeper. Some visitors from Oakland liked her makeshift dining camp so well they put up a sign—"Palace Hotel"—naming it after the burned-out downtown luxury establishment that was reputedly once the largest hotel in the world. Humorous signs were common around the camps and street-side shelters. Nearby on Oak Street a few women ran "The Oyster Loaf" and the "Chat Noir"—two little shacks with their names in fancy cursive. A shack in Jefferson Square was titled "The House of Mirth," with additional signs jokingly offering rooms for rent with steam heat and elevators. The inscription on the side of "Hoffman's Café," another little street-side shack, read "Cheer up, have one on me . . . come in and spend a quiet evening." A menu chalked on the door of "Camp Necessity," a tiny shack, included the items "fleas eyes raw, 98¢, pickled eels, nails fried, 13¢, flies legs on toast, .09¢, crab's tongues, stewed," ending with "rain water fritters with umbrella sauce, $9.10." "The Appetite Killery" may be the most ironic name, but the most famous inscription read, "Eat, drink, and be merry, for tomorrow we may have to go to Oakland." Many had already gone there or to hospitable Berkeley, and the railroads carried many much farther away for free.

About three thousand people had died, at least half the city was homeless, families were shattered, the commercial district was smoldering ashes, and the army from the military base at the city's north end was terrorizing many citizens. As soon as the newspapers resumed printing, they began to publish long lists of missing people and of the new locations at which displaced citizens and sundered families could be found. Despite or perhaps because of this, the people were for the most part calm and cheerful, and many survived the earthquake with gratitude and generosity. Edwin Emerson recalled that after the quake, "when the tents of the refugees, and the funny street kitchens, improvised from doors and shutters and pieces of roofing, overspread all the city, such merriment became an accepted thing. Everywhere, during those long moonlit evenings, one could hear the tinkle of guitars and mandolins, from among the tents. Or, passing by the grotesque rows of curbstone kitchens, one became dimly aware of the low murmurings of couples who had sought refuge in those dark recesses as in bowers of love. It was at this time that the droll signs and inscriptions began to appear on walls and tent flaps, which soon became one of the familiar sights of reconstructing San Francisco. The overworked marriage license clerk has deposed that the fees collected by him for issuing such licenses during April and May 1906 far exceeded the totals for the same months of any preceding years in San Francisco." Emerson had rushed to the scene of disaster from New

York, pausing to telegraph a marriage proposal of his own to a young woman in San Francisco, who wrote a letter of rejection that was still in the mail when she met her suitor in person amid the wreckage and accepted. They were married a few weeks later.

Disaster requires an ability to embrace contradiction in both the minds of those undergoing it and those trying to understand it from afar. In each disaster, there is suffering, there are psychic scars that will be felt most when the emergency is over, there are deaths and losses. Satisfactions, newborn social bonds, and liberations are often also profound. Of course one factor in the gap between the usual accounts of disaster and actual experience is that those accounts focus on the small percentage of people who are wounded, killed, orphaned, and otherwise devastated, often at the epicenter of the disaster, along with the officials involved. Surrounding them, often in the same city or even neighborhood, is a periphery of many more who are largely undamaged but profoundly disrupted—and it is the disruptive power of disaster that matters here, the ability of disasters to topple old orders and open new possibilities. This broader effect is what disaster does to society. In the moment of disaster, the old order no longer exists and people improvise rescues, shelters, and communities. Thereafter, a struggle takes place over whether the old order with all its shortcomings and injustices will be reimposed or a new one, perhaps more oppressive or perhaps more just and free, like the disaster utopia, will arise.

Of course people who are deeply and devastatingly affected may yet find something redemptive in their experience, while those who are largely unaffected may be so rattled they are immune to the other possibilities (curiously, people farther from the epicenter of a disaster are often more frightened, but this seems to be because what you imagine as overwhelming or terrifying while at leisure becomes something you can cope with when you must—there is no time for fear). There are no simple rules for the emotions. We speak mostly of happy and sad emotions, a divide that suggests a certain comic lightness to the one side and pure negativity to the other, but perhaps we would navigate our experiences better by thinking in terms of deep and shallow, rich and poor. The very depth of emotion, the connecting to the core of one's being, the calling into play one's strongest feelings and abilities, can be rich, even on deathbeds, in wars and emergencies, while what is often assumed to be the circumstance of happiness sometimes is only insulation from the depths, or so the plagues of ennui and angst among the comfortable suggest.

Next door to Holshouser's kitchen, an aid team from the mining boomtown of Tonopah, Nevada, set up and began to deliver wag-onloads of supplies to the back of Holshouser's tent. The Nevadans got on so well with the impromptu cook and hostess they gave her a guest register whose inscription read in part: "in cordial appreciation of her prompt, philanthropic, and efficient service to the people in general, and particularly to the Tonopah Board of Trade Relief Com-mittee. . . . May her good deeds never be forgotten." Thinking that the place's "Palace Hotel" sign might cause confusion, they rebap-tized it the Mizpah Café after the Mizpah Saloon in Tonopah, and a new sign was installed. The ornamental letters spelled out above the name "One Touch of Nature Makes the Whole World Kin" and those below "Established April 23, 1906." The Hebrew word *mizpah*, says one encyclopedia, "is an emotional bond between those who are separated (either physically or by death)." Another says it was the Old Testament watchtower "where the people were accustomed to meet in great national emergencies." Another source describes it as "symbol-izing a sanctuary and place of hopeful anticipation." The ramshackle material reality of Holshouser's improvised kitchen seemed to matter not at all in comparison with its shining social role. It ran through June of 1906, when Holshouser wrote her memoir of the earthquake. Her piece is as remarkable for what it doesn't say: it doesn't speak of fear, enemies, conflict, chaos, crime, despondency, or trauma.

Just as her kitchen was one of many spontaneously launched com-munity centers and relief projects, so her resilient resourcefulness represents the ordinary response in many disasters. In them, strang-ers become friends and collaborators, goods are shared freely, people improvise new roles for themselves. Imagine a society where money plays little or no role, where people rescue each other and then care for each other, where food is given away, where life is mostly out of doors in public, where the old divides between people seem to have fallen away, and the fate that faces them, no matter how grim, is far less so for being shared, where much once considered impossible, both good and bad, is now possible or present, and where the moment is so pressing that old complaints and worries fall away, where people feel important, purposeful, at the center of the world. It is by its very nature unsustainable and evanescent, but like a lightning flash it illuminates ordinary life, and like lightning it sometimes shatters the old forms. It is utopia itself for many people, though it is only a brief moment during terrible times. And at the time they manage to hold both irreconcilable experiences, the joy and the grief.

A MAP OF UTOPIA

This utopia matters, because almost everyone has experienced some version of it and because it is not the result of a partisan agenda but rather a broad, unplanned effort to salvage society and take care of the neighbors amid the wreckage. "A map of the world that does not include Utopia is not worth even glancing at, for it leaves out the one country at which humanity is always heading," wrote Oscar Wilde fifteen years before San Francisco's great quake. The utopias built by citizens like Anna Holshouser are not yet on that map. But they should be. They could change the map of our own beliefs, our sense of what is possible and who we are. Utopia is in trouble these days. Many no longer believe that a better world, as opposed to a better life, is possible, and the rhetoric of private well-being trumps public good, at least in the English-speaking world. And yet the yearning remains—all the riches piled up, the security gates and stock options, are only defenses against a world of insecurity and animosity, piecemeal solutions to a pervasive problem. Sometimes it seems as though home improvement has trumped the idealistic notion of a better world. Sometimes. But utopia flares up in other parts of the world, where hope is fiercer and dreams are larger.

"There is no alternative," the conservative British prime minister Margaret Thatcher liked to say, but there is, and it appears where it is least expected, as well as where it is most diligently cultivated. Changing the world is the other way to imagine salvaging the self—and others, for the utopian impulse is generous even when it's wrongheaded. And utopias of sorts arise in the present, in Argentina, in Mexico, in countless social, economic, and agricultural experiments in Europe, in India, and in the United States; among other places. The map of utopias is cluttered nowadays with experiments by other names, and the very idea is expanding. It needs to open up a little more to contain disaster communities. These remarkable societies suggest that, just as many machines reset themselves to their original settings after a power outage, so human beings reset themselves to something altruistic, communitarian, resourceful, and imaginative after a disaster, that we revert to something we already know how to do. The possibility of paradise is already within us as a default setting.

The two most basic goals of social utopias are to eliminate deprivation—hunger, ignorance, homelessness—and to forge a society in which no one is an outsider, no one is alienated. By this standard, Holshouser's free food and warm social atmosphere achieved both, on however tiny a scale, and versions of the Mizpah Café sprung up all over the ruined city.

Some religious attempts at utopia are authoritarian, led by a charismatic leader, by elders, by rigid rules that create outcasts, but the secular utopias have mostly been committed to liberty, democracy, and shared power. The widespread disdain for revolution and utopia takes as its object lesson the Soviet-style attempts at coercive utopias, in which the original ideals of leveling and sharing go deeply awry, the achievement critiqued in George Orwell's *Animal Farm* and *1984* and other dystopian novels. Many fail to notice that it is not the ideals, the ends, but the coercive and authoritarian means that poison paradise. There are utopias whose ideals pointedly include freedom from coercion and dispersal of power to the many. Most utopian visions nowadays include many worlds, many versions, rather than a coercive one true way. The anthropologist David Graeber writes, "Stalinists and their ilk did not kill because they dreamed great dreams—actually, Stalinists were famous for being rather short on imagination—but because they mistook their dreams for scientific certainties. This led them to feel they had a right to impose their visions through a machinery of violence." There are plenty of failed revolutions and revolutions such as the French Revolution that lapse into bloodbaths—and yet when that revolution was over, France would never be dominated by an absolutist monarchy again; ordinary French people had more rights, and people around the world had an enlarged sense of the possible. All revolutions fail because they set their sights heaven-high, but none of them fail to do something, and many increase the amount of liberty, justice, and hope for their heirs.

Unpoliced utopian experiments have arisen often in the United States. The ascetic rural Shakers have lasted from 1775, when they arrived in New York from England, into—by the tenuous thread of a few older survivors—the present. Less stable experiments proliferated in the nineteenth century. There was, for example, Brook Farm in Massachusetts in the 1840s, in which a lot of bookish idealists tried, not very effectively, to till the earth to realize an ideal union of mental and physical labor and collective life. There was also the socialist Kaweah Colony in the mountains of California in the 1880s and 1890s (the land they homesteaded is now part of Sequoia National Park, and the giant tree they named the Karl Marx Tree is now the General Sherman sequoia). Many argue that the United States was founded on utopian dreams, from the conquistador fantasies of a gold-drenched El Dorado to the pioneer reading of the American West as an unfallen Eden the woodsman entered as an ax-swinging Adam. Some even include the seventeenth-century New England Puritans among the Utopians, though their regime of sober piety, stern patriarchs, and enforced conformity resembles a lot of other peoples' gulags. And the Puritans were not social experimentalists; the pervasive utopian preoccupation with sharing wealth and finding a communal mode of dealing with practical needs and social goals had little to do with them, though it surfaced in other conservative religious movements, such as Mormonism.

I often argue with my friend Sam about what has become of the dream of Utopia. He believes it has faded with the end of communist and universalist fantasies; I believe it has evolved into more viable, modest versions. A certain kind of twentieth-century utopian idealism has died, the kind that believed we could and should erase everything and start over: new language, new society, new ways of organizing power, work, even family, home, and more. Projects for abandoning the past wholesale and inventing a whole new human being seem, like the idea of one-size-fits-all universalism, more ominous than utopian to us now. It may be because *we* now includes people who forcibly lost their language, whether it was Yiddish in Poland or Cree in Canada, that as we lose the past, we cherish it more and look at the devouring mouth of the future with more apprehension. But we have also learned that you can reinvent the government but not human nature in one fell stroke, and the process of reinventing human nature is a much more subtle, personal, incremental process. Mostly nowadays we draw our hopes from fragments and traditions from a richly varied past rather than an imagined future. But disaster throws us into the temporary utopia of a transformed human nature and society, one that is bolder, freer, less attached and divided than in ordinary times, not blank, but not tied down.

Utopianism was a driving force in the nineteenth century. Union activists sought to improve working conditions and wages for the vast majority of laborers, and many were radicals who also hoped for or worked for a socialist or anarchist revolution that would change the whole society and eliminate the causes of suffering, poverty, and powerlessness rather than merely mitigate some of the effects (how viable and desirable their versions of the ideal were is another story). The socialist-anarchist Kaweah commune included many union members, while the French commune Icaria-Speranza, eighty miles north of San Francisco, included refugees from the 1848 revolution in France and the Paris Commune, the populist takeover of that city for two months in 1871.

This list of utopian possibilities leaves off the underground utopias, the odd ways in which people improvise their hopes or just improve their lives in the most adverse circumstances. I once met a young Polish émigré who told me that many Poles were nostalgic, not for the Communist regime that fell in 1989 but for the close-knit communities that developed to survive that malevolent era, circulating black-market goods and ideas, helping each other with the long food lines and other tasks of survival, banding together to survive. In the democratic-capitalist regime that replaced Poland's communism, such alliances were no longer necessary, and people drifted apart, free at last but no longer a community. Finding the balance between independence and fellowship is one of the ongoing utopian struggles. And under the false brotherhood of Soviet-style communism, a true communal solidarity of resistance was born (as well as an independent Polish labor union, Solidarity, that eventually brought down that system). This nostalgia for a time that was in many ways much harder but is remembered as better, morally and socially, is common. And it brings us to the ubiquitous fleeting utopias that are neither coerced nor countercultural but universal, albeit overlooked: disaster utopias, the subject of this book.

You don't have to subscribe to a political ideology, move to a commune, or join the guerrillas in the mountains; you wake up in a society suddenly transformed, and chances are good you will be part of that transformation in what you do, in whom you connect to, in how you feel. Something changes. Elites and authorities often fear the changes of disaster or anticipate that the change means chaos and destruction, or a least the undermining of the foundations of their power. So a power struggle often takes place in disaster—and real political and social change can result, from that struggle or from the new sense of self and society that emerges. Too, the elite often believe that if they themselves are not in control, the situation is out of control, and in their fear, take repressive measures that become secondary disasters. But many others who don't hold radical ideas, don't believe in revolution, don't consciously desire profound social change find themselves in a transformed world leading a life they could not have imagined and rejoice in it.

The future holds many more disasters because of such factors as climate change and the likelihood of large earthquakes on long-dormant or semidormant faults, as well as increases in the vulnerability of populations who have moved to coasts, to cities, to areas at risk, to flimsy housing, to deeper poverty, shallower roots, and frailer support networks. The relief organization Oxfam reported in 2007, "The number of weather-related disasters has quadrupled over the past twenty years and the world should do more to prepare for them. The report argues that climate change is responsible for the growing number of weather-related disasters—more intense rain, combined with frequent droughts, make damaging floods much more likely." Disaster is never terribly far away. Knowing how people behave in disasters is fundamental to knowing how to prepare for them. And what can be learned about resilience, social and psychological response, and possibility from sudden disasters is relevant as well for the slower disasters of poverty, economic upheaval, and incremental environmental degradation as well as the abiding questions about social possibilities.

The Mizpah Café was at once nothing special and a miracle, chaos and deprivation turned into order and abundance by will, empathy, and one woman's resourcefulness. It is a miniature of the communities that often arise out of disasters. [. . .] Disasters are extraordinarily generative, and though disaster utopias recur again and again, there is no simple formula for what arises: it has everything to do with who or what individuals or communities were before the disaster and the circumstances they find themselves in. But those circumstances are far richer and stranger than has ever been accounted for.

QUESTIONS FOR DISCUSSION

According to Solnit, why do disasters create brief utopias of "transformed human nature and society"? (73)

1. What answer does Solnit offer to her question, "What is this feeling that crops up during so many disasters?" (60)

2. What does Solnit mean in saying that disaster "requires an ability to embrace contradiction both in the minds of those undergoing it and those trying to understand it from afar"? (68)

3. Why does Solnit believe that finding "the balance between independence and fellowship" is a recurring challenge of attempts to create utopias? (73)

4. According to Solnit, how are lessons learned from disasters relevant to the "slower disasters of poverty, economic upheaval, and incremental environmental degradation as well as the abiding questions about social possibilities"? (74) What lessons does she think are to be learned?

What is the main reason why the utopias that emerge in disasters are by their "very nature unsustainable and evanescent," according to Solnit? (70)

1. If "social ties and meaningful work are deeply desired, readily improvised, and intensely rewarding," why does Solnit say that the "very structure of our economy and society prevents these goals from being achieved"? (61)

2. Does Solnit believe that human nature or elites and authorities bear more responsibility for our failure to sustain the brief paradises that emerge in disasters?

3. If, as Solnit asserts, "The possibility of paradise is already within us as a default setting" during times of disaster, what is it about human nature that Solnit believes needs to be improved in a slow "process of reinvention"? (71)

FOR FURTHER REFLECTION

1. Do you agree with Solnit that the human desire for social ties and meaningful work are prevented by the "very structure of our economy and society"?

2. If feeling joy in the midst of pain is a common human experience, do you agree with Solnit that "We don't even have a language for this emotion"?

3. How would you respond to Cain's question, "Am I my brother's keeper?" What does it mean to be your "brother's keeper" in today's world?

Time

Riichi Yokomitsu

The manager of our troupe failed to return for a whole week after stepping out one evening. Takagi decided to open the suitcase he had left behind. It was empty. Then we were really at our wits' end. When the truth dawned on us—our manager had run off, leaving us without a penny—we were all too dumbfounded to make any suggestion as to how to deal with the room and board bill. I was finally chosen as delegate for the group to face the landlord. I asked him please to allow us to continue as we were for the time being, and assured him that remittances would be forthcoming from our families. I earned us thus a temporary reprieve. Two or three money orders did in fact come, and each time we acclaimed them with joyous shouts. What happened, however, was that the money which arrived was the exclusive possession of the man receiving it, and it simply led to his making off immediately with whichever actress of the company he liked best.

Finally there were twelve of us left—eight men and four women: six-feet tall, amply built Takagi, who assumed as a matter of course that women had eyes for no one but him; Kinoshita, who liked gambling better than three meals a day and whose every thought was directed toward inventing a means of seeing dice through the box; pale, gentle Sasa, whom everyone called Buddha, and who, mysteriously enough, licked the windowpanes when he was drunk; Yagi, who was a little peculiar, and collected women's underwear; Matsugi, a champion at hand and foot wrestling, always on the lookout for billiard parlors in whatever town we went to; Kurigi, who was forever forgetting and mislaying his belongings, and whose only talent was for losing whatever came into his hands; Yashima, who, miser that he was, hated to return borrowed articles; and myself—eight men, plus the four women, Namiko, Shinako, Kikue, and Yukiko. In our cases it was not so much that remittances were unconscionably slow in arriving, as that little or no possibility existed of any money coming to us. Knowing this all along, we had placed our hopes on the money of others more likely to receive it.

The landlord's looks turned unfriendly, as he too began to doubt whether he would see his money, however much longer he waited. His surveillance over the remaining twelve of us was eagle-eyed, to say the least. For our part, we each felt that it was preferable for no money to arrive at all than to have some come to any one of us—whoever received it was sure to sneak off by himself, and make the burden on those who remained all the heavier. Our suspicions grew so strong that soon we were spying on one another secretly, wondering who would be the next to run off. But it was only at the beginning that we could afford the luxury of this mutual spying. Before long we had more pressing matters on our minds than who would be the next to escape—the landlord stopped giving us even one meal a day. We gradually turned pallid and unwell, and our days were spent drinking water to fill our stomachs and discussing interminably what we should do. At length we reached agreement: we would all escape together. If, as we reasoned, we escaped in a group, we would have little to worry about even if a couple of men were sent in pursuit of us. There lurked also in our minds the specter of the fate which lay in store for anyone who happened by mischance to be the last left behind. These considerations led us to swear up and down to make a joint escape. However, if we were simply to make a wild break for it, or in any way attract the attention of the local bullies in the landlord's employ, we would have no chance of success. We decided therefore to take advantage of our visits to the public bath, the one freedom we were allowed, and some rainy night when the watch over us was least strict to make our escape. We would have to follow the road along the coast rather than an easier route, for unless the way we took was the most difficult and unlikely, we were certain to be caught. With these matters settled by way of preliminaries, we resolved to await a rainy night.

In the room next to the one where our escape plans were being discussed, Namiko lay all alone. She had suffered a severe attack of some female sickness during a performance, and was still unable to move from her bed. Whenever the question of what to do with her arose, we all fell silent. On this one topic, no one had a word to say. It was quite clearly—if tacitly—understood that we had no alternative but to abandon her. As a matter of fact, I was also of the opinion that we would have to sacrifice Namiko for the sake of the eleven others of us, but after we had finished our discussion I happened to pass through her room. She suddenly thrust out her arms and seized my foot. She begged me in tears to take her along, insisting that she must escape when we did. I managed eventually to extricate my foot by promising to discuss the matter with the others.

I called everyone together again to reopen our discussion. They were all perfectly aware of my reason for summoning them. In their eyes flashed repeated warnings not to propose anything foolish. I asked if they would not consent to taking Namiko along. First of all, I explained, she was passionately anxious to escape with the rest of us. There was also the sentimental consideration that, after all, she had shared rice from the same pot with us for such a long time. Yukiko, who was standing next to me, capitulated first. She declared that she didn't feel right about leaving Namiko behind. She had once received a pair of stockings from her. Shinako remembered that she had been given some lace cuffs, and Kikue had been given a comb. The women thus were at least not opposed to taking Namiko along. Not one of the men spoke openly. Instead, one after another they took me aside to urge that I drop the subject. "Come on," I said, in an attempt to persuade them, "let's take her. Something good is bound to come of it." They began for the first time to come around to my point of view, and finally agreed that we might as well take her.

When we actually reached the point of making our escape, we faced the necessity of following a trail over the cliffs along the sea for some fifteen or twenty miles before we could get through the pass. The thought of carrying a sick woman on our backs loomed as a staggering undertaking. In order to fool that scoundrel of a landlord we would have to leave the rooming house one by one, swinging our towels as part of the pretense of visiting the public bath in a storm. If we took too much time over our departure we would have no chance to eat, and would be obliged to set out with empty stomachs. In that case we would have no choice but to risk making our way, under cover of darkness, to the next station.

I asked Namiko to try and stand, as a test of her ability to walk. She made an effort, but immediately collapsed limply over the bedding, moaning that her eyes felt as if they were swimming in her head. She seemed utterly without bones. I, who in a moment of sympathy had urged the others to take Namiko along, now could not help thinking that in her condition it would be best for all of us to leave her behind. "Wouldn't you really prefer to remain here by yourself?" I said. "I can't imagine that the landlord would do anything bad to a sick person like yourself. We promise to send you money." Namiko burst into tears. "I'd rather you killed me than left me here alone." She persisted, and I could do nothing to change her mind. After having convinced the others to take Namiko along, I could not bring myself to be so irresponsible as to propose now that we abandon her. So, I too began to wait for the next rainy night. I made no mention of Namiko again. But even waiting for the rain was not easy for us. Anyone who went to the public bath would always pawn an article of clothing and buy buns to be shared with the rest of us. We realized, however, at this rate we might use up the money needed for our train fare, and then face real disaster. We stopped smoking altogether, and limited ourselves to only one bun a day. The whole time was spent lolling around, drinking water to keep ourselves going. There was nothing else to do. Fortunately, the autumn rains began to fall a few mornings later, and by late afternoon an increasingly violent storm had developed. We determined to stage our escape that night, and each of us completed whatever preparations were necessary. We waited for the dark. One thought obsessed me—assuming that we all managed to reach the railway station safely, which man would eventually go off with which woman. The fact that eight men had remained behind with the four women was not only because they had no money. Each of the women had had relations with two or even three of the men, I rather suspected, which made separation extremely difficult. I felt certain that sooner or later, somewhere, there would be trouble. However, no one betrayed any presentiment of this as night approached and the time set for our escape drew upon us. Soon, one or two at a time, the members of the troupe began going out, towels in hand. It crossed my mind that, unknown to me, the matter of which man would go with which woman had already been decided. My share of the escape preparations consisted merely of bundling together changes of clothes for all of us and throwing the bundles over the wall to the others waiting on the opposite side. I was conscious of the danger that, if I was the last to leave, since it had been my idea to take Namiko along, I might well be left to figure out an escape for the two of us. Were such a proposal to be made, the others were only too likely to agree with it. I therefore contrived that Takagi should be the last to leave. With my towel slung over my shoulder I took Namiko on my back and set out in the rain for the bamboo thicket where I was to join the others.

There were about ten of us huddled together in the thicket, protected only by three oil-paper umbrellas. We waited for the others. Kinoshita, who had taken our bundles to the pawnshop, did not appear. No one actually voiced anything, but an expression of uneasiness gradually crept over our faces, as much as to say, "Kinoshita has run off with the money." We stood in silence, staring at each other. Soon, Kinoshita returned with ten yen in his hand. Our next problem was to eat before we started. Takagi was the last to arrive and suggested we all go together to a restaurant. Matsugi pointed out that it would be best to go one at a time, since we were sure to be discovered if we went in a crowd. We agreed to this. We decided to divide the money, but all we had was a ten yen bill. We could have sent someone to change it, but the unspoken fear that anyone who went for change might run off with the money prevented us from letting the money out of our sight. Someone said, "Having the money is just the same as not having it. What are we going to do?" For a while there was silence, then another remarked that if we delayed any longer people from the rooming house would catch up with us. And still another voice: "What could we do if they really came after us? I'm too hungry to move." When we reached this impasse Yashima suggested that the money be turned over to me, since I was the one person who could not run away or hide, what with a sick woman on my back. To this everyone assented. However, I knew that if I were entrusted with the money the others would constantly be spying on me, and this would be extremely disagreeable. I thought it would be better if in front of everybody I gave the money to Namiko. As guardian of our money, she would certainly, at least for the time being, be carefully protected. I thrust the bill into her kimono. With this, the sick woman, who up until now had been treated as a disgusting nuisance, suddenly became an object of value, a reassuringly dependable safe-deposit vault. Automatically we began to formulate regulations around her. First of all, the men in the group were to take turns carrying Namiko on their back, each one taking a hundred steps. The women were not required to carry the burden, but to take turns counting. Next we settled the order of carrying her, while the women laughingly watched and backed one or another of us in our choosing games. Those of us who were to go in front began to walk out of the bamboo thicket.

There were only three umbrellas for the twelve of us, and the rain whipped by a gale beat headlong into our faces. We struggled forward in single file, four to an umbrella, and drenched by the rain. In the middle was Namiko, guarded like a holy image in procession, immediately behind her the women, and farther back some of the men. Sasa, who was near the middle, suddenly called out, "We seem to have forgotten all about eating." There were cries of assent, and again the column came to a halt. But there was hardly time now for eating: if we were overtaken we would be finished. Several favored making a desperate attempt to cross the pass tonight in the hope that tomorrow would be safe, and by tacit consent our column began to wriggle caterpillar-like ahead in the darkness. The starch had drained from the women's felt hats, which began to make a loud spattering noise. At first we thought in terror that it might be the sound of pursuers. From time to time, as if by a prearranged signal, we all would turn to look behind us. But as Kurigi said, even supposing that the landlord discovered what had happened and sent people out after us, they would never choose this terrible road at first. This observation was reassuring, but the fact remained that none of us had ever traveled on the road before. We had not the least idea what lay ahead, not even whether we were to pass through cultivated land or barren desolation. The road, from which the sand had been washed by the rain to expose frequently the raised heads of stones, was only dimly visible at out feet. Uneasiness akin to desperation mounted steadily within us. Only Kinoshita, who chattered on with his usual socialistic talk, displayed any energy. "The next time I meet that damned manager who's responsible for all our suffering, I will really give him a beating," he swore, and at his words the hatred of the group for the already half-forgotten manager suddenly flared up again. "Beat him? I'll shove him in the ocean!" shouted someone else; and another voice chimed in, "The ocean's too good for him! I'll split his head open with a rock." "I'll stick burning hot prongs down his throat!" "Burning hot prongs are too good for him," another man was saying when the sick woman, who up until that moment had not uttered a sound, suddenly burst into loud wails. Yagi, who was carrying her on his back, stopped in his tracks. There were cries from behind. "What's the matter? Can't you move any faster?" Namiko was weeping convulsively, and she began now to beg us to go on without her. At first we were at a loss to tell what had caused this outburst, when we discovered that she was losing blood. We stood there in the rain, bewildered and helpless. I suggested that the women be left to deal with this female disorder, and one of the women thereupon said that a dry cloth was needed immediately. I felt obliged to offer my undershirt. The sick woman felt sorry for us, and all the while that Matsugi, whose turn was next, was carrying her, she begged him in tears again and again to go on without her. Matsugi finally lost his temper and threatened to leave her then and there if she kept whining, and this only made her wail all the more hysterically. Uppermost in our minds, however, was the fear of being overtaken. Finally we reached a point where even that ceased to worry us, when thoughts of our hunger assailed us. "Tomorrow," began one of us, "when we get to a town the first thing I'm going to do is eat pork cutlets." "I'll take fish." "I'd rather have eels than fish." "I'd like a steak." Then we all started to talk about food, not listening to what anyone else had to say, but elaborating on what we liked to eat and places where we had once had a good meal. We were becoming like voracious beasts.

I was as desperate as the others, at least as far as hunger was concerned. I looked for something to eat along the road, but ever since we had emerged from the bamboo thicket we had not passed a single cultivated field. There was hardly much point in searching here: to the right was a wall of sheer rock, and to the left, at the foot of a cliff that dropped several hundred feet, we could hear the sound of waves.

It was all we could do to avoid a misstep from the path, which was a bare four feet wide. We lurched ahead tied to one another with our belts, following whichever way the umbrella in front led. The road twisted up and down. Sometimes the rain unexpectedly swept up on us from below, and before we knew it we would be pasted against the edge of the rock face. Our column staggered ahead over the endless cliff, now stretching out, now contracting, and we began to collide with each other: we obviously could not allow stories of food to dull our faculties. Presently the pleasant remembrances of food turned into grim reminders of the fact that we had nothing to eat. One after another of us dropped out of the discussion. Then we were silent, and all that could be heard between the roar of the waves and the sound of the wind was the monotonous voice of the woman counting the number of paces. There were no sighs now, nor even so much as a cough. The silence which pressed on every one of us, the mute fear of what would happen if things continued this way much longer, was almost tangible enough to touch. At this juncture Namiko's losses of blood became severe. The confusion of removing our undershirts and the wailing of Namiko restored our animation, and with it talk about food. Some protested that so much talk about food worked up our appetites all the more, but the others answered that talk was now the only means at our disposal for blunting our hunger. Water was better than nothing, and some began to lick the drops of rain which trickled from the umbrellas, or else to chew on pine needles pulled from the stunted trees along our way. We looked like so many ravenous demons, but this occasioned no laughter. My clothes were soaked through and through, but my throat was parched. When the rain blew against me I would turn my head away from the umbrella into the rain with my mouth open. And when it came my turn to carry Namiko again, however much I tried to remind myself that the weight on my back was a woman, I was so hungry that I could scarcely keep my feet moving. Everything grew misty before my eyes as I ran more and more out of breath. My arms became numb, and my legs trembled under me. I could go on only by biting my tongue and leaning my head into the back of the man in front of me who carried the umbrella. By the time that the woman had counted up to about ninety, I felt like tossing Namiko over the edge, but I steeled myself against betraying any emotion, for I knew that if she detected it she would start her screeching again. My eyelids became so stiff that when I opened them I heard a click. Even though the burden was eventually shifted to the next man, it came back every eight hundred yards, after each man had performed his stint, and there was pitiful little time to recuperate from the strain. To make matters worse, every minute increased my hunger, and with it the sick woman on my back became heavier. This was unbearable enough, but Namiko took it into her head to insist that we carry her at the front of the column because she couldn't bear being sandwiched in the middle. This was probably more agreeable to Namiko, for it reduced her fear of being abandoned, but we who were doing the carrying were additionally fatigued by the constant pushing from behind. I recalled that everyone was being made to suffer simply because I had brought the sick woman along, and I resolved that if ever we became so exhausted as to reach the verge of collapse, I would either hurl Namiko into the ocean or remain with her and ask the others to go on without us.

But in point of fact we had already reached the "verge of collapse" and such thoughts obviously served no useful purpose. Our faces were livid and stained with a greasy sweat, our eyes had begun to glaze, and there were some who after protracted yawns would suddenly let out strange, unnerving cries. When one of us, as if broken by the wind, collapsed over a projecting ledge of the rock wall, Namiko again began to weep and beg us to leave her there. Water was streaming from the women's hair and clothes, and they walked like specters, with their wet hair plastered over their faces. The color of their underwear had seeped through and stained their kimonos. By the time water had soaked their compacts and purses, a heavy calm fell over them. Kikue said, "We're going to die soon, anyway; I wish it were all over." "Why don't you jump over the edge then? It'd be perfectly simple," snapped Yagi. This crude joke apparently got on the nerves of Kurigi, who was already at the end of his tether. He snarled, "What do you mean by joking when people are suffering?" and closed in on Yagi. Yagi drew himself up, as if startled at being so unexpectedly threatened, and blurted out, "You needn't get so angry, no matter how much I joke with Kikue. You may be in love with her, but you haven't got a chance—I've seen her with Takagi myself." Gentle Sasa, who up to now had kept absolutely silent, suddenly pulled a knife from his pocket and lunged at Takagi. Takagi deftly avoided the point of Sasa's knife, and made a headlong dash along the cliff. Sasa ran in pursuit, lurching heavily. Kurigi, who for a while had remained dumbfounded by this development, now realizing that his enemy was actually not Yagi but Takagi and Sasa, ran off after them. Dimly visible through the dark beside me, I could see and hear Kikue, sobbing that it was all her fault. "Go at once," I said, "and stop the fight." But she answered, "Unless you go too I can't stop them." Then, and this came as an entirely unexpected event, Namiko suddenly thrust out her arms and, fastening herself on the neck of the weeping Kikue, began to gnash her teeth. Apparently she had realized for the first time that her lover—whichever one of the three he was—had been taken from her. Soon even Yagi, who had caused the quarrel, was in a rage, and I was amazed to see him drag Shinako to the ground and demand that she reveal her lover's name. It was obvious that the fight could soon involve us all, and if anyone got hurt and could not proceed farther, we were all without question doomed. I was appalled at our horrible plight; my only comfort came from the fact that nobody around me had a weapon. But one of the men up the road had a knife, and I could not very well leave things at that. Shaking all over, I ran along the black cliff, shouting again and again, "Wait! Wait!" When I had gone about two hundred yards I saw the three of them lying motionless by the side of the road, flat on their backs. I thought that they must be dead, but I noticed then that they were all staring at my face, their eyes popping from their sockets. I asked what had happened. "We decided that to get hurt fighting over a woman in a place like this wouldn't do us any good, and we stopped. But don't make us talk for a while—we're so exhausted that breathing is painful."

"You are very wise," I said, and returned to the sick woman. There the fight seemed just beginning. Yagi and Kinoshita were grappling and snarling on the road near the shrieking Namiko. Even the women had evidently lost all track of who had stolen their man and whose man they themselves had stolen. They were in such a state of bewilderment that they did not even bother to ask me what had happened in the fight up the road. The fights had not actually come as a great surprise to me, but I never imagined that they would explode with such violence here. The detached calm with which I had contemplated the quarrels was now rudely shattered by the realization that our progress might be halted because of them. Yagi and Kinoshita had long been on bad terms and rivals in love. There was not much likelihood therefore that they would separate even if I tried to force my way in and stop the fight. In any case, it was certainly pleasanter for them to be lying on the ground hitting each other than to be on their feet walking and obliged to carry a sick woman. They seemed in fact to be hitting each other merely in order to rest their grappling legs. I thought that the best plan was to let them fight all they could, as long as they did not cause each other any real harm. I sat on the ground to rest myself while the two of them continued to wrestle weakly. As I watched, suddenly both Yagi and Kinoshita ceased moving altogether, both apparently utterly exhausted, and capable now only of panting furiously. This, I thought, was a good point to intervene. I said, "You can't go on lying there indefinitely. If you want to fight, go ahead and fight. If you've had enough, break it up now, and let's get moving again. The three of them up the road have had the sense to realize that nothing is so stupid as fighting over a woman, and now they've made up." Yagi and Kinoshita slowly got to their feet and began to walk.

When our procession joined the three men up the road, the sick woman was shifted to another back. There were no more undershirts left among us to wipe her bleeding, and now as we walked along peacefully, our shorts one by one were used. In spite of the fact that the result of the immorality of the women had been to excite violent quarrels among the men, when the various relations had become so excessively complicated as to upset all judgments, a balance was restored, and a kind of calm monotony ensued. This to me was at once fascinating and terrifying. But soon afterward, as hunger began to assail us more fiercely than ever, our peace was turned into a bestial stupor from which all individuality had been stripped. I became incapable of speech. The skin of my abdomen stuck to my spine. There was no saliva left in my mouth. Sour juices welled up from my stomach, bringing with them a griping pain. The rims of my eyes burned. My incessant yawns reeked of bitter tobacco. No doubt as a result of our exhaustion from the scuffles, not a word was said as we proceeded in the soaking rain, with our heads down. Our helplessness was so manifest, that Namiko, now weeping quietly to herself, began to appear the strongest of us. We were plunged into despair and doubted we could ever manage to cross the cliff which extended limitlessly before us in the dark. We could no longer think in terms so remote as hope or a happier future. Our heads held no other thoughts but of the moments of time that kept pressing in on us, one after another: what would our hunger be like in another two minutes, how could we last out another minute. The time which I could conceive of came to be filled entirely with sensations of hunger, and I began to feel as if what was trudging forward in the endless darkness was not myself but only a stomach. I could feel already that time as far as I was concerned was nothing but a measure of my stomach.

We must have walked ten or twelve miles since nightfall. Just about when the men were turning over the last of their underclothes to the sick woman, we discovered a small hut on the rock face somewhat above the road. Those who were in the lead could not be sure at first whether it was a boulder or a hut. While they were still arguing, we saw that it was an abandoned water mill. We decided that it would be a good idea to rest there a bit, if only to escape from the rain, and we went in. It was evident that no human being had made his way here for a very long time: cobwebs that crisscrossed the hut clung to our faces. There was space enough to shelter us from the rain, a musty little room into which the twelve of us squeezed. "There must be water somewhere, this is a mill. I'm going to look," Yagi said, and wandered outside the hut. But the pipes which should have carried water had rotted into pieces, and the blades of the water wheel were covered with white mold. It was impossible to find any water here. The sweat on our skins turned icy, and the dampness in our clothes made us shiver. To our fatigue and hunger now was added the biting cold of the late autumn night, so sharp that anyone who separated himself from the others could not have endured it. We wished to make a fire, but no one had matches. The best we could do was remove our coats, spread them out on the floor, and arrange ourselves together so as to share one another's warmth. The sick woman was placed in the center with the three other women around her, and the men spread their arms around the women making an effect something like an artichoke. But such measures did not suffice. The cold assaulted us even more keenly.

Then our teeth began to chatter so badly that we could not form words but only stammer. Tears came but not a sound from the lips. We were shaking like jellyfish in the water. Soon the sick woman in the center lost even the strength to shiver, and in the midst of our trembling she lay shrunken and motionless. One of the women moaned, "When I die, please cut off my hair and send it to my mother. I can't stand any more." Then another voice cried, "I'm finished too. When I die, cut off my thumb and send it home." "Send back my glasses." Even while they spoke our knees grew numb, our thighs grew numb, and soon the pain reached our heads. Kurigi suddenly burst out, "I'm being punished now because when I was a boy I threw stones at the village god." And Takagi said, "I'm being punished for having deceived so many women," a remark which seemed to transfix men and women alike. They joined in with affirmative exclamations amidst their tears. The extreme mercilessness they all displayed rather amused me, but at the same time I could not detach myself from the conviction that we would die there. I was sitting on a wooden support next to the millstone, and I wondered when the next disaster would strike us. It proved to be something which we might have foreseen: an insidious drowsiness began to overtake us. Our shivering imperceptibly had died away. I realized with a shock that if we once permitted ourselves to fall asleep the end would come. I began to shout, to shake people's heads, to strike them. I told them if we fell asleep we were finished; I urged them to hit at once anyone who dozed. What made our struggle so difficult against the strange enemy was that the very consciousness we were losing was the only weapon we could employ in our defense. Even as I exhorted the others, I felt myself growing increasingly drowsy, and my thoughts wandered to reveries on the nature of sleep. I dimly realized that soon I too would be dropping off. But that thought itself made me leap up, ready to kick that thing, whatever it was, that was trying to steal my consciousness. Then I came face to face with something even stranger—in the midst of this frantic shuttling between life and death I sensed time, milder than ever I had experienced it, and I felt that I should like to go that one step further and peep at the instant of time when my consciousness was extinguished. Abruptly I opened my eyes and looked around me. In front the others were all dropping off to sleep, their heads hanging lifelessly.

I rushed from one to another, striking violently, and shouting warnings to wake up. Each opened his vacant eyes, some only again to lean senselessly against the person next to them, others, aware suddenly of the mortal danger threatening them, gazed around in bewilderment, blinking their eyes. Still others thought that having been struck by me gave them the right to hit anyone else who was asleep, and there soon began a wild melee. At each slight letup sleep crept back to suck up all consciousness. I pulled each by the hair, I shook their heads wildly, I slapped them so hard on the cheeks that the imprint of my fingers remained. But even if I had struck so hard that they tasted the bones of my fist, even if I had had a fist of iron, no sooner would my violent actions stop for a moment than all would plummet toward death. Even while I went on pummeling the eleven others, watching intently their every movement, I felt suddenly buoyed up by the infinite pleasure into which my consciousness was melting. Pleasure—indeed there is nothing to compare with the gaiety and transparency of the pleasure before death. The heart begins to choke from its extremity of pleasure, as if it were licking some luscious piece of fruit. It holds no melancholy, like a forgetting of the self. What is this thing between life and death, this wave which surges up in ever shifting colors with a vapor joyous as the sky? I wonder if it is not the face of that dreadful monster no human being has ever seen—time? It gave me pleasure to think that when I died and disappeared every other man in the whole world would vanish at the same time with me. This temptation to kill every human being, this game with death enticed me, and I wavered on the point of yielding myself without further struggle to sleep. And yet, when I observed the others I would pound them with both hands, scarcely caring where I struck. To fight to keep others from death—why should such a harmful act prove beneficial? Even supposing that we managed to escape death now, it was impossible to imagine that when we were dying at some future time we could do so without the least worry, so neatly and so pleasantly as now. And yet I seemed to want them to live again. I pulled the women by the hair and beat them, kicked the men over and over. Could that be called love, I wonder? Or was it more properly to be termed habit? I was so painfully aware of the unhappy future that awaited us all that I felt like strangling each to death, and yet I was compelled by helping them to prolong their sufferings. And was this action to be called salvation?—My lips formed the words, "Go ahead and die!" but I continued to tear frantically through their sleep as though struggling with some misfortune from long years past which had never ceased in it depredations. Gradually they awakened and then, with exactly the expression of "Which one of you has destroyed my happiness?" fell to hitting those around them more savagely than ever. It seemed impossible that anyone could now sleep undisturbed. Some kept moving even while asleep, with only their hands flailing the air in motions of striking. The others, even as they were stamping, kicking, hitting, wildly pounding one another in this scene of inferno, began to fall asleep again. What at first had been round and gathered together steadily disintegrated as heads dropped between legs and trunks became interlocked. In this coagulating, amorphous mass, it was no longer possible to tell whom one struck or where the blow fell. I ranged over as large an area as I could, furiously striking everyone, for I knew that anyone who escaped would die. But lethargy is filled with a submerged terror that attacks with a ferocity only second to that of brute violence; an instant, it would seem, after arousing someone I would open my eyes to find him striking my head or thrusting his knee into my groin. Each time I awoke I would wriggle my way among the bodies around me and sink into them. Thus we moved again and again from sleep to waking.

Outside the hut changes had also been taking place. The rain had stopped, and in the moonlight streaming in through holes in the crumbling walls we could see the spider webs etched with absolute clarity. We tried to make our way outside in the hope of shaking off our drowsiness, but our legs refused to move. So we crawled out on our bellies and stared at the mountains and the sea illuminated by moonlight. Then Sasa, who was beside me, wordlessly tugged at my sleeve and pointed dementedly at a place down the cliff. I looked, my mind a blank—a thin stream of water was flowing from the rocks, making a faint splashing sound as it sparkled in the moonlight. I tried to shout "Water!" but I had no voice. Sasa went down the cliff, rubbing his knees painfully. After a few minutes he reached the spring and began to drink. His spirits were suddenly restored, and he shouted "Water! Water!" I too faintly called out at the same time.

We were saved. The others, incapable as they were of moving their legs, crawled out of the hut, each man for himself, and headed for the spring. One after another, their pale cobweb-covered faces exposed by the moonlight, they pressed their noses into the rock. The clear water filled with the smell of the rock soaked through from the throat to the stomach and down to the toes, with the sharpness of a knife. Then, as the force of life first began to operate, we all let out cries of wonder at the moon, as if we felt that this is what it meant to be really alive, and we pressed our mouths again to the rock. Suddenly I remembered the sick woman in the hut. I wondered if she might not have fallen asleep and died already. I asked the others to think of some way of getting water to her. Takagi had the idea of carrying water in a hat. We filled his soft hat with water, but after taking a few steps the water leaked out of it. Then we tried putting five hats together, one inside the other, and filled them with water. This time it did not leak noticeably, but it was obvious that by the time we got the hat to Namiko the water would be gone. "Wouldn't the quickest way," Sasa suggested, "be to pass the hat along in a relay?" The eleven of us distributed ourselves in the moonlight at intervals of about twenty feet apart. I was chosen to be the last in line, the one to give the water to Namiko. While I waited for the hat to be passed up, I kept shaking the sick woman. Although her skin still bore red marks where she had been struck, her body was crumbling into sleep under my shaking, and she showed no signs of returning to consciousness. I took her by the hair and shook her head violently. Her eyes opened, but it was no more than that, for they remained fixed in a dull stare. Just then the hat arrived, with almost all the water gone. I poured into her mouth the few remaining drops, and for the first time she seemed to open her eyes of her own volition. She placed her hand on my knee and looked around the hut. I said, "It's water. You must drink it or you'll die." I lay her over my knee and waited for the next hat. Another came and again I poured the drops into her mouth. As I repeated this over and over I seemed to see the others, shouting as they scrambled one after another back up the steep cliff from the spring, their weary bodies caught in the moonlight, and exactly as though I were pouring distilled moonlight I poured the drops of water into the sick woman's mouth.

QUESTIONS FOR DISCUSSION

Why does the group change from being suspicious of one another to trying to keep one another alive?

1. Even though Namiko will slow the others down, why do they agree to take her along? After the narrator puts the group's money in her kimono, why do they automatically begin to "formulate regulations around her"? (84)

2. After the violent quarrels on the cliff, why is it "at once fascinating and terrifying" that "a balance was restored, and a kind of calm monotony ensued"? (89)

3. Why does the narrator fight to keep himself and the others alive even though he believes "there is nothing to compare with the gaiety and transparency of the pleasure before death"? (92) Why does he wonder if wanting the others "to live again" is "love" or "habit"? (92)

4. At the end of the story, why does the group frantically work together to bring water to Namiko?

Why does the narrator call time a "monster" and "this thing between life and death"? (92)

1. Why does it give the narrator pleasure "to think that when I died and disappeared every other man in the whole world would vanish at the same time with me"? (92)

2. Why is the narrator convinced that an "unhappy future" awaits them all? Why does he think that helping them to "prolong their sufferings" might be called "salvation"? (92–93)

3. After drinking water from the stream, why do the members of the group "let out cries of wonder at the moon"? (94)

4. Why does the narrator imagine that the life-saving water he pours into Namiko's mouth is like "distilled moonlight"? (94)

FOR FURTHER REFLECTION

1. When do we have a moral obligation to help someone in need, even if by doing so we endanger ourselves? Should a weak individual be sacrificed if he or she imperils the well-being of the group?

2. In what situations have you been acutely aware of "what it meant to be really alive"? Were you alone or with others at the time?

3. Does it take hardship or the danger of death to prompt us to act for the greater benefit of society and our fellow citizens?

On the Cannibals

Michel de Montaigne

When King Pyrrhus crossed into Italy, after noting the excellent formation of the army which the Romans had sent ahead toward him he said, "I do not know what kind of barbarians these are" (for the Greeks called all foreigners barbarians) "but there is nothing barbarous about the ordering of the army which I can see!" The Greeks said the same about the army which Flaminius brought over to their country, as did Philip when he saw from a hilltop in his kingdom the order and plan of the Roman encampment under Publius Sulpicius Galba. We should be similarly wary of accepting common opinions; we should judge them by the ways of reason, not by popular vote.

I have long had a man with me who stayed some ten or twelve years in that other world which was discovered in our century when Villegaignon made his landfall and named it La France Antartique. This discovery of a boundless territory seems to me worthy of reflection. I am by no means sure that some other land may not be discovered in the future, since so many persons, greater than we are, were wrong about this one! I fear that our eyes are bigger than our bellies, our curiosity more than we can stomach. We grasp at everything but clasp nothing but wind.

Plato brings in Solon to relate that he had learned from the priests of the town of Saïs in Egypt how, long ago before the Flood, there was a vast island called Atlantis right at the mouth of the Straits of Gibraltar, occupying an area greater than Asia and Africa combined; the kings of that country, who not only possessed that island but had spread on to the mainland across the breadth of Africa as far as Egypt and the length of Europe as far as Tuscany, planned to stride over into Asia and subdue all the peoples bordering on the Mediterranean as far as the Black Sea. To this end they had traversed Spain, Gaul, and Italy and had reached as far as Greece when the Athenians withstood them; but soon afterward those Athenians, as well as the people of Atlantis and their island, were engulfed in that Flood.

It is most likely that that vast inundation should have produced strange changes to the inhabitable areas of the world; it is maintained that it was then that the sea cut off Sicily from Italy—

> Those places, they say, were once wrenched apart by a
> violent convulsion, whereas they had formerly been one
> single land. [VIRGIL]

—as well as Cyprus from Syria, and the island of Negropontus from the Boeotian mainland, while elsewhere lands once separated were joined together by filling in the trenches between them with mud and sand:

> Barren swamps which you could row a boat through
> now feed neighboring cities and bear the heavy plough.
> [HORACE]

Yet there is little likelihood of that island's being the New World which we have recently discovered, for it was virtually touching Spain; it would be unbelievable for a flood to force it back more than twelve hundred leagues to where it is now; besides, our modern seamen have already all but discovered that it is not an island at all but a mainland, contiguous on one side with the East Indies and on others with lands lying beneath both the Poles—or that if it is separated from them, it is by straits so narrow that it does not deserve the name of "island" on that account.

It seems that large bodies such as these are subject, as are our own, to changes, some natural, some feverish. When I consider how my local river the Dordogne has, during my own lifetime, been encroaching on the right-hand bank going downstream and has taken over so much land that it has robbed many buildings of their foundation, I realize that it has been suffering from some unusual upset: for if it had always gone on like this or were to do so in the future, the whole face of the world would be distorted. But their moods change: some-times they incline one way, then another: and sometimes they restrain themselves. I am not discussing those sudden floodings whose causes we know. By the coastline in Médoc, my brother the Sieur d'Arsac can see lands of his lying buried under sand spewed up by the sea: the tops of some of the buildings are still visible: his rents and arable fields have been changed into very sparse grazing. The locals say that the sea has been thrusting so hard against them for some time now that they have lost four leagues of land. These sands are the sea's pio-neer corps: and we can see those huge shifting sand dunes marching a half-league ahead in the vanguard, capturing territory.

The other testimony from antiquity which some would make rele-vant to this discovery is in Aristotle—if that little book about unheard wonders is really his. He tells how some Carthaginians struck out across the Atlantic beyond the Straits of Gibraltar, sailed for a long time and finally discovered a large fertile island entirely clothed in woodlands and watered by great deep rivers but very far from any mainland; they and others after them, attracted by the richness and fertility of the soil, emigrated with their wives and children and started living there. The Carthaginian lords, seeing that their country was being gradually depopulated, expressly forbade any more to go there on pain of death and drove out those new settlers, fearing it is said that they would in time increase so greatly that they would sup-plant them and bring down their state.

But that account in Aristotle cannot apply to these new lands either.

That man of mine was a simple, rough fellow—qualities which make for a good witness: those clever chaps notice more things more carefully but are always adding glosses; they cannot help changing their story a little in order to make their views triumph and be more persuasive; they never show you anything purely as it is: they bend it and disguise it to fit in with their own views. To make their judgment more credible and to win you over they emphasize their own side, amplify it, and extend it. So you need either a very trustworthy man or else a man so simple that he has nothing in him on which to build such false discoveries or make them plausible; and he must be wed-ded to no cause. Such was my man; moreover on various occasions he showed me several seamen and merchants whom he knew on that voyage. So I am content with what he told me, without inquiring what the cosmographers have to say about it.

What we need is topographers who would make detailed accounts of the places which they had actually been to. But because they have the advantage of visiting Palestine, they want to enjoy the right of telling us tales about all the rest of the world! I wish everyone would write only about what he knows—not in this matter only but in all others. A man may well have detailed knowledge or experience of the nature of one particular river or stream, yet about all the others he knows only what everyone else does; but in order to trot out his little scrap of knowledge he will write a book on the whole of physics! From this vice many great inconveniences arise.

Now to get back to the subject, I find (from what has been told me) that there is nothing savage or barbarous about those peoples, but that every man calls barbarous anything he is not accustomed to; it is indeed the case that we have no other criterion of truth or right-reason than the example and form of the opinions and customs of our own country. There we always find the perfect religion, the perfect polity, the most developed and perfect way of doing anything! Those "savages" are only wild in the sense that we call fruits wild when they are produced by Nature in her ordinary course: whereas it is fruit which we have artificially perverted and misled from the common order which we ought to call savage. It is in the first kind that we find their true, vigorous, living, most natural, and most useful properties and virtues, which we have bastardized in the other kind by merely adapting them to our corrupt tastes. Moreover, there is a delicious savor which even our taste finds excellent in a variety of fruits produced in those countries without cultivation: they rival our own. It is not sensible that artifice should be reverenced more than Nature, our great and powerful Mother. We have so overloaded the richness and beauty of her products by our own ingenuity that we have smothered her entirely. Yet wherever her pure light does shine, she wondrously shames our vain and frivolous enterprises:

> Ivy grows best when left untended; the strawberry tree
> flourishes more beautifully in lonely grottoes, and birds
> sing the sweeter for their artlessness. [PROPERTIUS]

All our strivings cannot even manage to reproduce the nest of the smallest little bird, with its beauty and appropriateness to its purpose; we cannot even reproduce the web of the wretched spider. Plato says that all things are produced by nature, fortune, or art, the greatest and fairest by the first two, the lesser and least perfect by the last.

Those peoples, then, seem to me to be barbarous only in that they have been hardly fashioned by the mind of man, still remaining close neighbors to their original state of nature. They are still governed by the laws of Nature and are only very slightly bastardized by ours; but their purity is such that I am sometimes seized with irritation at their not having been discovered earlier, in times when there were men who could have appreciated them better than we do. It irritates me that neither Lycurgus nor Plato had any knowledge of them, for it seems to me that what experience has taught us about those peoples surpasses not only all the descriptions with which poetry has beautifully painted the Age of Gold and all its ingenious fictions about Man's blessed early state, but also the very conceptions and yearnings of philosophy. They could not even imagine a state of nature so simple and so pure as the one we have learned about from experience; they could not even believe that societies of men could be maintained with so little artifice, so little in the way of human solder. I would tell Plato that those people have no trade of any kind, no acquaintance with writing, no knowledge of numbers, no terms for governor or political superior, no practice of subordination or of riches or poverty, no contracts, no inheritances, no divided estates, no occupation but leisure, no concern for kinship—except such as is common to them all—no clothing, no agriculture, no metals, no use of wine or corn. Among them you hear no words for treachery, lying, cheating, avarice, envy, backbiting or forgiveness. How remote from such perfection would Plato find that Republic which he thought up—"men fresh from the gods" [SENECA].

These are the ways which Nature first ordained. [VIRGIL]

In addition they inhabit a land with a most delightful countryside and a temperate climate, so that, from what I have been told by my sources, it is rare to find anyone ill there; I have been assured that they never saw a single man bent with age, toothless, blear-eyed, or tottering. They dwell along the seashore, shut in to landwards by great lofty mountains, on a stretch of land some hundred leagues in width. They have fish and flesh in abundance which bear no resemblance to ours; these they eat simply cooked. They were so horror-struck by the first man who brought a horse there and rode it that they killed him with their arrows before they could recognize him, even though he had had dealings with them on several previous voyages. Their dwellings are immensely long, big enough to hold two or three hundred souls; they are covered with the bark of tall trees which are fixed into the earth, leaning against each other in support at the top, like some of our barns where the cladding reaches down to the ground and acts as a side. They have a kind of wood so hard that they use it to cut with, making their swords from it as well as grills to cook their meat. Their beds are woven from cotton and slung from the roof like hammocks on our ships; each has his own, since wives sleep apart from their husbands. They get up at sunrise and have their meal for the day as soon as they do so; they have no other meal but that one. They drink nothing with it, like those Eastern peoples who, according to Suidas, only drink apart from meals. They drink together several times a day, and plenty of it. This drink is made from a certain root and has the color of our claret. They always drink it lukewarm; it only keeps for two or three days; it tastes a bit sharp, is in no ways heady, and is good for the stomach; for those who are not used to it it is laxative but for those who are, it is a very pleasant drink. Instead of bread they use a certain white product resembling coriander cakes. I have tried some: it tastes sweet and somewhat insipid.

They spend the whole day dancing; the younger men go off hunting with bow and arrow. Meanwhile some of the womenfolk are occupied in warming up their drink: that is their main task. In the morning, before their meal, one of their elders walks from one end of the building to the other, addressing the whole barnful of them by repeating one single phrase over and over again until he has made the rounds, their building being a good hundred yards long. He preaches two things only: bravery before their enemies and love for their wives. They never fail to stress this second duty, repeating that it is their wives who season their drink and keep it warm. In my own house, as in many other places, you can see the style of their beds and rope-work as well as their wooden swords and the wooden bracelets with which they arm their wrists in battle, and the big open-ended canes to the sound of which they maintain the rhythm of their dances. They shave off all their hair, cutting it more cleanly than we do, yet with razors made of only wood or stone. They believe in the immortality of the soul: souls which deserve well of the gods dwell in the sky where the sun rises; souls which are accursed dwell where it sets. They have some priests and prophets or other, but they rarely appear among the people since they live in the mountains. When they do appear they hold a great festival and a solemn meeting of several villages—each of the barns which I have described constituting a village situated about one French league distant from the next. The prophet then addresses them in public, exhorting them to be virtuous and dutiful, but their entire system of ethics contains only the same two articles: resoluteness in battle and love for their wives. He foretells what is to happen and the results they must expect from what they undertake; he either incites them to war or deflects them from it, but only on condition that if he fails to divine correctly and if things turn out other than he foretold, then—if they can catch him—he is condemned as a false prophet and hacked to pieces. So the prophet who gets it wrong once is seen no more.

Prophecy is a gift of God. That is why abusing it should be treated as a punishable deceit. Among the Scythians, whenever their soothsayers got it wrong they were shackled hand and foot and laid in ox carts full of bracken where they were burned. Those who treat subjects under the guidance of human limitations can be excused if they have done their best; but those who come and cheat us with assurances of powers beyond the natural order and then fail to do what they promise, should they not be punished for it and for the foolhardiness of their deceit?

These peoples have their wars against others further inland beyond their mountains; they go forth naked, with no other arms but their bows and their wooden swords sharpened to a point like the blades of our pig stickers. Their steadfastness in battle is astonishing and always ends in killing and bloodshed: they do not even know the meaning of fear or flight. Each man brings back the head of the enemy he has slain and sets it as a trophy over the door of his dwelling. For a long period they treat captives well and provide them with all the comforts which they can devise; afterward the master of each captive summons a great assembly of his acquaintances; he ties a rope to one of the arms of his prisoner and holds him by it, standing a few feet away for fear of being caught in the blows, and allows his dearest friend to hold the prisoner the same way by the other arm: then, before the whole assembly, they both hack at him with their swords and kill him. This done, they roast him and make a common meal of him, sending chunks of his flesh to absent friends. This is not as some think done for food—as the Scythians used to do in antiquity—but to symbolize ultimate revenge. As a proof of this, when they noted that the Portuguese who were allied to their enemies practiced a different kind of execution on them when taken prisoner—which was to bury them up to the waist, to shoot showers of arrows at their exposed parts, and then to hang them— they thought that these men from the Other World, who had scattered a knowledge of many a vice throughout their neighborhood and who were greater masters than they were of every kind of revenge, which must be more severe than their own; so they began to abandon their ancient method and adopted that one. It does not sadden me that we should note the horrible barbarity in a practice such as theirs: what does sadden me is that, while judging correctly of their wrongdoings we should be so blind to our own. I think there is more barbarity in eating a man alive than in eating him dead; more barbarity in lacerating by rack and torture a body still fully able to feel things, in roasting him little by little and having him bruised and bitten by pigs and dogs (as we have not only read about but seen in recent memory, not among enemies in antiquity but among our fellow citizens and neighbors— and, what is worse, in the name of duty and religion) than in roasting him and eating him after his death.

Chrysippus and Zeno, the leaders of the Stoic school, certainly thought that there was nothing wrong in using our carcasses for whatever purpose we needed, even for food—as our own forebears did when, beleaguered by Caesar in the town of Alesia, they decided to relieve the hunger of the besieged with the flesh of old men, women, and others who were no use in battle:

> By the eating of such food it is notorious that the
> Gascons prolonged their lives. [SEXTUS EMPIRICUS]

And our medical men do not flinch from using corpses in many ways, both internally and externally, to cure us. Yet no opinion has ever been so unruly as to justify treachery, disloyalty, tyranny, and cruelty, which are everyday vices in us. So we can indeed call those folk barbarians by the rules of reason but not in comparison with ourselves, who surpass them in every kind of barbarism. Their warfare is entirely noble and magnanimous; it has as much justification and beauty as that human malady allows: among them it has no other foundation than a zealous concern for courage. They are not striving to conquer new lands, since without toil or travail they still enjoy that bounteous Nature who furnishes them abundantly with all they need, so that they have no concern to push back their frontiers. They are still in that blessed state of desiring nothing beyond what is ordained by their natural necessities: for them anything further is merely superfluous. The generic term which they use for men of the same age is "brother"; younger men they call "sons." As for the old men, they are the "fathers" of everyone else; they bequeath all their goods, indivisibly, to all these heirs in common, there being no other entitlement than that with which Nature purely and simply endows all her creatures by bringing them into this world. If the neighboring peoples come over the mountains to attack them and happen to defeat them, the victors' booty consists in fame and in the privilege of mastery in virtue and valor: they have no other interest in the goods of the vanquished and so return home to their own land, which lacks no necessity; nor do they lack that great accomplishment of knowing how to enjoy their mode of being in happiness and to be content with it. These people do the same in their turn: they require no other ransom from their prisoners of war than that they should admit and acknowledge their defeat—yet there is not one prisoner in a hundred years who does not prefer to die rather than to derogate from the greatness of an invincible mind by look or by word; you cannot find one who does not prefer to be killed and eaten than merely to ask to be spared. In order to make their prisoners love life more they treat them generously in every way, but occupy their thoughts with the menaces of the death awaiting all of them, of the tortures they will have to undergo and of the preparations being made for it, of limbs to be lopped off and of the feast they will provide. All that has only one purpose: to wrench some weak or unworthy word from their lips or to make them wish to escape, so as to enjoy the privilege of having frightened them and forced their constancy.

Indeed, if you take it the right way, true victory consists in that alone:

> There is no victory unless you subjugate the minds of
> the enemy and make them admit defeat. [CLAUDIAN]

In former times those warlike fighters the Hungarians never pressed their advantage beyond making their enemy throw himself on their mercy. Once having wrenched this admission from him, they let him go without injury or ransom, except at most for an undertaking never again to bear arms against them.

Quite enough of the advantages we do gain over our enemies are mainly borrowed ones not truly our own. To have stronger arms and legs is the property of a porter not of valor; agility is a dead and physical quality, for it is chance which causes your opponent to stumble and which makes the sun dazzle him; to be good at fencing is a matter of skill and knowledge which may light on a coward or a worthless individual. A man's worth and reputation lie in the mind and in the will: his true honor is found there. Bravery does not consist in firm arms and legs but in firm minds and souls: it is not a matter of what our horse or our weapons are worth but of what we are. The man who is struck down but whose mind remains steadfast, "if his legs give way, then on his knees doth he fight" [SENECA]; the man who relaxes none of his mental assurance when threatened with imminent death and who faces his enemy with inflexible scorn as he gives up the ghost is beaten by fortune, not by us: he is slain but not vanquished. Sometimes it is the bravest who may prove most unlucky. So there are triumphant defeats rivaling victories; Salamis, Plataea, Mycale, and Sicily are the fairest sister victories which the sun has ever seen, yet they would never dare to compare their combined glory with the glorious defeat of King Leonidas and his men at the defile of Thermopylae. Who has ever run into battle with a greater desire and ambition for victory than did Captain Ischolas when he was defeated? Has any man ever assured his safety more cleverly or carefully than he assured his destruction? His task was to defend against the Arcadians a certain pass in the Peleponnesus. He realized that he could not achieve this because of the nature of the site and of the odds against him, concluding that every man who faced the enemy must of necessity die in the battlefield; on the other hand he judged it unworthy of his own courage, of his greatness of soul, and of the name of Sparta to fail in his duty; so he chose the middle path between these two extremes and acted thus: he saved the youngest and fittest soldiers of his unit to serve for the defense of their country and sent them back there. He then determined to defend that pass with men whose loss would matter less and who would, by their death, make the enemy purchase their breakthrough as dearly as possible. And so it turned out. After butchering the Arcadians who beset them on every side, they were all put to the sword. Was ever a trophy raised to a victor which was not better due to those who were vanquished? True victory lies in your role in the conflict, not in coming through safely: it consists in the honor of battling bravely, not battling through.

To return to my tale, those prisoners, far from yielding despite all that was done to them during the two or three months of their captivity, maintain on the contrary a joyful countenance: they urge their captors to hurry up and put them to the test; they defy them, insult them, and reproach them for cowardice and for all the battles they have lost against their country. I have a song made by one such prisoner which contains the following: Let them all dare to come and gather to feast on him, for with him they will feast on their own fathers and ancestors who have served as food and sustenance for his body. "These sinews," he said, "this flesh and these veins—poor fools that you are—are your very own; you do not realize that they still contain the very substance of the limbs of your forebears: savor them well, for you will find that they taste of your very own flesh!" There is nothing "barbarous" in the contriving of that topic. Those who tell how they die and who describe the act of execution show the prisoners spitting at their killers and pulling faces at them. Indeed, until their latest breath, they never stop braving them and defying them with word and look. It is no lie to say that these men are indeed savages—by our standards; for either they must be or we must be: there is an amazing gulf between their souls and ours.

The husbands have several wives: the higher their reputation for valor the more of them they have. One beautiful characteristic of their marriages is worth noting: just as our wives are zealous in thwarting our love and tenderness for other women, theirs are equally zealous in obtaining them for them. Being more concerned for their husband's reputation than for anything else, they take care and trouble to have as many fellow wives as possible, since that is a testimony to their husband's valor.

Our wives will scream that that is a marvel, but it is not: it is a virtue proper to matrimony, but at an earlier stage. In the Bible, Leah, Rachel, Sarah, and the wives of Jacob all made their fair handmaidens available to their husbands; Livia, to her own detriment, connived at the lusts of Augustus, and Stratonice the consort of King Deiotarus not only provided her husband with a very beautiful chambermaid who served her but carefully brought up their children and lent a hand in enabling them to succeed to her husband's rank.

Lest anyone should think that they do all this out of a simple slavish subjection to convention or because of the impact of the authority of their ancient customs without any reasoning or judgment on their part, having minds so dulled that they could never decide to do anything else, I should cite a few examples of what they are capable of.

Apart from that war song which I have just given an account of, I have another of their songs, a love song, which begins like this:

> O Adder, stay: stay O Adder! From your colors
>   let my sister take the pattern for a girdle
>   she will make for me to offer to my love;
> So may your beauty and your speckled hues be for
>   ever honored above all other snakes.

This opening couplet serves as the song's refrain. Now I know enough about poetry to make the following judgment: not only is there nothing "barbarous" in this conceit but it is thoroughly Anacreontic. Their language incidentally is a pleasant one with an agreeable sound and has terminations rather like Greek.

Three such natives, unaware of what price in peace and happiness they would have to pay to buy a knowledge of our corruptions, and unaware that such commerce would lead to their downfall—which I suspect to be already far advanced—pitifully allowing themselves to be cheated by their desire for novelty and leaving the gentleness of their regions to come and see ours, were at Rouen at the same time as King Charles IX. The king had a long interview with them: they were shown our manners, our ceremonial, and the layout of a fair city. Then someone asked them what they thought of all this and wanted to know what they had been most amazed by. They made three points; I am very annoyed with myself for forgetting the third, but I still remember two of them. In the first place they said (probably referring to the Swiss Guard) that they found it very odd that all those full-grown bearded men, strong and bearing arms in the king's entourage, should consent to obey a boy rather than choosing one of themselves as a commander; secondly—since they have an idiom in their language which calls all men "halves" of one another—that they had noticed that there were among us men fully bloated with all sorts of comforts while their halves were begging at their doors, emaciated with poverty and hunger: they found it odd that those destitute halves should put up with such injustice and did not take the others by the throat or set fire to their houses.

I had a very long talk with one of them (but I used a stupid interpreter who was so bad at grasping my meaning and at understanding my ideas that I got little joy from it). When I asked the man (who was a commander among them, our sailors calling him a king) what advantage he got from his high rank, he told me that it was to lead his troops into battle; asked how many men followed him, he pointed to an open space to signify as many as it would hold—about four or five thousand men; questioned whether his authority lapsed when the war was over, he replied that he retained the privilege of having paths cut for him through the thickets in their forests, so that he could easily walk through them when he visited villages under his sway.

Not at all bad, that.—Ah! But they wear no breeches. . . .

QUESTIONS FOR DISCUSSION

Why does Montaigne use the culture and habits of the cannibals to criticize his own society?

1. Why is Montaigne saddened more by the "wrongdoings" of his own society than by the barbarity of the cannibals? (104)

2. What evidence does Montaigne present to support his suspicion that the cannibals have already been "bastardized" and "cheated" by contact with his own society? (100, 108)

3. Why does Montaigne say that "we can indeed call those folk barbarians by the rules of reason but not in comparison with ourselves"? (105) What does Montaigne mean by "the rules of reason"?

4. What does Montaigne mean when he says that the cannibals are "indeed savages—by our standards; for either they must be or we must be; there is an amazing gulf between their souls and ours"? (107)

Is Montaigne one of those untrustworthy "clever chaps" who gives more weight to his own point of view "to make their judgment more credible and to win you over"? (99)

1. Why does Montaigne begin by reviewing and then dismissing theories about where the cannibals might have lived?

2. Why does Montaigne say we should "be wary of accepting common opinions" but include well-known Latin quotations throughout his essay? (97)

3. Why does Montaigne say he wishes that "everyone would write only about what he knows," and then write about a place and a group of people he has only heard about from a "simple, rough fellow"? (99)

4. Why does Montaigne end his essay with the comment, "Not at all bad, that.—Ah! But they wear no breeches. . . ."? (109)

FOR FURTHER REFLECTION

1. Do you agree with Montaigne that Nature is always superior to art and man-made things?

2. Does Montaigne's argument and his critique of his own society apply in any way to our own?

3. Should ideas of morality be relative, or should there be universally applied moral standards? If you believe certain moral standards should apply to all societies irrespective of cultural differences, which ones would you apply?

The Dream of a Ridiculous Man

A Fantastic Story

Fyodor Dostoevsky

I

am a ridiculous man. They call me a madman now. That would be a distinct rise in my social position were it not that they still regard me as being as ridiculous as ever. But that does not make me angry any more. They are all dear to me now even while they laugh at me— yes, even then they are for some reason particularly dear to me. I shouldn't have minded laughing with them—not at myself, of course, but because I love them—had I not felt so sad as I looked at them. I feel sad because they do not know the truth, whereas I know it. Oh, how hard it is to be the only man to know the truth! But they won't understand that. No, they will not understand.

And yet in the past I used to be terribly distressed at appearing to be ridiculous. No, not appearing to be, but being. I've always cut a ridiculous figure. I suppose I must have known it from the day I was born. At any rate, I've known for certain I was ridiculous ever since I was seven years old. Afterward I went to school, then to the university, and—well—the more I learned, the more conscious did I become of the fact that I was ridiculous. So that for me my years of hard work at the university seem in the end to have existed for the sole purpose of demonstrating and proving to me, the more deeply engrossed I became in my studies, that I was an utterly absurd person. And as during my studies, so all my life. Every year the same consciousness that I was ridiculous in every way strengthened and intensified in my mind. They always laughed at me. But not one of them knew or suspected that if there were one man on earth who knew better than anyone else that he was ridiculous, that man was I. And this—I mean, the fact that they did not know it—was the bitterest pill for me to swallow. But there I was myself at fault. I was always so proud that I never wanted to confess it to anyone. No, I wouldn't do that for anything in the world. As the years passed, this pride increased in me so that I do believe that if ever I had by chance confessed it to any one I should have blown my brains out the same evening. Oh, how I suffered in the days of my youth from the thought that I might not myself resist the impulse to confess it to my schoolfellows. But ever since I became a man I grew for some unknown reason a little more composed in my mind, though I was more and more conscious of that awful characteristic of mine. Yes, most decidedly for some unknown reason, for to this day I have not been able to find out why that was so. Perhaps it was because I was becoming terribly disheartened owing to one circumstance which was beyond my power to control, namely, the conviction which was gaining upon me that nothing in the whole world *made any difference*. I had long felt it dawning upon me, but I was fully convinced of it only last year, and that, too, all of a sudden, as it were. I suddenly felt that it made *no* difference to me whether the world existed or whether nothing existed anywhere at all. I began to be acutely conscious that *nothing existed in my own lifetime*. At first I couldn't help feeling that at any rate in the past many things had existed; but later on I came to the conclusion that there had not been anything even in the past, but that for some reason it had merely seemed to have been. Little by little I became convinced that there would be nothing in the future, either. It was then that I suddenly ceased to be angry with people and almost stopped noticing them. This indeed disclosed itself in the smallest trifles. For instance, I would knock against people while walking in the street. And not because I was lost in thought—I had nothing to think about—I had stopped thinking about anything at that time: it made no difference to me. Not that I had found an answer to all the questions. Oh, I had not settled a single question, and there were thousands of them! But *it made no difference to me*, and all the questions disappeared.

And, well, it was only after that that I learned the truth. I learned the truth last November, on the third of November, to be precise, and every moment since then has been imprinted indelibly on my mind. It happened on a dismal evening, as dismal an evening as could be imagined. I was returning home at about eleven o'clock and I remember thinking all the time that there could not be a more dismal evening. Even the weather was foul. It had been pouring all day, and the rain too was the coldest and most dismal rain that ever was, a sort of menacing rain—I remember that—a rain with a distinct animosity toward people. But about eleven o'clock it had stopped suddenly, and a horrible dampness descended upon everything, and it became much damper and colder than when it had been raining. And a sort of steam was rising from everything, from every cobble in the street, and from every side street if you peered closely into it from the street as far as the eye could reach. I could not help feeling that if the gaslight had been extinguished everywhere, everything would have seemed much more cheerful, and that the gaslight oppressed the heart so much just because it shed a light upon it all. I had had scarcely any dinner that day. I had been spending the whole evening with an engineer who had two more friends visiting him. I never opened my mouth, and I expect I must have got on their nerves. They were discussing some highly controversial subject, and suddenly got very excited over it. But it really did not make any difference to them. I could see that. I knew that their excitement was not genuine. So I suddenly blurted it out. "My dear fellows," I said, "you don't really care a damn about it, do you?" They were not in the least offended, but they all burst out laughing at me. That was because I had said it without meaning to rebuke them, but simply because it made no difference to me. Well, they realized that it made no difference to me, and they felt happy.

When I was thinking about the gaslight in the streets, I looked up at the sky. The sky was awfully dark, but I could clearly distinguish the torn wisps of cloud and between them fathomless dark patches. All of a sudden I became aware of a little star in one of those patches and I began looking at it intently. That was because the little star gave me an idea: I made up my mind to kill myself that night. I had made up my mind to kill myself already two months before and, poor as

I am, I bought myself an excellent revolver and loaded it the same day. But two month had elapsed and it was still lying in the drawer. I was so utterly indifferent to everything that I was anxious to wait for the moment when I would not be so indifferent and then kill myself. Why—I don't know. And so every night during these two months I thought of shooting myself as I was going home. I was only waiting for the right moment. And now the little star gave me an idea, and I made up my mind then and there that it should *most certainly* be that night. But why the little star gave me the idea—I don't know.

And just as I was looking at the sky, this little girl suddenly grasped me by the elbow. The street was already deserted and there was scarcely a soul to be seen. In the distance a cabman was fast asleep on his box. The girl was about eight years old. She had a kerchief on her head, and she wore only an old, shabby little dress. She was soaked to the skin, but what stuck in my memory was her little torn wet boots. I still remember them. They caught my eye especially. She suddenly began tugging at my elbow and calling me. She was not crying, but saying something in a loud, jerky sort of voice, something that did not make sense, for she was trembling all over and her teeth were chattering from cold. She seemed to be terrified of something and she was crying desperately, "Mummy! Mummy!" I turned round to look at her, but did not utter a word and went on walking. But she ran after me and kept tugging at my clothes, and there was a sound in her voice which in very frightened children signifies despair. I know that sound. Though her words sounded as if they were choking her, I realized that her mother must be dying somewhere very near, or that something similar was happening to her, and that she had run out to call someone, to find someone who would help her mother. But I did not go with her; on the contrary, something made me drive her away. At first I told her to go and find a policeman. But she suddenly clasped her hands and, whimpering and gasping for breath, kept running at my side and would not leave me. It was then that I stamped my foot and shouted at her. She just cried, "Sir! Sir! . . ." and then she left me suddenly and rushed headlong across the road: another man appeared there and she evidently rushed from me to him.

I climbed to the fifth floor. I live apart from my landlord. We all have separate rooms as in an hotel. My room is very small and poor.

My window is a semicircular skylight. I have a sofa covered with American cloth, a table with books on it, two chairs and a comfortable armchair, a very old armchair indeed, but low-seated and with a high back serving as a headrest. I sat down in the armchair, lighted the candle, and began thinking. Next door in the other room behind the partition, the usual bedlam was going on. It had been going on since the day before yesterday. A retired army captain lived there, and he had visitors—six merry gentlemen who drank vodka and played faro with an old pack of cards. Last night they had a fight and I know that two of them were for a long time pulling each other about by the hair. The landlady wanted to complain, but she is dreadfully afraid of the captain. We had only one more lodger in our rooms, a thin little lady, the wife of an army officer, on a visit to Petersburg with her three little children who had all been taken ill since their arrival at our house. She and her children were simply terrified of the captain and they lay shivering and crossing themselves all night long, and the youngest child had a sort of nervous attack from fright. This captain (I know that for a fact) sometimes stops people on Nevsky Avenue and asks them for a few coppers, telling them he is very poor. He can't get a job in the Civil Service, but the strange thing is (and that's why I am telling you this) that the captain had never once during the month he had been living with us made me feel in the least irritated. From the very first, of course, I would not have anything to do with him, and he himself was bored with me the very first time we met. But however big a noise they raised behind their partition and however many of them there were in the captain's room, it makes no difference to me. I sit up all night and, I assure you, I don't hear them at all—so completely do I forget about them. You see, I stay awake all night till daybreak, and that has been going on for a whole year now. I sit up all night in the armchair at the table—doing nothing. I read books only in the daytime. At night I sit like that without even thinking about anything in particular: some thoughts wander in and out of my mind, and I let them come and go as they please. In the night the candle burns out completely.

I sat down at the table, took the gun out of the drawer, and put it down in front of me. I remember asking myself as I put it down, "It is to be then?" and I replied with complete certainty, "It is!" That is to say, I was going to shoot myself. I knew I should shoot myself that night for certain. What I did not know was how much longer I should go on sitting at the table till I shot myself. And I should of course have shot myself, had it not been for the little girl.

II

You see, though nothing made any difference to me, I could feel pain, for instance, couldn't I? If anyone had struck me, I should have felt pain. The same was true so far as my moral perceptions were concerned. If anything happened to arouse my pity, I should have felt pity, just as I used to do at the time when things did make a difference to me. So I had felt pity that night: I should most decidedly have helped a child. Why then did I not help the little girl? Because of a thought that had occurred to me at the time: when she was pulling at me and calling me, a question suddenly arose in my mind and I could not settle it. It was an idle question, but it made me angry. What made me angry was the conclusion I drew from the reflection that if I had really decided to do away with myself that night, everything in the world should have been more indifferent to me than ever. Why then should I have suddenly felt that I was not indifferent and be sorry for the little girl? I remember that I was very sorry for her, so much so that I felt a strange pang which was quite incomprehensible in my position. I'm afraid I am unable better to convey that fleeting sensation of mine, but it persisted with me at home when I was sitting at the table, and I was very much irritated. I had not been so irritated for a long time past. One train of thought followed another. It was clear to me that so long as I was still a human being and not a meaningless cipher, and till I became a cipher, I was alive, and consequently able to suffer, be angry, and feel shame at my actions. Very well. But if, on the other hand, I were going to kill myself in, say, two hours, what did that little girl matter to me and what did I care for shame or anything else in the world? I was going to turn into a cipher, into an absolute cipher. And surely the realization that I should soon cease to exist *altogether*, and hence everything would cease to exist, ought to have had some slight effect on my feeling of pity for the little girl or on my feeling of shame after so mean an action. Why after all did I stamp and shout so fiercely at the little girl? I did it because I thought that not only did I feel no pity, but that it wouldn't matter now if I were guilty of the most inhuman baseness, since in another two hours everything would become extinct. Do you believe me when I tell you that that was the only reason why I shouted like that? I am almost convinced of it now. It seemed clear to me that life and the world in some way or other depended on me now. It might almost be said that the world seemed to be created for me alone. If I were to shoot myself, the world would cease to exist—for me at any rate. To say nothing of the possibility that nothing would in fact exist for anyone after me and the whole world would dissolve as soon as my consciousness became extinct, would disappear in a twinkling like a phantom, like some integral part of my consciousness, and vanish without leaving a trace behind, for all this world and all these people exist perhaps only in my consciousness.

I remember that as I sat and meditated, I began to examine all these questions which thronged in my mind one after another from quite a different angle, and thought of something quite new. For instance, the strange notion occurred to me that if I had lived before on the moon or on Mars and had committed there the most shameful and dishonorable action that can be imagined, and had been so disgraced and dishonored there as can be imagined and experienced only occasionally in a dream, a nightmare, and if, finding myself afterward on earth, I had retained the memory of what I had done on the other planet, and moreover knew that I should never in any circumstances go back there—if that were to have happened, should I or should I not have felt, as I looked from the earth upon the moon, that *it made no difference* to me? Should I or should I not have felt ashamed of that action? The questions were idle and useless, for the gun was already lying before me and there was not a shadow of doubt in my mind that *it* was going to take place for certain, but they excited and maddened me. It seemed to me that I could not die now without having settled something first. The little girl, in fact, had saved me, for by these questions I put off my own execution.

Meanwhile things had grown more quiet in the captain's room: they had finished their card game and were getting ready to turn in for the night, and now were only grumbling and swearing at each other in a halfhearted sort of way. It was at that moment that I suddenly fell asleep in my armchair at the table, a thing that had never happened to me before.

I fell asleep without being aware of it at all. Dreams, as we all know, are very curious things: certain incidents in them are presented with quite uncanny vividness, each detail executed with the finishing touch of a jeweller, while others you leap across as though entirely unaware of, for instance, space and time. Dreams seem to be induced not by reason but by desire, not by the head but by the heart, and yet what clever tricks my reason has sometimes played on me in dreams! And furthermore what incomprehensible things happen to it in a dream. My brother, for instance, died five years ago. I sometimes dream about him: he takes a keen interest in my affairs, we are both very interested, and yet I know very well all through my dream that my brother is dead and buried. How is it that I am not surprised that, though dead, he is here beside me, doing his best to help me? Why does my reason accept all this without the slightest hesitation? But enough. Let me tell you about my dream. Yes, I dreamed that dream that night. My dream of the third of November. They are making fun of me now by saying that it was only a dream. But what does it matter whether it was a dream or not, so long as that dream revealed the Truth to me? For once you have recognized the truth and seen it, you know it is the one and only truth and that there can be no other, whether you are asleep or awake. But never mind. Let it be a dream, but remember that I had intended to cut short by suicide the life that means so much to us, and that my dream—my dream—oh, it revealed to me a new, grand, regenerated, strong life!

Listen.

III

I have said that I fell asleep imperceptibly and even while I seemed to be revolving the same thoughts again in my mind. Suddenly I dreamed that I picked up the gun and, sitting in my armchair, pointed it straight at my heart—at my heart, and not at my head. For I had firmly resolved to shoot myself through the head, through the right temple, to be precise. Having aimed the gun at my breast, I paused for a second or two, and suddenly my candle, the table and the wall began moving and swaying before me. I fired quickly.

In a dream you sometimes fall from a great height, or you are being murdered or beaten, but you never feel any pain unless you really manage somehow or other to hurt yourself in bed, when you feel pain and almost always wake up from it. So it was in my dream: I did not feel any pain, but it seemed as though with my shot everything within me was shaken and everything was suddenly extinguished, and a terrible darkness descended all around me. I seemed to have become blind and dumb. I was lying on something hard, stretched out full length on my back. I saw nothing and could not make the slightest movement. All round me people were walking and shouting. The captain was yelling in his deep bass voice, the landlady was screaming and—suddenly another hiatus, and I was being carried in a closed coffin. I could feel the coffin swaying and I was thinking about it, and for the first time the idea flashed through my mind that I was dead, dead as a doornail, that I knew it, that there was not the least doubt about it, that I could neither see nor move, and yet I could feel and reason. But I was soon reconciled to that and, as usually happens in dreams, I accepted the facts without questioning them.

And now I was buried in the earth. They all went away, and I was left alone, entirely alone. I did not move. Whenever before I imagined how I should be buried in a grave, there was only one sensation I actually associated with the grave, namely, that of damp and cold. And so it was now. I felt that I was very cold, especially in the tips of my toes, but I felt nothing else.

I lay in my grave and, strange to say, I did not expect anything, accepting the idea that a dead man had nothing to expect as an incontestable fact. But it was damp. I don't know how long a time passed, whether an hour, or several days, or many days. But suddenly a drop of water, which had seeped through the lid of the coffin, fell on my closed left eye. It was followed by another drop a minute later, then after another minute by another drop, and so on. One drop every minute. All at once deep indignation blazed up in my heart, and I suddenly felt a twinge of physical pain in it. "That's my wound," I thought. "It's the shot I fired. There's a bullet there. . . ." And drop after drop still kept falling every minute on my closed eyelid. And suddenly I called (not with my voice, for I was motionless, but with the whole of my being) upon Him who was responsible for all that was happening to me:

"Whoever Thou art, and if anything more rational exists than what is happening here, let it, I pray Thee, come to pass here too. But if Thou art revenging Thyself for my senseless act of self-destruction by the infamy and absurdity of life after death, then know that no torture that may be inflicted upon me can ever equal the contempt which I shall go on feeling in silence, though my martyrdom last for aeons upon aeons!"

I made this appeal and was silent. The dead silence went on for almost a minute, and one more drop fell on my closed eyelid, but I knew, I knew and believed infinitely and unshakably that everything would without a doubt change immediately. And then my grave was opened. I don't know, that is, whether it was opened or dug open, but I was seized by some dark and unknown being and we found ourselves in space. I suddenly regained my sight. It was a pitch-black night. Never, never had there been such darkness! We were flying through space at a terrific speed and we had already left the earth behind us. I did not question the being who was carrying me. I was proud and waited. I was telling myself that I was not afraid, and I was filled with admiration at the thought that I was not afraid. I cannot remember how long we were flying, nor can I give you an idea of the time; it all happened as it always does happen in dreams when you leap over space and time and the laws of nature and reason, and only pause at the points which are especially dear to your heart. All I remember is that I suddenly beheld a little star in the darkness.

"Is that Sirius?" I asked, feeling suddenly unable to restrain myself, for I had made up my mind not to ask any questions.

"No," answered the being who was carrying me, "that is the same star you saw between the clouds when you were coming home."

I knew that its face bore some resemblance to a human face. It is a strange fact but I did not like that being, and I even felt an intense aversion for it. I had expected complete non-existence and that was why I had shot myself through the heart. And yet there I was in the hands of a being, not human of course, but which *was*, which existed. "So there is life beyond the grave!" I thought with the curious irrelevance of a dream, but at heart I remained essentially unchanged. "If I must *be* again," I thought, "and live again at someone's unalterable behest, I won't be defeated and humiliated!"

"You know I'm afraid of you and that's why you despise me," I said suddenly to my companion, unable to refrain from the humiliating remark with its implied admission, and feeling my own humiliation in my heart like the sharp prick of a needle.

He did not answer me, but I suddenly felt that I was not despised, that no one was laughing at me, that no one was even pitying me, and that our journey had a purpose, an unknown and mysterious purpose that concerned only me. Fear was steadily growing in my heart. Something was communicated to me from my silent companion—mutely but agonizingly—and it seemed to permeate my whole being. We were speeding through dark and unknown regions of space. I had long since lost sight of the constellations familiar to me. I knew that there were stars in the heavenly spaces whose light took thousands and millions of years to reach the earth. Possibly we were already flying through those spaces. I expected something in the terrible anguish that wrung my heart. And suddenly a strangely familiar and incredibly nostalgic feeling shook me to the very core: I suddenly caught sight of our sun! I knew that it could not possibly be *our* sun that gave birth to our earth, and that we were millions of miles away from our sun, but for some unknown reason I recognized with every fiber of my being that it was precisely the same sun as ours, its exact copy and twin. A sweet, nostalgic feeling filled my heart with rapture: the old familiar power of the same light which had given me life stirred an echo in my heart and revived it, and I felt the same life stirring within me for the first time since I had been in the grave.

"But if it is the sun, if it's exactly the same sun as ours," I cried, "then where is the earth?"

And my companion pointed to a little star twinkling in the darkness with an emerald light. We were making straight for it.

"But are such repetitions possible in the universe? Can that be nature's law? And if that is an earth there, is it the same earth as ours? Just the same poor, unhappy, but dear, dear earth, and beloved forever and ever? Arousing like our earth the same poignant love for herself even in the most ungrateful of her children?" I kept crying, deeply moved by an uncontrollable, rapturous love for the dear old earth I had left behind.

The face of the poor little girl I had treated so badly flashed through my mind.

"You shall see it all," answered my companion, and a strange sadness sounded in his voice.

But we were rapidly approaching the planet. It was growing before my eyes. I could already distinguish the ocean, the outlines of Europe, and suddenly a strange feeling of some great and sacred jealousy blazed up in my heart.

"How is such a repetition possible and why? I love, I can only love the earth I've left behind, stained with my blood when, ungrateful wretch that I am, I extinguished my life by shooting myself through the heart. But never, never have I ceased to love that earth, and even on the night I parted from it I loved it perhaps more poignantly than ever. Is there suffering on this new earth? On our earth we can truly love only with suffering and through suffering! We know not how to love otherwise. We know no other love. I want suffering in order to love. I want and thirst this very minute to kiss, with tears streaming down my cheeks, the one and only earth I have left behind. I don't want, I won't accept life on any other! . . ."

But my companion had already left me. Suddenly, and without as it were being aware of it myself, I stood on this other earth in the bright light of a sunny day, fair and beautiful as paradise. I believe I was standing on one of the islands which on our earth form the Greek archipelago, or somewhere on the coast of the mainland close to this archipelago. Oh, everything was just as it is with us, except that everything seemed to be bathed in the radiance of some public festival and of some great and holy triumph attained at last. The gentle emerald sea softly lapped the shore and kissed it with manifest, visible, almost conscious love. Tall, beautiful trees stood in all the glory of their green luxuriant foliage, and their innumerable leaves (I am sure of that) welcomed me with their soft, tender rustle, and seemed to utter sweet words of love. The lush grass blazed with bright and fragrant flowers. Birds were flying in flocks through the air and, without being afraid of me, alighted on my shoulders and hands and joyfully beat against me with their sweet fluttering wings. And at last I saw and came to know the people of this blessed earth. They came to me themselves. They surrounded me. They kissed me. Children of the sun, children of their sun—oh, how beautiful they were! Never on our earth had I beheld such beauty in man. Only perhaps in our children during the very first years of their life could one have found a remote, though faint, reflection of this beauty. The eyes of these happy people shone with a bright luster. Their faces were radiant with understanding and a serenity of mind that had reached its greatest fulfilment. Those faces were joyous; in the words and voices of these people there was a childlike gladness. Oh, at the first glance at their faces I at once understood all, all! It was an earth unstained by the Fall, inhabited by people who had not sinned and who lived in the same paradise as that in which, according to the legends of mankind, our first parents lived before they sinned, with the only difference that all the earth here was everywhere the same paradise. These people, laughing happily, thronged round me and overwhelmed me with their caresses; they took me home with them, and each of them was anxious to set my mind at peace. Oh, they asked me no questions, but seemed to know everything already (that was the impression I got), and they longed to remove every trace of suffering from my face as soon as possible.

IV

Well, you see, again let me repeat: All right, let us assume it was only a dream! But the sensation of the love of those innocent and beautiful people has remained with me forever, and I can feel that their love is even now flowing out to me from over there. I have seen them myself. I have known them thoroughly and been convinced. I loved them and I suffered for them afterward. Oh, I knew at once even all the time that there were many things about them I should never be able to understand. To me, a modern Russian progressive and a despicable citizen of Petersburg, it seemed inexplicable that, knowing so much, they knew nothing of our science, for instance. But I soon realized that their knowledge was derived from, and fostered by emotions other than those to which we were accustomed on earth, and that their aspirations, too, were quite different. They desired nothing. They were at peace with themselves. They did not strive to gain knowledge of life as we strive to understand it because their lives were full. But their knowledge was higher and deeper than the knowledge we derive from our science; for our science seeks to explain what life is and strives to understand it in order to teach others how to live, while they knew how to live without science. I understood that, but I couldn't understand their knowledge. They pointed out their trees to me and I could not understand the intense love with which they looked on them; it was as though they were talking with beings like themselves. And, you know, I don't think I am exaggerating in saying that they talked with them! Yes, they had discovered their language, and I am sure the trees understood them. They looked upon all nature like that—the animals which lived peaceably with them and did not attack them, but loved them, conquered by their love for them. They pointed out the stars to me and talked to me about them in a way that I could not understand, but I am certain that in some curious way they communed with the stars in the heavens, not only in thought, but in some actual, living way. Oh, these people were not concerned whether I understood them or not; they loved me without it. But I too knew that they would never be able to understand me, and for that reason I hardly ever spoke to them about our earth. I merely kissed the earth of which they lived in their presence, and worshipped them without any words. And they saw that and let me worship them without being ashamed that I was worshipping them, for they themselves loved much. They did not suffer for me when, weeping, I sometimes kissed their feet, for in their hearts they were joyfully aware of the strong affection with which they would return my love. At times I asked myself in amazement how they had managed never to offend a person like me and not once arouse in a person like me a feeling of jealousy and envy. Many times I asked myself how I—a braggart and a liar—could refrain from telling them all I knew of science and philosophy, of which of course they had no idea? How it had never occurred to me to impress them with my store of learning, or impart my learning to them out of the love I bore them?

They were playful and high-spirited like children. They wandered about their beautiful woods and groves, they sang their beautiful songs, they lived on simple food—the fruits of their trees, the honey from their woods, and the milk of the animals that loved them. To obtain their food and clothes, they did not work very hard or long. They knew love and they begot children, but I never noticed in them those outburst of *cruel* sensuality which overtake almost everybody on our earth, whether man or woman, and are the only source of almost every sin of our human race. They rejoiced in their newborn children as new sharers in their bliss. There were no quarrels or jealousy among them, and they did not even know what the words meant. Their children were the children of them all, for they were all one family. There was scarcely any illness among them, though there was death; but their old people died peacefully, as though falling asleep, surrounded by the people who took leave of them, blessing them and smiling at them, and themselves receiving with bright smiles the farewell wishes of their friends. I never saw grief or tears on those occasions. What I did see was love that seemed to reach the point of rapture, but it was a gentle, self-sufficient, and contemplative rapture. There was reason to believe that they communicated with the departed after death, and that their earthly union was not cut short by death. They found it almost impossible to understand me when I questioned them about life eternal, but apparently they were so convinced of it in their minds that for them it was no question at all. They had no places of worship, but they had a certain awareness of a constant, uninterrupted, and living union with the Universe at large. They had no specific religions, but instead they had a certain knowledge that when their earthly joy had reached the limits imposed upon it by nature, they—both the living and the dead—would reach a state of still closer communion with the Universe at large. They looked forward to that moment with joy, but without haste and without pining for it, as though already possessing it in the vague stirrings of their hearts, which they communicated to each other.

In the evening, before going to sleep, they were fond of gathering together and singing in melodious and harmonious choirs. In their songs they expressed all the sensations the parting day had given them. They praised it and bade it farewell. They praised nature, the earth, the sea, and the woods. They were also fond of composing songs about one another, and they praised each other like children. Their songs were very simple, but they sprang straight from the heart and they touched the heart. And not only in their songs alone, but they seemed to spend all their lives in perpetual praise of one another. It seemed to be a universal and all-embracing love for each other. Some of their songs were solemn and ecstatic, and I was scarcely able to understand them at all. While understanding the words, I could never entirely fathom their meaning. It remained somehow beyond the grasp of my reason, and yet it sank unconsciously deeper and deeper into my heart. I often told them that I had had a presentiment of it years ago and that all that joy and glory had been perceived by me while I was still on our earth as a nostalgic yearning, bordering at times on unendurably poignant sorrow; that I had had a presentiment of them all and of their glory in the dreams of my heart and in the reveries of my soul; that often on our earth I could not look at the setting sun without tears. . . . That there always was a sharp pang of anguish in my hatred of the men of our earth; why could I not hate them without loving them too? Why could I not forgive them? And in my love for them, too, there was a sharp pang of anguish: why could I not love them without hating them? They listened to me, and I could tell that they did not know what I was talking about. But I was not sorry to have spoken to them of it, for I knew that they appreciated how much and how anxiously I yearned for those I had forsaken. Oh yes, when they looked at me with their dear eyes full of love, when I realized that in their presence my heart, too, became as innocent and truthful as theirs, I did not regret my inability to understand them, either. The sensation of the fullness of life left me breathless, and I worshipped them in silence.

Oh, everyone laughs in my face now and everyone assures me that I could not possibly have seen and felt anything so definite, but was merely conscious of a sensation that arose in my own feverish heart, and that I invented all those details myself when I woke up. And when I told them that they were probably right, good Lord, what mirth that admission of mine caused and how they laughed at me! Why, of course, I was overpowered by the mere sensation of that dream and it alone survived in my sorely wounded heart. But nonetheless the real shapes and forms of my dream, that is, those I actually saw at the very time of my dream, were filled with such harmony and were so enchanting and beautiful, and so intensely true, that on awakening I was indeed unable to clothe them in our feeble words so that they

were bound as it were to become blurred in my mind; so is it any wonder that perhaps unconsciously I was myself afterward driven to make
up the details which I could not help distorting, particularly in view
of my passionate desire to convey some of them at least as quickly as I
could. But that does not mean that I have no right to believe that it all
did happen. As a matter of fact, it was quite possibly a thousand times
better, brighter, and more joyful than I describe it. What if it was only
a dream? All that couldn't possibly not have been. And do you know,
I think I'll tell you a secret: perhaps it was no dream at all! For what
happened afterward was so awful, so horribly true, that it couldn't
possibly have been a mere coinage of my brain seen in a dream.
Granted that my heart was responsible for my dream, but could my
heart alone have been responsible for the awful truth of what happened to me afterward? Surely my paltry heart and my vacillating and
trivial mind could not have risen to such a revelation of truth! Oh,
judge for yourselves: I have been concealing it all the time, but now I
will tell you the whole truth. The fact is, I—corrupted them all!

V

Yes, yes, it ended in my corrupting them all! How it could have
happened I do not know, but I remember it clearly. The dream encom-
passed thousands of years and left in me only a vague sensation of
the whole. I only know that the cause of the Fall was I. Like a horrible
trichina, like the germ of the plague infecting whole kingdoms, so
did I infect with myself all that happy earth that knew no sin before
me. They learned to lie, and they grew to appreciate the beauty of a
lie. Oh, perhaps, it all began *innocently*, with a jest, with a desire to
show off, with amorous play, and perhaps indeed only with a germ,
but this germ made its way into their hearts and they liked it. The
voluptuousness was soon born, voluptuousness begot jealousy, and
jealousy—cruelty. . . . Oh, I don't know, I can't remember, but soon,
very soon the first blood was shed: they were shocked and horrified,
and they began to separate and to shun one another. They formed
alliances, but it was one against another. Recriminations began,
reproaches. They came to know shame, and they made shame into a
virtue. The conception of honor was born, and every alliance raised

its own standard. They began torturing animals, and the animals ran away from them into the forests and became their enemies. A struggle began for separation, for isolation, for personality, for mine and thine. They began talking in different languages. They came to know sorrow, and they loved sorrow. They thirsted for suffering, and they said that Truth could only be attained through suffering. It was then that science made its appearance among them. When they became wicked, they began talking of brotherhood and humanity and understood the meaning of those ideas. When they became guilty of crimes, they invented justice, and drew up whole codes of law, and to ensure the carrying out of their laws they erected a guillotine. They only vaguely remembered what they had lost, and they would not believe that they ever were happy and innocent. They even laughed at the possibility of their former happiness and called it a dream. They could not even imagine it in any definite shape or form, but the strange and wonderful thing was that though they had lost faith in their former state of happiness and called it a fairy tale, they longed so much to be happy and innocent once more that, like children, they succumbed to the desire of their hearts, glorified this desire, built temples, and began offering up prayers to their own idea, their own "desire," and at the same time firmly believed that it could not be realized and brought about, though they still worshipped it and adored it with tears. And yet if they could have in one way or another returned to the state of happy innocence they had lost, and if someone had shown it to them again and had asked them whether they desired to go back to it, they would certainly have refused. The answer they gave me was, "What if we are dishonest, cruel, and unjust? We *know* it and we are sorry for it, and we torment ourselves for it, and inflict pain upon ourselves, and punish ourselves more perhaps than the merciful Judge who will judge us and whose name we do not know. But we have science and with its aid we shall again discover truth, though we shall accept it only when we perceive it with our reason. Knowledge is higher than feeling, and the consciousness of life is higher than life. Science will give us wisdom. Wisdom will reveal to us the laws. And the knowledge of the laws of happiness is higher than happiness." That is what they said to me, and having uttered those words, each of them began to love himself better than anyone else, and indeed they could not do otherwise. Every one of them became so jealous of his own personality that he strove with might and main to belittle and humble it in others; and therein he saw the whole purpose of his life. Slavery made its appearance, even voluntary slavery: the weak eagerly submitted themselves to the will of the strong on condition that the strong helped them to oppress those who were weaker than themselves. Saints made their appearance, saints who came to these people with tears and told them of their pride, of their loss of proportion and harmony, of their loss of shame. They were laughed to scorn and stoned to death. Their sacred blood was spilled on the threshold of the temples. But then men arose who began to wonder how they could all be united again, so that everybody should, without ceasing to love himself best of all, not interfere with everybody else and so that all of them should live together in a society which would at least seem to be founded on mutual understanding. Whole wars were fought over this idea. All the combatants at one and the same time firmly believed that science, wisdom, and the instinct of self-preservation would in the end force mankind to unite into a harmonious and intelligent society, and therefore, to hasten matters, the "very wise" did their best to exterminate as rapidly as possible the "not so wise" who did not understand their idea, so as to prevent them from interfering with its triumph. But the instinct of self-preservation began to weaken rapidly. Proud and voluptuous men appeared who frankly demanded all or nothing. In order to obtain everything they did not hesitate to resort to violence, and if it failed—to suicide. Religions were founded to propagate the cult of non-existence and self-destruction for the sake of the everlasting peace in nothingness. At last these people grew weary of their senseless labors and suffering appeared on their faces, and these people proclaimed that suffering was beauty, for in suffering alone was there thought. They glorified suffering in their songs. I walked among them, wringing my hands and weeping over them, but I loved them perhaps more than before when there was no sign of suffering in their faces and when they were innocent and—oh, so beautiful! I loved the earth they had polluted even more than when it had been a paradise, and only because sorrow had made its appearance on it. Alas, I always loved sorrow and affliction, but only for myself, only for myself; for them I wept now, for I pitied them. I stretched out my hands to them, accusing, cursing, and despising myself. I told them that I alone was responsible for it all—I alone; that it was I who had brought them corruption, contamination, and lies! I implored them to crucify me, and I taught them how to make the cross. I could not kill myself; I had not the courage to do it; but I longed to receive martyrdom at their hands. I thirsted for martyrdom, I yearned for my blood to be shed to the last drop in torment and suffering. But they only laughed at me, and in the end they began looking upon me as a madman. They justified me. They said that they had got what they themselves wanted and that what was now could not have been otherwise. At last they told me that I was becoming dangerous to them and that they would lock me up in a lunatic asylum if I did not hold my peace. Then sorrow entered my soul with such force that my heart was wrung and I felt as though I were dying, and then—well, then I awoke.

It was morning, that is, the sun had not risen yet, but it was about six o'clock. When I came to, I found myself in the same armchair, my candle had burned out, in the captain's room they were asleep, and silence, so rare in our house, reigned around. The first thing I did was to jump up in great amazement. Nothing like this had ever happened to me before, not even so far as the most trivial details were concerned. Never, for instance, had I fallen asleep like this in my armchair. Then, suddenly, as I was standing and coming to myself, I caught sight of my gun lying there ready and loaded. But I pushed it away from me at once! Oh, how I longed for life, life! I lifted up my hands and called upon eternal Truth—no, not called upon, but wept. Rapture, infinite and boundless rapture intoxicated me. Yes, life and—preaching! I made up my mind to preach from that very moment and, of course, to go on preaching all my life. I am going to preach, I want to preach. What? Why, truth. For I have beheld truth, I have beheld it with mine own eyes, I have beheld it in all its glory!

And since then I have been preaching. Moreover, I love all who laugh at me more than all the rest. Why that is so, I don't know and cannot explain, but let it be so. They say that even now I often get muddled and confused and that if I am getting muddled and confused now, what will be later on? It is perfectly true. I do get muddled and confused and it is quite possible that I shall be getting worse later. And, of course, I shall get muddled several times before I find out how to preach, that is, what words to use and what deeds to perform, for that is all very difficult! All this is even now as clear to me as daylight, but, pray, tell me who does not get muddled and confused? And yet all follow the same path, at least all strive to achieve the same thing, from the philosopher to the lowest criminal, only by different roads. It is an old truth, but this is what is new: I cannot even get very much muddled and confused. For I have beheld the Truth. I have beheld it and I know that people can be happy and beautiful without losing their ability to live on earth. I will not and I cannot believe that evil is the normal condition among men. And yet they all laugh at this faith of mine. But how can I help believing it? I have beheld it—the Truth— it is not as though I had invented it with my mind: I have beheld it, I have beheld it, and the *living image* of it has filled my soul forever. I have beheld it in all its glory and I cannot believe that it cannot exist among men. So how can I grow muddled and confused? I shall of course lose my way and I'm afraid that now and again I may speak with words that are not my own, but not for long: the living image of what I beheld will always be with me and it will always correct me and lead me back on to the right path. Oh, I'm in fine fettle, and I am of good cheer. I will go on and on for a thousand years, if need be. Do you know, at first I did not mean to tell you that I corrupted them, but that was a mistake—there you have my first mistake! But Truth whispered to me that I was *lying*, and preserved me and set me on the right path. But I'm afraid I do not know how to establish a heaven on earth, for I do not know how to put it into words. After my dream I lost the knack of putting things into words. At least, onto the most necessary and most important words. But never mind, I shall go on and I shall keep on talking, for I have indeed beheld it with my own eyes, though I cannot describe what I saw. It is this the scoffers do not understand. "He had a dream," they say, "a vision, a hallucination!" Oh dear, is this all they have to say? Do they really think that is very clever? And how proud they are! A dream! What is a dream? And what about our life? Is that not a dream too? I will say more: even— yes, even if this never comes to pass, even if there never is a heaven on earth (that, at any rate, I can see very well!), even then I shall go on preaching. And really how simple it all is: in one day, *in one hour*, everything could be arranged at once! The main thing is to love your neighbor as yourself—that is the main thing, and that is everything, for nothing else matters. Once you do that, you will discover at once how everything can be arranged. And yet it is an old truth, a truth that has been told over and over again, but in spite of that it finds no place among men! "The consciousness of life is higher than life, the knowledge of happiness is higher than happiness"—that is what we have to fight against! And I shall, I shall fight against it! If only we all wanted it, everything could be arranged immediately.

And—I did find that little girl. . . . And I shall go on! I shall go on!

QUESTIONS FOR DISCUSSION

Why does the narrator refer to himself as "ridiculous" and "an utterly absurd person"? (113)

1. Why does the narrator know "better than anyone else" that he is ridiculous? (114)

2. After his encounter with the little girl, what does the narrator mean when he says, "It might almost be said that the world seemed to be created for me alone"? (119)

3. If the narrator has "lost the knack of putting things into words," why does he become a preacher? (133)

Why does the narrator believe he was the cause of the Fall that occurred in his dream? (129)

1. Why does the narrator feel an "intense aversion" to the being who carries him through space? (122)

2. Why does the narrator dream that after the Fall he loved the people "perhaps more than before when there was no sign of suffering in their faces and when they were innocent"? (131)

3. Why does the narrator say that it was a mistake to reveal that he corrupted the people in his dream? (133)

4. What does the narrator mean when he says we have to fight against the belief that the "consciousness of life is higher than life, the knowledge of happiness is higher than happiness"? (130)

FOR FURTHER REFLECTION

1. Why does Dostoevsky make the narrator, a self-described "absurd person" and a "braggart and liar," come to the conclusion that "the main thing is to love your neighbor as yourself"? (113, 133–134)

2. What is the difference between wisdom and knowledge? Is it necessary to suffer in order to become wise? Do you agree with the narrator when he says, "On our earth we can truly love only with suffering and through suffering"? (124)

3. Is it possible to truly love those we cannot fully understand?

The Best Life Possible

Much utopian thinking can be viewed as political philosophy, investigating such fundamental questions as what elements constitute the best communities for satisfying human needs and what alterations are conducive to the realization of these communities. From this perspective, almost any regional plan, partisan agenda, legislative effort, reform movement, policy formation, or revolutionary manifesto that aims to improve society can be considered utopian in spirit. However, most utopian proposals are more comprehensive and envision communities in which most of the social and institutional arrangements that provide for human well-being are taken into consideration, both in theory and in practice.

As philosophical propositions, utopian proposals are based on sets of principles from which the characteristics of ideal communities are derived. They also often provide criteria for evaluating whether, and to what extent, the ideal is realized.

Many utopian proposals that fall within the realm of political philosophy are also concerned with highly pragmatic questions such as how ideal communities should be geographically situated, how their centers of population should be laid out, how their governing bodies should be structured, and how their citizens should be educated. The three selections in this section frame their considerations of utopian communities in abstract terms that should be generally applicable to many of the selections in other sections of this book.

Very little is known for certain about the Chinese philosopher **Mencius** (371–289 BCE). It is said that he studied with the grandson of the eminent philosopher Confucius and that he spent many years as an itinerant, visiting heads of state and attempting to persuade them to effect fundamental reforms in how their communities were governed. Mencius, through his eponymous book, is considered one of the principal interpreters of Confucian philosophy. The selection included here is from Book I of *Mencius,* and, like most of his writings, it takes the form of brief dialogues between himself and various kings. In these dialogues, he asks his interlocutors—and his readers—to address what kinds of interventions into a society's existing conditions hold potential for setting things on a new and better course, ultimately leading to an ideal state of affairs.

The selection from Book VII of Greek philosopher **Aristotle's** (384–322 BCE) *The Politics* comes after a lengthy discussion of what constitutes the best life for humans, the nature of human happiness, and the conditions conducive to it. Thus, he derives his very specific recommendations for an ideal community in Book VII from the foundational principles of his philosophical system. In the selection included here, Aristotle proposes the material and organizational conditions that he thinks will result in a well-ordered community, which he defines as one that holds the greatest possibilities for the happiness of its citizens. How are members of the community to be educated in the role of citizen so that they can fully partake of these possibilities?

"A Framework for Utopia" is taken from a chapter in *Anarchy, State, and Utopia* (1974), written by the American philosopher **Robert Nozick** (1938–2002). Nozick's "framework for utopia" is intended to provide a solution to one of the central quandaries of utopian thinking: that individuals differ and that no one ideal community is likely to be acceptable to all. In his framework for utopia, Nozick argues that the ultimate utopia is a collection of utopias that individuals can pick and choose among, depending on their preferences. In light of this idea of a framework, then, is the notion of a single community that is usually associated with utopian thinking really one of its necessary attributes?

Mencius

(selection)

Mencius

M encius went to see King Hui of Liang. "You, sir," said the king, "have come all this distance, thinking nothing of a thousand *li*. You must surely have some way of profiting my state?"

"Your Majesty," answered Mencius. "What is the point of mentioning the word *profit*? All that matters is that there should be benevolence and rightness. If Your Majesty says, "How can I profit my state?" and the counselors say, "How can I profit my family?" and the gentlemen and commoners say, "How can I profit my person?" then those above and those below will be vying with each other for profit and the state will be imperiled. When regicide is committed in a state of ten thousand chariots, it is certain to be by a vassal with a thousand chariots, and when it is committed in a state of a thousand chariots, it is certain to be by a vassal with a hundred chariots. A share of a thousand in ten thousand or a hundred in a thousand is by no means insignificant, yet if profit is put before rightness, there is no satisfaction short of total usurpation. No benevolent man ever abandons his parents, and no dutiful man ever puts his prince last. Perhaps you will now endorse what I have said, "All that matters is that there should be benevolence and rightness. What is the point of mentioning the word *profit*?"

Mencius went to see King Hui of Liang. The king was standing over a pond. "Are such things enjoyed even by a good and wise man?" said he, looking round at his wild geese and deer.

"Only if a man is good and wise," answered Mencius, "is he able to enjoy them. Otherwise he would not, even if he had them.

"The *Odes* say,

> He surveyed and began the Sacred Terrace.
> He surveyed it and measured it;
> The people worked at it;
> In less than no time they finished it.
> He surveyed and began without haste;
> The people came in ever increasing numbers.
> The King was in the Sacred Park.
> The doe lay down;
> The doe were sleek;
> The white birds glistened.
> The King was at the Sacred Pond.
> Oh! how full it was of leaping fish!

It was with the labor of the people that King Wen built his terrace and pond, yet so pleased and delighted were they that they named his terrace the "Sacred Terrace" and his pond the "Sacred Pond," and rejoiced in his possession of deer, fish, and turtles. It was by sharing their enjoyments with the people that men of antiquity were able to enjoy themselves.

"The *T'ang shih* says,

> O Sun, when wilt thou perish?
> We care not if we have to die with thee.

When the people were prepared "to die with" him, even if the tyrant had a terrace and pond, birds and beasts, could he have enjoyed them all by himself?"

King Hui of Liang said, "I have done my best for my state. When crops failed in Ho Nei I moved the population to Ho Tung and the grain to Ho Nei, and reversed the action when crops failed in Ho Tung. I have not noticed any of my neighbors taking as much pains over his government. Yet how is it the population of the neighboring states has not decreased and mine has not increased?"

"Your Majesty is fond of war," said Mencius. "May I use an analogy from it? After weapons were crossed to the rolling of drums, some soldiers fled, abandoning their armor and trailing their weapons. One stopped after a hundred paces, another after fifty paces. What would you think if the latter, as one who ran only fifty paces, were to laugh at the former who ran a hundred?"

"He had no right to," said the king. "He did not quite run a hundred paces. That is all. But all the same, he ran."

"If you can see that," said Mencius, "you will not expect your own state to be more populous than the neighboring states.

"If you do not interfere with the busy seasons in the fields, then there will be more grain than the people can eat; if you do not allow nets with too fine a mesh to be used in large ponds, then there will be more fish and turtles than they can eat; if hatchets and axes are permitted in the forests on the hills only in the proper seasons, then there will be more timber than they can use. When the people have more grain, more fish and turtles than they can eat, and more timber than they can use, then in the support of their parents when alive and in the mourning of them when dead, they will be able to have no regrets over anything left undone. For the people not to have any regrets over anything left undone, whether in the support of their parents when alive or in the mourning of them when dead, is the first step along the kingly way.

"If the mulberry is planted in every homestead of five *mu* of land, then those who are fifty can wear silk; if chickens, pigs, and dogs do not miss their breeding season, then those who are seventy can eat meat; if each lot of a hundred *mu* is not deprived of labor during the busy season, then families with several mouths to feed will not go hungry. Exercise due care over the education provided by village schools, and reinforce this by teaching them the duties proper to sons and younger brothers, and those whose heads have turned hoary will not be carrying loads on the roads. When those who are seventy wear silk and eat meat and the masses are neither cold nor hungry, it is impossible for their prince not to be a true king.

"Now when food meant for human beings is so plentiful as to be thrown to dogs and pigs, you fail to realize that it is time for collection, and when men drop dead from starvation by the wayside, you fail to realize that it is time for distribution. When people die, you simply say, 'It is none of my doing. It is the fault of the harvest.' In what way is that different from killing a man by running him through, while saying all the time, "It is none of my doing. It is the fault of the weapon." Stop putting the blame on the harvest and the people of the whole empire will come to you."

King Hui of Liang said, "I shall listen willingly to what you have to say."

"Is there any difference," said Mencius, "between killing a man with a staff and killing him with a knife?"

"There is no difference."

"Is there any difference between killing him with a knife and killing him with misrule?"

"There is no difference."

"There is fat meat in your kitchen and there are well-fed horses in your stables, yet the people look hungry and in the outskirts of cities men drop dead from starvation. This is to show animals the way to devour men. Even the devouring of animals by animals is repugnant to men. If, then, one who is father and mother to the people cannot, in ruling over them, avoid showing animals the way to devour men, wherein is he father and mother to the people?

"When Confucius said, 'The inventor of burial figures in human form deserves not to have any progeny,' he was condemning him for the use of something modeled after the human form. How, then, can the starving of this very people be countenanced?"

King Hui of Liang said, "As you know, the state of Chin was second to none in power in the empire. But when it came to my own time we suffered defeat in the east by Ch'i when my eldest son died, and we lost territory to the extent of seven hundred *li* to Ch'in in the west, while to the south we were humiliated by Ch'u. I am deeply ashamed of this and wish, in what little time I have left in this life, to wash away all this shame. How can this be done?"

"A territory of a hundred *li* square," answered Mencius, "is sufficient to enable its ruler to become a true king. If Your Majesty practices benevolent government toward the people, reduces punishment and taxation, gets the people to plough deeply and weed promptly, and if the able-bodied men learn, in their spare time, to be good sons and good younger brothers, loyal to their prince and true to their word, so that they will, in the family, serve their fathers and elder brothers, and outside the family, serve their elders and superiors, then they can be made to inflict defeat on the strong armor and sharp weapons of Ch'in and Ch'u, armed with nothing but staves.

"These other princes take the people away from their work during the busy seasons, making it impossible for them to till the land and so minister to the needs of their parents. Thus parents suffer cold and hunger while brothers, wives, and children are separated and scattered. These princes push their people into pits and into water. If you should go and punish such princes, who is there to oppose you? Hence it is said, 'The benevolent man has no match.' I beg of you not to have any doubts."

Mencius saw King Hsiang of Liang. Coming away, he said to someone, "When I saw him at a distance he did not look like a ruler of men and when I went close to him I did not see anything that commanded respect. Abruptly he asked me, "Through what can the empire be settled?"

" 'Through unity,' I said.

" 'Who can unite it?'

" 'One who is not fond of killing can unite it,' I said.

" 'Who can give it to him?'

" 'No one in the empire will refuse to give it to him. Does Your Majesty not know about the young seedling? Should there be a drought in the seventh or eighth month, it will wilt. If clouds begin to gather in the sky and rain comes pouring down, then it will spring up again. This being the case, who can stop it? Now in the empire amongst the shepherds of men there is not one who is not fond of killing. If there is one who is not, then the people in the empire will crane their necks to watch for his coming. This being truly the case, the people will turn to him like water flowing downwards with a tremendous force. Who can stop it?' "

King Hsüan of Ch'i asked, "Can you tell me about the history of Duke Huan of Ch'i and Duke Wen of Chin?"

"None of the followers of Confucius," answered Mencius, "spoke of the history of Duke Huan and Duke Wen. It is for this reason that no one in after ages passed on any accounts, and I have no knowledge of them. If you insist, perhaps I may be permitted to tell you about becoming a true king."

"How virtuous must a man be before he can become a true king?"

"He becomes a true king by tending the people. This is something no one can stop."

"Can someone like myself tend the people?"

"Yes."

"How do you know that I can?"

"I heard the following from Hu He:

> The king was sitting in the hall. He saw someone
> passing below, leading an ox. The king noticed this and
> said, "Where is the ox going?" "The blood of the ox is to
> be used for consecrating a new bell." "Spare it. I cannot
> bear to see it shrinking with fear, like an innocent
> man going to the place of execution." "In that case,
> should the ceremony be abandoned?" "That is out of the
> question. Use a lamb instead."

"I wonder if this is true?"

"It is."

"The heart behind your action is sufficient to enable you to become a true king. The people all thought that you grudged the expense, but, for my part, I have no doubt that you were moved by pity for the animal."

"You are right," said the king. "How extraordinary that there should be such people! Ch'i may be a small state, but I am not quite so miserly as to grudge the use of an ox. It was simply because I could not bear to see it shrink with fear, like an innocent man going to the place of execution, that I used a lamb instead."

"You must not be surprised that the people thought you miserly. You used a small animal in place of a big one. How were they to know? If you were pained by the animal going innocently to its death, what was there to choose between an ox and a lamb?"

The king laughed and said, "What was really in my mind, I wonder? It is not true that I grudged the expense, but I *did* use a lamb instead of the ox. I suppose it was only natural that the people should have thought me miserly."

"There is no harm in this. It is the way of a benevolent man. You saw the ox but not the lamb. The attitude of a gentleman toward animals is this: once having seen them alive, he cannot bear to see them die, and once having heard their cry, he cannot bear to eat their flesh. That is why the gentleman keeps his distance from the kitchen."

The king was pleased and said, "The *Odes* say,

> The heart is someone else's,
> But it is I who have surmised it.

"This describes you perfectly. For though the deed was mine, when I looked into myself I failed to understand my own heart. You described it for me and your words struck a chord in me. What made you think that my heart accorded with the way of a true king?"

"Should someone say to you, 'I am strong enough to lift a hundred *chün* but not a feather; I have eyes that can see the tip of a new down but not a cartload of firewood,' would you accept the truth of such a statement?"

"No."

"Why should it be different in your own case? Your bounty is sufficient to reach the animals, yet the benefits of your government fail to reach the people. That a feather is not lifted is because one fails to make the effort; that a cartload of firewood is not seen is because one fails to use one's sight. Similarly, that the people have not been tended is because you fail to practice kindness. Hence your failure to become a true king is due to a refusal to act, not to an inability to act."

"What is the difference in form between refusal to act and inability to act?"

"If you say to someone, 'I am unable to do it,' when the task is one of striding over the North Sea with Mount T'ai under your arm, then this is a genuine case of inability to act. But if you say, "I am unable to do it," when it is one of making an obeisance to your elders, then this is a case of refusal to act, not of inability. Hence your failure to become a true king is not the same in kind as 'striding over the North Sea with Mount T'ai under your arm,' but the same as 'making an obeisance to your elders.'

"Treat the aged of your own family in a manner befitting their venerable age and extend this treatment to the aged of other families; treat your own young in a manner befitting their tender age and extend this to the young of other families, and you can roll the empire on your palm.

"The *Odes* say,

> He set an example for his consort
> And also for his brothers,
> And so ruled over the family and the state.

"In other words, all you have to do is take this very heart here and apply it to what is over there. Hence one who extends his bounty can tend those within the four seas; one who does not cannot tend even his own family. There is just one thing in which the ancients greatly surpassed others, and that is the way they extended what they did. Why is it then that your bounty is sufficient to reach animals yet the benefits of your government fail to reach the people? "It is by weighing a thing that its weight can be known and by measuring it that its length can be ascertained. It is so with all things, but particularly so with the heart. Your Majesty should measure his own heart.

"Perhaps you find satisfaction only in starting a war, imperiling your subjects and incurring the enmity of other feudal lords?"

"No. Why should I find satisfaction in such acts? I only wish to realize my supreme ambition."

"May I be told what this is?"

The king smiled, offering no reply.

"Is it because your food is not good enough to gratify your palate, and your clothes not good enough to gratify your body? Or perhaps the sights and sounds are not good enough to gratify your eyes and ears and your close servants not good enough to serve you? Any of your various officials surely could make good these deficiencies. It cannot be because of these things."

"No. It is not because of these things."

"In that case one can guess what your supreme ambition is. You wish to extend your territory, to enjoy the homage of Ch'in and Ch'u, to rule over the central kingdoms and to bring peace to the barbarian tribes on the four borders. Seeking the fulfillment of such an ambition by such means as you employ is like looking for fish by climbing a tree."

"Is it as bad as that?" asked the king.

"It is likely to be worse. If you look for fish by climbing a tree, though you will not find it, there is no danger of this bringing disasters in its train. But if you seek the fulfillment of an ambition like yours by such means as you employ, after putting all your heart and might into the pursuit, you are certain to reap disaster in the end."

"Can I hear about this?"

"If the men of Tsou and the men of Ch'u were to go to war, who do you think would win?"

"The men of Ch'u."

"That means that the small is no match for the big, the few no match for the many, and the weak no match for the strong. Within the seas there are nine areas of ten thousand *li* square, and the territory of Ch'i makes up one of these. For one to try to overcome the other eight is no different from Tsou going to war with Ch'u. Why not go back to fundamentals?

"Now if you should practice benevolence in the government of your state, then all those in the empire who seek office would wish to find a place at your court, all tillers of land to till the land in outlying parts of your realm, all merchants to enjoy the refuge of your marketplace, all travelers to go by way of your roads, and all those who hate their rules to lay their complaints before you. This being so, who can stop you from becoming a true king?"

"I am dull-witted," said the king, "and cannot see my way beyond this point. I hope you will help me toward my goal and instruct me plainly. Though I am slow, I shall make an attempt to follow your advice."

"Only a gentleman can have a constant heart in spite of a lack of constant means of support. The people, on the other hand, will not have constant hearts if they are without constant means. Lacking constant hearts, they will go astray and fall into excesses, stopping at nothing. To punish them after they have fallen foul of the law is to set a trap for the people. How can a benevolent man in authority allow himself to set a trap for the people? Hence when determining what means of support the people should have, a clear-sighted ruler ensures that these are sufficient, on the one hand, for the care of parents, and, on the other, for the support of wife and children, so that the people always have sufficient food in good years and escape starvation in bad; only then does he drive them toward goodness; in this way the people find it easy to follow him.

"Nowadays, the means laid down for the people are sufficient neither for the care of parents nor for the support of wife and children. In good years life is always hard, while in bad years there is no way of escaping death. Thus simply to survive takes more energy than the people have. What time can they spare for learning about rites and duty?

"If you wish to put this into practice, why not go back to fundamentals? If the mulberry is planted in every homestead of five *mu* of land, then those who are fifty can wear silk; if chickens, pigs, and dogs do not miss their breeding season, then those who are seventy can eat meat; if each lot of a hundred *mu* is not deprived of labor during the busy season, then families with several mouths to feed will not go hungry. Exercise due care over the education provided by village schools, and reinforce this by teaching them duties proper to sons and younger brothers, and those whose heads have turned hoary will not be carrying loads on the roads. When the aged wear silk and eat meat and the masses are neither cold nor hungry, it is impossible for their prince not to be a true king."

QUESTIONS FOR DISCUSSION

Does King Hui make progress in becoming a true king as a result of his encounters with Mencius?

1. Why does Mencius say that benevolence and rightness are "all that matters"? (141)

2. Why does Mencius tell King Hui, "For the people not to have any regrets over anything left undone" is "the first step along the kingly way"? (143)

3. Why is King Hui eager "to wash away all this shame" of battle defeats but not ashamed of having starving subjects? (144)

4. If King Hui does not finally become a true king, what would Mencius say keeps him from that goal?

According to Mencius, what is the answer to King Hsüan's question, "How virtuous must a man be before he can become a true king"? (146)

1. Why does Mencius say to King Hui, "The benevolent man has no match"? (145)

2. Why does Mencius think King Hsüan has the heart to enable him to become a true king?

3. Why does Mencius think that King Hsüan's failure to become a true king "is due to a refusal to act, not to an inability to act"? (147)

FOR FURTHER REFLECTION

1. In your opinion, what is the most effective aspect of Mencius's way of teaching?

2. Why do people who govern often seem to be out of touch with the needs of the people?

3. Are benevolence and rightness "all that matters" for world leaders today?

The Politics

(selection)

Aristotle

Now that our introduction to these matters is finished and since we have earlier discussed the other constitutions, the first part of what remains to be discussed will deal with the question, "What are the fundamental postulates for a state which is to be constructed exactly as one would wish, one provided with all the appropriate material equipment, without which it would not be the best state?" We must therefore postulate everything as we would wish it to be, remembering however that nothing must be outside the bounds of possibility. I am thinking for example of population and territory; these are part of the essential material. A weaver or a boatmaker must have a supply of the materials necessary for the exercise of his craft, and the better the provision for these, the finer will be the result which his skill will produce. So too a statesman or lawgiver must have the proper material in sufficient quantities.

For the making of a state the first essential is a supply of men and we must consider both how many they shall be and of what kind. The second is territory; we shall need to determine both its extent and its quality. Most people think that if a city is to be happy it must needs be great. This may be true, but they do not know how to judge greatness and smallness in a city. They judge greatness by the number of people living in it; but one ought to look not at numbers merely but at power and effectiveness. A city has a function to perform and the city which is most capable of discharging that function must be regarded as greatest, rather in the same way that one might say that Hippocrates was "a bigger man," not as a man but as a physician, than one of great bodily size. However, even granting that we must have regard to size of population, we must not do so without discrimination; we must allow for the presence in the states of many slaves and many foreigners, residents, or visitors. Our concern is only with those who form part of the state, with those sections of population of which a state properly consists. Great numbers of these is a mark of a great city, but a city cannot possibly be great which can put into the field only a handful of citizen-soldiers along with a large rabble of inferior persons. A great city and a populous one are not the same. Moreover, experience has shown that it is difficult, if not impossible, for an over-large population to be well and lawfully governed; at any rate I know of no well-constituted city that does not restrict its numbers. The language itself makes this certain. For law is itself a kind of order and to live under good laws is to live in good order. But an excessively large number cannot be orderly; that would require the power of the divine force which holds the universe together, where to be sure we do find order and beauty conjoined with size and multiplicity. Therefore that city will be finest which, though large, conforms to the limitations just mentioned. But there must also be a proper norm for the size of a city, as there is a normal size for everything else—animals, plants, instruments, and so on. Each of these can only perform its proper function if it is neither too large nor too small; otherwise its true raison d'être will be either entirely lost or seriously impaired. Thus a boat a few inches long will not really be a boat at all, nor one half a mile long. If it reaches a certain size, it may be long enough (or small enough) to be called a boat, but still be too small (or too large) to be navigated. It is just the same with a city; if it has too few people it cannot serve its own needs as a city should; if it has too many it can certainly meet all its essential requirements, but as an ethnic conglomerate not as a city. Such size makes it difficult for any constitution to subsist. For who will be military commander of the excessive population? Who will be their crier unless he has the voice of a stentor? Therefore, when first the population becomes large enough to be able to provide for itself all that is needed for living the good life after the manner of the city-state community, then we can begin to speak of a city. It is possible to go on from there; a city greater in population than that will be a larger city, but as we have said this process is not unlimited. What the limit of size should be can easily be determined by an examination of the facts. The activities of a city are those of the rulers and those of the ruled, and the functions of the ruler are decision and direction. In order to give decisions on matters of justice and for the purpose of distributing offices in accordance with the work of the applicants, it is necessary that the citizens should know each other and know what kind of people they are. Where this condition does not exist, both elections and decisions at law are bound to suffer; it is not right in either of these matters to vote at haphazard, which is clearly what takes place where the population is excessive. Another drawback is that it becomes easy for noncitizens, foreigners resident in the country, to become possessed of citizenship; the great size of the population makes detection difficult. Here then we have ready to hand the best definition of a city: it must have a population large enough to cater for all the needs of a self-sufficient existence, but not so large that it cannot be easily supervised. Let that be our way of defining the size of a city.

The case is similar when we turn our attention to territory. As regards quality of land, everyone would choose the most self-sufficient, that is to say the most universally productive; to have everything to hand and nothing lacking is the height of self-sufficiency. As to size and extent, these should be such that the citizens can live a life that involves no manual labor, a life of a free man but one without extravagance. The general configuration of the land is not difficult to state, though there are some points on which we must take the opinion of those who have experience of conducting operations of war; it ought to be hard for a hostile force to invade, easy for an expeditionary force to depart from. Apart from that, just as we remarked that the population ought to be easily supervised, so we say the same of the territory; in a country that can easily be seen it is easy to bring military assistance at any point. Next, the position of the city: if we are to put it exactly where we would like best, it should be conveniently situated for both sea and land. This will give three advantages: first the point mentioned above, it will be equally well-placed for operations in all directions; also it will form an entrepôt for the receipt of incoming foodstuffs; and it will have access to timber and whatever other raw materials the land may be able to produce.

There is a good deal of argument about communication with the sea and whether it is a help or a hindrance in good government of states. Some say that to open one's city to foreigners, brought up in a different code of behavior, is detrimental to good order and makes for overcrowding. They say that the use of the sea leads to much coming and going of large numbers of traders and that this is inimical to the good life of the citizens. If these evil consequences can be avoided, it is obviously better both for economic and for defensive reasons that the city and its territory should have access to the sea. To facilitate resistance to an enemy a successful defender needs to be in a position to use both sea and land, and even if he cannot strike a blow against invaders on both elements, it will be easier to strike on one, if he has access to both. So too in the economic sphere; people must import the things which they do not themselves produce and export those of which they have a surplus. For when a city becomes a trading city it must do so in its own interest and not in others'. Some throw their city open as a market for all comers for the sake of the money they bring in; but a city which regards this kind of profit-making as illegitimate ought not to possess that kind of open market at all.

Again, we see in modern times many cities and territories in possession of docks and harbors conveniently situated, not too far away but not so near as to encroach upon the town itself, and dominated by walls and other such defense-works. It is therefore clear that if this intercommunication is productive of good, the city will derive advantage from it; if of evil, it is easy to guard against that by laying down regulations and stating who are and who are not to be allowed to enter the area. Then there is this matter of naval forces; clearly it is desirable that there should be a certain amount of these; for it is important that by sea as well as by land a state should be able to make its power felt or to render aid, not only internally but in relation to certain neighbors. The number of ships and the size of the naval force will have to be decided in the light of the circumstances and way of living of the state concerned. If it is to play a big part as a leading state, it will need naval as well as land forces large enough for such activities. The addition to population, which the enlistment of large numbers of seamen will make necessary, need not swell the membership of the cities; there is no reason why they should have a share in the state as if they were soldiers. The troops that are carried on board are free men belonging to the infantry; they are in authority and take precedence over the crews. But the rowers need not be members of the state; and a potential source of manpower for them is sure to exist wherever the outlying dwellers and agricultural laborers are plentiful. We can see examples of this today: at Heraclea, though their city is of modest size, they find crews for many triremes. So much then for territory, harbors, cities, sea, naval forces; we pass now to the citizens and population.

We have already spoken about limiting the number of citizens; we must now ask what kind of natural qualities they should have. We could form a fair notion of the answer if we glanced first at the most famous Greek states and then at the racial divisions of the whole world. The races that live in cold regions and those of Europe are full of courage and passion but somewhat lacking in skill and brain-power; for this reason, while remaining generally independent, they lack political cohesion and the ability to rule over others. On the other hand the Asiatic races have both brains and skill but are lacking in courage and willpower; so they have remained enslaved and sub-ject. The Hellenic race, occupying a midposition geographically, has a measure of both. Hence it continues to be free, to have the best political institutions, and to be capable of ruling all others, given a single constitution. But we do observe the same differences among the Greeks themselves when we compare one set with another; some are by nature one-sided, in others the qualities of head and of heart are combined. Both are clearly needed if men are to be as we want them—the kind of person who can easily be molded by a lawgiver and brought to a high degree of excellence. Some say that to feel friendly at the sight of familiar faces and hostile at the approach of strangers is a requirement for guardians of the state. Now friendliness springs from the heart, from that power in our souls whereby we love. We see this from the fact that our feelings are more likely to be aroused if those whom we love neglect us than by the conduct of those whom we do not know. Hence the lines of Archilochus, reproaching his friends but addressed to his own heart, are aptly spoken: "About your friends you torture yourself." The power to command and the spirit of freedom have their source in this faculty, which is masterful and unsubdued. But what he says about harshness to strangers is, I think, quite wrong; there is no need to behave thus to anyone and fierceness is not a mark of greatness of mind except toward wrongdoers. Rather, as we have said, is indignation aroused by the sight of friends when we believe ourselves to have been wrongly used by them. And this is understandable; where men expect to receive kindness as their due, they are indignant at being deprived of it and at losing the benefit. Hence the proverbial sayings, "Grievous is fraternal strife" and "Excessive love turns to excessive hate."

So much for the members of the state, their number, and their kind, so much for the size and kind of territory; we need say no more because one cannot expect the same attention to detail in theoretical discussions as one would if the case were presented before our eyes.

Just as, in considering any other object that exists in nature, we do not call "parts" all those indispensable things without which the whole would not be itself, so too we must not list as parts of a city the indispensable conditions of its existence, nor would we in relation to any other form of community that made up a single definite kind; to all its members, irrespective of their degree of participation, the community is the community, one single identical whole. Food supply, an amount of territory, and the like, these are indispensable but they are not the things that give a specific character to any form of human society. Whenever one thing is a means and another an end, there can be no other relation between them than this—that the one acts, the other is acted upon. Take any set of tools and consider it along with its users in relation to the work which they produce; for example a house and its builders. There is no other relation between house and builders, nothing that can be called cooperation, but the builder's skill with his tools is a means toward building a house. So too a state needs to own property, but property is no part of the state, though many parts of the property are living creatures. When we speak of city or state, we mean a community of like persons whose end or aim is the best life possible. The best is happiness and this consists in the exercise of all good qualities and their fullest possible use. Life is such that some can get a share of happiness, while others get little or none. Here then we clearly have a reason for the existence of different kinds of cities and the variety of constitutions. Different sets of people seek their happiness in different ways and by different means; little wonder that their lives are different or that they have different political constitutions.

We must also ask how many are those things without which there can be no city. (We include what we call *parts* of the state, because their presence too is essential.) Let us therefore make a count of all the things and actions needed, for that will show the answer. They are (1) food, (2) handicrafts and their tools, (3) arms. Arms are included because members of the constitution must carry them even among themselves, both for internal government in the event of civil disobedience and to repel external aggression. (4) Wealth too is required both for war and for all the internal needs. Then (5) the needs of religion (this might have been put first) and (6) (most essential of all) a method of arriving at decisions, both about policy and about matters of right and wrong as between one person and another. These then are the essentials; every state, we may say, has need of these. For a state is not a chance agglomeration but, we repeat, a body of men aiming at a self-sufficient life; and if any of these six is lacking, it will be impossible for that community to be thoroughly self-sufficing. It is therefore essential in setting up a city to make provision for all these activities. Quite a number of agricultural workers will be needed to supply food; skilled craftsmen will be required, and fighting men, and wealthy men, and priests, and judges of what is right and expedient.

This enumeration of classes being finished, it remains to consider whether they shall all take part in all these activities, everybody being, as occasion requires, farmer and craftsman and councilor and judge (for this is not impossible) or shall we postulate a different set of persons for each task? Or again, are not some of the jobs necessarily confined to one set of people, while others may be thrown open to all? The situation is not the same in every form of constitution; for as we have said it is equally possible for all to share in everything and for some to share in some. These are what make differences in constitutions; in democracies all share in all, in oligarchies the reverse is true.

But since our present inquiry is directed toward the best constitution, that is to say, that by which a city would be most happy, and we have already said that happiness cannot exist apart from virtue, it becomes clear that in the best state with the best constitution, one that possesses just men who are just absolutely and not simply relatively to some postulated standard, the citizens must not live a banausic or commercial life. Such a life is not noble and not conducive to virtue. Nor will those who are to be citizens live an agricultural life; for they must have leisure to cultivate their virtue and talents, time for the activities of a citizen. Now both defense and deliberation, whether about policy or about questions of justice, are at the heart and center of the state. And when we ask whether these are to be assigned to different persons or to be kept together in the hands of the same body, our answer is partly one and partly the other. In so far as the tasks themselves differ in the best time of life for their performance, one requiring wisdom, the other strength, they should be assigned to different people. But as it is impossible to secure that those who are strong enough to enforce their will shall always tolerate being ruled by others, to that extent they must be assigned to the same people. For those who possess and can wield arms are in a position to decide whether the constitution is to continue or not. So we are left with this conclusion: that this constitution, both in its military and its civil functions, should be put into the hands of the same class of persons, but not both simultaneously. Rather we should follow nature, the young have strength, the older have understanding, so it is both right and expedient that the distribution of tasks should be made on this basis; it takes into account fitness for the work. Property too must belong to this class; it is essential that citizens should have ample subsistence, and these are citizens. The lower-class element has no part in the state nor any other class that is not productive of virtue. This is evident from our postulates; being happy must occur in conjunction with virtue, and in pronouncing a city happy we must have regard not to part of it but to all its citizens. It is also clear that property must belong to these; the agricultural workers will be slaves or non-Greeks dwelling in the country roundabout.

Of the list which we made earlier there remains the class of priests. Their position is clear: no agricultural or commercial worker could be made a priest, since it is only right and proper that the gods should be worshipped by citizens. As we have divided citizens and their duties into military and civil, it is also right and proper that citizens who have thus spent themselves in long service should both enjoy their retirement and serve the gods. These then should be appointed to priestly offices.

We have now stated what are the essential requirements of a state and what are its parts. There must be agricultural workers and craftsmen and paid laborers; but as to parts of the state, these are the military and deliberative elements, which may be separated either permanently or successively.

. . . We stated above that the land ought to be possessed by those who have arms and enjoy full participation in the constitution, and why the cultivators should be different from the owners, also the nature and extent of the territory required. We must speak first about the division of the land for the purposes of cultivation and about those who will cultivate it, who and of what type they will be. We do not agree with those who have said that all land should be communally owned, but we do believe that there should be a friendly arrangement for sharing the usufruct and that none of the citizens should be without means of support. Next as to communal feeding, it is generally agreed that this is a very useful institution in a well-ordered society; why we too are of this opinion we will say later. In any case, where communal meals exist, all citizens should partake of them, though it is not easy for those who are badly off to pay the contribution fixed and keep a household going at the same time. Another thing that should be a charge on the whole community is the public worship of the gods. Thus it becomes necessary to divide the land into two parts, one publicly owned, the other privately. Each of these has to be further divided into two. One part of the public land will support the service of the gods, the other the communal feeding. Of the privately owned land one part will be near the frontier, the other near the city, so that every citizen will have two portions, one in each locality. This is not only in accordance with justice and equality but makes also for greater unity in the face of wars with bordering states. Without this dual arrangement some make too little of hostilities on the border, others too much, some underestimate the dangers of frontier quarrels, others take them too seriously, even sacrificing honor in order to avoid them. Hence in some countries it is the custom that when war against a neighbor is under consideration, those who live near to the border should be excluded from the discussion as being too closely involved to be able to give honest advice. It is therefore important that the territory should for the reasons given be divided in the manner stated. As for those who are to till the land, they should, if possible, be slaves (and we are building as we would wish). They should not be all of one stock nor men of spirit; this will ensure that they will be good workers and not prone to revolt. An alternative to slaves is foreigners settled on the countryside, men of the same type as the slaves just mentioned. They fall into two groups according to whether they work privately on the land of individual owners of property, or publicly on the common land. I hope later on to say how slaves ought to be used in agriculture and why it is a good thing that all slaves should have before them the prospect of receiving their freedom as a reward.

We have already noted that a city should have easy access both to the sea and to the interior, and, so far as conditions allow, be equally accessible to the whole of its territory. The land upon which the city itself is to be sited should be sloping. That is something that we must just hope to find, but we should keep four considerations in mind. First and most essential the situation must be a healthy one. A slope facing east, with winds blowing from the direction of sunrise, gives a healthy site, rather better than one on the lee side of north though this gives good weather. Next, it should be well situated for carrying out all its civil and military activities. For the purposes of defense the site should be one from which defenders can easily make a sally but which attackers will find difficult to approach and difficult to surround. Water, and especially spring water, should be abundant and if possible under immediate control in time of war; alternatively a way has been discovered of catching rain water in large quantities in vessels numerous enough to ensure a supply when fighting prevents the defenders from going far afield.

Since consideration must be given to the health of the inhabitants, which is partly a matter of siting in the best place and facing the right way, partly also dependent on a supply of pure water, this too must receive careful attention. I mention situation and water supply in particular because air and water, being just those things that we make most frequent and constant use of, have the greatest effect on our bodily condition. Hence, in a state which has welfare at heart, water for human consumption should be separated from water for all other purposes, unless of course all the water is alike and there are plenty of springs that are drinkable.

In the matter of defensive positions it should be remembered that what is best for one type of government is not so good for another. A lofty central citadel suits both oligarchy and monarchy, a level plain democracy; neither suits an aristocracy, which prefers a series of strongly held points. In laying out areas for private dwelling houses, the modern or Hippodamean method has the advantage of regularity; it is also more attractive and for all purposes save one, more practical. For ease of defense, the old-fashioned irregular siting of houses was better, hard for foreign mercenaries to get out of and for attackers to penetrate. It follows that both methods should be used and this is quite possible: arrange the buildings in the same pattern as is used for planting vines, not in rows but in quincunx, and do not lay out the whole city with geometric regularity but only certain parts. This will meet the needs both of safety and good appearance.

As for walls, it is quite out of date to say, as some do, that cities that lay claim to valor have no need of walls; we have only to look at what in fact has happened to cities that made that boast. Doubtless there is something not quite honorable in seeking safety behind solid walls, at any rate against an enemy equal in numbers or only very slightly superior. But it may happen, and does happen, that the numerical superiority of the attackers is too much for the courage of the defenders, both of the average man and of a chosen few. If then we are to save our city and avoid the miseries of cruelty and oppression, we must concede that the greatest degree of protection that walls can afford is also the best military measure. The truth of this is emphasized by all the modern improvements in missiles and artillery for attacking a besieged town. Deliberately to give cities no walls at all is like choosing an easily attacked position and clearing away the surrounding high ground. It is as if we were to refrain from putting walls round private property for fear of rending the inhabitants unmanly. Another thing that should not be lost sight of is that those who have provided their city with a wall are in a position to regard that city in both ways, to treat it either as a fortified or an unfortified city. Those who have no walls have no such choice. And if this is so, then it is a duty not only to build walls but also to maintain them in a manner suitable both for the city's appearance and for its defensive needs, which in these days are very numerous. Just as the attacking side is always on the lookout for methods which will give them an advantage, so too the defenders must seek additional means of defense by the aid of scientific inquiry. An enemy will not even attempt an attack on those who are really well prepared to meet it.

We have seen that the greater number of the citizens should be distributed over a number of feeding centers and also that the walls should be furnished at suitable intervals with forts each manned by a garrison. Hence it would seem reasonable that some of the feeding centers should be located in the same places as the garrisons. For the rest, institutions devoted to the service of the gods and the chief feeding places of government offices should have a central position on the same site, unless the sacral law or some pronouncement of Apollo at Delphi requires the sacred building in the case to be erected somewhere apart. Our purpose would be well served by a site which gives a frontage commensurate with our ideas of good siting and is at the same time easily defended in relation to the neighboring parts of the city. Just below this is a good place to build a square of the kind which in Thessaly is given the name Free Market. Here nothing may be bought or sold and no member of the lower orders or countryman may be admitted unless summoned by the authorities. The amenities of this area would be enhanced if the gymnasiums of the older folk were situated there; for in the taking of exercise also there should be separation of age groups, the younger in one place, the older in another; government personnel should go in with the latter but should also mingle with the young men, since the presence of authority's watchful eye is the best way to instill a real feeling of deference and of respect for the upper classes. The market proper, where buying and selling are done, must be in quite a separate place, conveniently situated both for goods sent up from the harbor and for people coming in from the country.

The authorities of the state being divided into secular and religious, it is right that the priests too should have their eating places near the sacred buildings. As for the minor offices of government—those concerned with contracts, with suits-at-law, summonses, and the ordering of such matters generally (also surveillance of markets and what is called "astynomy")—these should all be located near a market and general meeting place. This will, of course, be the area of the dealers' market, which is intended for the exchange of necessary commodities: the upper area that we mentioned is intended for recreation. A similar arrangement should be followed in country districts; for there too the officials, forest wardens, or field wardens, or whatever they may be called, must have eating places and garrison posts to enable them to carry out their work of protection; likewise shrines of gods and heroes situated all over the countryside.

But it is really not necessary now to go on mentioning all these things in detail. It is not at all difficult to think what things are needed; it is quite another matter to provide them. Our talk is the mirror of our desires, but the outcome is in fortune's hands. Therefore we will say no more about these matters now and turn to the *politeia* itself.

We must now discuss the constitution itself and ask ourselves what people and what kind of people ought to form the material out of which is to be made a happy and well-governed city. All men's well-being depends on two things; one is the right choice of target, of the end to which actions should tend, the other lies in finding the actions that lead to that end. These two may just as easily conflict with each other as coincide. Sometimes for example the aim is well-chosen, but in action men fail to attain it. At other times they successfully perform everything that conduces to the end, but the end itself was badly chosen. Or they may fail in and be wrong about both, as sometimes happens in the practice of medicine, when doctors neither rightly discern what kind of condition is a healthy one for the body nor discover the means which will enable their self-set goal to be attained.

Wherever professional skill and knowledge come into play, these two must both be mastered—the end and the means to the end.

It is clear then that all men desire to have happiness and the good life, but some men are in a position to get it, others are not. This may be due to fortune or to their natural disposition; both play a part; the good life needs *some* material goods at any time, but when the natural disposition is good, fortune will need to provide a lesser amount of these, a greater amount when it is bad. Some indeed, who start with excellent opportunities, fail from the very beginning in the pursuit of happiness. But as our object is to find the *best* constitution, and that means the one whereby a city will be best ordered, and we call that city best ordered in which the possibilities of happiness are greatest; it is clear that we must keep our conception of happiness constantly in mind. We defined this in our *Ethics* and we may be permitted to make use of the definition here: happiness is activity and the complete utilization of all our powers, our goodness, not conditionally but absolutely. By "conditionally" in this connection I refer to actions necessary in the conditions and by "absolutely" I mean moral or noble. For example actions relating to justice, the just recovery of damages, and the infliction of just punishment spring from the virtue justice, but they are necessary or conditional and whatever good is in them is there by necessity. But actions directed toward honors and high standards of living are noble actions absolutely. For the former actions are but the removal of evil, the latter are not; they are on the contrary the creation and the begetting of positive good.

A good man will nobly bear ill health, poverty, and other misfortunes, but happiness requires the opposite of these. Hence men imagine that the causes of happiness lie in external goods and not within our minds. This is as if we were to ascribe brilliant lyre playing to the quality of the instrument rather than to the skill of the player.

From what has been said it is clear that some things must be there from the start, others must be provided by a lawgiver. We wish for our city good fortune in all that fortune has it in her power to bestow, that is all we can expect of her. It is not in fortune's power to make a city good; that is a matter of scientific planning and deliberate policy. On the other hand, a city's being good rests on the citizens who share in the constitution being good; and for us all the citizens share in the constitution. The question then is, How does a man become good? Of course if it is possible for all to be good (and not just the citizens taken individually), then that is better, since all includes each. But in fact men are good and virtuous because of three things. These are nature, habit or training, reason. First, nature: a man must be born, and he must be born a man and not something else; he must have the body and the mind of a man. It may be of no advantage to be born with certain qualities, because habit and training cause changes. There are some qualities which have a dual possibility; subsequent habits may make them either good or bad. The majority of creatures live by nature only; some live by habit also to some extent. Man lives by reason as well, he alone has the faculty of reason. To make a good man requires all three working concertedly. Reason causes men to do many things contrary to habit and to nature, whenever they are convinced that this is the better course. In an earlier chapter we described what nature can do to make men such that they will easily respond to the handling of the legislator. After that it becomes a matter of education. Men learn partly by training, partly by listening.

Since every association of persons forming a state consists of rulers and ruled, we must ask whether those who rule and those who are ruled ought to be different persons or the same for life; for the education which will be needed will depend upon which way we answer that question. If one group of persons were as far superior to all the rest as we deem gods and heroes to be superior to men, having to begin with great physical and bodily excellence and equally great mental and spiritual superiority, so much so that the superiority of the rulers is indisputable and quite evident to those ruled by them, then, I say, it is better that the same set of persons should always rule and the others always be ruled. But since this is not a condition that can easily be obtained, and since kings are not so greatly superior to their subjects as the writer Scylax says they were in India, it follows that, for a variety of causes, all alike must share in the business of ruling and being ruled by turns. For equality means the same not for all indiscriminately but for those who are like; this is fair and the established constitution can hardly be long maintained if it is contrary to justice. Otherwise there will be a large revolutionary element among the ruled all over the country, and it becomes quite impossible for even a strong governing class to withstand such a combination.

Again it cannot be disputed that rulers have to be superior to those who are ruled. It therefore becomes the duty of the lawgiver to consider how this distinction is to be made and how they shall share in government. We noted earlier that Nature herself has provided one distinction: that class which in respect of birth is all the same she has divided into older and younger, the former being more fit for ruling, the latter for being ruled. No one really objects to this method of command by seniority or thinks himself too good for it; after all he knows that once he reaches the required age, he will get what he has earned by waiting. There is then a sense in which we must say "the same persons rule and are ruled" and a sense in which we must say that they are different persons. So too their education must be in one sense the same, in another different; for, as is often said, one who is to become a good ruler must first himself be ruled. But since we hold that the same qualities are needed for citizen and for ruler and for the best man, and that the same man should be first ruled and later ruler, it immediately becomes an essential task of the planner of a constitution to ensure that men shall be good men, to consider what practices will make them so, and what is the end or aim of the best life.

Two parts of the soul are distinguished, one possessing reason in itself, the other not so possessing reason but capable of listening to reason. To these belong, we think, the virtues because of which a good man is called good. To those who accept our division of the soul there is no difficulty in answering the question, "To which of the parts does the concept of *end* belong?" For the inferior is always but a means to the superior; and this is no less clear in matters that have to be planned by human skill than it is in those which belong to the sphere of nature; and the superior in this case is that which is possessed of reason. It is our custom to make a distinction between practical reason and theoretical reason, and so we must similarly divide the rational part of the soul. Actions too will follow suit; there will be three kinds in all and those springing from that which is by nature better, that is, from the two rational parts, must be regarded as preferable by all who are in a position to make a choice from among three kinds or even from among two. For each man, that is to be chosen which is the very best that he can attain.

Again, all life can be divided into work and leisure, war and peace, and of things done some belong to the class of actions that have moral worth, while others are necessary but have no such value. In the choice of these the same principle, the lesser for the sake of the greater, must be followed in actions as in parts of the soul; that is to say, we choose war for the sake of peace, work for the sake of leisure, menial and useful acts for the sake of the noble. The statesman therefore in making laws must have an eye to all these things, with reference both to the parts of the soul and to the actions to which these give rise, and an eye even more to better things and to ends in view. In the same way too he must regard men's lives and their choice of what they shall do. For one must be able to work and to fight, but even more to be at peace and lead a life of cultivated leisure, to do the necessary and useful things, but still more those of intrinsic worth. These then are the targets at which education should be aimed, whether children's education or that of those requiring it at a later age.

QUESTIONS FOR DISCUSSION

Why does Aristotle say that "happiness cannot exist apart from virtue"? (160)

1. Why does Aristotle assume that citizens, but not "the lower-class element," are "productive of virtue"? (160)

2. If happiness cannot exist apart from virtue, why does Aristotle later suggest that a person whose "natural disposition" is not good may require more "material goods" to achieve happiness and the good life? (166)

3. Does Aristotle think that a city can be "happy" if "some men are in a position to get [happiness], others are not"? (166)

4. According to Aristotle, how much responsibility does an individual have to make sure that nature, habit, and reason are "working concertedly"? (167)

Does Aristotle believe that a happy city is a realistic possibility or only an ideal worth striving for?

1. What does Aristotle mean when he says that the "best state" is "one that possesses just men who are just absolutely and not simply relatively to some postulated standard"? (160)

2. Why does Aristotle acknowledge, "It is not at all difficult to think what things are needed; it is quite another matter to provide them"? (165)

3. Why does Aristotle say that "the outcome is in fortune's hands" but also say, "It is not in fortune's power to make a city good; that is a matter of scientific planning and deliberate policy"? (165, 166)

4. Why does Aristotle qualify his discussion of the best-ordered city by saying only that the "possibilities of happiness are greatest," not that everyone is happy? (166)

FOR FURTHER REFLECTION

1. Do you agree with Aristotle that "happiness cannot exist apart from virtue"?

2. In contemporary society, to what degree does the well-being of the state depend on the happiness of the individual?

3. How would you define a well-ordered city today? Do any cities or towns in the United States meet your criteria?

4. How do you define happiness? Is it personally achievable?

A Framework for Utopia

Robert Nozick

N o state more extensive than the minimal state can be justified. But doesn't the idea, or ideal, of the minimal state lack luster? Can it thrill the heart or inspire people to struggle or sacrifice? Would anyone man barricades under its banner? It seems pale and feeble in comparison with, to pick the polar extreme, the hopes and dreams of utopian theorists. Whatever its virtues, it appears clear that the minimal state is no utopia. We would expect then that an investigation into utopian theory should more than serve to highlight the defects and shortcomings of the minimal state as the end of political philosophy. Such an investigation also promises to be intrinsically interesting. Let us then pursue the theory of utopia to where it leads.

The totality of conditions we would wish to impose on societies which are (preeminently) to qualify as utopias, taken jointly, are inconsistent. That it is impossible simultaneously and continually to realize all social and political goods is a regrettable fact about the human condition, worth investigating and bemoaning. Our subject here, however, is the best of all possible worlds. For whom? The best of all possible worlds for me will not be that for you. The world, of all those I can imagine, which I would most prefer to live in, will not be precisely the one you would choose. Utopia, though, must be, in some restricted sense, the best for all of us; the best world imaginable, for each of us. In what sense can this be? . . .

THE FRAMEWORK

It would be disconcerting if there were only one argument or connected set of reasons for the adequacy of a particular description of
utopia. Utopia is the focus of so many different strands of aspiration
that there must be many theoretical paths leading to it. Let us sketch
some of these alternate, mutually supporting, theoretical routes.

The first route begins with the fact that people are different. They
differ in temperament, interests, intellectual ability, aspirations, natural bent, spiritual quests, and the kind of life they wish to lead. They
diverge in the values they have and have different weightings for the
values they share. (They wish to live in different climates—some in
mountains, plains, deserts, seashores, cities, towns.) There is no reason to think that there is *one* community which will serve as ideal for
all people and much reason to think that there is not.

We may distinguish among the following theses:

I. For each person there is a kind of life that objectively is the
best for him.
   a. People are similar enough, so that there is one kind of
   life which objectively is the best for each of them.
   b. People are different, so that there is *not* one kind of life
   which objectively is the best for everyone, and,
      1. The different kinds of life are similar enough so
      that there *is* one kind of community (meeting cer-
      tain constraints) which objectively is the best for
      everyone.
      2. The different kinds of life are so different that there
      is *not* one kind of community (meeting certain con-
      straints) which objectively is the best for everyone
      (no matter which of these different lives is best for
      them).
II. For each person, so far as objective criteria of goodness can
tell (insofar as these exist), there is a wide range of very
different kinds of life that tie as best; no other is objectively
better for him than any one in this range, and no one within
the range is objectively better than any other. And there
is not one community which objectively is the best for the

living of each selection set from the family of sets of not-objectively inferior lives.

For our purposes at this point either of I.b.2 or II will serve.

Wittgenstein, Elizabeth Taylor, Bertrand Russell, Thomas Merton, Yogi Berra, Allen Ginsburg, Harry Wolfson, Thoreau, Casey Stengel, The Lubavitcher Rebbe, Picasso, Moses, Einstein, Hugh Hefner, Socrates, Henry Ford, Lenny Bruce, Baba Ram Dass, Gandhi, Sir Edmund Hillary, Raymond Lubitz, Buddha, Frank Sinatra, Columbus, Freud, Norman Mailer, Ayn Rand, Baron Rothschild, Ted Williams, Thomas Edison, H. L. Mencken, Thomas Jefferson, Ralph Ellison, Bobby Fischer, Emma Goldman, Peter Kropotkin, you, and your parents. Is there really *one* kind of life which is best for each of these people? Imagine all of them living in any utopia you've ever seen described in detail. Try to describe the society which would be best for all of these persons to live in. Would it be agricultural or urban? Of great material luxury or of austerity with basic needs satisfied? What would relations between the sexes be like? Would there be any institution similar to marriage? Would it be monogamous? Would children be raised by their parents? Would there be private property? Would there be a serene secure life or one with adventures, challenges, dangers, and opportunities for heroism? Would there be one, many, any religion? How important would it be in people's lives? Would people view their life as importantly centered about private concerns or about public action and issues of public policy? Would they be single-mindedly devoted to particular kinds of accomplishments and work or jacks-of-all-trades and pleasures or would they concentrate on full and satisfying leisure activities? Would children be raised permissively, strictly? What would their education concentrate upon? Will sports be important in people's lives (as spectators, participants)? Will art? Will sensual pleasures or intellectual activities predominate? Or what? Will there be fashions in clothing? Will great pains be taken to beautify appearance? What will the attitude toward death be? Would technology and gadgets play an important role in society? And so on.

The idea that there is one best composite answer to all of these questions, one best society for *everyone* to live in, seems to me to be an incredible one. (And the idea that, if there is one, we now know enough to describe it is even more incredible.) No one should attempt to describe a utopia unless he's recently reread, for example, the works of Shakespeare, Tolstoy, Jane Austen, Rabelais and Dostoevsky to remind himself of how different people are. (It will also serve to remind him of how complex they are; see the third route below.)

Utopian authors, each very confident of the virtues of his own vision and of its singular correctness, have differed among themselves (no less than the people listed above differ) in the institutions and kinds of life they present for emulation. Though the picture of an idea society that each presents is much too simple (even for the component communities to be discussed below), we should take the fact of the differences seriously. No utopian author has everyone in his society leading exactly the same life, allocating exactly the same amount of time to exactly the same activities. *Why not?* Don't the reasons also count against just one kind of community?

The conclusion to draw is that there will not be *one* kind of community existing and one kind of life led in utopia. Utopia will consist of utopias, of many different and divergent communities in which people lead different kinds of lives under different institutions. Some kinds of communities will be more attractive to most than others; communities will wax and wane. People will leave some for others or spend their whole lives in one. Utopia is a framework for utopias, a place where people are at liberty to join together voluntarily to pursue and attempt to realize their own vision of the good life in the ideal community but where no one can *impose* his own utopian vision upon others. The utopian society is the society of utopianism. (Some of course may be content where they are. Not *everyone* will be joining special experimental communities, and many who abstain at first will join the communities later, after it is clear how they actually are working out.) Half of the truth I wish to put forth is that utopia is meta-utopia: the environment in which utopian experiments may be tried out; the environment in which people are free to do their own thing; the environment which must, to a great extent, be realized first if more particular utopian visions are to be realized stably.

If, as we noted at the beginning of this chapter, not all goods can be realized simultaneously, then trade-offs will have to be made. The second theoretical route notes that there is little reason to believe that one unique system of trade-offs will command universal assent. Different communities, each with a slightly different mix, will provide a range from which each individual can choose that community which best approximates *his* balance among competing values. (Its opponents will call this the smorgasbord conception of utopia, preferring restaurants with only one dinner available, or, rather, preferring a one-restaurant town with one item on the menu.)

DESIGN DEVICES AND FILTER DEVICES

The third theoretical route to the framework for utopia is based on the fact that people are complex. As are the webs of possible relationships among them. Suppose (falsely) that the earlier arguments are mistaken and that *one* kind of society *is* best for all. How are we to find out what this society is like? Two methods suggest themselves, which we shall call design devices and filter devices.

Design devices construct something (or its description) by some procedure which does not essentially involve constructing descriptions of others of its type. The result of the process is one object. In the case of societies, the result of the design process is a description of one society, obtained by people (or a person) sitting down and thinking about what the best society is. After deciding, they set about to pattern everything on this one model.

Given the enormous complexity of man, his many desires, aspirations, impulses, talents, mistakes, loves, sillinesses, given the *thickness* of his intertwined and interrelated levels, facets, relationships (compare the thinness of the social scientists' description of man to that of the novelists), and given the complexity of interpersonal institutions and relationships, and the complexity of coordination of the actions of many people, it is enormously unlikely that, even if there were one ideal pattern for society, it could be arrived at in this a priori (relative to current knowledge) fashion. And even supposing that some great genius *did* come along with the blueprint, who could have confidence that it would work out well?

Sitting down at this late stage in history to dream up a description of the perfect society is not of course the same as starting from scratch. We have available to us partial knowledge of the results of application of devices other than design devices, including partial application of the filter device to be described below. It is helpful to imagine cavemen sitting together to think up what, for all time, will be the best possible society and then setting out to institute it. Do none of the reasons that make you smile at this apply to us?

Filter devices involve a process which eliminates (filters out) many from a large set of alternatives. The two key determinants of the end result(s) are the particular nature of the filtering out process (and what qualities it selects against) and the particular nature of the set of alternatives it operates upon (and how this set is generated). Filtering processes are especially appropriate for designers having limited knowledge who do not know precisely the nature of a desired end product. For it enables them to utilize their knowledge of specific conditions they don't want violated in judiciously building a filter to reject the violators. It might turn out to be impossible to design an appropriate filter, and one might try another filter process for this task of design. But generally, it seems, less knowledge (including knowledge of what is desirable) will be required to produce an appropriate filter, even one that converges uniquely upon a particular kind of product, than would be necessary to construct only the product(s) from scratch.

Furthermore, if the filtering process is of the type that involves a variable method of generating new candidates, so that their quality improves as the quality of the members remaining after previous filtering operations improves, and it also involves a variable filter that becomes more selective as the quality of the candidates sent into it improves (that is, it rejects some candidates which previously had passed successfully through the filter), then one legitimately may expect that the merits of what will remain after long and continued operation of the process will be very high indeed. We should not be *too* haughty about the results of filter processes, being one ourselves. From the vantage point of the considerations leading us to recommend a filter process in the constructing of societies, evolution is a process for creating living beings appropriately chosen by a modest deity, who does not know precisely what the being he wishes to create is like.

A filtering process for specifying a society which might come to mind is one in which the people planning out the ideal society consider many different kinds of societies and criticize some, eliminate some, modify the descriptions of others, until they come to the one they consider best. This no doubt is how any design team would work, and so it should not be assumed that design devices exclude filtering features. (Nor need filter devices exclude design aspects, especially in the generating process.) But one cannot determine in advance which people will come up with the best ideas, and all ideas must be tried out (and not merely simulated on a computer) to see how they will work. And some ideas will come only as we are (post facto) trying to describe what patterns have evolved from the spontaneous coordination of the actions of many people.

If the ideas must actually be tried out, there must be many communities trying out different patterns. The filtering process, the process of eliminating communities, that our framework involves is very simple: people try out living in various communities, and they leave or slightly modify the ones they don't like (find defective). Some communities will be abandoned, others will struggle along, others will split, others will flourish, gain members, and be duplicated elsewhere. Each community must win and hold the voluntary adherence of its members. No pattern is *imposed* on everyone, and the result will be one pattern if and only if everyone voluntarily chooses to live in accordance with that pattern of community.

The design device comes in at the stage of generating specific communities to be lived in and tried out. Any group of people may devise a pattern and attempt to persuade others to participate in the adventure of a community in that pattern. Visionaries and crackpots, maniacs and saints, monks and libertines, capitalists and communists and participatory democrats, proponents of phalanxes (Fourier), palaces of labor (Flora Tristan), villages of unity and cooperation (Owen), mutualist communities (Proudhon), time stores (Josiah Warren), Bruderhof, kibbutzim, kundalini yoga ashrams, and so forth, may all have their try at building their vision and setting an alluring example. It should not be thought that every pattern tried will be explicitly designed de novo. Some will be planned modifications, however slight, of others already existing (when it is seen where they rub), and the details of many will be built up spontaneously in communities that leave some leeway. As communities become more attractive for their inhabitants, patterns previously adopted as the best available will be rejected. And as the communities which people live in improve (according to their lights), ideas for new communities often will improve as well.

The operation of the framework for utopia we present here thus realizes the advantages of a filtering process incorporating mutually improving interaction between the filter and the surviving products of the generating process, so that the quality of generated and non-rejected products improves. Furthermore, given people's historical memories and records, it has the feature that an already rejected alternative (or its slight modification) can be *retried*, perhaps because new or changed conditions make it now seem more promising or appropriate. This is unlike biological evolution where previously rejected mutations cannot easily be recalled when conditions change. Also, evolutionists point out the advantages of genetic heterogeneity (polytypic and polymorphic) when conditions change greatly. Similar advantages adhere to a system of diverse communities, organized along different lines and perhaps encouraging different types of character, and different patterns of abilities and skills.

THE FRAMEWORK AS UTOPIAN COMMON GROUND

The use of a filter device dependent upon people's individual decisions to live in or leave particular communities is especially appropriate. For the ultimate purpose of utopian construction is to get communities that people will want to live in and will choose voluntarily to live in. Or at least this must be a side effect of successful utopian construction. The filtering process proposed will achieve this. Furthermore, a filtering device dependent upon people's decisions has certain advantages over one which operates mechanically, given our inability to formulate explicitly principles which adequately handle, in advance, all of the complex, multifarious situations which arise. We often state prima facie principles without thinking that we can mark off in advance all of the exceptions to the principle. But though we cannot describe in advance all of the exceptions to the principle, we do think that very often we will be able to recognize that a particular situation we are presented with *is* an exception.

Similarly, we will not be able in advance to program automatically a filtering device to reject all and only what should be rejected (either objectively, or in our view now, or in our view then). We will have to leave room for people's judging each particular instance. This is not by itself an argument for each person's judging for himself. Nor is the only alternative to the mechanical application of explicitly formulated rules the operation of a system *wholly* dependent upon choices without any guidelines at all, as it is clear from the existence of our legal system. So the fact of not being able to state or program exceptionless principles in advance does not, *by itself*, suffice to get to my preferred alternative of *everyone's* choice, and *no* guidelines set up in advance (except for those guidelines that protect this preferred argument).

We have argued that even if there is one kind of community that is best for each and every person, the framework set out is the best means for finding out the nature of that community. Many more arguments can and should be offered for the view that, even if there is one kind of society that is best for everyone, the operation of the framework (1) is best for anyone's coming up with a picture of what the society is like, (2) is best for anyone's becoming convinced that the picture is indeed one of the best society, (3) is best for large numbers of people's becoming so convinced, and (4) is the best way to stabilize such a society with people living securely and enduringly under that particular pattern. I cannot offer these other arguments here. (And I could not offer all of them anywhere; understanding *why* supports the correctness of the position.) However, I do wish to note that the arguments for the framework offered and mentioned here are even more potent when we drop the (false) assumption that there is *one* kind of society best for everyone, and so stop misconstruing the problem as one of which one type of community every individual person should live in.

The framework has two advantages over every other kind of description of utopia: first, it will be acceptable to almost every utopian at some future point in time, whatever his particular vision; and second, it is compatible with the realization of almost all particular utopian visions, though it does not guarantee the realization or universal triumph of any particular utopian vision. Any utopian will agree that our framework is an appropriate one for a society of good men. For good men, he thinks, voluntarily will choose to live under the particular pattern he favors, if they are as rational as he is and thus are able equally to see its excellence. And most utopians will agree that at *some* point in time our framework is an appropriate one, for at some point (after people have been made good, and uncorrupt generations have been produced) people voluntarily will choose to live under the favored pattern. Thus our framework is now admitted, among a wide range of utopians and their opponents, to be appropriate common ground, *sooner or later.* For each thinks his own particular vision would be realized under it.

Those with different utopian visions who believe the framework is an appropriate *path* to their vision (as well as being permissible after their vision is realized) might well cooperate in attempting to realize the framework, even given mutual knowledge of their different predictions and predilections. Their different hopes conflict only if they involve universal realization of one particular pattern. We may distinguish three utopian positions: *imperialistic* utopianism, which countenances the forcing of everyone into one pattern of community; *missionary* utopianism, which hopes to persuade or convince everyone to live in one particular kind of community, but will not force them to do so; and *existential* utopianism, which hopes that a particular pattern of community will exist (will be viable), though not necessarily universally, so that those who wish to do so may live in accordance with it. Existential utopians can wholeheartedly support the framework. With full knowledge of their differences, adherents of diverse visions may cooperate in realizing the framework. Missionary utopians, though their aspirations are universal, will join them in supporting the framework, viewing fully voluntary adherence to their preferred pattern as crucial. They will not, however, especially admire the framework's additional virtue of allowing the simultaneous realization of many diverse possibilities. Imperialistic utopians, on the other hand, will oppose the framework so long as some others do not agree with them. (Well, you can't satisfy everybody; especially if there are those who will be dissatisfied unless not everybody is satisfied.) Since any particular community may be established within the framework, it is compatible with all particular utopian visions, while guaranteeing none. Utopians should view this as an enormous virtue; for their particular view would not fare as well under utopian schemes other than their own.

COMMUNITY AND NATION

The operation of the framework has many of the virtues, and few of the defects, people find in the libertarian vision. For though there is great liberty to choose among communities, many particular communities internally may have many restrictions unjustifiable on libertarian grounds: that is, restrictions which libertarians would condemn if they were enforced by a central state apparatus. For example, paternalistic intervention into people's lives, restrictions on the range of books which may circulate in the community, limitations on the kinds of sexual behavior, and so on. But this is merely another way of pointing out that in a free society people may contract into various restrictions which the government may not legitimately impose upon them. Though the framework is libertarian and laissez faire, *individual communities within it need not be*, and perhaps no community within it will choose to be so. Thus, the characteristics of the framework need not pervade the individual communities. In *this* laissez-faire system it could turn out that though they are permitted, there are no actually functioning "capitalist" institutions; or that some communities have them and others don't or some communities have some of them, or what you will.

In previous chapters, we have spoken of a person's opting out of particular provisions of certain arrangements. Why now do we say that various restrictions may be imposed in a particular community? Mustn't the community allow its members to opt out of these restrictions? No; founders and members of a small communist community may, quite properly, refuse to allow anyone to opt out of equal sharing, even though it would be possible to arrange this. It is not a general principle that every community or group must allow internal opting out when that is feasible. For sometimes such internal opting out would itself change the character of the group from that desired. Herein lies an interesting theoretical problem. A nation or protective agency may not compel redistribution between one community and another, yet a community such as a kibbutz may redistribute within itself (or give to another community or to outside individuals). Such a community needn't offer its members an opportunity to opt out of these arrangements while remaining a member of the community. Yet, I have argued, a nation should offer this opportunity; people have a right to so opt out of a nation's requirements. Wherein lies the difference between a community and a nation that makes the difference in the legitimacy of imposing a certain pattern upon all of its members?

A person will swallow the imperfections of a package P (which may be a protective arrangement, a consumer good, a community) that is desirable on the whole rather than purchase a different package (a completely different package, or P with some changes), when no more desirable attainable different package is worth to him its greater costs over P, including the costs of inducing enough others to participate in making the alternative package. One assumes that the cost calculation for nations is such as to permit internal opting out. But this is not the whole story for two reasons. First, it may be feasible in individual communities also to arrange internal opting out at little administrative cost (which he may be willing to pay), yet this needn't always be done. Second, nations differ from other packages in that the individual himself isn't to bear the administrative costs of opting out of some otherwise compulsory provision. The other people must pay for finely designing their compulsory arrangements so that they don't apply to those who wish to opt out. Nor is the difference merely a matter of there being many alternative kinds of communities while there are many fewer nations. Even if almost everyone wished to live in a communist community, so that there weren't any viable noncommunist communities, no particular community need also (though it is to be hoped that one would) allow a resident individual to opt out of their sharing arrangement. The recalcitrant individual has no alternative but to conform. Still, the others do not force him to conform, and his rights are not violated. He has no right that the others cooperate in making his nonconformity feasible.

The difference seems to me to reside in the difference between a face-to-face community and a nation. In a nation, one knows that there are nonconforming individuals, but one need not be directly confronted by these individuals or by the fact of their nonconformity. Even if one finds it offensive that others do not conform, even if the knowledge that there exist nonconformists rankles and makes one very unhappy, this does not constitute being harmed by the others or having one's rights violated. Whereas in a face-to-face community one cannot avoid being directly confronted with what one finds to be offensive. How one lives in one's immediate environment is affected.

This distinction between a face-to-face community and one that is not generally runs parallel to another distinction. A face-to-face community can exist on land jointly owned by its members, whereas the land of a nation is not so held. The community will be entitled then, as a body, to determine what regulations are to be obeyed on its land; whereas the citizens of a nation do not jointly own its land and so cannot in this way regulate its use. If *all* the separate individuals who own land coordinate their actions in imposing a common regulation (for example, no one may reside on this land who does not contribute *n* percent of his income to the poor), the same *effect* will be achieved as if the nation had passed legislation requiring this. But since unanimity is only as strong as its weakest link, even with the use of secondary boycotts (which are perfectly legitimate), it would be impossible to maintain such a unanimous coalition in the face of the blandishments to some to defect.

But some face-to-face communities will not be situated on jointly held land. May the majority of the voters in a small village pass an ordinance against things that they find offensive being done on the *public* streets? May they legislate against nudity or fornication or sadism (on consenting masochists) or hand-holding by racially mixed couples on the streets? Any private owner can regulate his premises as he chooses. But what of the public thoroughfares, where people cannot easily avoid sights they find offensive? Must the vast majority cloister themselves against the offensive minority? If the majority may determine the limits on detectable behavior in public, may they, in addition to requiring that no one appear in public without wearing clothing, also require that no one appear in public without wearing a badge certifying that he has contributed *n* percent of his income to the needy during the year, on the grounds that they find it offensive to look at someone not wearing this badge (not having contributed)? And whence this emergent right of the majority to decide? Or are there to be no "public" places or ways? (Some dangers of this, noted in Chapter 2, would be avoided by the Lockean proviso of Chapter 7.) Since I do not see my way clearly through these issues, I raise them here only to leave them.

COMMUNITIES WHICH CHANGE

The individual communities may have *any* character compatible with the operation of the framework. If a person finds the character of a particular community uncongenial, he needn't choose to live in it. This is all well and good for an individual deciding which community to enter. But suppose a particular community is *changing* in its character and becoming one of a sort an individual dislikes. "If you don't like it here, don't join" has more force than "If you don't like it here, leave." After a person has spent much of his life in a community, sent down roots, made friends, and contributed to the community, the choice to pick up and leave is a difficult one. Such a community's establishing a new restriction, or abolishing an old one, or seriously changing its character, will affect its individual members in something like the way in which a *nation's* changing its laws will affect its citizens. Shouldn't one, therefore, be less willing to grant the communities such great latitude in ordering their internal affairs; shouldn't there be limits on their imposing restrictions that, if imposed by a state, would constitute a violation of an individual's rights? Friends of liberty never thought that the existence of America made legitimate the practices of Czarist Russia. Why should there be a difference of kind in the case of the communities?

Various remedies suggest themselves; I shall discuss one here. Anyone may start *any* sort of new community (compatible with the operation of the framework) they wish. For no one need enter it. (No community may be excluded, on paternalistic grounds, nor may lesser paternalistic restrictions geared to nullify supposed defects in people's decision processes be imposed—for example, compulsory information programs, waiting periods.) Modifying an already existing community is held to be a different matter. The wider society may pick some preferred internal structure for communities (which respects certain rights, and so on) and may require that communities somehow compensate the community's dissenters for changes away from this structure, for those changes it chooses to make. Having described this solution to the problem, we see that it is *unnecessary*. For, to accomplish the same end individuals need only include in the explicit terms of an agreement (contract) with any community they enter the stipulation that any member (including themselves) will be so compensated for deviations from a specified structure (which need not be society's preferred norm) in accordance with specified conditions. (One may use the compensation to finance leaving the community.)

TOTAL COMMUNITIES

Under the framework, there will be groups and communities covering all aspects of life, though limited in membership. (Not everyone, I assume, will choose to join one big commune or federation of communes.) Some things about some aspects of life extend to everyone; for example, everyone has various rights that may not be violated, various boundaries that may not be crossed without another's consent. Some people will find this covering of all aspects of some person's lives and some aspects of all person's lives to be insufficient. These people will desire a doubly total relationship that covers all people and all aspects of their lives, for example, all people in all their behavior (none is excluded in principle) showing certain feelings of love, affection, willingness to help others; all being engaged together in some common and important task.

Consider the members of a basketball team, all caught up in playing basketball well. (Ignore the fact that they are trying to win, though is it an accident that such feelings often arise when some unite *against* others?) They do not play primarily for money. They have a primary *joint* goal, and each subordinates himself to achieving this common goal, scoring fewer points himself than he otherwise might. If all are tied together by joint participation in an activity toward a common goal that each ranks as his most important goal, then fraternal feeling will flourish. They will be united and unselfish; *they* will be *one*. But basketball players, of course, do not have a common highest goal; they have separate families and lives. Still we might imagine a society in which all work together to achieve a common highest goal. Under the framework, any group of persons can so coalesce, form a movement, and so forth. But the structure itself is diverse; it does not itself provide or guarantee that there will be any common goal that all pursue jointly. It is borne in upon one, in contemplating such an issue, how appropriate it is to speak of "individualism" and (the word coined in opposition to it) "socialism." It goes without saying that any persons may attempt to unite kindred spirits, but, whatever their hopes and longings, none have the right to impose their vision of unity upon the rest.

UTOPIAN MEANS AND ENDS

How do the well-known objections to "utopianism" apply to the conception presented here? Many criticisms focus upon utopians' lack of discussion of *means* for achieving their vision or their concentration upon means that will not achieve their ends. In particular, critics contend that utopians often believe that they can bring about new conditions and nurture forth their particular communities by voluntary actions within the existing structure of society. They believe this for three reasons. First, because they believe that when certain persons or groups have an interest in the continuance of a pattern far from the ideal one (because they occupy a privileged position in it, and benefit from specific injustices or defects in the actual pattern which would be eliminated in the ideal one), then if their cooperation is necessary in order to realize the ideal pattern through voluntary actions, these people can be convinced voluntarily to perform the actions (against their interests) which will aid in bringing about the ideal patterns. Through argument and other rational means, utopians hope to convince people of the desirability and justice of the ideal pattern and of the injustice and unfairness of their special privileges, thereby getting them to act differently. Second, their critics continue, utopians believe that even when the framework of the existing society allows joint voluntary actions that would be sufficient to bring about a great change in the society by those not benefiting from defects and injustices in the actual society, then those whose privileges are threatened will not intervene actively, violently, and coercively to crush the experiment and changes. Third, critics assert that utopians are naive to think, even when the cooperation of the especially privileged is not required and when such persons will abstain from violently interfering in the process, that it is possible to establish through voluntary cooperation the particular experiment in the very different external environment, which often is hostile to the goals of the experiment. How can small communities overcome the whole thrust of the society; aren't isolated experiments doomed to failure? On this last point, we saw in Chapter 8 how a worker-controlled factory could be established in a free society. The point generalizes: there *is* a means of realizing various micro-situations through the voluntary actions of persons in a free society. Whether people *will* choose to perform those actions is another matter. Yet, in a free system any large, popular, revolutionary movement should be able to bring about its ends by such a voluntary process. As more and more people see how it works, more and more will wish to participate in or support it. And so it will grow, without being necessary to force everyone or a majority or anyone into the pattern.

Even if none of these objections hold, some will object to reliance on the voluntary actions of persons, holding that people are now so corrupt that they will not choose to cooperate voluntarily with experiments to establish justice, virtue, and the good life. (Even though if they did choose to do so, the experiments would succeed in a wholly voluntary environment, or in some current one.) Furthermore, if they weren't corrupt (after they're not corrupt) they would (will) cooperate. So, the argument continues, people must be forced to act in accordance with the good pattern; and persons trying to lead them along the bad old ways must be silenced. This view deserves an extended discussion, which it cannot be given here. Since the proponents of this view are themselves so obviously fallible, presumably few will choose to give them, or allow them to have, the dictatorial powers necessary for stamping out views they think are corrupt. What is desired is an organization of society optimal for people who are far less than ideal, optimal also for much better people, and which is such that living under such organization itself tends to make people better and more ideal. Believing with Tocqueville that it is only by being free that people will come to develop and exercise the virtues, capacities, responsibilities, and judgments appropriate to free men, that being free encourages such development, and that current people are not close to being so sunken in corruption as possibly to constitute an extreme exception to this, the voluntary framework is the appropriate one to settle upon.

Whatever the justice of these criticisms of the views about means of writers in the utopian tradition, we make no assumption that people can be gotten voluntarily to give up privileged positions based upon illegitimate interventions, directly or through government, into other people's lives; nor do we assume that in the face of the permissible voluntary actions of persons refusing any longer to have their rights violated, those other persons whose illegitimate privileges are threatened will stand by peacefully. It is true that I do not discuss here what legitimately may be done and what tactics would be best in such circumstances. Readers hardly will be interested in such discussion until they accept the libertarian framework.

Many particular criticisms have been made of the particular *ends* of writers in the utopian tradition and of the particular societies they describe. But two criticisms have seemed to apply to all.

First, utopians want to make all of society over in accordance with one detailed plan, formulated in advance and never before approximated. They see as their object a perfect society, and hence they describe a static and rigid society, with no opportunity or expectation of change or progress and no opportunity for the inhabitants of the society themselves to choose new patterns. (For if a change is a change for the better, then the previous state of the society, because surpassable, wasn't perfect; and if a change is a change for the worse, the previous state of society, allowing deterioration, wasn't perfect. And why make a change which is neutral?)

Second, utopians assume that the particular society they describe will operate without certain problems arising, that social mechanisms and institutions will function as they predict, and that people will not act from certain motives and interests. They blandly ignore certain obvious problems that anyone with any experience of the world would be struck by or make the most wildly optimistic assumptions about how these problems will be avoided or surmounted. (The utopian tradition is maximax.)

We do not detail the character of each particular community within the society, and we imagine the nature and composition of these constituent communities changing over time. No utopian writers actually fix *all* of the details of their communities. Since details about the framework would have to be fixed, how does our procedure differ from theirs? They wish to fix in advance all of the *important* social details, leaving undetermined only the trivial details, about which they either don't care or which raise no interesting issues of principle. Whereas, in our view, the nature of the various communities is very important, these questions are so important that they should not be settled by anyone for anyone else. Do we, however, wish to describe in specific detail the nature of the framework, which is to be fixed in character and unchanging? Do we assume that the framework will operate without problems? I do wish to describe the *kind* of framework, namely, one which leaves liberty for experimentation of varied sorts. But all of the details of the framework will not be set down in advance. (It would be easier to do this than to design in advance the details of a perfect society.)

Nor do I assume that all problems about the framework are solved. Let us mention a few here. There will be problems about the role, if any, to be played by some central authority (or protective association); how will this authority be selected, and how will it be ensured that the authority does, and does only, what it is supposed to do? The major role, as I see it, would be to enforce the operation of the framework— for example, to prevent some communities from invading and seizing others, their persons or assets. Furthermore, it will adjudicate in some reasonable fashion conflicts between communities which cannot be settled by peaceful means. What the best form of such a central authority is I would not wish to investigate here. It seems desirable that one not be fixed permanently but that room be left for improvements of detail. I ignore here the difficult and important problems of the controls on a central authority powerful enough to perform its appropriate functions, because I have nothing special to add to the standard literature on federations, confederations, decentralization of power, checks and balances, and so on.

One persistent strand in utopian thinking, as we have mentioned, is the feeling that there is some set of principles obvious enough to be accepted by all men of good will, precise enough to give unambiguous guidance in particular situations, clear enough so that all will realize its dictates, and complete enough to cover all problems which actually will arise. Since I do not assume that there are such principles, I do not assume that the political realm will wither away. The messiness of the details of a political apparatus and the details of how *it* is to be controlled and limited do not fit easily into one's hopes for a sleek, simple utopian scheme.

Apart from the conflict between communities, there will be other tasks for a central apparatus or agency, for example, enforcing an individual's right to leave a community. But problems arise if an individual can plausibly be viewed as *owing* something to the other members of a community he wishes to leave: for example, he has been educated at their expense on the explicit agreement that he would use his acquired skills and knowledge in the home community. Or, he has acquired certain family obligations that he will abandon by shifting communities. Or, without such ties, he wishes to leave. What may he take out with him? Or, he wishes to leave after he's committed some punishable offense for which the community wishes to punish him. Clearly the principles will be complicated ones. Children present yet more difficult problems. In some way it must be ensured that they are *informed* of the range of alternatives in the world. But the home community might view it as important that their youngsters not be exposed to the knowledge that one hundred miles away is a community of great sexual freedom. And so on. I mention these problems to indicate a fraction of the thinking that needs to be done on the details of a framework and to make clear that I do not think its nature can be settled finally now either.

Even though the details of the framework aren't settled, won't there be some rigid limits about it, some things inalterably fixed? Will it be possible to shift to a nonvoluntary framework permitting the forced exclusion of various styles of life? If a framework could be devised that could not be transformed into a nonvoluntary one, would we wish to institute it? If we institute such a permanently voluntary general framework, are we not, to some extent, ruling out certain possible choices? Are we not saying in advance that people cannot choose to live in a certain way; are we setting a rigid range in which people can move and thus committing the usual fault of the static utopians? The comparable question about an individual is whether a free system will allow him to sell himself into slavery. I believe that it would. (Other writers disagree.) It also would allow him permanently to commit himself never to enter into such a transaction. But some things individuals may choose for themselves, no one may choose for another. So long as it is realized at what a *general* level the rigidity lies, and what diversity of particular lives and communities it allows, the answer is, "Yes, the framework should be fixed as voluntary." But remember that any individual may contract into any particular constraints over himself and so may use the voluntary framework to contract himself out of it. (If all individuals do so, the voluntary framework will not operate until the next generation, when others come of age.)

HOW UTOPIA WORKS OUT

"Well, what exactly will it all turn out to be like? In what directions will people flower? How large will the communities be? Will there be some large cities? How will economies of scale operate to fix the size of the communities? Will all of the communities be geographical, or will there be many important secondary associations, and so on? Will most communities follow particular (though diverse) utopian visions, or will many communities themselves be open, animated by no such particular vision?"

I do not know, and you should not be interested in my guesses about what would occur under the framework in the near future. As for the long run, I would not attempt to guess.

"So is this all it comes to: utopia is a free society?" Utopia is *not* just a society in which the framework is realized. For who could believe that ten minutes after the framework was established, we would have utopia? Things would be no different than now. It is what grows spontaneously from the individual choices of many people over a long period of time that will be worth speaking eloquently about. (Not that any particular stage of the process is an end state which all our desires are aimed at. The utopian process is substituted for the utopian end state of other static theories of utopias.) Many communities will achieve many different characters. Only a fool, or a prophet, would try to prophesy the range and limits and characters of the communities after, for example, 150 years of the operation of this framework.

Aspiring to neither role, let me close by emphasizing the dual nature of the conception of utopia being presented here. There is the framework of utopia, and there are the particular communities within the framework. Almost all of the literature on utopia is, according to our conception, concerned with the character of the particular communities within the framework. The fact that I have not propounded some particular description of a constituent community does *not* mean that (I think) doing so is unimportant, or less important, or uninteresting.

How could that be? We *live* in particular communities. It is here that one's nonimperialistic vision of the ideal or good society is to be propounded and realized. Allowing us to do that is what the framework is *for*. Without such visions impelling and animating the creation of particular communities with particular desired characteristics, the framework will lack life. Conjoined with many persons' particular visions, the framework enables us to get the best of all possible worlds.

The position expounded here totally rejects planning in detail, in advance, one community in which everyone is to live yet sympathizes with voluntary utopian experimentation and provides it with the background in which it can flower; does this position fall within the utopian or the antiutopian camp? My difficulty in answering this question encourages me to think the framework captures the virtues and advantages of each position. (If instead it blunders into combining the errors, defects, and mistakes of both of them, the filtering process of free and open discussion will make this clear.)

UTOPIA AND THE MINIMAL STATE

The framework for utopia that we have described is equivalent to the minimal state. . . .

. . . This morally favored state, the only morally legitimate state, the only morally tolerable one, we now see is the one that best realizes the utopian aspirations of untold dreamers and visionaries. It preserves what we all can keep from the utopian tradition and opens the rest of that tradition to our individual aspirations. Recall now the question with which this chapter began. Is not the minimal state, the framework for utopia, an inspiring vision?

The minimal state treats us as inviolate individuals, who may not be used in certain ways by others as means or tools or instruments or resources; it treats us as persons having individual rights with the dignity this constitutes. Treating us with respect by respecting our rights, it allows us, individually or with whom we choose, to choose our life and to realize our ends and our conception of ourselves, insofar as we can, aided by the voluntary cooperation of other individuals possessing the same dignity. How *dare* any state or group of individuals do more. Or less.

QUESTIONS FOR DISCUSSION

Why does Nozick believe that the framework for utopia must be "realized first if more particular utopian visions are to be realized stably"? (176)

1. Why does Nozick argue "that even if there is one kind of community that is best for each and every person, the framework set out is the best means for finding out the nature of that community "? (181)

2. Why does Nozick think his "filtering process" will achieve "communities that people will want to live in and will choose voluntarily to live in"? (180)

3. According to Nozick, how would a framework like the one he describes come about?

4. Why does Nozick think that once a framework for utopia is established, a utopia will grow "spontaneously from the individual choices of many people over a long period of time"? (193)

What does Nozick mean that the framework for utopia is "equivalent to" the minimal state? (194)

1. Does Nozick believe that the framework for utopia is a minimal state, or only that it is equivalent to a minimal state?

2. If, as Nozick says, it is an "incredible" idea that there is "one best society for *everyone* to live in," why does he believe the minimal state is the best form of government for everyone to live in? (175)

3. Why does Nozick think the framework must be voluntary? According to Nozick, how is the framework conducive to utopia if people—possibly all people—can choose to opt out of it?

4. In highlighting "the defects and shortcomings of the minimal state as the end of political philosophy," what does Nozick mean by "the end of political philosophy"? (173) Does Nozick think the framework is an end in itself?

FOR FURTHER REFLECTION

1. Do you agree with Nozick that his concept of a framework for utopia is an inspiring vision?

2. How would you answer Nozick's question about whether the concept of a framework for utopia falls "within the utopian or antiutopian camp"?

3. Is an organization of society that "tends to make people better and more ideal" a possibility or an unrealizable ideal?

4. Is the U.S. Constitution an example of filters and designs in the creation of a democratic utopia? Is the United States the opposite of a minimal state or a framework for utopia in progress?

Of Which He Is a Citizen

Most utopian proposals are prompted by the contemporary historical and cultural conditions in which the authors live, and look primarily to an improved future that makes a break from the past. Some proposals, however, are strongly influenced by and grounded in older traditions and systems of belief, and are intended to restore and sustain the values of those traditions. These movements derive their principles, moral direction, and justification from adherence to religious creeds and narratives that hold out the promise of an ideal world not only here and now but also in realms transcending earthly existence.

Among the many variations of the belief-based form of utopianism are Christian communities that through the centuries have sprung up, run their course, and dissolved, such as the Shakers. In addition, there are communities that have persisted through centuries of external social change and continue to assert their faith-based identity even into the twenty-first century, such as the Amish communities in rural North America, but also the Church of Jesus Christ of Latter Day Saints, even as they fully engage with the modern urban, secular world.

Other forms of utopianism that look backward for their foundational principles place less emphasis on religious dogma and more on a tradition of divinely mandated covenants related in sacred narratives that promise the establishment of just and equitable earthly communities. Among these are the Zionist settlements established in Palestine from the latter half of the nineteenth century onward, prior to the founding of Israel in 1948. While reaffirming their basis in Jewish traditions, they also represented a highly strategic political movement in response to what their founders viewed as an untenable anti-Semitic climate in Europe.

The two selections in this section of *Imperfect Ideal* represent different aspects of this kind of tradition-based utopianism.

The selection from the early Christian philosopher **Saint Augustine** of Hippo (354–430), taken from Books XIV and XIX of his magisterial work *The City of God* (413–427), investigates a fundamental problem that arises when a utopian vision is informed by teachings believed to carry divine authority. Since such a vision is generally intended to take hold and lead to the establishment of a political community in the world, the challenge for such proposals is to account for how the religious foundations of such a community can coexist with the harsh realities of governance and remain solid and stable. For Augustine, this was not merely a theoretical problem, but a living reality in the waning days of the Roman Empire as the Christian church struggled to maintain its central place in the political life of an increasingly fragmented world. Augustine asks us to consider the complex and often ambivalent relationship between what he terms the divine City of God and the secular City of Man and to think about what it means to simultaneously be a citizen of both.

Austrian Jewish leader **Theodor Herzl** (1860–1904) was the pre-eminent force behind the Jewish political and social movement known as Zionism in the late nineteenth century. The selection included here is from his highly influential pamphlet *The Jewish State* (1896), which controversially proposed the large-scale emigration of Jews from Europe to a place where they could establish a nation free from the stress of anti-Semitism that had persisted for centuries, in spite of the relatively successful assimilation of many Jews into European society. Though secular in tone and professing not to be utopian in intent, Herzl's manifesto and rallying cry in *The Jewish State*, as evidenced by the prominent use of the archaic and venerable term "Zion," drew its inspiration from centuries of Jewish religious tradition. In doing so, Herzl prompts us to ask how the assertion of a divinely ordained promised land can be the founding principle of a community that has strong religious underpinnings, while at the same time maintaining its fundamentally secular identity.

The City of God

(selection)

Saint Augustine

We have already stated in the preceding books that God, desiring not only that the human race might be able by their similarity of nature to associate with one another, but also that they might be bound together in harmony and peace by the ties of relationship, was pleased to derive all men from one individual, and created man with such a nature that the members of the race should not have died, had not the two first (of whom the one was created out of nothing, and the other out of him) merited this by their disobedience; for by them so great a sin was committed that by it human nature was altered for the worse, and was transmitted also to their posterity, liable to sin and subject to death. And the kingdom of death so reigned over men, that the deserved penalty of sin would have hurled all headlong even into the second death, of which there is no end, had not the undeserved grace of God saved some therefrom. And thus it has come to pass that, though there are very many and great nations all over the earth, whose rites and customs, speech, arms, and dress, are distinguished by marked differences, yet there are no more than two kinds of human society, which we may justly call two cities, according to the language of our scriptures. The one consists of those who wish to live after the flesh, the other of those who wish to live after the spirit; and when they severally achieve what they wish, they live in peace, each after its kind.

Accordingly, two cities have been formed by two loves: the earthly by the love of self, even to the contempt of God; the heavenly by the love of God, even to the contempt of self. The former, in a word, glories in itself, the latter in the Lord. For the one seeks glory from men, but the greatest glory of the other is God, the witness of conscience. The one lifts up its head in its own glory; the other says to its God, "Thou art my glory, and the lifter up of mine head." (Ps. 3:4) In the one, the princes and the nations it subdues are ruled by the love of ruling; in the other, the princes and the subjects serve one another in love, the latter obeying, while the former take thought of all. The one delights in its own strength, represented in the persons of its rulers; the other says to its God, "I will love Thee, O Lord, my strength." (Ps. 17:1) And therefore the wise men of the one city, living according to man, have sought for profit to their own bodies or souls or both, and those who have known God "glorified Him not as God, neither were thankful, but became vain in their imaginations, and their foolish heart was darkened; professing themselves to be wise"—that is, glorying in their own wisdom, and being possessed by pride—"they became fools, and changed the glory of the incorruptible God into an image made like to corruptible man, and to birds, and four-footed beasts, and creeping things." For they were either leaders or followers of the people in adoring images, "and worshipped and served the creature more than the Creator, who is blessed forever." (Rom. 1:21–25) But in the other city there is no human wisdom, but only godliness, which offers due worship to the true God, and looks for its reward in the society of the saints, of holy angels as well as holy men, "that God may be all in all." (1 Cor. 15:28)

■ ■ ■

But the families which do not live by faith seek their peace in the earthly advantages of this life; while the families which live by faith look for those eternal blessings which are promised, and use as pilgrims such advantages of time and of earth as do not fascinate and divert them from God, but rather aid them to endure with greater ease, and to keep down the number of those burdens of the corruptible body which weigh upon the soul. Thus the things necessary for this mortal life are used by both kinds of men and families alike, but each has its own peculiar and widely different aim in using them. The earthly city, which does not live by faith, seeks an earthly peace, and the end it proposes, in the well-ordered concord of civic obedience and rule, is the combination of men's wills to attain the things which are helpful to this life. The heavenly city, or rather the part of it which sojourns on earth and lives by faith, makes use of this peace only because it must, until this mortal condition which necessitates it shall pass away. Consequently, so long as it lives like a captive and a stranger in the earthy city, though it has already received the promise of redemption, and the gift of the Spirit as the earnest of it, it makes no scruple to obey the laws of the earthly city, whereby the things necessary for the maintenance of this mortal life are administered; and thus, as this life is common to both cities, so there is a harmony between them in regard to what belongs to it. But, as the earthly city has had some philosophers whose doctrine is condemned by the divine teaching, and who, being deceived either by their own conjectures or by demons, supposed that many gods must be invited to take an interest in human affairs, and assigned to each a separate function and a separate department—to one the body, to another the soul; and in the body itself, to one the head, to another the neck, and each of the other members to one of the gods; and in like manner, in the soul, to one god the natural capacity was assigned, to another education, to another anger, to another lust; and so the various affairs of life were assigned—cattle to one, corn to another, wine to another, oil to another, the woods to another, money to another, navigation to another, wars and victories to another, marriages to another, births and fecundity to another, and other things to other gods: and as the celestial city, on the other hand, knew that one God only was to be worshipped, and that to him alone was due that service which the Greeks call *latreia*, and which can be given only to a god, it has come to pass that the two cities could not have common laws of religion, and that the heavenly city has been compelled in this matter to dissent and to become obnoxious to those who think differently, and to stand the brunt of their anger and hatred and persecutions, except insofar as the minds of their enemies have been alarmed by the multitude of the Christians and quelled by the manifest protection of God accorded to them. This heavenly city, then, while it sojourns on earth, calls citizens out of all nations, and gathers together a society of pilgrims of all languages, not scrupling about diversities in the manners, laws, and institutions whereby earthly peace is secured and maintained, but recognizing that, however various these are, they all tend to one and the same end of earthly peace. It therefore is so far from rescinding and abolishing these diversities, that it even preserves and adopts them, so long only as no hindrance to the worship of the one supreme and true God is thus introduced. Even the heavenly city, therefore, while in its state pilgrimage, avails itself of the peace of earth, and, so far as it can without injuring faith and godliness, desires and maintains a common agreement among men regarding the acquisition of the necessaries of life, and makes this earthly peace bear upon the peace of heaven; for this alone can be truly called and esteemed the peace of the reasonable creatures, consisting as it does in the perfectly ordered and harmonious enjoyment of God and of one another in God. When we shall have reached that peace, this mortal life shall give place to one that is eternal, and our body shall be no more this animal body which by its corruption weighs down the soul, but a spiritual body feeling no want and in all its members subjected to the will. In its pilgrim state the heavenly city possesses this peace by faith; and by this faith it lives righteously when it refers to the attainment of that peace every good action toward God and man; for the life of the city is a social life.

It is a matter of no moment in the city of God whether he who adopts the faith that brings men to God adopts it in one dress and manner of life or another, so long only as he lives in conformity with the commandments of God. And hence, when philosophers themselves become Christians, they are compelled, indeed, to abandon their erroneous doctrines, but not their dress and mode of living, which are no obstacle to religion. So that we make no account of the distinction of sects which Varro adduced in connection with the Cynic school, provided always nothing indecent or self-indulgent is retained. . . .

. . . And therefore, where there is not this righteousness whereby the one supreme God rules the obedient city according to his grace, so that it sacrifices to none but him, and whereby, in all the citizens of this obedient city, the soul consequently rules the body and reason the vices in the rightful order, so that, as the individual just man, so also the community and people of the just, live by faith, which works by love, that love whereby man loves God as he ought to be loved, and his neighbor as himself—there, I say, there is not an assemblage associated by a common acknowledgment of right, and by a community of interests. But if there is not this, there is not a people, if our definition be true, and therefore there is no republic; for where there is no people there can be no republic.

But if we discard this definition of a people, and assuming another, say that a people in an assemblage of reasonable beings bound together by a common agreement as to the objects of their love, then, in order to discover the character of any people, we have only to observe what they love. Yet whatever it loves, if only it is an assemblage of reasonable beings and not of beasts, and is bound together by an agreement as to the objects of love, it is reasonably called a people; and it will be a superior people in proportion as it is bound together by higher interests, inferior in proportion as it is bound together by lower. According to this definition of ours, the Roman people is a people, and its weal is without doubt a commonwealth or republic. But what its tastes were in its early and subsequent days, and how it declined into sanguinary seditions and then to social and civil wars, and so burst asunder or rotted off the bond of concord in which the health of a people consists, history shows, and in the preceding books I have related at large. And yet I would not on this account say either that it was not a people, or that its administration was not a republic, so long as there remains an assemblage of reasonable beings bound together by a common agreement as to the objects of love. But what I say of this people and of this republic I must be understood to think and say of the Athenians or any Greek state, of the Egyptians, of the early Assyrian Babylon, and of every other nation, great or small, which had a public government. For, in general, the city of the ungodly, which did not obey the command of God that it should offer no sacrifice save to him alone, and which, therefore, could not give to the soul its proper command over the body, nor to the reason its just authority over the vices, is void of true justice.

And thus we may say of peace, as we have said of eternal life, that it is the end of our good; and the rather because [sic] the psalmist says of the city of God, the subject of this laborious work, "Praise the Lord, O Jerusalem, praise thy God, O Zion; for He hath strengthened the bars of thy gates, He hath blessed thy children within thee, who hath made thy borders peace." (Ps. 147:12-14) For when the bars of her gates shall be strengthened, none shall go in or come out from her; consequently we ought to understand the peace of her borders as that final peace we are wishing to declare. For even the mystical name of the city itself, that is, Jerusalem, means, as I have already said, "Vision of Peace." But as the word peace is employed in connection with things in this world in which certainly life eternal has no place, we have preferred to call the end or supreme good of this city life eternal rather than peace. Of this end the apostle says, "But now, being freed from sin, and become servants to God, ye have your fruit unto holiness, and the end life eternal." (Rom. 6:22) But on the other hand, as those who are not familiar with Scripture may suppose that the life of the wicked is eternal life, either because of the immortality of the soul, which some of the philosophers even have recognized, or because of the endless punishment of the wicked, which forms a part of our faith, and which seems impossible unless the wicked live forever, it may therefore be advisable, in order that everyone may readily understand what we mean, to say that the end or supreme good of this city is either peace in eternal life, or eternal life in peace. For peace is a good so great, that even in this earthly and mortal life there is no word we hear with such pleasure, nothing we desire with such zest or find to be more thoroughly gratifying. So that if we dwell for a little longer on this subject, we shall not in my opinion be wearisome to our readers, who will attend both for the sake of understanding what is the end of this city of which we speak, and for the sake of the sweetness of peace which is dear to all.

Whoever gives even moderate attention to human affairs and to our common nature, will recognize that if there is no man who does not wish to be joyful, neither is there anyone who does not wish to have peace. For even they who make war desire nothing but victory—desire, that is to say, to attain to peace with glory. For what else is victory than the conquest of those who resist us? And when this is done there is peace. It is therefore with the desire for peace that wars are waged, even by those who take pleasure in exercising their warlike nature in command and battle. And hence it is obvious that peace is the end sought for by war. For every man seeks peace by waging war, but no man seeks war by making peace. For even they who intentionally interrupt the peace in which they are living have no hatred of peace, but only wish it changed into a peace that suits them better. They do not, therefore, wish to have no peace, but only one more to their mind. And in the case of sedition, when men have separated themselves from the community, they yet do not effect what they wish, unless they maintain some kind of peace with their fellow-conspirators. And therefore even robbers take care to maintain peace with their comrades, that they may with greater effect and greater safety invade the peace of other men. And if an individual happens to be of such unrivaled strength, and to be so jealous of partnership that he trusts himself with no comrades but makes his own plots and commits depredations and murders on his own account, yet he maintains some shadow of peace with such persons as he is unable to kill and from whom he wishes to conceal his deeds. In his own home too he makes it his aim to be at peace with his wife and children and any other members of his household; for unquestionably their prompt obedience to his every look is a source of pleasure to him. And if this be not rendered, he is angry, he chides and punishes; and even by this storm he secures the calm peace of his own home as occasion demands. For he sees that peace cannot be maintained unless all the members of the same domestic circle be subject to one head, such as he himself is in his own house. And therefore if a city or nation offered to submit itself to him, to serve him in the same style as he had made his household serve him, he would no longer lurk in a brigand's hiding places, but lift his head in open day as a king, though the same covetousness and wickedness should remain in him. And thus all men desire to have peace with their own circle whom they wish to govern as suits themselves. For even those whom they make war against they wish to make their own, and impose on them the laws of their own peace.

But let us suppose a man such as poetry and mythology speak of—a man so insociable and savage as to be called rather a semi-man than a man. Although, then, his kingdom was the solitude of a dreary cave, and he himself was so singularly bad-hearted that he was named Kakos, which is the Greek word for *bad*; though he had no wife to sooth him with endearing talk, no children to play with, no sons to do his bidding, no friend to enliven him with intercourse, not even his father Vulcan (though in one respect he was happier than his father, not having begotten a monster like himself); although he gave to no man, but took as he wished whatever he could, from whomsoever he could, when he could; yet in that solitary den, the floor of which, as Virgil (*Aeneid*, 8.195) says, was always reeking with recent slaughter, there was nothing else than peace sought, a peace in which no one should molest him, or disquiet him with any assault or alarm. With his own body he desired to be at peace, and he was satisfied only in proportion as he had this peace. For he ruled his members, and they obeyed him; and for the sake of pacifying his mortal nature, which rebelled when it needed anything, and of allaying the sedition of hunger which threatened to banish the soul from the body, he made forays, slew, and devoured, but used the ferocity and savageness he displayed in these actions only for the preservation of his own life's peace. So that, had he been willing to make with other men the same peace which he made with himself in his own cave, he would neither have been called bad, nor a monster, nor a semi-man. Or if the appearance of his body and his vomiting smoky fires frightened men from having any dealings with him, perhaps his fierce ways arose not from a desire to do mischief, but from the necessity of finding a living. But he may have had no existence, or, at least, he was not such as the poets fancifully describe him, for they had to exalt Hercules, and did so at the expense of Cacus. It is better, then, to believe that such a man or semi-man never existed, and that this, in common with many other fancies of the poets, is mere fiction. For the most savage animals (and he is said to have been almost a wild beast) encompass their own species with a ring of protecting peace. They cohabit, beget, produce, suckle, and bring up their young, though very many of them are not gregarious, but solitary—not like sheep, deer, pigeons, starlings, bees, but such as lions, foxes, eagles, bats. For what tigress does not gently purr over her cubs, and lay aside her ferocity to fondle them? What kite, solitary as he is when circling over his prey, does not seek a mate, build a nest, hatch the eggs, bring up the young birds, and maintain with the mother of his family as peaceful a domestic alliance as he can? How much more powerfully do the laws of man's nature move him to hold fellowship and maintain peace with all men so far as in him lies, since even wicked men wage war to maintain the peace of their own circle, and wish that, if possible, all men belonged to them, that all men and things might serve but one head, and might, either through love or fear, yield themselves to peace with him! It is thus that pride in its perversity apes God. It abhors equality with other men under him, but, instead of his rule, it seeks to impose a rule of its own upon its equals. It abhors, that is to say, the just peace of God, and loves its own unjust peace, but it cannot help loving peace of one kind or other. For there is no vice so clean contrary to nature that it obliterates even the faintest traces of nature.

He, then, who prefers what is right to what is wrong, and what is well-ordered to what is perverted, sees that the peace of unjust men is not worthy to be called peace in comparison with the peace of the just. And yet even what is perverted must of necessity be in harmony with, and in dependence on, and in some part of the order of things, for otherwise it would have no existence at all. Suppose a man hangs with his head downward, this is certainly a perverted attitude of body and arrangement of its members; for that which nature requires to be above is beneath, and vice versa. This perversity disturbs the peace of the body, and is therefore painful. Nevertheless the spirit is at peace with its body and labors for its preservation, and hence the suffering; but if it is banished from the body by its pains, then, so long as the bodily framework holds together, there is in the remains a kind of peace among the members and hence the body remains suspended. And inasmuch as the earthly body tends toward the earth and rests on the bond by which it is suspended, it tends thus to its natural peace, and the voice of its own weight demands a place for it to rest; and though now lifeless and without feeling, it does not fall from the peace that is natural to its place in creation, whether it already has it or is tending toward it. For if you apply embalming preparations to prevent the bodily frame from moldering and dissolving, a kind of peace still unites part to part and keeps the whole body in a suitable place on the earth—in other words, in a place that is at peace with the body. If, on the other hand, the body receives no such care but be left to the natural course, it is disturbed by exhalations that do not harmonize with one another and that offend our senses; for it is this which is perceived in putrefaction until it is assimilated to the elements of the world, and particle by particle enters into peace with them. Yet throughout this process the laws of the most high Creator and Governor are strictly observed, for it is by him the peace of the universe is administered. For although minute animals are produced from the carcass of a larger animal, all these little atoms, by the law of the same Creator, serve the animals they belong to in peace. And although the flesh of dead animals be eaten by others, no matter where it be carried nor what it be brought into contact with nor what it be converted and changed into, it still is ruled by the same laws which pervade all things for the conservation of every mortal race and which bring things that fit one another into harmony.

The peace of the body then consists in the duly proportioned arrangement of its parts. The peace of the irrational soul is the harmonious repose of the appetites, and that of the rational soul the harmony of knowledge and action. The peace of body and soul is the well-ordered and harmonious life and health of the living creature. Peace between man and God is the well-ordered obedience of faith to eternal law. Peace between man and man is well-ordered concord. Domestic peace is the well-ordered concord between those of the family who rule and those who obey. Civil peace is a similar concord among the citizens. The peace of the celestial city is the perfectly ordered and harmonious enjoyment of God, and of one another in God. The peace of all things is the tranquillity of order. Order is the distribution which allots things equal and unequal, each to its own place. And hence, though the miserable, insofar as they are such, do certainly not enjoy peace, but are severed from that tranquillity of order in which there is no disturbance, nevertheless, inasmuch as they are deservedly and justly miserable, they are by their very misery connected with order. They are not, indeed, conjoined with the blessed, but they are disjoined from them by the law of order. And though they are disquieted, their circumstances are notwithstanding adjusted to them, and consequently they have some tranquillity of order, and therefore some peace. But they are wretched because, although not wholly miserable, they are not in that place where any mixture of misery is impossible. They would, however, be more wretched if they had not had that peace which arises from being in harmony with the natural order of things. When they suffer, their peace is insofar disturbed; but their peace continues insofar as they do not suffer, and insofar as their nature continues to exist. As, then, there may be life without pain, while there cannot be pain without some kind of life, so there may be peace without war, but there cannot be war without some kind of peace, because war supposes the existence of some natures to wage it, and these natures cannot exist without peace of one kind or other.

And therefore there is a nature in which evil does not or even cannot exist; but there cannot be a nature in which there is no good. Hence not even the nature of the devil himself is evil, insofar as it is nature, but it was made evil by being perverted. Thus he did not abide in the truth, but could not escape the judgment of the truth; he did not abide in the tranquillity of order, but did not therefore escape the power of the Ordainer. The good imparted by God to his nature did not screen him from the justice of God by which order was preserved in his punishment; neither did God punish the good which he had created, but the evil which the devil had committed. God did not take back all he had imparted to his nature, but something he took and something he left, that there might remain enough to be sensible of the loss of what was taken. And this very sensibility to pain is evidence of the good which has been taken away and the good which has been left. For, were nothing good left, there could be no pain on account of the good which had been lost. For he who sins is still worse if he rejoices in his loss of righteousness. But he who is in pain, if he derives no benefit from it, mourns at least the loss of health. And as righteousness and health are both good things, and as the loss of any good thing is a matter of grief, not of joy—if, at least, there is no compensation, as spiritual righteousness may compensate for the loss of bodily health—certainly it is more suitable for a wicked man to grieve in punishment than to rejoice in his fault. As, then, the joy of a sinner who has abandoned what is good is evidence of a bad will, so his grief for the good he has lost when he is punished is evidence of a good nature. For he who laments the peace his nature has lost is stirred to do so by some relics of peace which make his nature friendly to itself. And it is very just that in the final punishment the wicked and godless should in anguish bewail the loss of the natural advantages they enjoyed, and should perceive that they were most justly taken from them by that God whose benign liberality they had despised. God, then, the most wise Creator and most just Ordainer of all natures, who placed the human race upon earth as its greatest ornament, imparted to men some good things adapted to this life, to wit, temporal peace, such as we can enjoy in this life from health and safety and human fellowship, and all things needful for the preservation and recovery of this peace, such as the objects which are accommodated to our outward senses, light, night, the air, and waters suitable for us, and everything the body requires to sustain, shelter, heal, or beautify it; and all under this most equitable condition, that every man who made a good use of these advantages suited to the peace of this mortal condition, should receive ampler and better blessings, namely, the peace of immortality, accompanied by glory and honor in an endless life made fit for the enjoyment of God and of one another in God, but that he who used the present blessings badly should both lose them and should not receive the others.

QUESTIONS FOR DISCUSSION

Why does Augustine make a point of saying that when both the heavenly city and the earthly city achieve their goals they can "live in peace"? (201)

1. According to Augustine, how does "earthly peace bear upon the peace of heaven"? (204) Why does he say that the heavenly city "makes use of [earthly] peace only because it must"? (203)

2. Does Augustine think that earthly peace is a path to heavenly peace?

3. What does Augustine mean by "the peace of the just"? (209)

4. What does Augustine mean when he says, "Peace between man and God is the well-ordered obedience of faith to eternal law"? (210)

According to Augustine, what is the relationship between his concept of the two cities and the "natural order of things"? (211)

1. What does Augustine mean by "the natural order of things"? (211)

2. What does Augustine mean when he says that in the heavenly city there is "no human wisdom, but only godliness"? (202)

3. According to Augustine, how are "all nations" in the city of God? (204)

4. Why does Augustine say, "The life of the [heavenly] city is a social life"? (204)

5. Does Augustine think that people in the earthly city can be good?

FOR FURTHER REFLECTION

1. How useful is Augustine's concept of two cities in understanding the world today?

2. Should people be striving for Augustine's "just peace of God" as opposed to mere "peace on earth"?

3. Would Augustine have approved of the concept of utopia?

The Jewish State

(selection)

Theodor Herzl

Preface

The idea which I have developed in this pamphlet is a very old one: it is the restoration of the Jewish State.

The world resounds with outcries against the Jews, and these outcries have awakened the slumbering idea.

I wish it to be clearly understood from the outset that no portion of my argument is based on a new discovery. I have discovered neither the historic condition of the Jews nor the means to improve it. In fact, every man will see for himself that the materials of the structure I am designing are not only in existence, but actually already in hand. If, therefore, this attempt to solve the "Jewish question" is to be designated by a single word, let it be said to be the result of an inescapable conclusion rather than that of a flighty imagination.

I must, in the first place, guard my scheme from being treated as utopian by superficial critics who might commit this error of judgment if I did not warn them. I should obviously have done nothing to be ashamed of if I had described a utopia on philanthropic lines; and I should also, in all probability, have obtained literary success more easily if I had set forth my plan in the irresponsible guise of a romantic tale. But this utopia is far less attractive than any one of those portrayed by Sir Thomas More and his numerous forerunners and successors. And I believe that the situation of the Jews in many countries is grave enough to make such preliminary trifling superfluous.

An interesting book, *Freiland*, by Dr. Theodor Hertzka, which appeared a few years ago, may serve to mark the distinction I draw between my conception and a utopia. His is the ingenious invention of a modern mind thoroughly schooled in the principles of political economy, it is as remote from actuality as the equatorial mountain on which his dream state lies. Freiland is a complicated piece of mechanism with numerous cogged wheels fitting into each other; but there is nothing to prove that they can be set in motion. Even supposing "Freiland societies" were to come into existence, I should look on the whole thing as a joke.

The present scheme, on the other hand, includes the employment of an existent propelling force. In consideration of my own inadequacy, I shall content myself with indicating the cogs and wheels of the machine to be constructed, and I shall rely on more skilled mechanicians than myself to put them together.

Everything depends on our propelling force. And what is that force? The misery of the Jews.

Who would venture to deny its existence? We shall discuss it fully in the chapter on the causes of anti-Semitism.

Everybody is familiar with the phenomenon of steam power, generated by boiling water, which lifts the kettle lid. Such tea-kettle phenomena are the attempts of Zionist and kindred associations to check anti-Semitism.

I believe that this power, if rightly employed, is powerful enough to propel a large engine and to move passengers and goods: the engine having whatever form men may choose to give it.

I am absolutely convinced that I am right, though I doubt whether I shall live to see myself proved to be so. Those who are the first to inaugurate this movement will scarcely live to see its glorious close. But the inauguration of it is enough to give them a feeling of pride and the joy of spiritual freedom.

I shall not be lavish in artistically elaborated descriptions of my project, for fear of incurring the suspicion of painting a utopia. I anticipate, in any case, that thoughtless scoffers will caricature my sketch and thus try to weaken its effect. A Jew, intelligent in other respects, to whom I explained my plan, was of the opinion that "a utopia was a project whose future details were represented as already extant." This is a fallacy. Every chancellor of the exchequer calculates in his budget estimates with assumed figures, and not only with such as are based on the average returns of past years, or on previous revenues in other states, but sometimes with figures for which there is no precedent whatever; as for example, in instituting a new tax. Everybody who studies a budget knows that this is the case. But even if it were known that the estimates would not be rigidly adhered to, would such a financial draft be considered utopian?

But I am expecting more of my readers. I ask the cultivated men whom I am addressing to set many preconceived ideas entirely aside. I shall even go so far as to ask those Jews who have most earnestly tried to solve the Jewish question to look upon their previous attempts as mistaken and futile.

I must guard against a danger in setting forth my idea. If I describe future circumstances with too much caution I shall appear to doubt their possibility. If, on the other hand, I announce their realization with too much assurance I shall appear to be describing a chimera.

I shall therefore clearly and emphatically state that I believe in the practical outcome of my scheme, though without professing to have discovered the shape it may ultimately take. The Jewish State is essential to the world; it will therefore be created.

The plan would, of course, seem absurd if a single individual attempted to do it; but if worked by a number of Jews in cooperation it would appear perfectly rational, and its accomplishment would present no difficulties worth mentioning. The idea depends only on the number of its supporters. Perhaps our ambitious young men, to whom every road of progress is now closed, seeing in this Jewish State a bright prospect of freedom, happiness, and honors opening to them, will ensure the propagation of the idea.

I feel that with the publication of this pamphlet my task is done. I shall not again take up the pen, unless the attacks of noteworthy antagonists drive me to do so, or it becomes necessary to meet unforeseen objections and to remove errors.

Am I stating what is not yet the case? Am I before my time? Are the sufferings of the Jews not yet grave enough? We shall see.

It depends on the Jews themselves whether this political pamphlet remains for the present a political romance. If the present generation is too dull to understand it rightly, a future, finer, and a better generation will arise to understand it. The Jews who wish for a state shall have it, and they will deserve to have it.

Introduction

It is astonishing how little insight into the science of economics many of the men who move in the midst of active life possess. Hence it is that even Jews faithfully repeat the cry of the anti-Semites: "We depend for sustenance on the nations who are our hosts, and if we had no hosts to support us we should die of starvation." This is a point that shows how unjust accusations may weaken our self-knowledge. But what are the true grounds for this statement concerning the nations that act as "hosts"? Where it is not based on limited physiocratic views it is founded on the childish error that commodities pass from hand to hand in continuous rotation. We need not wake from long slumber, like Rip van Winkle, to realize that the world is considerably altered by the production of new commodities. The technical progress made during this wonderful era enables even a man of most limited intelligence to note with his short-sighted eyes the appearance of new commodities all around him. The spirit of enterprise has created them.

Labor without enterprise is the stationary labor of ancient days; and typical of it is the work of the husbandman, who stands now just where his progenitors stood a thousand years ago. All our material welfare has been brought about by men of enterprise. I feel almost ashamed of writing down so trite a remark. Even if we were a nation of entrepreneurs—such as absurdly exaggerated accounts make us out to be—we should not require another nation to live on. We do not depend on the circulation of old commodities, because we produce new ones.

The world possesses slaves of extraordinary capacity for work, whose appearance has been fatal to the production of handmade goods: these slaves are the machines. It is true that workmen are required to set machinery in motion; but for this we have men in plenty, in superabundance. Only those who are ignorant of the conditions of Jews in many countries of Eastern Europe would venture to assert that Jews are either unfit or unwilling to perform manual labor.

But I do not wish to take up the cudgels for the Jews in this pamphlet. It would be useless. Everything rational and everything sentimental that can possibly be said in their defense has been said already. If one's hearers are incapable of comprehending them, one is a preacher in a desert. And if one's hearers are broad and high-minded enough to have grasped them already, then the sermon is superfluous. I believe in the ascent of man to higher and yet higher grades of civilization; but I consider this ascent to be desperately slow. Were we to wait till average humanity had become as charitably inclined as was Lessing when he wrote *Nathan the Wise*, we should wait beyond our day, beyond the days of our children, of our grandchildren, and of our great-grandchildren. But the world's spirit comes to our aid in another way.

This century has given the world a wonderful renaissance by means of its technical achievements; but at the same time its miraculous improvements have not been employed in the service of humanity. Distance has ceased to be an obstacle, yet we complain of insufficient space. Our great steamships carry us swiftly and surely over hitherto unvisited seas. Our railways carry us safely into a mountain-world hitherto tremblingly scaled on foot. Events occurring in countries undiscovered when Europe confined the Jews in ghettos are known to us in the course of an hour. Hence the misery of the Jews is an anachronism—not because there was a period of enlightenment one hundred years ago, for that enlightenment reached in reality only the choicest spirits.

I believe that electric light was not invented for the purpose of illuminating the drawing rooms of a few snobs, but rather for the purpose of throwing light on some of the dark problems of humanity. One of these problems, and not the least of them, is the Jewish question. In solving it we are working not only for ourselves, but also for many other overburdened and oppressed beings.

The Jewish question still exists. It would be foolish to deny it. It is a remnant of the Middle Ages, which civilized nations do not even yet seem able to shake off, try as they will. They certainly showed a generous desire to do so when they emancipated us. The Jewish question exists wherever Jews live in perceptible numbers. Where it does not exist, it is carried by Jews in the course of their migrations. We naturally move to those places where we are not persecuted, and there our presence produces persecution. This is the case in every country, and will remain so, even in those highly civilized—for instance, France—until the Jewish question finds a solution on a political basis. The unfortunate Jews are now carrying the seeds of anti-Semitism into England; they have already introduced it into America.

I believe that I understand anti-Semitism, which is really a highly complex movement. I consider it from a Jewish standpoint, yet without fear or hatred. I believe that I can see what elements there are in it of vulgar sport, of common trade jealousy, of inherited prejudice, of religious intolerance, and also of pretended self-defense. I think the Jewish question is no more a social than a religious one, notwithstanding that it sometimes takes these and other forms. It is a national question, which can only be solved by making it a political world-question to be discussed and settled by the civilized nations of the world in council.

We are a people—one people.

We have honestly endeavored everywhere to merge ourselves in the social life of surrounding communities and to preserve the faith of our fathers. We are not permitted to do so. In vain are we loyal patriots, our loyalty in some places running to extremes; in vain do we make the same sacrifices of life and property as our fellow citizens; in vain do we strive to increase the fame of our native land in science and art, or her wealth by trade and commerce. In countries where we have lived for centuries we are still cried down as strangers, and often by those whose ancestors were not yet domiciled in the land where Jews had already had experience of suffering. The majority may decide which are the strangers; for this, as indeed every point which arises in the relations between nations, is a question of might. I do not here surrender any portion of our prescriptive right, when I make this statement merely in my own name as an individual. In the world as it now is and for an indefinite period will probably remain, might precedes right. It is useless, therefore, for us to be loyal patriots, as were the Huguenots who were forced to emigrate. If we could only be left in peace. . . .

But I think we shall not be left in peace.

Oppression and persecution cannot exterminate us. No nation on earth has survived such struggles and sufferings as we have gone through. Jew-baiting has merely stripped off our weaklings; the strong among us were invariably true to their race when persecution broke out against them. This attitude was most clearly apparent in the period immediately following the emancipation of the Jews. Those Jews who were advanced intellectually and materially entirely lost the feeling of belonging to their race. Wherever our political well-being has lasted for any length of time, we have assimilated with our surroundings. I think this is not discreditable. Hence, the statesman who would wish to see a Jewish strain in his nation would have to provide for the duration of our political well-being; and even a Bismarck could not do that.

For old prejudices against us still lie deep in the hearts of the people. He who would have proofs of this need only listen to the people where they speak with frankness and simplicity: proverb and fairy tale are both anti-Semitic. A nation is everywhere a great child, which can certainly be educated; but its education would, even in most favorable circumstances, occupy such a vast amount of time that we could, as already mentioned, remove our own difficulties by other means long before the process was accomplished.

Assimilation, by which I understood not only external conformity in dress, habits, customs, and language, but also identity of feeling and manner—assimilation of Jews could be effected only by intermarriage. But the need for mixed marriages would have to be felt by the majority; their mere recognition by law would certainly not suffice.

The Hungarian Liberals, who have just given legal sanction to mixed marriages, have made a remarkable mistake which one of the earliest cases clearly illustrates; a baptized Jew married a Jewess. At the same time the struggle to obtain the present form of marriage accentuated distinctions between Jews and Christians, thus hindering rather than aiding the fusion of races.

Those who really wished to see the Jews disappear through inter-mixture with other nations, can only hope to see it come about in one way. The Jews must previously acquire economic power sufficiently great to overcome the old social prejudice against them. The aristocracy may serve as an example of this, for in its ranks occur the proportionately largest numbers of mixed marriages. The Jewish families which regild the old nobility with their money become gradually absorbed. But what form would this phenomenon assume in the middle classes, where (the Jews being a bourgeois people) the Jewish question is mainly concentrated? A previous acquisition of power could be synonymous with that economic supremacy which Jews are already erroneously declared to possess. And if the power they now possess creates rage and indignation among the anti-Semites, what outbreaks would such an increase of power create? Hence the first step toward absorption will never be taken, because this step would involve the subjection of the majority to a hitherto scorned minority, possessing neither military nor administrative power of its own. I think, therefore, that the absorption of Jews by means of their prosperity is unlikely to occur. In countries which now are anti-Semitic my view will be approved. In others, where Jews now feel comfortable, it will probably be violently disputed by them. My happier co-religionists will not believe me till Jew-baiting teaches them the truth; for the longer anti-Semitism lies in abeyance the more fiercely will it break out. The infiltration of immigrating Jews, attracted to a land by apparent security, and the ascent in the social scale of native Jews, combine powerfully to bring about a revolution. Nothing is plainer than this rational conclusion.

Because I have drawn this conclusion with complete indifference to everything but the quest of truth, I shall probably be contradicted and opposed by Jews who are in easy circumstances. Insofar as private interests alone are held by their anxious or timid possessors to be in danger, they can safely be ignored, for the concerns of the poor and oppressed are of greater importance than theirs. But I wish from the outset to prevent any misconception from arising, particularly the mistaken notion that my project, if realized, would in the least degree injure property now held by Jews. I shall therefore explain everything connected with rights of property very fully. Whereas, if my plan never becomes anything more than a piece of literature, things will merely remain as they are. It might more reasonably be objected that I am giving a handle to anti-Semitism when I say we are a people—one people; that I am hindering the assimilation of Jews where it is about to be consummated, and endangering it where it is an accomplished fact, insofar as it is possible for a solitary writer to hinder or endanger anything.

This objection will be especially brought forward in France. It will probably also be made in other countries, but I shall answer only the French Jews beforehand, because these afford the most striking example of my point.

However much I may worship personality—powerful individual personality in statesmen, inventors, artists, philosophers, or leaders, as well as the collective personality of a historic group of human beings, which we call a nation—however much I may worship personality, I do not regret its disappearance. Whoever can, will, and must perish, let him perish. But the distinctive nationality of Jews neither can, will, nor must be destroyed. It cannot be destroyed, because external enemies consolidate it. It will not be destroyed; this is shown during two thousand years of appalling suffering. It must not be destroyed, and that, as a descendant of numberless Jews who refused to despair, I am trying once more to prove in this pamphlet. Whole branches of Judaism may wither and fall, but the trunk will remain.

Hence, if all or any of the French Jews protest against this scheme on account of their own "assimilation," my answer is simple: The whole thing does not concern them at all. They are Jewish Frenchmen, well and good! This is a private affair for the Jews alone.

The movement toward the organization of the State I am proposing would, of course, harm Jewish Frenchmen no more than it would harm the "assimilated" of other countries. It would, on the contrary, be distinctly to their advantage. For they would no longer be disturbed in their "chromatic function," as Darwin puts it, but would be able to assimilate in peace, because the present anti-Semitism would have been stopped forever. They would certainly be credited with being assimilated to the very depths of their souls, if they stayed where they were after the new Jewish State, with its superior institutions, had become a reality.

The "assimilated" would profit even more than Christian citizens by the departure of faithful Jews; for they would be rid of the disquieting, incalculable, and unavoidable rivalry of a Jewish proletariat, driven by poverty and political pressure from place to place, from land to land. This floating proletariat would become stationary. Many Christian citizens—whom we call anti-Semites—can now offer determined resistance to the immigration of foreign Jews. Jewish citizens cannot do this, although it affects them far more directly; for on them they feel first of all the keen competition of individuals carrying on similar branches of industry, who, in addition, either introduce anti-Semitism where it does not exist, or intensify it where it does. The "assimilated" give expression to this secret grievance in "philanthropic" undertakings. They organize emigration societies for wandering Jews. There is a reverse to the picture which would be comic, if it did not deal with human beings. For some of these charitable institutions are created not for, but against, persecuted Jews; they are created to despatch these poor creatures just as fast and far as possible. And thus, many an apparent friend of the Jews turns out, on careful inspection, to be nothing more than an anti-Semite of Jewish origin, disguised as a philanthropist.

But the attempts at colonization made even by really benevolent men, interesting attempts though they were, have so far been unsuccessful. I do not think that this or that man took up the matter merely as an amusement, that they engaged in the emigration of poor Jews as one indulges in the racing of horses. The matter was too grave and tragic for such treatment. These attempts were interesting, in that they represented on a small scale the practical forerunners of the idea of a Jewish State. They were even useful, for out of their mistakes may be gathered experience for carrying the idea out successfully on a larger scale. They have, of course, done harm also. The transportation of anti-Semitism to new districts, which is the inevitable consequence of such artificial infiltration, seems to me to be the least of these evils. Far worse is the circumstance that unsatisfactory results tend to cast doubts on intelligent men. What is impractical or impossible to simple argument will remove this doubt from the minds of intelligent men. What is impractical or impossible to accomplish on a small scale, need not necessarily be so on a larger one. A small enterprise may result in loss under the same conditions which would make a large one pay. A rivulet cannot even be navigated by boats, the river into which it flows carries stately iron vessels.

No human being is wealthy or powerful enough to transplant a nation from one habitation to another. An idea alone can achieve that and this idea of a state may have the requisite power to do so. The Jews have dreamt this kingly dream all through the long nights of their history. "Next year in Jerusalem" is our old phrase. It is now a question of showing that the dream can be converted into a living reality.

For this, many old, outgrown, confused, and limited notions must first be entirely erased from the minds of men. Dull brains might, for instance, imagine that this exodus would be from civilized regions into the desert. That is not the case. It will be carried out in the midst of civilization. We shall not revert to a lower stage, we shall rise to a higher one. We shall not dwell in mud huts; we shall build new more beautiful and more modern houses, and possess them in safety. We shall not lose our acquired possessions; we shall realize them. We shall surrender our well-earned rights only for better ones. We shall not sacrifice our beloved customs; we shall find them again. We shall not leave our old home before the new one is prepared for us. Those only will depart who are sure thereby to improve their position; those who are now desperate will go first, after them the poor; next the prosperous, and, last of all, the wealthy. Those who go in advance will raise themselves to a higher grade, equal to those whose representatives will shortly follow. Thus the exodus will be at the same time an ascent of the class.

The departure of the Jews will involve no economic disturbances, no crises, no persecutions; in fact, the countries they abandon will revive to a new period of prosperity. There will be an inner migration of Christian citizens into the positions evacuated by Jews. The outgoing current will be gradual, without any disturbance, and its initial movement will put an end to anti-Semitism. The Jews will leave as honored friends, and if some of them return, they will receive the same favorable welcome and treatment at the hands of civilized nations as is accorded to all foreign visitors. Their exodus will have no resemblance to a flight, for it will be a well-regulated movement under control of public opinion. The movement will not only be inaugurated with absolute conformity to law, but it cannot even be carried out without the friendly cooperation of interested governments, who would derive considerable benefits from it.

Security for the integrity of the idea and the vigor of its execution will be found in the creation of a body corporate, or corporation. This corporation will be called "The Society of Jews." In addition to it there will be a Jewish company, an economically productive body.

An individual who attempted even to undertake this huge task alone would be either an impostor or a madman. The personal character of the members of the corporation will guarantee its integrity, and the adequate capital of the company will prove its stability.

These prefatory remarks are merely intended as a hasty reply to the mass of objections which the very words "Jewish State" are certain to arouse. Henceforth we shall proceed more slowly to meet further objections and to explain in detail what has been as yet only indicated; and we shall try in the interests of this pamphlet to avoid making it a dull exposition. Short aphoristic chapters will therefore best answer the purpose.

If I wish to substitute a new building for an old one, I must demolish before I construct. I shall therefore keep to this natural sequence. In the first and general part, I shall explain my ideas, remove all prejudices, determine essential political and economic conditions, and develop the plan.

In the special part, which is divided into three principal sections, I shall describe its execution. These three sections are: "The Jewish Company," "Local Groups," and the "Society of Jews." The society is to be created first, the company last; but in this exposition the reverse order is preferable, because it is the financial soundness of the enterprise which will chiefly be called into question, and doubts on this score must be removed first.

In the conclusion, I shall try to meet every further objection that could possibly be made. My Jewish readers will, I hope, follow me patiently to the end. Some will naturally make their objections in an order of succession other than that chosen for their refutation. But whoever finds his doubts dispelled should give allegiance to the cause.

Although I speak of reason, I am fully aware that reason alone will not suffice. Old prisoners do not willingly leave their cells. We shall see whether the youth whom we need are at our command—the youth, who irresistibly draw on the old, carry them forward on strong arms, and transform rational motives into enthusiasm.

QUESTIONS FOR DISCUSSION

Why does Herzl believe that the creation of a Jewish state is an "inescapable conclusion"? (215)

1. Why does Herzl say that the misery of the Jews is a "propelling force" sufficient to bring about the creation of a Jewish state? (216)

2. Why does Herzl believe that the electric light was invented "for the purpose of throwing light on some of the dark problems of humanity"? (219)

3. What does Herzl mean when he says "the distinctive nationality" of the Jews "cannot be destroyed, because external enemies consolidate it"? (223)

4. According to Herzl, how can the very idea of a Jewish State "have the requisite power" to bring it about? (225)

5. Why does Herzl argue that the countries Jews abandon "will revive to a new period of prosperity"? (225)

Does Herzl believe that the Jewish state he envisions is for all Jews or only those who have not already achieved economic freedoms?

1. If Herzl believes the Jewish question is a "national question," why does he say, "This is a private affair for the Jews alone"? (220, 223)

2. Why does Herzl believe that "the absorption of Jews by means of their prosperity is unlikely to occur?" (223)

3. Why does Herzl say that the concerns of the "poor and oppressed are of greater importance" than the concerns of "Jews who are in easy circumstances"? (222)

4. Why does Herzl think that his plan will be "contradicted and opposed by Jews in easy circumstances," rather than merely be ignored by them? (222)

FOR FURTHER REFLECTION

1. Is Herzl's description of how the phrase "Next year in Jerusalem" can be "converted into a living reality" a utopian ideal?

2. What does the term anti-Semitism mean today? In your opinion, is anti-Semitism increasing or decreasing in American society?

3. What defines "a people"? Do Americans think of themselves as "a people"?

Our Incomplete State

Utopian writers have often explored the nature of community and communal experience. Some have dreamt of a utopia based on strongly socialistic societies of collective ownership and forbidden private property, while others have explored communitarian social organization built around small cooperative groups. Since the nineteenth century both utopian and dystopian visions have been informed by socialism and its detractors, and vexed reactions to perceived centralization have gradually become a key element of the contested response to planned societies.

Robert Owen (1771–1858), a successful textile mill owner in New Lanark, Scotland, looked to radical ideas of communitarianism when modeling an ideal environment for his employees. In his third essay from "A New View of Society; or Essays on the Principle of the Formation of the Human Character, and the Application of the Principle to Practice" (1813–1816), he emphasizes the importance of children's play, opportunities for lifelong learning, and a secure, funded retirement. He enacted his proposals and principles in the factories and homes he established for over two thousand workers. Owen's efforts became a model for early socialists, but the sustainability of his model has been challenged. How could such radical notions, drawn from Enlightenment thinkers, function in the wider society of the time? How are his attitudes toward the welfare of his workers implemented or ignored today?

Later in the nineteenth century, Irish playwright **Oscar Wilde** (1854–1900) also asserted that socialism could foster creativity among workers in his essay "The Soul of Man Under Socialism" (1891). In contrast to Owen, Wilde's brand of socialism pointed toward an almost anarchical utopia. For Wilde, the abolition of private property would lead to greater individualism, and, in effect, to the freedom and time to devote one-self to art. With greater technological progress, machinery would take the place of menial labor, thus removing poverty and ugliness from the world. In his vision, as a consequence of the implementation of social-ism, all mankind would be free to focus on art and creativity. Did Wilde overestimate the benefits of industrialization, or can mechanization still offer an escape from poverty and a path to greater free time?

Vladimir Lenin (1870–1924), founder of the Russian Communist Party, saw implicit in the projected transition from capitalism to com-munism a necessary interim stage of "revolutionary dictatorship of the proletariat." In the selection included here, from chapter five of *The State and Revolution* (1917), he argues that this period of dictatorship by armed workers and peasants will be brief, prior to the achievement of true democracy. Lenin admits a "defect" to the change he advocates, and consciously dissociates himself from utopian thought. Does his preemptive defense against charges of utopianism prefigure some of the flaws with which opponents later charged the Soviet Union?

In his novel *We* (1924), Russian author **Yevgeny Zamyatin** (1884–1937) describes a futuristic society deeply repressive to the individual and to human relationships. Ruled by the totalitarian Well-Doer, the protago-nist D-503 can record his thoughts only in private "Records" that chart his periodic involvement with individuals attempting to overthrow the system. Zamyatin's satirical depiction was controversial at the time and not published in the Soviet Union until the 1950s. Yet, in his 1946 essay on *We*, George Orwell observed, "Writing at about the time of Lenin's death, he cannot have had the Stalin dictatorship in mind, and conditions in Russia in 1923 were not such that anyone would revolt against them on the ground that life was becoming too safe and comfortable. What Zamyatin seems to be aiming at is not any particular country, but the implied aims of industrial civilisation." Are these same issues of freedom and control at stake in all utopian and dystopian writing?

With strictly socialist societies now largely in demise around the world, other forms of shared community effort now similarly channel utopian thought. Are political movements such as Occupy and anti-globalization groups the new expressions of the socialist urge for shared communal values? Or are these movements themselves fundamentally opposed to socialism?

A New View of Society

(selection)

Robert Owen

Third Essay

The Principles of the Former Essays applied to a Particular Situation

Truth must ultimately prevail over error.

At the conclusion of the Second Essay, a promise was made that an account should be given of the plans which were in progress at New Lanark for the further improvement of its inhabitants; and that a practical system should be sketched, by which equal advantages might be generally introduced among the poor and working classes throughout the United Kingdom.

This account became necessary, in order to exhibit even a limited view of the principles on which the plans of the author are founded, and to recommend them generally to practice.

That which has been hitherto done for the community at New Lanark, as described in the Second Essay, has chiefly consisted in *withdrawing some of those circumstances which tended to generate, continue, or increase early bad habits; that is to say, undoing that which society had from ignorance permitted to be done.*

To effect this, however, was a far more difficult task than to train up a child from infancy in the way he should go; for that is the most easy process for the formation of character; while to unlearn and to change long acquired habits is a proceeding directly opposed to the most tenacious feelings of human nature.

Nevertheless, the proper application steadily pursued did effect beneficial changes on these old habits, even beyond the most sanguine expectations of the party by whom the task was undertaken.

The principles were driven from the study of human nature itself and they could not fail of success.

Still, however, very little, comparatively speaking, had been done for them. They had not been taught the most valuable domestic and social habits: such as the most economical method of preparing food; how to arrange their dwellings with neatness, and to keep them always clean and in order; but, what was of infinitely more importance, they had not been instructed how to train their children to form them into valuable members of the community, or to know that principles existed, which, when properly applied to practice from infancy, would ensure from man to man, without chance of failure, a just, open, sincere, and benevolent conduct.

It was in this stage of the progress of improvement, that it became necessary to form arrangements for surrounding them with circumstances which should gradually prepare the individuals to receive and firmly retain those domestic and social acquirements and habits. For this purpose a building, which may be termed the 'new institution', was erected in the centre of the establishment, with an enclosed area before it. The area is intended for a playground for the children of the villagers, from the time they can walk alone until they enter the school.

It must be evident to those who have been in the practice of observing children with attention, that much of good or evil is taught to or acquired by a child at a very early period of its life; that much of temper or disposition is correctly or incorrectly formed before he attains his second year; and that many durable impressions are made at the termination of the first twelve or even six months of his existence. The children, therefore, of the uninstructed and ill-instructed, suffer material injury in the formation of their characters during these and the subsequent years of childhood and of youth.

It was to prevent, or as much as possible to counteract, these primary evils, to which the poor and working classes are exposed when infants, that the area became part of the New Institution.

Into this playground the children are to be received as soon as they can freely walk alone; to be superintended by persons instructed to take charge of them.

As the happiness of man chiefly, if not altogether, depends on his own sentiments and habits, as well as those of the individuals around him; and as any sentiments and habits may be given to all infants, it becomes of primary importance that those alone should be given to them which can contribute to their happiness. Each child, therefore, on his entrance into the playground, is to be told in language which he can understand, that 'he is never to injure his playfellows; but that, on the contrary, he is to contribute all in his power to make them happy.' This simple precept, when comprehended in all its bearings, and the habits which will arise from its early adoption into practice, *if no counteracting principle be forced upon the young mind*, will effectually supersede all the errors which have hitherto kept the world in ignorance and misery. So simple a precept, too, will be easily taught, and as easily acquired; for the chief employment of the superintendents will be to prevent any deviation from it in practice. The older children, when they shall have experienced the endless advantages from acting on this principle, will, by their example, soon enforce the practice of it on the young strangers: and the happiness, which the little groups will enjoy from this rational conduct, will ensure its speedy and general and willing adoption. The habit also which they will acquire at this early period of life by continually acting on the principle, will fix it firmly; it will become easy and familiar to them, or, as it is often termed, natural.

Thus, by merely attending to the evidence of our senses respecting human nature, and disregarding the wild, inconsistent, and absurd theories in which man has been hitherto trained in all parts of the earth, we shall accomplish with ease and certainty the supposed Herculean labour of forming a rational character in man, and that, too, chiefly before the child commences the ordinary course of education.

The character thus early formed will be as durable as it will be advantageous to the individual and to the community; for by the constitution of our nature, when once the mind fully understands that which is true, the impression of that truth cannot be erased except by mental disease or death; while error must be relinquished at every period of life, whenever it can be made manifest to the mind in which it has been received. This part of the arrangement, therefore, will effect the following purposes:

The child will be removed, so far as is at present practicable, from the erroneous treatment of the yet untrained and untaught parents.

The parents will be relieved from the loss of time and from the care and anxiety which are now occasioned by attendance on their children from the period when they can go alone to that at which they enter the school.

The child will be placed in a situation of safety, where, with its future schoolfellows and companions, it will acquire the best habits and principles, while at mealtimes and at night it will return to the caresses of its parents; and the affections of each are likely to be increased by the separation.

The area is also to be a place of meeting for the children from five to ten years of age, previous to and after school-hours, and to serve for a drill-ground, the object of which will be hereafter explained; and a shade will be formed, under which in stormy weather the children may retire for shelter.

These are the important purposes to which a playground attached to a school may be applied.

Those who have derived a knowledge of human nature from observation know that man in every situation requires relaxation from his constant and regular occupations, whatever they be: and that if he shall not be provided with or permitted to enjoy innocent and uninjurious amusements, he must and will partake of those which he can obtain, to give him temporary relief from his exertions, although the means of gaining that relief should be most pernicious. For man, irrationally instructed, is ever influenced far more by immediate feelings than by remote considerations.

Those, then, who desire to give mankind the character which it would be for the happiness of all that they should possess, will not fail to make careful provision for their amusement and recreation.

The Sabbath was originally so intended. It was instituted to be a day of universal enjoyment and happiness to the human race. It is frequently made, however, from the opposite extremes of error, either a day of superstitious gloom and tyranny over the mind, or of the most destructive intemperance and licentiousness. The one of these has been the cause of the other; the latter the certain and natural consequence of the former. Relieve the human mind from useless and superstitious restraints; train it on those principles which facts, ascertained from the first knowledge of time to this day, demonstrate to be the only principles which are true; and intemperance and licentiousness will not exist; for such conduct in itself is neither the immediate nor the future interest of man; and he is ever governed by one or other of these considerations, according to the habits which have been given to him from infancy.

The Sabbath, in many parts of Scotland, is not a day of innocent and cheerful recreation to the labouring man; nor can those who are confined all the week to sedentary occupations, freely partake, without censure, of the air and exercise to which nature invites them, and which their health demands.

The errors of the times of superstition and bigotry still hold some sway, and compel those who wish to preserve a regard to their respectability in society, to an overstrained demeanour; and this demeanour sometimes degenerates into hypocrisy, and is often the cause of great inconsistency. It is destructive of every open, honest, generous, and manly feeling. It disgusts many, and drives them to the opposite extreme. It is sometimes the cause of insanity. It is founded on ignorance, and defeats its own object.

While erroneous customs prevail in any country, it would evince an ignorance of human nature in any individual to offend against them, until he has convinced the community of their error.

To counteract, in some degree, the inconvenience which arose from the misapplication of the Sabbath, it became necessary to introduce on the other days of the week some innocent amusement and recreation for those whose labours were unceasing, and in winter almost uniform. In summer, the inhabitants of the village of New Lanark have their gardens and potato grounds to cultivate; they have walks laid out to give them health and the habit of being gratified with the ever-changing scenes of nature—for those scenes afford not only the most economical, but also the most innocent pleasures which man can enjoy; and all men may be easily trained to enjoy them.

In winter the community are deprived of these healthy occupations and amusements; they are employed ten hours and three-quarters every day in the week, except Sunday, and generally every individual continues during that time at the same work: and experience has shown that the average health and spirits of the community are several degrees lower in winter than in summer; and this in part may be fairly attributed to that cause.

These considerations suggested the necessity of rooms for innocent amusements and rational recreation.

Many well-intentioned individuals, unaccustomed to witness the conduct of those among the lower orders who have been rationally treated and trained, may fancy such an assemblage will necessarily become a scene of confusion and disorder; instead of which, however, it proceeds with uniform propriety; it is highly favourable to the health, spirits, and dispositions of the individuals so engaged; and if any irregularity should arise, the cause will be solely owing to the parties who attempt to direct the proceedings being deficient in a practical knowledge of human nature.

It has been and ever will be found far more easy to lead mankind to virtue, or to rational conduct, by providing them with well-regulated innocent amusements and recreations, than by forcing them to submit to useless restraints, which tend only to create disgust, and often to connect such feelings even with that which is excellent in itself, merely because it has been judiciously associated.

Hitherto, indeed, in all ages and in all countries, man seems to have blindly conspired against the happiness of man, and to have remained as ignorant of himself as he was of the solar system prior to the days of Copernicus and Galileo.

Many of the learned and wise among our ancestors were conscious of this ignorance, and deeply lamented its effects; and some of them recommended the partial adoption of those principles which can alone relieve the world from the miserable effects of ignorance.

The time, however, for the emancipation of the human mind had not then arrived: the world was not prepared to receive it. The history of humanity shows it to be an undeviating law of nature, that man shall not prematurely break the shell of ignorance; that he must patiently wait until the principle of knowledge has pervaded the whole mass of the interior, to give it life and strength sufficient to bear the light of day.

Those who have duly reflected on the nature and extent of the mental movements of the world for the last half-century, must be conscious that great changes are in progress; that man is about to advance another important step towards that degree of intelligence which his natural powers seem capable of attaining. Observe the transactions of the passing hours; see the whole mass of mind in full motion; behold it momentarily increasing in vigour, and preparing ere long to burst its confinement. But what is to be the nature of this change? A due attention to the facts around us, and to those transmitted by the invention of printing from former ages, will afford a satisfactory reply.

From the earliest ages it has been the practice of the world to act on the supposition that each individual man forms his own character, and that therefore he is accountable for all his sentiments and habits, and consequently merits reward for some and punishment for others. Every system which has been established among men has been founded on these erroneous principles. When, however, they shall be brought to the test of fair examination, they will be found not only unsupported, but in direct opposition to all experience, and to the evidence of our senses.

This is not a slight mistake, which involves only trivial consequences; it is a fundamental error of the highest possible magnitude; it enters into all our proceedings regarding man from his infancy; and it will be found to be the true and sole origin of evil. It generates and perpetuates ignorance, hatred, and revenge, where, without such error, only intelligence, confidence, and kindness, would exist. It has hitherto been the Evil Genius of the world. It severs man from man throughout the various regions of the earth; and makes enemies of those who, but for this gross error, would have enjoyed each other's kind offices and sincere friendship. It is, in short, an error which carries misery in all its consequences.

This error cannot much longer exist; for every day will make it more and more evident *that the character of man is, without a single exception, always formed for him; that it may be, and is, chiefly created by his predecessors; that they give him, or may give him, his ideas and habits, which are the powers that govern and direct his conduct.*

Man, therefore, never did, nor is it possible he ever can, form his own character.

The knowledge of this important fact has not been derived from any of the wild and heated speculations of an ardent and ungoverned imagination; on the contrary, it proceeds from a long and patient study of the theory and practice of human nature, under many varied circumstances; it will be found to be a deduction drawn from such a multiplicity of facts, as to afford the most complete demonstration.

Had not mankind been misinstructed from infancy on this subject, making it necessary that they should unlearn what they have been taught, the simple statement of this truth would render it instantly obvious to every rational mind. Men would know that their predecessors might have given them the habits of ferocious cannibalism, or of the highest known benevolence and intelligence; and by the acquirement of this knowledge they would soon learn that, as parents, preceptors, and legislators united, they possess the means of training the rising generations to either of those extremes; that they may with the greatest certainty make them the conscientious worshippers of Juggernaut, or of the most pure spirit, possessing the essence of every excellence which the human imagination can conceive; that they may train the young to become effeminate, deceitful, ignorantly selfish, intemperate, revengeful, murderous—of course ignorant, irrational, and miserable; or to be manly, just, generous, temperate, active, kind, and benevolent—that is intelligent, rational, and happy. The knowledge of these principles having been derived from facts which perpetually exist, they defy ingenuity itself to confute them; nay, the most severe scrutiny will make it evident that they are utterly unassailable.

Is it then wisdom to think and to act in opposition to the facts which hourly exhibit themselves around us, and in direct contradiction to the evidence of our senses? Inquire of the most learned and wise of the present day, ask them to speak with sincerity, and they will tell you that they have long known the principles on which society has been found to be false. Hitherto, however, the tide of public opinion, in all countries, has been directed by a combination of prejudice, bigotry, and fanaticism, derived from the wildest imaginations of ignorance; and the most enlightened men have not dared to expose those errors which to them were offensive, prominent, and glaring.

Happily for man this reign of ignorance rapidly approaches to dissolution; its terrors are already on the wing, and soon they will be compelled to take their flight, never more to return. For now the knowledge of the existing errors is not only possessed by the learned and reflecting, but it is spreading far and wide throughout society; and ere long it will be fully comprehended even by the most ignorant.

Attempts may indeed be made by individuals, who through ignorance mistake their real interests, to retard the progress of this knowledge; but as it will prove itself to be in unison with the evidence of our senses, and therefore true beyond the possibility of disproof, it cannot be impeded, and in its course will overwhelm all opposition.

These principles, however, are not more true in theory than beneficial in practice, whenever they are properly applied. Why, then, should all their substantial advantages be longer withheld from the mass of mankind? Can it, by possibility, be a crime to pursue the only practical means which a rational being can adopt to diminish the misery of man, and increase his happiness?

These questions, of the deepest interest to society, are now brought to the fair test of public experiment. It remains to be proved, whether the character of man shall continue to be formed under the guidance of the most inconsistent notions, the errors of which for centuries past have been manifest to every reflecting rational mind; or whether it shall be moulded under the direction of uniformly consistent principles, derived from the unvarying facts of the creation; principles, the truth of which no sane man will now attempt to deny.

It is then by the full and complete disclosure of these principles, that the destruction of ignorance and misery is to be effected, and the reign of reason, intelligence, and happiness, is to be firmly established.

It was necessary to give this development of the principles advocated, that the remaining parts of the New Institution, yet to be described, may be clearly understood. We now proceed to explain the several purposes intended to be accomplished by the School, Lecture Room, and Church.

It must be evident to those who have any powers of reason yet undestroyed, that man is now taught and trained in a theory and practice directly opposed to each other. Hence the perpetual inconsistencies, follies, and absurdities, which everyone can readily discover in his neighbour, without being conscious that he also possesses similar incongruities. The instruction to be given in the School, Lecture Room, and Church, is intended to counteract and remedy this evil; and to prove the incalculable advantages which society would derive from the introduction of a theory and practice consistent with each other. The uppermost storey of the New Institution is arranged to serve for a School, Lecture Room, and Church. And these are intended to have a direct influence in forming the character of the villagers.

It is comparatively of little avail to give to either young or old 'precept upon precept, and line upon line', *except the means shall be also prepared to train them in good practical habits*. Hence an education for the untaught and ill-taught becomes of the first importance to the welfare of society; and it is this which has influenced all the arrangements connected with the New Institution.

The time the children will remain under the discipline of the playground and school, will afford all the opportunity that can be desired to create, cultivate, and establish, those habits and sentiments which tend to the welfare of the individual and of the community. And in conformity to this plan of proceeding, the precept which was given to the child of two years old, on coming into the playground, 'that he must endeavour to make his companions happy', is to be renewed and enforced on his entrance into the school: and the first duty of the schoolmaster will be to train his pupils to acquire the practice of always acting on this principle. It is a simple rule, the plain and obvious reasons for which children at an early age may be readily taught to comprehend, and as they advance in years, become familiarized with its practice, and experience the beneficial effects to themselves, they will better feel and understand all its important consequences to society.

Such then being the foundation on which the practical habits of the children are to be formed, we proceed to explain the superstructure.

In addition to the knowledge of the principle and practice of the above-mentioned precept, the boys and girls are to be taught in the school to read well, and to understand what they read; to write expeditiously a good legible hand; and to learn correctly, so that they may comprehend and use with facility the fundamental rules of arithmetic. The girls are also to be taught to sew, cut out, and make up useful family garments; and, after acquiring a sufficient knowledge of these, they are to attend in rotation in the public kitchen and eating rooms, to learn to prepare wholesome food in an economical manner, and to keep a house neat and well arranged.

It was said that the children are to be taught to read well, and to understand what they read.

In many schools, the children of the poor and labouring classes are never taught to understand what they read; the time therefore which is occupied in the mockery of the instruction is lost. In other schools, the children, through the ignorance of their instructors, are taught to believe without reasoning, and thus never to think or to reason correctly. These truly lamentable practices cannot fail to indispose the young mind for plain, simple, and rational instruction.

The books by which it is now the common custom to teach children to read, inform them of anything except that which, at their age, they ought to be taught; hence the inconsistencies and follies of adults. It is full time that this system should be changed. *Can man, when possessing the full vigour of his faculties, form a rational judgement on any subject, until he has first collected all the facts respecting it which are known? Has not this been, and will not this ever remain, the only path by which human knowledge can be obtained?* Then children ought to be instructed on the same principles. They should first be taught the knowledge of facts, commencing with those which are most familiar to the young mind, and gradually proceeding to the most useful and necessary to be known by the respective individuals in the rank of life in which they are likely to be placed; and in all cases the children should have as clear an explanation of each fact as their minds can comprehend, rendering those explanations more detailed as the child acquires strength and capacity of intellect.

As soon as the young mind shall be duly prepared for such instruction, the master should not allow any opportunity to escape, that would enable him to enforce the clear and inseparable connection which exists between the interest and happiness of each individual and the interest and happiness of every other individual. This should be the beginning and end of all instruction; and by degrees it will be so well understood by his pupils, that they will receive the same conviction of its truth, that those familiar with mathematics now entertain of the demonstrations of Euclid. And when thus comprehended, the all prevailing principle of known life, the desire of happiness, will compel them without deviation to pursue it in practice.

It is much to be regretted that the strength and capacity of the minds of children are yet unknown; their faculties have been hitherto estimated by the folly of instruction which has been given to them; while, if they were never taught to acquire error, they would speedily exhibit such powers of mind, as would convince the most incredulous how much the human intellect has been injured by the ignorance of former and present treatment.

It is therefore indeed important that the mind from its birth should receive those ideas only which are consistent with each other, which are in unison with all the known facts of the creation, and which are therefore true. Now, however, from the day they are born, the minds of children are impressed with false notions of themselves and of mankind; and in lieu of being conducted into the plain path leading to health and happiness, the utmost pains are taken to compel them to pursue an opposite direction, in which they can attain only inconsistency and error.

Let the plan which has now been recommended be steadily put in practice from infancy, *without counteraction from the systems of education which now exist*, and characters, even in youth, may be formed, that in true knowledge, and in every good and valuable quality, will not only greatly surpass the wise and learned of the present and preceding times, but will appear, as they really will be, a race of rational or superior beings. It is true, this change cannot be instantaneously established; it cannot be created by magic, or by a miracle; it must be effected gradually—and to accomplish it finally will prove a work of labour and of years. For those who have been misinstructed from infancy, who have now influence and are active in the world, and whose activity is directed by the false notions of their forefathers, will of course endeavour to obstruct the change. Those who have been systematically impressed with early errors, and conscientiously think them to be truths, will of necessity, while such errors remain, endeavour to perpetuate them in their children. Some simple but general method, therefore, becomes necessary to counteract as speedily as possible an evil of so formidable a magnitude.

It was this view of the subject which suggested the utility of preparing the means to admit of evening lectures in the New Institution; and it is intended they should be given, during winter, three nights in the week, alternately with dancing.

To the ill-trained and ill-taught these lectures may be made invaluable; and these are now numerous; for the far greater part of the population of the world has been permitted to pass the proper season for instruction without being trained to be rational; and they have acquired only the ideas and habits which proceed from ignorant association and erroneous instruction.

It is intended that the lectures should be familiar discourses, delivered in plain impressive language, to instruct the adult part of the community in the most useful practical parts of knowledge in which they are deficient, particularly in the proper method of training their children to become rational creatures; how to expend the earnings of their own labour to advantage; and how to appropriate the surplus gains which will be left to them, in order to create a fund which will relieve them from the anxious fear of future want, and thus give them, under the many errors of the present system, that rational confidence in their own exertions and good conduct, without which, consistency of character or domestic comfort cannot be obtained, and ought not to be expected. The young people may be also questioned relative to their progress in useful knowledge, and allowed to ask for explanations. In short, these lectures may be made to convey, in an amusing and agreeable manner, highly valuable and substantial information to those who are now the most ignorant in the community; and by similar means, which at a trifling expense may be put into action over the whole kingdom, the most important benefits may be given to the labouring classes, and through them, to the whole mass of society.

For it should be considered that *the far greater part of the population belong to or have risen from the labouring classes; and by them the happiness and comfort of all ranks, not excluding the highest, are very essentially influenced*: because even much more of the character of children in all families is formed by the servants, than is ever supposed by those unaccustomed to trace with attention the human mind from earliest infancy. It is indeed impossible that children in any situation can be correctly trained, until those who surround them from infancy shall be previously well instructed; and the value of good servants may be duly appreciated by those who have experienced the difference between the very good and very bad.

The last part of the intended arrangement of the New Institution remains yet to be described. This is the Church and its doctrines; and they involve considerations of the highest interest and importance; inasmuch as a knowledge of truth on the subject of religion would permanently establish the happiness of man; for it is the inconsistencies alone, proceeding from the want of this knowledge, which have created, and still create, a great proportion of the miseries which exist in the world.

The only certain criterion of truth is, that it is ever consistent with itself; it remains one and the same under every view and comparison of it which can be made; while error will not stand the test of this investigation and comparison, because it ever leads to absurd conclusions.

Those whose minds are equal to the subject will, ere this, have discovered, that the principles in which mankind have been hitherto instructed, and by which they have been governed, will not bear the test of this criterion. Investigate and compare them; they betray absurdity, folly, and weakness; hence the infinity of jarring opinions, dissensions, and miseries, which have hitherto prevailed.

Had any one of the various opposing systems which have governed the world and disunited man from man, been true, without any mixture of error—that system, very speedily after its public promulgation, would have pervaded society, and compelled all men to have acknowledged its truth.

The criterion, however, which has been stated, shows, that they are all, without an exception, in part inconsistent with the works of nature; that is, with the facts which exist around us. Those systems therefore must have contained some fundamental errors; and it is utterly impossible for man to become rational, or enjoy the happiness he is capable of attaining, until those errors are exposed and annihilated.

Each of those systems contains some truth with more error; hence it is that no one of them has gained, or is likely to gain, universality.

The truth which the several systems possess, serves to cover and perpetuate the errors which they contain; but those errors are most obvious to all who have not from infancy been taught to receive them.

Is proof demanded? Ask, in succession, those who are esteemed the most intelligent and enlightened of every sect and party, what is their opinion of every other sect and party throughout the world. Is it not evident that, without one exception, the answer will be, that they all contain errors so clearly in opposition to reason and equity, that he can only feel pity and deep commiseration for the individuals whose minds have been thus perverted and rendered irrational? And this reply they will all make, unconscious that they themselves are of the number whom they commiserate.

The doctrines which have been taught to every known sect, combined with the external circumstances by which they have been surrounded, have been directly calculated, and could not fail, to produce the characters which have existed. And the doctrines in which the inhabitants of the world are now instructed, combined with the external circumstances by which they are surrounded, form the characters which at present pervade society.

The doctrines which have been and now are taught throughout the world, must necessarily create and perpetuate, and they do create and perpetuate, a total want of mental charity among men. They also generate superstitions, bigotry, hypocrisy, hatred, revenge, wars, and all their evil consequences. For it has been and is a fundamental principle in every system hitherto taught, with exceptions more nominal than real, 'That man will possess merit, and receive eternal reward, by believing the doctrines of that peculiar system; that he will be eternally punished if he disbelieves them; that all those innumerable individuals also, who, through time, have been taught to believe other than the tenets of this system, must be doomed to eternal misery.' Yet nature itself, in all its works, is perpetually operating to convince man of such gross absurdities.

Yes, my deluded fellow men, believe me, for your future happiness, that the facts around us, when you shall observe them aright, will make it evident, even to demonstration, that all such doctrines must be erroneous, because THE WILL OF MAN HAS NO POWER WHATEVER OVER HIS OPINIONS; HE MUST, AND EVER DID, AND EVER WILL BELIEVE WHAT HAS

BEEN, IS, OR MAY BE IMPRESSED ON HIS MIND BY HIS PREDECESSORS AND THE CIRCUMSTANCES WHICH SURROUND HIM. It becomes therefore the essence of irrationality to suppose that any human being, from the creation to this day, could deserve praise or blame, reward or punishment, for the prepossessions of early education.

It is from these fundamental errors, in all systems which have been hitherto taught to the mass of mankind, that the misery of the human race has to so great an extent proceeded; for, in consequence of them, man has been always instructed from infancy to believe impossibilities—he is still taught to pursue the same insane course, and the result still is misery. Let this source of wretchedness, the most lamentable of all errors, this scourge of the human race, be publicly exposed; and let those just principles be introduced, which prove themselves true by their uniform consistency and the evidence of our senses; hence insincerity, hatred, revenge, and even a wish to injure a fellow creature, will ere long be unknown; and mental charity, heartfelt benevolence, and acts of kindness to one another, will be the distinguished characters of human nature.

Shall then misery most complicated and extensive be experienced, from the prince to the peasant, in all nations throughout the world, and shall its cause and prevention be known, and yet withheld? The knowledge of this cause, however, cannot be communicated to mankind without offending against the deep-rooted prejudices of all. The work is therefore replete with difficulties, which can alone be overcome by those who, foreseeing all its important practical advantages, may be induced to contend against them.

Yet, difficult as it may be to establish this grand truth generally throughout society, on account of the dark and gross errors in which the world to this period has been instructed, it will be found, whenever the subject shall undergo a full investigation, that the principles now brought forward cannot, by possibility, injure any class of men, or even a single individual. On the contrary, there is not one member of the great family of the world, from the highest to the lowest, that will not derive the most important benefits from its public promulgation. And when such incalculable, substantial, and permanent advantages are clearly seen and strongly felt, shall individual considerations be for a moment put in competition with its attainment? No!

Ease, comfort, the good opinion of part of society, and even life itself, may be sacrificed to those prejudices; and yet the principles on which this knowledge is founded must ultimately and universally prevail.

This high event, of unequalled magnitude in the history of humanity, is thus confidently predicted, because the knowledge whence that confidence proceeds is not derived from any of the uncertain legends of the days of dark and gross ignorance, but from the plain and obvious facts which now exist throughout the world. Due attention to these facts, to these truly revealed works of nature, will soon instruct, or rather compel mankind to discover the universal errors in which they have been trained.

The principle, then, on which the doctrines taught in the New Institution are proposed to be founded, is, that they shall be in unison with universally revealed facts, which cannot but be true.

The following are some of the facts, which, with a view to this part of the undertaking, may be deemed fundamental:

That man is born with a desire to obtain happiness, which desire is the primary cause of all his actions, continues through life, and, in popular language, is called self-interest.

That he is also born with the germs of animal propensities, or the desire to sustain, enjoy, and propagate life; and which desires, as they grow and develop themselves, are termed his natural inclinations.

That he is born likewise with faculties which, in their growth, receive, convey, compare, and become conscious of receiving and comparing ideas.

That the ideas so received, conveyed, compared, and understood, constitute human knowledge, or mind, which acquires strength and maturity with the growth of the individual.

That the desire of happiness in man, the germs of his natural inclinations, and the faculties by which he acquires knowledge, are formed unknown to himself in the womb; and whether perfect or imperfect, they are alone the immediate work of the Creator, and over which the infant and future man have no control.

That these inclinations and faculties are not formed exactly alike in any two individuals; hence the diversity of talents, and the varied impressions called liking and disliking which the same external objects make on different persons, and the lesser varieties which exist among men whose characters have been formed apparently under similar circumstances.

That the knowledge which man receives is derived from the objects around him, and chiefly from the example and instruction of his immediate predecessors.

That this knowledge may be limited or extended, erroneous or true; limited, when the individual receives few, and extended when he receives many ideas; erroneous, when those ideas are inconsistent with the facts which exist around him, and true when they are uniformly consistent with them.

That the misery which he experiences, and the happiness which he enjoys, depend on the kind and degree of knowledge which he receives, and on that which is possessed by those around him.

That when the knowledge which he receives is true and unmixed with error, although it be limited, if the community in which he lives possesses the same kind and degree of knowledge, he will enjoy happiness in proportion to the extent of that knowledge. On the contrary, when the opinions which he receives are erroneous, and the opinions possessed by the community in which he resides are equally erroneous, his misery will be in proportion to the extent of those erroneous opinions.

That when the knowledge which man receives shall be extended to its utmost limit, and true without any mixture of error, then he may and will enjoy all the happiness of which his nature will be capable.

That it consequently becomes of the first and highest importance that man should be taught to distinguish truth from error.

That man has no other means of discovering what is false, except by his faculty of reason, or the power of acquiring and comparing the ideas which he receives.

That when this faculty is properly cultivated or trained from infancy, and the child is rationally instructed to retain no impressions or ideas which by his powers of comparing them appear to be inconsistent, then the individual will acquire real knowledge, or those ideas only which will leave an impression of their consistency or truth on all minds which have not been rendered irrational by an opposite procedure.

That the reasoning faculty may be injured and destroyed during its growth, by reiterated impressions being made upon it of notions not derived from realities, and which it therefore cannot compare with the ideas previously received from the objects around it. And when the mind receives these notions which it cannot comprehend, along with those ideas which it is conscious are true and which yet are inconsistent with such notions, then the reasoning faculties become injured, the individual is taught or forced to believe, and not to think or reason, and partial insanity or defective powers of judging ensue.

That all men are thus erroneously trained at present, and hence the inconsistencies and misery of the world.

That the fundamental errors now impressed from infancy on the minds of all men, and from whence all their other errors proceed, are, that they form their own individual characters, and possess merit or demerit for the peculiar notions impressed on the mind during its early growth, before they have acquired strength and experience to judge of or resist the impression of those notions or opinions, which, on investigation, appear contradictions to facts existing around them, and which are therefore false.

That these false notions have ever produced evil and misery in the world; and that they still disseminate them in every direction.

That the sole cause of their existence hitherto has been man's ignorance of human nature: while their consequences have been all the evil and misery, except those of accidents, disease, and death, with which man has been and is afflicted: and that the evil and misery which arise from accidents, disease, and death, are also greatly increased and extended by man's ignorance of himself.

That, in proportion as man's desire of self-happiness, or his self-love, is directed by true knowledge, those actions will abound which are virtuous and beneficial to man; that in proportion as it is influenced by false notions, or the absence of true knowledge, those actions will prevail which generate crimes, from whence arises an endless variety of misery; and, consequently, that every rational means should be now adopted to detect error, and to increase true knowledge among men.

That when these truths are made evident, every individual will necessarily endeavour to promote the happiness of every other individual within his sphere of action; because he must clearly, and without any doubt, comprehend such conduct to be the essence of self-interest, or the true cause of self-happiness.

Here, then, is a firm foundation on which to erect vital religion, pure and undefiled, and the only one which, without any counteracting evil, can give peace and happiness to man.

It is to bring into practical operation, in forming the character of men, these most important of all truths, that the religious part of the Institution at New Lanark will be chiefly directed, and such are the fundamental principles upon which the Instructor will proceed. They are thus publicly avowed before all men, that they may undergo discussion and the most severe scrutiny and investigation.

Let those, therefore, who are esteemed the most learned and wise, throughout the various states and empires in the world, examine them to their foundation, compare them with every fact which exists, and if the shadow of inconsistency and falsehood be discovered, let it be publicly exposed, that error may not more abound.

But should they withstand this extended ordeal, and prove themselves uniformly consistent with every known fact, and therefore true, then let it be declared, that man may be permitted by man to become rational, and that the misery of the world may be speedily removed.

Having alluded to the chief uses of the playground and exercise rooms, with the School, Lecture Room, and Church, it remains, to complete the account of the New Institution, that the object of the drill exercises mentioned when stating the purposes of the playground, should be explained; and to this we now proceed.

Were all men trained to be rational, the art of war would be rendered useless. While, however, any part of mankind shall be taught that they form their own characters, and shall continue to be trained from infancy to think and act irrationally—that is, to acquire feelings of enmity, and to deem it a duty to engage in war against those who have been instructed to differ from them in sentiments and habits—even the most rational must, for their personal security, learn the means of defence; and every community of such characters, while surrounded by men who have been thus improperly taught, should acquire a knowledge of this destructive art, that they may be enabled to overrule the actions of irrational beings, and maintain peace.

To accomplish these objects to the utmost practical limit, and with the least inconvenience, every male should be instructed how best to defend, when attacked, the community to which he belongs. And these advantages are only to be obtained by providing proper means for the instruction of all boys in the use of arms and the arts of war.

As an example how easily and effectually this might be accomplished over the British Isles, it is intended that the boys trained and educated at the Institution at New Lanark shall be thus instructed; that the person appointed to attend the children in the playground shall be qualified to drill and teach the boys the manual exercise, and that he shall be frequently so employed; that afterwards, firearms, of proportionate weight and size to the age and strength of the boys, shall be provided for them, when also they might be taught to practise and understand the more complicated military movements.

This exercise, properly administered, will greatly contribute to the health and spirits of the boys, give them an erect and proper form, and habits of attention, celerity, and order. They will, however, be taught to consider this exercise, an art, rendered absolutely necessary by the partial insanity of some of their fellow creatures who by the errors of their predecessors, transmitted through preceding generations, have been taught to acquire feelings of enmity, increasing to madness, against those who could not avoid differing from them in sentiments and habits; that this art should never be brought into practice except to restrain the violence of such madmen; and, in these cases, that it should be administered with the least possible severity, and solely to prevent the evil consequences of those rash acts of the insane, and, if possible, to cure them of their disease.

Thus, in a few years, by foresight and arrangement, may almost the whole expense and inconvenience attending the local military be superseded, and a permanent force created, which in numbers, discipline, and principles, would be superior, beyond all comparison, for the purposes of defence; always ready in case of need, yet without the loss which is now sustained by the community of efficient and valuable labour. The expenditure which would be saved by this simple expedient, would be far more than competent to educate the whole of the poor and labouring classes of these kingdoms.

There is still another arrangement in contemplation for the community at New Lanark, and without which the establishment will remain incomplete.

It is an expedient to enable the individuals, by their own foresight, prudence, and industry, to secure to themselves in old age a comfortable provision and asylum.

Those now employed at the establishment contribute to a fund which supports them when too ill to work, or superannuated. This fund, however, is not calculated to give them more than a bare existence; and it is surely desirable that, after they have spent nearly half a century in unremitting industry, they should, if possible, enjoy a comfortable independence.

To effect this object, it is intended that in the most pleasant situation near the present village, neat and convenient dwellings should be erected, with gardens attached; that they should be surrounded and sheltered by plantations, through which public walks should be formed; and the whole arranged to give the occupiers the most substantial comforts.

That these dwellings, with the privileges of the public walks, etc., shall become the property of those individuals who, without compulsion, shall subscribe each equitable sums monthly, as, in a given number of years will be equal to the purchase, and to create a fund from which, when these individuals become occupiers of their new residences they may receive weekly, monthly, or quarterly payments, sufficient for their support; the expenses of which may be reduced to a very low rate individually, by arrangements which may be easily formed to supply all their wants with little trouble to themselves; and by their previous instruction they will be enabled to afford the small additional subscription which will be required for these purposes.

This part of the arrangement would always present a prospect of rest, comfort, and happiness to those employed; in consequence, their daily occupations would be performed with more spirit and cheerfulness, and their labour would appear comparatively light and easy. Those still engaged in active operations would, of course, frequently visit their former companions and friends, who, after having spent their years of toil, were in the actual enjoyment of this simple retreat; and from this intercourse each party would naturally derive pleasure. The reflections of each would be most gratifying. The old would rejoice that they had been trained in habits of industry, temperance, and foresight, to enable them to receive and enjoy in their declining years every reasonable comfort which the present state of society will admit; the young and middle-aged, that they were pursuing the same course, and that they had not been trained to waste their money, time, and health, in idleness and intemperance. These and many similar reflections could not fail often to arise in their minds; and those who could look forward with confident hopes to such certain comfort and independence would, in part, enjoy by anticipation these advantages. In short, when this part of the arrangement is well considered, it will be found to be the most important to the community and to the proprietors; indeed, the extensively good effects of it will be experienced in such a variety of ways, that to describe them even below the truth would appear an extravagant exaggeration. They will not, however, prove the less true because mankind are yet ignorant of the practice, and of the principles on which it has been founded.

These, then, are the plans which are in progress or intended for the further improvement of the inhabitants of New Lanark. They have uniformly proceeded from the principles which have been developed through these Essays, restrained, however, hitherto, in their operations, by the local sentiments and unfounded notions of the community and neighbourhood, and by the peculiar circumstances of the establishment.

In every measure to be introduced at the place in question, for the comfort and happiness of man, the existing errors of the country were always to be considered; and as the establishment belonged to parties whose views were various, it became also necessary to devise means to create pecuniary gains from each improvement, sufficient to satisfy the spirit of commerce.

All, therefore, which has been done for the happiness of this community, which consists of between two and three thousand individuals, is far short of what might have been easily effected in practice had not mankind been previously trained in error. Hence, in devising these plans, the sole consideration was not, what were the measures dictated by these principles, which would produce the greatest happiness to man; but what could be effected in practice under the present irrational systems by which these proceedings were surrounded?

Imperfect, however, as these proceedings must yet be, in consequence of the formidable obstructions enumerated, they will yet appear, upon a full minute investigation by minds equal to the comprehension of such a system, to combine a greater degree of substantial comfort to the individuals employed in the manufactory, and of pecuniary profit to the proprietors, than has hitherto been found attainable.

But to whom can such arrangements be submitted? Not to the mere commercial character, in whose estimation to forsake the path of immediate individual gain would be to show symptoms of a disordered imagination; for the children of commerce have been trained to direct all their faculties to buy cheap and sell dear; and consequently, those who are the most expert and successful in this wise and noble art, are, in the commercial world, deemed to possess foresight and superior acquirements; while such as attempt to improve the moral habits and increase the comforts of those whom they employ, are termed wild enthusiasts.

Nor yet are they to be submitted to the mere men of the law; for these are necessarily trained to endeavour to make wrong appear right, or to involve both in a maze of intricacies, and to legalize injustice.

Nor to mere political leaders or their partisans; for they are embarrassed by the trammels of party, which mislead their judgement, and often constrain them to sacrifice the real well-being of the community and of themselves, to an apparent but most mistaken self-interest.

Nor to those termed heroes and conquerors, or to their followers; for their minds have been trained to consider the infliction of human misery, and the commission of military murders, a glorious duty, almost beyond reward.

Nor yet to the fashionable or splendid in their appearance; for these are from infancy trained to deceive and to be deceived, to accept shadows for substances, and to live a life of insincerity, and of consequent discontent and misery.

Still less are they to be exclusively submitted to the official expounders and defenders of the various opposing religious systems throughout the world; for many of these are actively engaged in propagating imaginary notions, which cannot fail to vitiate the rational powers of man, and to perpetuate his misery.

These principles, therefore, and the practical systems which they recommend, are not to be submitted to the judgement of those who have been trained under, and continue in, any of these unhappy combinations of circumstances. But they are to be submitted to the dispassionate and patient investigation and decision of those individuals of every rank and class and denomination of society, who have become in some degree conscious of the errors in which they exist; who have felt the thick mental darkness by which they are surrounded; who are ardently desirous of discovering and following truth wherever it may lead; and who can perceive the inseparable connection which exists between individual and general, between private and public good!

It has been said, and it is now repeated, that these principles, thus combined, will prove themselves unerringly true against the most insidious or open attack; and, ere long, they will, by their irresistible truth, pervade society to the utmost bounds of the earth; for 'silence will not retard their progress, and opposition will give increased celerity to their movements'. When they shall have dissipated in some degree, as they speedily will dissipate, the thick darkness in which the human mind has been and is still enveloped, the endless beneficial consequences which must follow the general introduction of them into practice may then be explained in greater detail, and urged upon minds to which they will then appear less questionable.

QUESTIONS FOR DISCUSSION

Why does Owen emphasize that New Lanark will put the principles he advocates "to the fair test of public experiment"? (241)

1. Why does Owen believe that the playground of the New Institution will "prevent" and "counteract" the "primary evils, to which the poor and working classes are exposed when infants"? (234)

2. Why are there rooms in New Lanark set aside "for innocent amusements and rational recreation"? (238)

3. Why does Owen highlight New Lanark's "School, Lecture Room, and Church"? (241)

4. Why does Owen believe that the boys of New Lanark need to be instructed in military drill exercises?

Why is Owen confident that the principles he outlines will create "a race of rational or superior beings"? (244)

1. Why does Owen suggest that "in all ages and in all countries, man seems to have blindly conspired against the happiness of man"? (238)

2. On what grounds does Owen believe that the time "for the emancipation of the human mind" is arriving? (238)

3. According to Owen, why is the belief that each individual forms his own character "the true and sole origin of evil"? (239)

4. Why does Owen believe that the "irresistible truth" of the principles he is explaining will overcome all opposition? (257)

FOR FURTHER REFLECTION

1. Do you agree with Owen that man *"never did, nor is it possible he ever can, form his own character"*?

2. Do you believe that today "man is about to advance another important step towards that degree of intelligence which his natural powers seem capable of attaining"?

3. Is the proper test of truth that "it is ever consistent with itself" and "remains one and the same under every view and comparison of it which can be made"?

4. Which of the "universally revealed facts" that Owen lists do you accept as true?

The Soul of Man Under Socialism

Oscar Wilde

The chief advantage that would result from the establishment of Socialism is, undoubtedly, the fact that Socialism would relieve us from that sordid necessity of living for others which, in the present condition of things, presses so hardly upon almost everybody. In fact, scarcely anyone at all escapes.

Now and then, in the course of the century, a great man of science, like Darwin; a great poet like Keats; a fine critical spirit like M. Renan; a supreme artist like Flaubert, has been able to isolate himself, to keep himself out of reach of the clamorous claims of others, to stand 'under the shelter of the wall', as Plato puts it, and so to realize the perfection of what was in him, to his own incomparable gain, and to the incomparable and lasting gain of the whole world. These, however, are exceptions. The majority of people spoil their lives by an unhealthy and exaggerated altruism—are forced, indeed, so to spoil them. They find themselves surrounded by hideous poverty, by hideous ugliness, by hideous starvation. It is inevitable that they should be strongly moved by all this. The emotions of man are stirred more quickly than man's intelligence; and, as I pointed out some time ago in an article on the function of criticism, it is much more easy to have sympathy with suffering than it is to have sympathy with thought. Accordingly, with admirable, though misdirected intentions, they very seriously and very sentimentally set themselves to the task of remedying the evils that they see. But their remedies do not cure the disease: they merely prolong it. Indeed, their remedies are part of the disease.

They try to solve the problem of poverty, for instance, by keeping the poor alive; or, in the case of a very advanced school, by amusing the poor.

But this is not a solution: it is an aggravation of the difficulty. The proper aim is to try and reconstruct society on such a basis that poverty will be impossible. And the altruistic virtues have really prevented the carrying out of this aim. Just as the worst slave-owners were those who were kind to their slaves, and so prevented the horror of the system being realized by those who suffered from it, and understood by those who contemplated it, so, in the present state of things in England, the people who do most harm are the people who try to do most good; and at last we have had the spectacle of men who have really studied the problem and know the life—educated men who live in the East End—coming forward and imploring the community to restrain its altruistic impulses of charity, benevolence, and the like. They do so on the ground that such charity degrades and demoralizes. They are perfectly right. Charity creates a multitude of sins.

There is also this to be said. It is immoral to use private property in order to alleviate the horrible evils that result from the institution of private property. It is both immoral and unfair.

Under Socialism all this will, of course, be altered. There will be no people living in fetid dens and fetid rags, and bringing up unhealthy, hunger-pinched children in the midst of impossible and absolutely repulsive surroundings. The security of society will not depend, as it does now, on the state of the weather. If a frost comes we shall not have a hundred thousand men out of work, tramping about the streets in a state of disgusting misery, or whining to their neighbours for alms, or crowding round the doors of loathsome shelters to try and secure a hunch of bread and a night's unclean lodging. Each member of the society will share in the general prosperity and happiness of the society, and if a frost comes no one will practically be anything the worse.

Upon the other hand, Socialism itself will be of value simply because it will lead to Individualism.

Socialism, Communism, or whatever one chooses to call it, by converting private property into public wealth, and substituting co-operation for competition, will restore society to its proper condition of a thoroughly healthy organism, and ensure the material well-being of each member of the community. It will, in fact, give Life its proper basis and its proper environment. But, for the full development of Life to its highest mode of perfection, something more is needed. What is needed is Individualism. If the Socialism is Authoritarian; if there are Governments armed with economic power as they are now with political power; if, in a word, we are to have Industrial Tyrannies, then the last state of man will be worse than the first. At present, in consequence of the existence of private property, a great many people are enabled to develop a certain very limited amount of Individualism. They are either under no necessity to work for their living, or are enabled to choose the sphere of activity that is really congenial to them, and gives them pleasure. These are the poets, the philosophers, the men of science, the men of culture—in a word, the real men, the men who have realized themselves, and in whom all Humanity gains a partial realization. Upon the other hand, there are a great many people who, having no private property of their own, and being always on the brink of sheer starvation, are compelled to do the work of beasts of burden, to do work that is quite uncongenial to them, and to which they are forced by the peremptory, unreasonable, degrading Tyranny of want. These are the poor; and amongst them there is no grace of manner, or charm of speech, or civilization, or culture, or refinement in pleasures, or joy of life. From their collective force Humanity gains much in material prosperity. But it is only the material result that it gains, and the man who is poor is in himself absolutely of no importance. He is merely the infinitesimal atom of a force that, so far from regarding him, crushes him: indeed, prefers him crushed, as in that case he is far more obedient.

Of course, it might be said that the Individualism generated under conditions of private property is not always, or even as a rule, of a fine or wonderful type, and that the poor, if they have not culture and charm, have still many virtues. Both these statements would be quite true. The possession of private property is very often extremely demoralizing, and that is, of course, one of the reasons why Socialism wants to get rid of the institution. In fact, property is really a nuisance. Some years ago people went about the country saying that property has duties. They said it so often and so tediously that, at last, the Church has begun to say it. One hears it now from every pulpit. It is perfectly true. Property not merely has duties, but has so many duties that its possession to any large extent is a bore. It involves endless claims upon one, endless attention to business, endless bother. If property had simply pleasures, we could stand it; but its duties make it unbearable. In the interest of the rich we must get rid of it. The virtues of the poor may be readily admitted, and are much to be regretted. We are often told that the poor are grateful for charity. Some of them are, no doubt, but the best amongst the poor are never grateful. They are ungrateful, discontented, disobedient, and rebellious. They are quite right to be so. Charity they feel to be a ridiculously inadequate mode of partial restitution, or a sentimental dole, usually accompanied by some impertinent attempt on the part of the sentimentalist to tyrannize over their private lives. Why should they be grateful for the crumbs that fall from the rich man's table? They should be seated at the board, and are beginning to know it. As for being discontented, a man who would not be discontented with such surroundings and such a low mode of life would be a perfect brute. Disobedience, in the eyes of anyone who has read history, is man's original virtue. It is through disobedience that progress has been made, through disobedience and through rebellion. Sometimes the poor are praised for being thrifty. But to recommend thrift to the poor is both grotesque and insulting. It is like advising a man who is starving to eat less. For a town or country labourer to practise thrift would be absolutely immoral. Man should not be ready to show that he can live like a badly fed animal. He should decline to live like that, and should either steal or go on the rates, which is considered by many to be a form of stealing. As for begging, it is safer to beg than to take, but it is finer to take than to beg. No: a poor man who is ungrateful, unthrifty, discontented, and rebellious, is probably a real personality, and has much in him. He is at any rate a healthy protest. As for the virtuous poor, one can pity them, of course, but one cannot possibly admire them. They have made private terms with the enemy, and sold their birthright for very bad pottage. They must also be extraordinarily stupid. I can quite understand a man accepting laws that protect private property, and admit of its accumulation, as long as he himself is able under those conditions to realize some form of beautiful and intellectual life. But it is almost incredible to me how a man whose life is marred and made hideous by such laws can possibly acquiesce in their continuance.

However, the explanation is not really difficult to find. It is simply this. Misery and poverty are so absolutely degrading, and exercise such a paralysing effect over the nature of men, that no class is ever really conscious of its own suffering. They have to be told of it by other people, and they often entirely disbelieve them. What is said by great employers of labour against agitators is unquestionably true. Agitators are a set of interfering, meddling people, who come down to some perfectly contented class of the community, and sow the seeds of discontent amongst them. That is the reason why agitators are so absolutely necessary. Without them, in our incomplete state, there would be no advance towards civilization. Slavery was put down in America, not in consequence of any action on the part of the slaves, or even any express desire on their part that they should be free. It was put down entirely through the grossly illegal conduct of certain agitators in Boston and elsewhere, who were not slaves themselves, nor owners of slaves, nor had anything to do with the question really. It was, undoubtedly, the Abolitionists who set the torch alight, who began the whole thing. And it is curious to note that from the slaves themselves they received, not merely very little assistance, but hardly any sympathy even; and when at the close of the war the slaves found themselves free, found themselves indeed so absolutely free that they were free to starve, many of them bitterly regretted the new state of things. To the thinker, the most tragic fact in the whole of the French Revolution is not that Marie Antoinette was killed for being a queen, but that the starved peasant of the Vendée voluntarily went out to die for the hideous cause of feudalism.

It is clear, then, that no Authoritarian Socialism will do. For while under the present system a very large number of people can lead lives of a certain amount of freedom and expression and happiness, under an industrial-barrack system, or a system of economic tyranny, nobody would be able to have any such freedom at all. It is to be regretted that a portion of our community should be practically in slavery, but to propose to solve the problem by enslaving the entire community is childish. Every man must be left quite free to choose his own work. No form of compulsion must be exercised over him. If there is, his work will not be good for him, will not be good in itself, and will not be good for others. And by work I simply mean activity of any kind.

I hardly think that any Socialist, nowadays, would seriously propose that an inspector should call every morning at each house to see that each citizen rose up and did manual labour for eight hours. Humanity has got beyond that stage, and reserves such a form of life for the people whom, in a very arbitrary manner, it chooses to call criminals. But I confess that many of the socialistic views that I have come across seem to me to be tainted with ideas of authority, if not of actual compulsion. Of course, authority and compulsion are out of the question. All association must be quite voluntary. It is only in voluntary associations that man is fine.

But it may be asked how Individualism, which is now more or less dependent on the existence of private property for its development, will benefit by the abolition of such private property. The answer is very simple. It is true that, under existing conditions, a few men who have had private means of their own, such as Byron, Shelley, Browning, Victor Hugo, Baudelaire, and others, have been able to realize their personality, more or less completely. Not one of these men ever did a single day's work for hire. They were relieved from poverty. They had an immense advantage. The question is whether it would be for the good of Individualism that such an advantage should be taken away. Let us suppose that it is taken away. What happens then to Individualism? How will it benefit?

It will benefit in this way. Under the new conditions Individualism will be far freer, far finer, and far more intensified than it is now. I am not talking of the great imaginatively realized Individualism of such poets as I have mentioned, but of the great actual Individualism latent and potential in mankind generally. For the recognition of private property has really harmed Individualism, and obscured it, by confusing a man with what he possesses. It has led Individualism entirely astray. It has made gain, not growth, its aim. So that man thought that the important thing was to have, and did not know that the important thing is to be. The true perfection of man lies, not in what man has, but in what man is. Private property has crushed true Individualism, and set up an Individualism that is false. It has debarred one part of the community from being individual by starving them. It has debarred the other part of the community from being individual by putting them on the wrong road, and encumbering them. Indeed, so completely has man's personality been absorbed by his possessions that the English law has always treated offences against a man's property with far more severity than offences against his person, and property is still the test of complete citizenship. The industry necessary for the making of money is also very demoralizing. In a community like ours, where property confers immense distinction, social position, honour, respect, titles, and other pleasant things of the kind, man, being naturally ambitious, makes it his aim to accumulate this property, and goes on wearily and tediously accumulating it long after he has got far more than he wants, or can use, or enjoy, or perhaps even know of. Man will kill himself by overwork in order to secure property, and really, considering the enormous advantages that property brings, one is hardly surprised. One's regret is that society should be constructed on such a basis that man has been forced into a groove in which he cannot freely develop what is wonderful, and fascinating, and delightful in him—in which, in fact, he misses the true pleasure and joy of living. He is also, under existing conditions, very insecure. An enormously wealthy merchant may be—often is—at every moment of his life at the mercy of things that are not under his control. If the wind blows an extra point or so, or the weather suddenly changes, or some trivial thing happens, his ship may go down, his speculations may go wrong, and he finds himself a poor man, with his social position quite gone. Now, nothing should be able to harm a man except himself. Nothing should be able to rob a man at all. What a man really has, is what is in him. What is outside of him should be a matter of no importance.

With the abolition of private property, then, we shall have true, beautiful, healthy Individualism. Nobody will waste his life in accumulating things, and the symbols for things. One will live. To live is the rarest thing in the world. Most people exist, that is all.

It is a question whether we have ever seen the full expression of a personality, except on the imaginative plane of art. In action, we never have. Caesar, says Mommsen, was the complete and perfect man. But how tragically insecure was Caesar! Wherever there is a man who exercises authority, there is a man who resists authority. Caesar was very perfect, but his perfection travelled by too dangerous a road. Marcus Aurelius was the perfect man, says Renan. Yes, the great emperor was a perfect man. But how intolerable were the endless claims upon him! He staggered under the burden of the empire. He was conscious how inadequate one man was to bear the weight of that Titan and too vast orb. What I mean by a perfect man is one who develops under perfect conditions; one who is not wounded, or worried, or maimed, or in danger. Most personalities have been obliged to be rebels. Half their strength has been wasted in friction. Byron's personality, for instance, was terribly wasted in its battle with the stupidity and hypocrisy and Philistinism of the English. Such battles do not always intensify strength; they often exaggerate weakness. Byron was never able to give us what he might have given us. Shelley escaped better. Like Byron, he got out of England as soon as possible. But he was not so well known. If the English had realized what a great poet he really was, they would have fallen on him with tooth and nail, and made his life as unbearable to him as they possibly could. But he was not a remarkable figure in society, and consequently he escaped, to a certain degree. Still, even in Shelley the note of rebellion is sometimes too strong. The note of the perfect personality is not rebellion, but peace.

It will be a marvellous thing—the true personality of man—when we see it. It will grow naturally and simply, flowerlike, or as a tree grows. It will not be at discord. It will never argue or dispute. It will not prove things. It will know everything. And yet it will not busy itself about knowledge. It will have wisdom. Its value will not be measured by material things. It will have nothing. And yet it will have everything, and whatever one takes from it, it will still have, so rich will it be. It will not be always meddling with others, or asking them to be like itself. It will love them because they will be different. And yet while it will not meddle with others, it will help all, as a beautiful thing helps us, by being what it is. The personality of man will be very wonderful. It will be as wonderful as the personality of a child.

In its development it will be assisted by Christianity, if men desire that; but if men do not desire that, it will develop none the less surely. For it will not worry itself about the past, nor care whether things happened or did not happen. Nor will it admit any laws but its own laws; nor any authority but its own authority. Yet it will love those who sought to intensify it, and speak often of them. And of these Christ was one.

'Know thyself!' was written over the portal of the antique world. Over the portal of the new world 'Be thyself' shall be written. And the message of Christ to man was simply 'Be thyself.' That is the secret of Christ.

When Jesus talks about the poor he simply means personalities, just as when he talks about the rich he simply means people who have not developed their personalities. Jesus moved in a community that allowed the accumulation of private property just as ours does, and the gospel that he preached was, not that in such a community it is an advantage for a man to live on scanty, unwholesome food, to wear ragged, unwholesome clothes, to sleep in horrid, unwholesome dwellings, and a disadvantage for a man to live under healthy, pleasant, and decent conditions. Such a view would have been wrong there and then, and would, of course, be still more wrong now and in England; for as man moves northward the material necessities of life become of more vital importance, and our society is infinitely more complex, and displays far greater extremes of luxury and pauperism than any society of the antique world. What Jesus meant was this. He said to man, 'You have a wonderful personality. Develop it. Be yourself. Don't imagine that your perfection lies in accumulating or possessing external things. Your affection is inside of you. If only you could realize that, you would not want to be rich. Ordinary riches can be stolen from a man. Real riches cannot. In the treasury-home of your soul, there are infinitely precious things, that may not be taken from you. And so, try to so shape your life that external things will not harm you. And try also to get rid of personal property. It involves sordid preoccupation, endless industry, continual wrong. Personal property hinders Individualism at every step.' It is to be noted that Jesus never says that impoverished people are necessarily good, or wealthy people necessarily bad. That would not have been true. Wealthy people are, as a class, better than impoverished people, more moral, more intellectual, more well-behaved. There is only one class in the community that thinks more about money than the rich, and that is the poor. The poor can think of nothing else. That is the misery of being poor. What Jesus does say, is that man reaches his perfection, not through what he has, not even through what he does, but entirely through what he is. And so the wealthy young man who comes to Jesus is represented as a thoroughly good citizen, who has broken none of the laws of his state, none of the commandments of his religion. He is quite respectable, in the ordinary sense of that extraordinary word. Jesus says to him, 'You should give up private property. It hinders you from realizing your perfection. It is a drag upon you. It is a burden. Your personality does not need it. It is within you, and not outside of you, that you will find what you really are, and what you really want.' To his own friends he says the same thing. He tells them to be themselves, and not to be always worrying about other things. What do other things matter? Man is complete in himself. When they go into the world, the world will disagree with them. That is inevitable. The world hates Individualism. But that is not to trouble them. They are to be calm and self-centred. If a man takes their cloak, they are to give him their coat, just to show that material things are of no importance. If people abuse them, they are not to answer back. What does it signify? The things people say of a man do not alter a man. He is what he is. Public opinion is of no value whatsoever. Even if people employ actual violence, they are not to be violent in turn. That would be to fall to the same low level. After all, even in prison, a man can be quite free. His soul can be free. His personality can be untroubled. He can be at peace. And, above all things, they are not to interfere with other people or judge them in any way. Personality is a very mysterious thing. A man cannot always be estimated by what he does. He may keep the law, and yet be worthless. He may break the law, and yet be fine. He may be bad, without ever doing anything bad. He may commit a sin against society, and yet realize through that sin his true perfection.

There was a woman who was taken in adultery. We are not told the history of her love, but that love must have been very great; for Jesus said that her sins were forgiven her, not because she repented, but because her love was so intense and wonderful. Later on, a short time before his death, as he sat at a feast, the woman came in and poured costly perfumes on his hair. His friends tried to interfere with her, and said that it was extravagance, and that the money that the perfume cost should have been expended on charitable relief of people in want, or something of that kind. Jesus did not accept that view. He pointed out that the material needs of Man were great and very permanent, but that the spiritual needs of Man were greater still, and that in one divine moment, and by selecting its own mode of expression, a personality might make itself perfect. The world worships the woman, even now, as a saint.

Yes, there are suggestive things in Individualism. Socialism annihilates family life, for instance. With the abolition of private property, marriage in its present form must disappear. This is part of the programme. Individualism accepts this and makes it fine. It converts the abolition of legal restraint into a form of freedom that will help the full development of personality, and make the love of man and woman more wonderful, more beautiful, and more ennobling. Jesus knew this. He rejected the claims of family life, although they existed in his day and community in a very marked form. 'Who is my mother? Who are my brothers?' he said, when he was told that they wished to speak to him. When one of his followers asked leave to go and bury his father, 'Let the dead bury the dead,' was his terrible answer. He would allow no claim whatsoever to be made on personality.

And so he who would lead a Christlike life is he who is perfectly and absolutely himself. He may be a great poet, or a great man of science, or a young student at a University, or one who watches sheep upon a moor; or a maker of dramas, like Shakespeare, or a thinker about God, like Spinoza; or a child who plays in a garden, or a fisherman who throws his net into the sea. It does not matter what he is, as long as he realizes the perfection of the soul that is within him. All imitation in morals and in life is wrong. Through the streets of Jerusalem at the present day crawls one who is mad and carries a wooden cross on his shoulders. He is a symbol of the lives that are marred by imitation. Father Damien was Christlike when he went out to live with the lepers, because in such service he realized fully what was best in him. But he was not more Christlike than Wagner when he realized his soul in music; or than Shelley, when he realized his soul in song. There is no one type for man. There are as many perfections as there are imperfect men. And while to the claims of charity a man may yield and yet be free, to the claims of conformity no man may yield and remain free at all.

Individualism, then, is what through Socialism we are to attain. As a natural result, the State must give up all idea of government. It must give it up because, as a wise man once said many centuries before Christ, there is such a thing as leaving mankind alone; there is no such thing as governing mankind. All modes of government are failures. Despotism is unjust to everybody, including the despot, who was probably made for better things. Oligarchies are unjust to the many, and ochlocracies are unjust to the few. High hopes were once formed of democracy; but democracy means simply the bludgeoning of the people by the people for the people. It has been found out. I must say that it was high time, for all authority is quite degrading. It degrades those who exercise it, and degrades those over whom it is exercised. When it is violently, grossly, and cruelly used, it produces a good effect, by creating, or at any rate bringing out, the spirit of revolt and Individualism that is to kill it. When it is used with a certain amount of kindness, and accompanied by prizes and rewards, it is dreadfully demoralizing. People, in that case, are less conscious of the horrible pressure that is being put on them, and so go through their lives in a sort of coarse comfort, like petted animals, without ever realizing that they are probably thinking other people's thoughts, living by other people's standards, wearing practically what one may call other people's second-hand clothes, and never being themselves for a single moment. 'He who would be free', says a fine thinker, 'must not conform.' And authority, by bribing people to conform, produces a very gross kind of overfed barbarism amongst us.

With authority, punishment will pass away. This will be a great gain—a gain, in fact, of incalculable value. As one reads history, not in the expurgated editions written for schoolboys and passmen, but in the original authorities of each time, one is absolutely sickened, not by the crimes that the wicked have committed, but by the punishments that the good have inflicted; and a community is infinitely more brutalized by the habitual employment of punishment than it is by the occasional occurrence of crime. It obviously follows that the more punishment is inflicted the more crime is produced, and most modern legislation has clearly recognized this, and has made it its task to diminish punishment as far as it thinks it can. Wherever it has really diminished it, the results have always been extremely good.

The less punishment, the less crime. When there is no punishment at all, crime will either cease to exist, or, if it occurs, will be treated by physicians as a very distressing form of dementia, to be cured by care and kindness. For what are called criminals nowadays are not criminals at all. Starvation, and not sin, is the parent of modern crime. That indeed is the reason why our criminals are, as a class, so absolutely uninteresting from any psychological point of view. They are not marvellous Macbeths and terrible Vautrins. They are merely what ordinary respectable, commonplace people would be if they had not got enough to eat. When private property is abolished there will be no necessity for crime, no demand for it; it will cease to exist. Of course, all crimes are not crimes against property, though such are the crimes that the English law, valuing what a man has more than what a man is, punishes with the harshest and most horrible severity (if we except the crime of murder, and regard death as worse than penal servitude, a point on which our criminals, I believe, disagree). But though a crime may not be against property, it may spring from the misery and rage and depression produced by our wrong system of property-holding, and so, when that system is abolished, will disappear. When each member of the community has sufficient for his wants, and is not interfered with by his neighbour, it will not be an object of any interest to him to interfere with anyone else. Jealousy, which is an extraordinary source of crime in modern life, is an emotion closely bound up with our conceptions of property, and under Socialism and Individualism will die out. It is remarkable that in communistic tribes jealousy is entirely unknown.

Now as the State is not to govern, it may be asked what the State is to do. The State is to be a voluntary association that will organize labour, and be the manufacturer and distributor of necessary commodities. The State is to make what is useful. The individual is to make what is beautiful. And as I have mentioned the word labour, I cannot help saying that a great deal of nonsense is being written and talked nowadays about the dignity of manual labour. There is nothing necessarily dignified about manual labour at all, and most of it is absolutely degrading. It is mentally and morally injurious to man to do anything in which he does not find pleasure, and many forms of labour are quite pleasureless activities, and should be regarded as such. To sweep a slushy crossing for eight hours on a day when the east wind is blowing is a disgusting occupation. To sweep it with mental, moral, or physical dignity seems to me to be impossible. To sweep it with joy would be appalling. Man is made for something better than disturbing dirt. All work of that kind should be done by a machine.

And I have no doubt that it will be so. Up to the present, man has been, to a certain extent, the slave of machinery, and there is something tragic in the fact that as soon as man had invented a machine to do his work he began to starve. This, however, is, of course, the result of our property system and our system of competition. One man owns a machine which does the work of five hundred men. Five hundred men are, in consequence, thrown out of employment, and, having no work to do, become hungry and take to thieving. The one man secures the produce of the machine and keeps it, and has five hundred times as much as he should have, and probably, which is of much more importance, a great deal more than he really wants. Were that machine the property of all, everybody would benefit by it. It would be an immense advantage to the community. All unintellectual labour, all monotonous, dull labour, all labour that deals with dreadful things, and involves unpleasant conditions, must be done by machinery. Machinery must work for us in coal mines, and do all sanitary services, and be the stoker of steamers, and clean the streets, and run messages on wet days, and do anything that is tedious or distressing. At present machinery competes against man. Under proper conditions machinery will serve man. There is no doubt at all that this is the future of machinery; and just as trees grow while the country gentleman is asleep, so while Humanity will be amusing itself, or enjoying cultivated leisure—which, and not labour, is the aim of man—or making beautiful things, or reading beautiful things, or simply contemplating the world with admiration and delight, machinery will be doing all the necessary and unpleasant work. The fact is, that civilization requires slaves. The Greeks were quite right there. Unless there are slaves to do the ugly, horrible, uninteresting work, culture and contemplation become almost impossible. Human slavery is wrong, insecure, and demoralizing. On mechanical slavery, on the slavery of the machine, the future of the world depends. And when scientific men are no longer called upon to go down to a depressing

East End and distribute bad cocoa and worse blankets to starving people, they will have delightful leisure in which to devise wonderful and marvellous things for their own joy and the joy of everyone else. There will be great storages of force for every city, and for every house if required, and this force man will convert into heat, light, or motion, according to his needs. Is this Utopian? A map of the world that does not include Utopia is not worth even glancing at, for it leaves out the one country at which Humanity is always landing. And when Humanity lands there, it looks out, and, seeing a better country, sets sail. Progress is the realization of Utopias.

Now, I have said that the community by means of organization of machinery will supply the useful things, and that the beautiful things will be made by the individual. This is not merely necessary, but it is the only possible way by which we can get either the one or the other. An individual who has to make things for the use of others, and with reference to their wants and their wishes, does not work with interest, and consequently cannot put into his work what is best in him. Upon the other hand, whenever a community or a powerful section of a community, or a government of any kind, attempts to dictate to the artist what he is to do, Art either entirely vanishes, or becomes stereotyped, or degenerates into a low and ignoble form of craft. A work of art is the unique result of a unique temperament. Its beauty comes from the fact that the author is what he is. It has nothing to do with the fact that other people want what they want. Indeed, the moment that an artist takes notice of what other people want, and tries to supply the demand, he ceases to be an artist, and becomes a dull or an amusing craftsman, an honest or a dishonest tradesman. He has no further claim to be considered as an artist. Art is the most intense mode of Individualism that the world has known. I am inclined to say that it is the only real mode of Individualism that the world has known. Crime, which, under certain conditions, may seem to have created Individualism, must take cognizance of other people and interfere with them. It belongs to the sphere of action. But alone, without any reference to his neighbours, without any interference the artist can fashion a beautiful thing; and if he does not do it solely for his own pleasure, he is not an artist at all.

And it is to be noted that it is the fact that Art is this intense form of Individualism that makes the public try to exercise over it an authority that is as immoral as it is ridiculous, and as corrupting as it is contemptible. It is not quite their fault. The public has always, and in every age, been badly brought up. They are continually asking Art to be popular, to please their want of taste, to flatter their absurd vanity, to tell them what they have been told before, to show them what they ought to be tired of seeing, to amuse them when they feel heavy after eating too much, and to distract their thoughts when they are wearied of their own stupidity. Now Art should never try to be popular. The public should try to make itself artistic. There is a very wide difference. If a man of science were told that the results of his experiments, and the conclusions that he arrived at, should be of such a character that they would not upset the received popular notions on the subject, or disturb popular prejudice, or hurt the sensibilities of people who knew nothing about science; if a philosopher were told that he had a perfect right to speculate in the highest spheres of thought, provided that he arrived at the same conclusions as were held by those who had never thought in any sphere at all—well, nowadays the man of science and the philosopher would be considerably amused. Yet it is really a very few years since both philosophy and science were subjected to brutal popular control, to authority in fact—the authority of either the general ignorance of the community, or the terror and greed for power of an ecclesiastical or governmental class. Of course, we have to a very great extent got rid of any attempt on the part of the community, or the Church, or the Government, to interfere with the individualism of speculative thought, but the attempt to interfere with the individualism of imaginative art still lingers. In fact, it does more than linger; it is aggressive, offensive, and brutalizing.

In England, the arts that have escaped best are the arts in which the public take no interest. Poetry is an instance of what I mean. We have been able to have fine poetry in England because the public do not read it, and consequently do not influence it. The public like to insult poets because they are individual, but once they have insulted them, they leave them alone. In the case of the novel and the drama, arts in which the public do take an interest, the result of the exercise of popular authority has been absolutely ridiculous. No country produces such badly written fiction, such tedious, common work in the novel form, such silly, vulgar plays as England. It must necessarily be so. The popular standard is of such a character that no artist can get to it. It is at once too easy and too difficult to be a popular novelist. It is too easy, because the requirements of the public as far as plot, style, psychology, treatment of life, and treatment of literature are concerned are within the reach of the very meanest capacity and the most uncultivated mind. It is too difficult, because to meet such requirements the artist would have to do violence to his temperament, would have to write not for the artistic joy of writing, but for the amusement of half-educated people, and so would have to suppress his individualism, forget his culture, annihilate his style, and surrender everything that is valuable in him. In the case of the drama, things are a little better: the theatre-going public like the obvious, it is true, but they do not like the tedious; and burlesque and farcical comedy, the two most popular forms, are distinct forms of art. Delightful work may be produced under burlesque and farcical conditions, and in work of this kind the artist in England is allowed very great freedom. It is when one comes to the higher forms of the drama that the result of popular control is seen. The one thing that the public dislike is novelty. Any attempt to extend the subject-matter of art is extremely distasteful to the public; and yet the vitality and progress of art depend in a large measure on the continual extension of subject-matter. The public dislike novelty because they are afraid of it. It represents to them a mode of Individualism, an assertion on the part of the artist that he selects his own subject, and treats it as he chooses. The public are quite right in their attitude. Art is Individualism, and Individualism is a disturbing and disintegrating force. Therein lies its immense value. For what it seeks to disturb is monotony of type, slavery of custom, tyranny of habit, and the reduction of man to the level of a machine. In Art, the public accept what has been, because they cannot alter it, not because they appreciate it. They swallow their classics whole, and never taste them. They endure them as the inevitable, and as they cannot mar them, they mouth about them. Strangely enough, or not strangely, according to one's own views, this acceptance of the classics does a great deal of harm. The uncritical admiration of the Bible and Shakespeare in England is an instance of what I mean. With regard to the Bible, considerations of ecclesiastical authority enter into the matter, so that I need not dwell upon the point.

But in the case of Shakespeare it is quite obvious that the public really see neither the beauties nor the defects of his plays. If they saw the beauties, they would not object to the development of the drama; and if they saw the defects, they would not object to the development of the drama either. The fact is, the public make use of the classics of a country as a means of checking the progress of Art. They degrade the classics into authorities. They use them as bludgeons for preventing the free expression of Beauty in new forms. They are always asking a writer why he does not write like somebody else, or a painter why he does not paint like somebody else, quite oblivious of the fact that if either of them did anything of the kind he would cease to be an artist. A fresh mode of Beauty is absolutely distasteful to them, and whenever it appears they get so angry and bewildered that they always use two stupid expressions—one is that the work of art is grossly unintelligible; the other, that the work of art is grossly immoral. What they mean by these words seems to me to be this. When they say a work is grossly unintelligible, they mean that the artist has said or made a beautiful thing that is new; when they describe a work as grossly immoral, they mean that the artist has said or made a beautiful thing that is true. The former expression has reference to style; the latter to subject-matter. But they probably use the words very vaguely, as an ordinary mob will use ready-made paving-stones. There is not a single real poet or prose-writer of this century, for instance, on whom the British public have not solemnly conferred diplomas of immorality, and these diplomas practically take the place, with us, of what in France is the formal recognition of an Academy of Letters, and fortunately make the establishment of such an institution quite unnecessary in England. Of course, the public are very reckless in their use of the word. That they should have called Wordsworth an immoral poet, was only to be expected. Wordsworth was a poet. But that they should have called Charles Kingsley an immoral novelist is extraordinary. Kingsley's prose was not of a very fine quality. Still, there is the word, and they use it as best they can. An artist is, of course, not disturbed by it. The true artist is a man who believes absolutely in himself, because he is absolutely himself. But I can fancy that if an artist produced a work of art in England that immediately on its appearance was recognized by the public, through their medium, which is the public Press, as a work that was quite intelligible and highly moral, he would begin seriously to question whether in its creation he had really been himself at all, and consequently whether the work was not quite unworthy of him, and either of a thoroughly second-rate order, or of no artistic value whatsoever.

Perhaps, however, I have wronged the public in limiting them to such words as 'immoral', 'unintelligible', 'exotic', and 'unhealthy'. There is one other word that they use. That word is 'morbid'. They do not use it often. The meaning of the word is so simple that they are afraid of using it. Still, they use it sometimes, and, now and then, one comes across it in popular newspapers. It is, of course, a ridiculous word to apply to a work of art. For what is morbidity but a mood of emotion or a mode of thought that one cannot express? The public are all morbid, because the public can never find expression for anything. The artist is never morbid. He expresses everything. He stands outside his subject, and through its medium produces incomparable and artistic effects. To call an artist morbid because he deals with morbidity as his subject-matter is as silly as if one called Shakespeare mad because he wrote *King Lear*.

On the whole, an artist in England gains something by being attacked. His individuality is intensified. He becomes more completely himself. Of course, the attacks are very gross, very impertinent, and very contemptible. But then no artist expects grace from the vulgar mind, or style from the suburban intellect. Vulgarity and stupidity are two very vivid facts in modern life. One regrets them, naturally. But there they are. They are subjects for study, like everything else. And it is only fair to state, with regard to modern journalists, that they always apologize to one in private for what they have written against one in public.

Within the last few years two other adjectives, it may be mentioned, have been added to the very limited vocabulary of art-abuse that is at the disposal of the public. One is the word 'unhealthy', the other is the word 'exotic'. The latter merely expresses the rage of the momentary mushroom against the immortal, entrancing, and exquisitely lovely orchid. It is a tribute, but a tribute of no importance. The word 'unhealthy', however, admits of analysis. It is a rather interesting word. In fact, it is so interesting that the people who use it do not know what it means.

What does it mean? What is a healthy or an unhealthy work of art? All terms that one applies to a work of art, provided that one applies them rationally, have reference to either its style or its subject, or to both together. From the point of view of style, a healthy work of art is one whose style recognizes the beauty of the material it employs, be that material one of words or of bronze, of colour or of ivory, and uses that beauty as a factor in producing the aesthetic effect. From the point of view of subject, a healthy work of art is one the choice of whose subject is conditioned by the temperament of the artist, and comes directly out of it. In fine, a healthy work of art is one that has both perfection and personality. Of course, form and substance cannot be separated in a work of art; they are always one. But for purposes of analysis, and setting the wholeness of aesthetic impression aside for a moment, we can intellectually so separate them. An unhealthy work of art, on the other hand, is a work whose style is obvious, old-fashioned and common, and whose subject is deliberately chosen, not because the artist has any pleasure in it, but because he thinks that the public will pay him for it. In fact, the popular novel that the public call healthy is always a thoroughly unhealthy production; and what the public call an unhealthy novel is always a beautiful and healthy work of art.

I need hardly say that I am not, for a single moment, complaining that the public and the public Press misuse these words. I do not see how, with their lack of comprehension of what Art is, they could possibly use them in the proper sense. I am merely pointing out the misuse; and as for the origin of the misuse and the meaning that lies behind it all, the explanation is very simple. It comes from the barbarous conception of authority. It comes from the natural inability of a community corrupted by authority to understand or appreciate Individualism. In a word, it comes from that monstrous and ignorant thing that is called Public Opinion, which, bad and well-meaning as it is when it tries to control action, is infamous and of evil meaning when it tries to control Thought or Art.

Indeed, there is much more to be said in favour of the physical force of the public than there is in favour of the public's opinion. The former may be fine. The latter must be foolish. It is often said that force is no argument. That, however, entirely depends on what one wants to prove. Many of the most important problems of the last few centuries, such as the continuance of personal government in England, or of feudalism in France, have been solved entirely by means of physical force. The very violence of a revolution may make the public grand and splendid for a moment. It was a fatal day when the public discovered that the pen is mightier than the paving-stone, and can be made as offensive as the brickbat. They at once sought for the journalist, found him, developed him, and made him their industrious and well-paid servant. It is greatly to be regretted, for both their sakes. Behind the barricade there may be much that is noble and heroic. But what is there behind the leading-article but prejudice, stupidity, cant and twaddle? And when these four are joined together they make a terrible force, and constitute the new authority.

In the old days men had the rack. Now they have the Press. That is an improvement certainly. But still it is very bad, and wrong, and demoralizing. Somebody—was it Burke?—called journalism the fourth estate. That was true at the time, no doubt. But at the present moment it really is the only estate. It has eaten up the other three. The Lords Temporal say nothing, the Lords Spiritual have nothing to say, and the House of Commons has nothing to say and says it. We are dominated by Journalism. In America the President reigns for four years, and Journalism governs for ever and ever. Fortunately, in America, Journalism has carried its authority to the grossest and most brutal extreme. As a natural consequence it has begun to create a spirit of revolt. People are amused by it, or disgusted by it, according to their temperaments. But it is no longer the real force it was. It is not seriously treated. In England, Journalism, except in a few well-known instances, not having been carried to such excesses of brutality, is still a great factor, a really remarkable power. The tyranny that it proposes to exercise over people's private lives seems to me to be quite extraordinary. The fact is that the public have an insatiable curiosity to know everything, except what is worth knowing. Journalism, conscious of this, and having tradesman-like habits, supplies their demands. In centuries before ours the public nailed the ears of journalists to the pump. That was quite hideous. In this century journalists have nailed their own ears to the keyhole. That is much worse. And what aggravates the mischief is that the journalists who are most to blame are not the amusing journalists who write for what are called Society papers. The harm is done by the serious, thoughtful, earnest journalists, who solemnly, as they are doing at present, will drag before the eyes of the public some incident in the private life of a great statesman, of a man who is a leader of political thought as he is a creator of political force, and invite the public to discuss the incident, to exercise authority in the matter, to give their views, and not merely to give their views, but to carry them into action, to dictate to the man upon all other points, to dictate to his party, to dictate to his country; in fact, to make themselves ridiculous, offensive, and harmful. The private lives of men and women should not be told to the public. The public have nothing to do with them at all.

In France they manage these things better. There they do not allow the details of the trials that take place in the divorce courts to be published for the amusement or criticism of the public. All that the public are allowed to know is that the divorce has taken place and was granted on petition of one or other or both of the married parties concerned. In France, in fact, they limit the journalist, and allow the artist almost perfect freedom. Here we allow absolute freedom to the journalist and entirely limit the artist. English public opinion, that is to say, tries to constrain and impede and warp the man who makes things that are beautiful in effect, and compels the journalist to retail things that are ugly, or disgusting, or revolting in fact, so that we have the most serious journalists in the world and the most indecent newspapers. It is no exaggeration to talk of compulsion. There are possibly some journalists who take a real pleasure in publishing horrible things, or who, being poor, look to scandals as forming a sort of permanent basis for an income. But there are other journalists, I feel certain, men of education and cultivation, who really dislike publishing these things, who know that it is wrong to do so, and only do it because the unhealthy conditions under which their occupation is carried on oblige them to supply the public with what the public wants, and to compete with other journalists in making that supply as full and satisfying to the gross popular appetite as possible. It is a very degrading position for any body of educated men to be placed in, and I have no doubt that most of them feel it acutely.

However, let us leave what is really a very sordid side of the subject, and return to the question of popular control in the matter of

Art, by which I mean Public Opinion dictating to the artist the form which he is to use, the mode in which he is to use it, and the materials with which he is to work. I have pointed out that the arts which have escaped best in England are the arts in which the public have not been interested. They are, however, interested in the drama, and as a certain advance has been made in the drama within the last ten or fifteen years, it is important to point out that this advance is entirely due to a few individual artists refusing to accept the popular want of taste as their standard, and refusing to regard Art as a mere matter of demand and supply. With his marvellous and vivid personality, with a style that has really a true colour-element in it, with his extraordinary power, not over mere mimicry but over imaginative and intellectual creation, Mr Irving, had his sole object been to give the public what they wanted, could have produced the commonest plays in the commonest manner, and made as much success and money as a man could possibly desire. But his object was not that. His object was to realize his own perfection as an artist, under certain conditions and in certain forms of Art. At first he appealed to the few: now he has educated the many. He has created in the public both taste and temperament. The public appreciate his artistic success immensely. I often wonder, however, whether the public understand that that success is entirely due to the fact that he did not accept their standard, but realized his own. With their standard the Lyceum would have been a sort of second-rate booth, as some of the popular theatres in London are at present. Whether they understand it or not, the fact however remains, that taste and temperament have, to a certain extent, been created in the public, and that the public is capable of developing these qualities. The problem then is, why do not the public become more civilized? They have the capacity. What stops them?

The thing that stops them, it must be said again, is their desire to exercise authority over the artists and over works of art. To certain theatres, such as the Lyceum and the Haymarket, the public seem to come in a proper mood. In both of these theatres there have been individual artists, who have succeeded in creating in their audiences—and every theatre in London has its own audience—the temperament to which Art appeals. And what is that temperament? It is the temperament of receptivity. That is all.

If a man approaches a work of art with any desire to exercise authority over it and the artist, he approaches it in such a spirit that he cannot receive any artistic impression from it at all. The work of art is to dominate the spectator: the spectator is not to dominate the work of art. The spectator is to be receptive. He is to be the violin on which the master is to play. And the more completely he can suppress his own silly views, his own foolish prejudices, his own absurd ideas of what Art should be, or should not be, the more likely he is to understand and appreciate the work of art in question. This is, of course, quite obvious in the case of the vulgar theatre-going public of English men and women. But it is equally true of what are called educated people. For an educated person's ideas of Art are drawn naturally from what Art has been, whereas the new work of art is beautiful by being what Art has never been; and to measure it by the standard of the past is to measure it by a standard on the rejection of which its real perfection depends. A temperament capable of receiving, through an imaginative medium, and under imaginative conditions, new and beautiful impressions, is the only temperament that can appreciate a work of art. And true as this is in the case of the appreciation of sculpture and painting, it is still more true of the appreciation of such arts as the drama. For a picture and a statue are not at war with Time. They take no account of its succession. In one moment their unity may be apprehended. In the case of literature it is different. Time must be traversed before the unity of effect is realized. And so, in the drama, there may occur in the first act of the play something whose real artistic value may not be evident to the spectator till the third or fourth act is reached. Is the silly fellow to get angry and call out, and disturb the play, and annoy the artists? No. The honest man is to sit quietly, and know the delightful emotions of wonder, curiosity, and suspense. He is not to go to the play to lose a vulgar temper. He is to go to the play to realize an artistic temperament. He is to go to the play to gain an artistic temperament. He is not the arbiter of the work of art. He is one who is admitted to contemplate the work of art, and, if the work be fine, to forget in its contemplation all the egotism that mars him—the egotism of his ignorance, or the egotism of his information. The point about the drama is hardly, I think, sufficiently recognized. I can quite understand that were *Macbeth* produced for the first time before a modern London audience, many of the people present would strongly and vigorously object to the introduction of the witches in the first act, with their grotesque phrases and their ridiculous words. But when the play is over one realizes that the laughter of the witches in *Macbeth* is as terrible as the laughter of madness in *Lear*, more terrible than the laughter of Iago in the tragedy of the Moor. No spectator of art needs a more perfect mood of receptivity than the spectator of a play. The moment he seeks to exercise authority he becomes the avowed enemy of Art, and of himself. Art does not mind. It is he who suffers.

With the novel it is the same thing. Popular authority and the recognition of popular authority are fatal. Thackeray's *Esmond* is a beautiful work of art because he wrote it to please himself. In his other novels, in *Pendennis*, in *Philip*, in *Vanity Fair* even, at times, he is too conscious of the public, and spoils his work by appealing directly to the sympathies of the public, or by directly mocking at them. A true artist takes no notice whatever of the public. The public are to him non-existent. He has no poppied or honeyed cakes through which to give the monster sleep or sustenance. He leaves that to the popular novelist. One incomparable novelist we have now in England, Mr George Meredith. There are better artists in France, but France has no one whose view of life is so large, so varied, so imaginatively true. There are tellers of stories in Russia who have a more vivid sense of what pain in fiction may be. But to him belongs philosophy in fiction. His people not merely live, but they live in thought. One can see them from myriad points of view. They are suggestive. There is soul in them and around them. They are interpretative and symbolic. And he who made them, those wonderful, quickly moving figures, made them for his own pleasure, and has never asked the public what they wanted, has never cared to know what they wanted, has never allowed the public to dictate to him or influence him in any way, but has gone on intensifying his own personality, and producing his own individual work. At first none came to him. That did not matter. Then the few came to him. That did not change him. The many have come now. He is still the same. He is an incomparable novelist.

With the decorative arts it is not different. The public clung with really pathetic tenacity to what I believe were the direct traditions of the Great Exhibition of international vulgarity, traditions that were so appalling that the houses in which people lived were only fit for blind people to live in. Beautiful things began to be made, beautiful colours came from the dyer's hand, beautiful patterns from the artist's brain, and the use of beautiful things and their value and importance were set forth. The public were really very indignant. They lost their temper. They said silly things. No one minded. No one was a whit the worse. No one accepted the authority of public opinion. And now it is almost impossible to enter any modern house without seeing some recognition of good taste, some recognition of the value of lovely surroundings, some sign of appreciation of beauty. In fact, people's houses are, as a rule, quite charming nowadays. People have been to a very great extent civilized. It is only fair to state, however, that the extraordinary success of the revolution in house-decoration and furniture and the like has not really been due to the majority of the public developing a very fine taste in such matters. It has been chiefly due to the fact that the craftsmen of things so appreciated the pleasure of making what was beautiful, and woke to such a vivid consciousness of the hideousness and vulgarity of what the public had previously wanted, that they simply starved the public out. It would be quite impossible at the present moment to furnish a room as rooms were furnished a few years ago, without going for everything to an auction of secondhand furniture from some third-rate lodging-house. The things are no longer made. However they may object to it, people must nowadays have something charming in their surroundings. Fortunately for them, their assumption of authority in these art-matters came to entire grief.

It is evident, then, that all authority in such things is bad. People sometimes inquire what form of government is most suitable for an artist to live under. To this question there is only one answer. The form of government that is most suitable to the artist is no government at all. Authority over him and his art is ridiculous. It has been stated that under despotism artists have produced lovely work. This is not quite so. Artists have visited despots, not as subjects to be tyrannized over, but as wandering wonder-makers, as fascinating vagrant personalities, to be entertained and charmed and suffered to be at peace, and allowed to create. There is this to be said in favour of the despot, that he, being an individual, may have culture, while the mob, being a monster, has none. One who is an Emperor and King may stoop down to pick up a brush for a painter, but when the democracy stoops down it is merely to throw mud. And yet the democracy have not so far to stoop as the emperor. In fact, when they want to throw mud they have not to stoop at all. But there is no necessity to separate the monarch from the mob; all authority is equally bad.

There are three kinds of despots. There is the despot who tyrannizes over the body. There is the despot who tyrannizes over the soul. There is the despot who tyrannizes over the soul and body alike. The first is called the Prince. The second is called the Pope. The third is called the People. The Prince may be cultivated. Many Princes have been. Yet in the Prince there is danger. One thinks of Dante at the bitter feast in Verona, of Tasso in Ferrara's madman's cell. It is better for the artist not to live with Princes. The Pope may be cultivated. Many Popes have been; the bad Popes have been. The bad Popes loved Beauty, almost as passionately, nay, with as much passion as the good Popes hated Thought. To the wickedness of the Papacy humanity owes much. The goodness of the Papacy owes a terrible debt to humanity. Yet, though the Vatican has kept the rhetoric of its thunders, and lost the rod of its lightning, it is better for the artist not to live with Popes. It was a Pope who said of Cellini to a conclave of Cardinals that common laws and common authority were not made for men such as he; but it was a Pope who thrust Cellini into prison, and kept him there till he sickened with rage, and created unreal visions for himself, and saw the gilded sun enter his room, and grew so enamoured of it that he sought to escape, and crept out from tower to tower, and falling through dizzy air at dawn, maimed himself, and was by a vine-dresser covered with vine leaves, and carried in a cart to one who, loving beautiful things, had care of him. There is danger in Popes. And as for the People, what of them and their authority? Perhaps of them and their authority one has spoken enough. Their authority is a thing blind, deaf, hideous, grotesque, tragic, amusing, serious, and obscene. It is impossible for the artist to live with the People. All despots bribe. The People bribe and brutalize. Who told them to exercise authority? They were made to live, to listen, and to love. Someone has done them a great wrong. They have marred themselves by imitation of their superiors. They have taken the sceptre of the Prince. How should they use it? They have taken the triple tiara of the Pope. How should they carry its burden? They are as a clown whose heart is broken. They are as a priest whose soul is not yet born. Let all who love Beauty pity them. Though they themselves love not Beauty, yet let them pity themselves. Who taught them the trick of tyranny?

There are many other things that one might point out. One might point out how the Renaissance was great, because it sought to solve no social problem, and busied itself not about such things, but suffered the individual to develop freely, beautifully, and naturally, and so had great and individual artists, and great and individual men. One might point out how Louis XIV, by creating the modern state, destroyed the individualism of the artist, and made things monstrous in their monotony of repetition, and contemptible in their conformity to rule, and destroyed throughout all France all those fine freedoms of expression that had made tradition new in beauty, and new modes one with antique form. But the past is of no importance. The present is of no importance. It is with the future that we have to deal. For the past is what man should not have been. The present is what man ought not to be. The future is what artists are.

It will, of course, be said that such a scheme as is set forth here is quite unpractical, and goes against human nature. This is perfectly true. It is unpractical, and it goes against human nature. This is why it is worth carrying out, and that is why one proposes it. For what is a practical scheme? A practical scheme is either a scheme that is already in existence, or a scheme that could be carried out under existing conditions. But it is exactly the existing conditions that one objects to; and any scheme that could accept these conditions is wrong and foolish. The conditions will be done away with, and human nature will change. The only thing that one really knows about human nature is that it changes. Change is the one quality we can predicate of it. The systems that fail are those that rely on the permanency of human nature, and not on its growth and development. The error of Louis XIV was that he thought human nature would always be the same. The result of his error was the French Revolution. It was an admirable result. All the results of the mistakes of governments are quite admirable.

It is to be noted that Individualism does not come to the man with any sickly cant about duty, which merely means doing what other people want because they want it; or any hideous cant about self-sacrifice, which is merely a survival of savage mutilation. In fact, it does not come to a man with any claims upon him at all. It comes naturally and inevitably out of man. It is the point to which all development tends. It is the differentiation to which all organisms grow. It is the perfection that is inherent in every mode of life, and towards which every mode of life quickens. And so Individualism exercises no compulsion over man. On the contrary, it says to man that he should suffer no compulsion to be exercised over him. It does not try to force people to be good. It knows that people are good when they are let alone. Man will develop Individualism out of himself. Man is now so developing Individualism. To ask whether Individualism is practical is like asking whether Evolution is practical. Evolution is the law of life, and there is no evolution except towards individualism. Where this tendency is not expressed, it is a case of artificially arrested growth, or of disease, or of death.

Individualism will also be unselfish and unaffected. It has been pointed out that one of the results of the extraordinary tyranny of authority is that words are absolutely distorted from their proper and simple meaning, and are used to express the obverse of their right signification. What is true about Art is true about Life. A man is called affected, nowadays, if he dresses as he likes to dress. But in doing that he is acting in a perfectly natural manner. Affectation, in such matters, consists in dressing according to the views of one's neighbour, whose views, as they are the view of the majority, will probably be extremely stupid. Or a man is called selfish if he lives in the manner that seems to him most suitable for the full realization of his own personality; if, in fact, the primary aim of his life is self-development. But this is the way in which everyone should live. Selfishness is not living as one wishes to live, it is asking others to live as one wishes to live. And unselfishness is letting other people's lives alone, not interfering with them. Selfishness always aims at creating around it an absolute uniformity of type. Unselfishness recognizes infinite variety of type as a delightful thing, accepts it, acquiesces in it, enjoys it. It is not selfish to think for oneself. A man who does not think for himself does not think at all. It is grossly selfish to require of one's neighbour that he should think in the same way, and hold the same opinions.

Why should he? If he can think, he will probably think differently. If he cannot think, it is monstrous to require thought of any kind from him. A red rose is not selfish because it wants to be a red rose. It would be horribly selfish if it wanted all the other flowers in the garden to be both red and roses. Under Individualism people will be quite natural and absolutely unselfish, and will know the meanings of the words, and realize them in their free, beautiful lives. Nor will men be egotistic as they are now. For the egotist is he who makes claims upon others, and the Individualist will not desire to do that. It will not give him pleasure. When man has realized Individualism, he will also realize sympathy and exercise it freely and spontaneously. Up to the present man has hardly cultivated sympathy at all. He has merely sympathy with pain, and sympathy with pain is not the highest form of sympathy. All sympathy is fine, but sympathy with suffering is the least fine mode. It is tainted with egotism. It is apt to become morbid. There is in it a certain element of terror for our own safety. We become afraid that we ourselves might be as the leper or as the blind, and that no man would have care of us. It is curiously limiting, too. One should sympathize with the entirety of life, not with life's sores and maladies merely, but with life's joy and beauty and energy and health and freedom. The wider sympathy is, of course, the more difficult. It requires more unselfishness. Anybody can sympathize with the sufferings of a friend, but it requires a very fine nature—it requires, in fact, that nature of a true Individualist—to sympathize with a friend's success. In the modern stress of competition and struggle for place, such sympathy is naturally rare, and is also very much stifled by the immoral ideal of uniformity of type and conformity to rule which is so prevalent everywhere, and is perhaps most obnoxious in England.

Sympathy with pain there will, of course, always be. It is one of the first instincts of man. The animals which are individual, the higher animals, that is to say, share it with us. But it must be remembered that while sympathy with joy intensifies the sum of joy in the world, sympathy with pain does not really diminish the amount of pain. It may make man better able to endure evil, but the evil remains. Sympathy with consumption does not cure consumption; that is what science does. And when Socialism has solved the problem of poverty, and Science solved the problem of disease, the area of the sentimentalists will be lessened, and the sympathy of man will be large, healthy and spontaneous. Man will have joy in the contemplation of the joyous life of others.

For it is through joy that the Individualism of the future will develop itself. Christ made no attempt to reconstruct society, and consequently the Individualism that he preached to man could be realized only through pain or in solitude. The Ideals that we owe to Christ are the ideals of the man who abandons society entirely, or of the man who resists society absolutely. But man is naturally social. Even the Thebaid became peopled at last. And though the cenobite realizes his personality, it is often an impoverished personality that he so realizes. Upon the other hand, the terrible truth that pain is a mode through which man may realize himself exercises a wonderful fascination over the world. Shallow speakers and shallow thinkers in pulpits and on platforms often talk about the world's worship of pleasure, and whine against it. But it is rarely in the world's history that its ideal has been one of joy and beauty. The worship of pain has far more often dominated the world. Medievalism, with its saints and martyrs, its love of self-torture, its wild passion for wounding itself, its gashing with knives, and its whipping with rods—Medievalism is real Christianity, and the medieval Christ is the real Christ. When the Renaissance dawned upon the world, and brought with it the new ideals of the beauty of life and the joy of living, men could not understand Christ. Even Art shows us that. The painters of the Renaissance drew Christ as a little boy playing with another boy in a palace or a garden, or lying back in his mother's arms, smiling at her, or at a flower, or at a bright bird; or as a noble, stately figure moving nobly through the world; or as a wonderful figure rising in a sort of ecstasy from death to life. Even when they drew him crucified they drew him as a beautiful God on whom evil men had inflicted suffering. But he did not preoccupy them much. What delighted them was to paint the men and women whom they admired, and to show the loveliness of this lovely earth. They painted many religious pictures—in fact they painted far too many, and the monotony of type and motive is wearisome, and was bad for art. It was the result of the authority of the public in art-matters, and is to be deplored. But their soul was not in the subject. Raphael was a great artist when he painted his portrait of the Pope.

When he painted his Madonnas and infant Christs, he was not a great artist at all. Christ had no message for the Renaissance, which was wonderful because it brought an ideal at variance with his, and to find the presentation of the real Christ we must go to medieval art. There he is one maimed and marred; one who is not comely to look on, because Beauty is a joy; one who is not in fair raiment, because that may be a joy also: he is a beggar who has a marvellous soul; he is a leper whose soul is divine; he needs neither property nor health; he is a God realizing his perfection through pain.

The evolution of man is slow. The injustice of men is great. It was necessary that pain should be put forward as a mode of self-realization. Even now, in some places in the world, the message of Christ is necessary. No one who lived in modern Russia could possibly realize his perfection except by pain. A few Russian artists have realized themselves in Art; in a fiction that is medieval in character, because its dominant note is the realization of men through suffering. But for those who are not artists, and to whom there is no mode of life but the actual life of fact, pain is the only door to perfection. A Russian who lives happily under the present system of government in Russia must either believe that man has no soul, or that, if he has, it is not worth developing. A Nihilist who rejects all authority because he knows authority to be evil, and welcomes all pain, because through that he realizes his personality, is a real Christian. To him the Christian ideal is a true thing.

And yet, Christ did not revolt against authority. He accepted the imperial authority of the Roman Empire and paid tribute. He endured the ecclesiastical authority of the Jewish Church, and would not repel its violence by any violence of his own. He had, as I said before, no scheme for the reconstruction of society. But the modern world has schemes. It proposes to do away with poverty, and the suffering that it entails. It desires to get rid of pain, and the suffering that pain entails. It trusts to Socialism and to Science as its methods. What it aims at is an Individualism expressing itself through joy. This Individualism will be larger, fuller, lovelier than any Individualism has ever been. Pain is not the ultimate mode of perfection. It is merely provisional and a protest. It has reference to wrong, unhealthy, unjust surroundings. When the wrong, and the disease, and the injustice are removed, it will have no further place. It was a great work, but it is almost over. Its sphere lessens every day.

Nor will man miss it. For what man has sought for is, indeed, neither pain nor pleasure, but simply Life. Man has sought to live intensely, fully, perfectly. When he can do so without exercising restraint on others, or suffering it ever, and his activities are all pleasurable to him, he will be saner, healthier, more civilized, more himself. Pleasure is Nature's test, her sign of approval. When man is happy, he is in harmony with himself and his environment. The new Individualism, for whose service Socialism, whether it wills it or not, is working, will be perfect harmony. It will be what the Greeks sought for, but could not, except in Thought, realize completely because they had slaves, and fed them; it will be what the Renaissance sought for, but could not realize completely except in Art, because they had slaves, and starved them. It will be complete, and through it each man will attain to his perfection. The new Individualism is the new Hellenism.

QUESTIONS FOR DISCUSSION

Why does Wilde believe that the value of Socialism is that it will "lead to Individualism"? (262)

1. Why does Wilde warn that if Socialism produces "Industrial Tyrannies," then "the last state of man will be worse than the first"? (263)

2. Why does Wilde think that it is "quite right" for the poor to be "ungrateful, discontented, disobedient, and rebellious" under capitalism? (264)

3. Why does Wilde believe that when Individualism is established people will be able to "live" fully rather than merely "exist"? (267)

4. Why does Wilde cite Jesus as an example of Individualism?

What does Wilde mean when he says, "Progress is the realization of Utopias"? (275)

1. According to Wilde, why has progress been made "through disobedience and through rebellion"? (264)

2. Why does Wilde insist that "every man must be left quite free to choose his own work," defining work as "activity of any kind"? (266)

3. According to Wilde, why will crime and punishment pass away once authority is abolished?

4. Why does Wilde declare that "a map of the world that does not include Utopia is not worth even glancing at, for it leaves out the one country at which Humanity is always landing"? (275)

FOR FURTHER REFLECTION

1. Do you agree with Wilde that charity necessarily "degrades and demoralizes"?

2. Do you agree or disagree with Wilde's argument that private property prevents people from realizing "the true pleasure and joy of living"?

3. Is society more brutalized by crime or by punishment?

4. How do you respond to Wilde's statement that "democracy means simply the bludgeoning of the people by the people for the people"?

The Economic Basis of the Withering Away of the State

Vladimir Lenin

1. PRESENTATION OF THE QUESTION BY MARX

From a superficial comparison of Marx's letter to Bracke of May 5, 1875, with Engels's letter to Bebel of March 28, 1875, which we examined above, it might appear that Marx was much more of a "champion of the state" than Engels, and that the difference of opinion between the two writers on the question of the state was very considerable.

Engels suggested to Bebel that all chatter about the state be dropped altogether, that the word "state" be eliminated from the program altogether and the word "community" substituted for it. Engels even declared that the Commune was no longer a state in the proper sense of the word. Yet Marx even spoke of the "future state in communist society," i.e., he would seem to recognize the need for the state even under communism.

But such a view would be fundamentally wrong. A closer examination shows that Marx's and Engels's views on the state and its withering away were completely identical, and that Marx's expression quoted above refers to the state in the process of *withering away*.

Clearly there can be no question of specifying the moment of the *future* "withering away," the more so since it will obviously be a lengthy process. The apparent difference between Marx and Engels is due to the fact that they dealt with different subjects and pursued different aims. Engels set out to show Bebel graphically, sharply, and in broad outline the utter absurdity of the current prejudices concerning the state (shared to no small degree by Lassalle). Marx only touched upon *this* question in passing, being interested in another subject, namely, the *development* of communist society.

The whole theory of Marx is the application of the theory of development—in its most consistent, complete, considered, and pithy form—to modern capitalism. Naturally, Marx was faced with the problem of applying this theory both to the *forthcoming* collapse of capitalism and to the *future* development of *future* communism.

On the basis of what *facts*, then, can the question of the future development of future communism be dealt with?

On the basis of the fact that it *has its origin* in capitalism, that it develops historically from capitalism, that it is the result of the action of a social force to which capitalism *gave birth*. There is no trace of an attempt on Marx's part to make up a utopia, to indulge in idle guess-work about what cannot be known. Marx treated the question of communism in the same way as a naturalist would treat the question of the development of, say, a new biological variety, once he knew that it had originated in such and such a way and was changing in such and such a definite direction.

To begin with, Marx brushed aside the confusion the Gotha Programme brought into the question of the relationship between state and society. He wrote:

> "Present-day society" is capitalist society, which exists in all civilized countries, being more or less free from medieval admixture, more or less modified by the particular historical development of each country, more or less developed. On the other hand, the "present-day state" changes with a country's frontier. It is different in the Prusso-German Empire from what it is in Switzerland, and different in England from what it is in the United States. "*The* present-day state" is, therefore, a fiction.
>
> Nevertheless, the different states of the different civilized countries, in spite of their motley diversity of form, all have this in common, that they are based on modern bourgeois society,

only one more or less capitalistically developed. They have, therefore, also certain essential characteristics in common. In this sense it is possible to speak of the "present-day state," in contrast with the future, in which its present root, bourgeois society, will have died off.

The question then arises: what transformation will the state undergo in communist society? In other words, what social functions will remain in existence there that are analogous to present state functions? This question can only be answered scientifically, and one does not get a flea-hop nearer to the problem by a thousandfold combination of the word "people" with the word "state."

After thus ridiculing all talk about a "people's state," Marx formulated the question and gave warning, as it were, that those seeking a scientific answer to it should use only firmly-established scientific data.

The first fact that has been established most accurately by the whole theory of development, by science as a whole—a fact that was ignored by the utopians, and is ignored by the present-day opportunists, who are afraid of the socialist revolution—is that, historically, there must undoubtedly be a special stage, or a special phase, of *transition* from capitalism to communism.

2. THE TRANSITION FROM CAPITALISM TO COMMUNISM

Marx continued: "Between capitalist and communist society lies the period of the revolutionary transformation of the one into the other. Corresponding to this is also a political transition period in which the state can be nothing but *the revolutionary dictatorship of the proletariat*." Marx bases this conclusion on an analysis of the role played by the proletariat in modern capitalist society, on the data concerning the development of this society, and on the irreconcilability of the antagonistic interests of the proletariat and the bourgeoisie.

Previously the question was put as follows: to achieve its emancipation, the proletariat must overthrow the bourgeoisie, win political power and establish its revolutionary dictatorship.

Now the question is put somewhat differently: the transition from capitalist society—which is developing toward communism—to communist society is impossible without a "political transition period," and the state in this period can only be the revolutionary dictatorship of the proletariat.

What, then, is the relation of this dictatorship to democracy?

We have seen that the *Communist Manifesto* simply places side by side the two concepts: "to raise the proletariat to the position of the ruling class" and "to win the battle of democracy." On the basis of all that has been said above, it is possible to determine more precisely how democracy changes in the transition from capitalism to communism.

In capitalist society, providing it develops under the most favorable conditions, we have a more or less complete democracy in the democratic republic. But this democracy is always hemmed in by the narrow limits set by capitalist exploitation, and consequently always remains, in effect, a democracy for the minority, only for the propertied classes, only for the rich. Freedom in capitalist society always remains about the same as it was in the ancient Greek republics: freedom for the slave-owners. Owing to the conditions of capitalist exploitation, the modern wage slaves are so crushed by want and poverty that "they cannot be bothered with democracy," "cannot be bothered with politics"; in the ordinary, peaceful course of events, the majority of the population is debarred from participation in public and political life.

The correctness of this statement is perhaps most clearly confirmed by Germany, because constitutional legality steadily endured there for a remarkably long time—nearly half a century (1871–1914)—and during this period the Social-Democrats were able to achieve far more than in other countries in the way of "utilizing legality," and organized a larger proportion of the workers into a political party than anywhere else in the world.

What is this largest proportion of politically conscious and active wage slaves that has so far been recorded in capitalist society? One million members of the Social-Democratic Party—out of fifteen million wage-workers! Three million organized in trade unions—out of fifteen million!

Democracy for an insignificant minority, democracy for the rich—that is the democracy of capitalist society. If we look more closely into the machinery of capitalist democracy, we see everywhere, in the "petty"—supposedly petty—details of the suffrage (residential qualification, exclusion of women, etc.), in the technique of the representative institutions, in the actual obstacles to the right of assembly (public buildings are not for "paupers"!), in the purely capitalist organization of the daily press, etc., etc.—we see restriction after restriction upon democracy. These restrictions, exceptions, exclusions, obstacles for the poor seem slight, especially in the eyes of one who has never known want himself and has never been in close contact with the oppressed classes in their mass life (and nine out of ten, if not ninety-nine out of a hundred, bourgeois publicists and politicians come under this category); but in their sum total these restrictions exclude and squeeze out the poor from politics, from active participation in democracy.

Marx grasped this *essence* of capitalist democracy splendidly when, in analyzing the experience of the Commune, he said that the oppressed are allowed once every few years to decide which particular representatives of the oppressing class shall represent and repress them in parliament!

But from this capitalist democracy—that is inevitably narrow and stealthily pushes aside the poor, and is therefore hypocritical and false through and through—forward development does not proceed simply, directly, and smoothly, toward "greater and greater democracy," as the liberal professors and petty-bourgeois opportunists would have us believe. No, forward development, i.e., development toward communism, proceeds through the dictatorship of the proletariat, and cannot do otherwise, for the *resistance* of the capitalist exploiters cannot be *broken* by anyone else or in any other way.

And the dictatorship of the proletariat, i.e., the organization of the vanguard of the oppressed as the ruling class for the purpose of suppressing the oppressors, cannot result merely in an expansion of democracy. *Simultaneously* with an immense expansion of democracy, which *for the first time* becomes democracy for the poor, democracy for the people, and not democracy for the money-bags, the dictatorship of the proletariat imposes a series of restrictions on the freedom of the oppressors, the exploiters, the capitalists. We must suppress them in order to free humanity from wage slavery, their resistance must be crushed by force; it is clear that there is no freedom and no democracy where there is suppression and where there is violence.

Engels expressed this splendidly in his letter to Bebel when he said, as the reader will remember, that "the proletariat needs the state, not in the interests of freedom but in order to hold down its adversaries, and as soon as it becomes possible to speak of freedom the state as such ceases to exist."

Democracy for the vast majority of the people, and suppression by force, i.e., exclusion from democracy, of the exploiters and oppressors of the people—this is the change democracy undergoes during the *transition* from capitalism to communism.

Only in communist society, when the resistance of the capitalists has been completely crushed, when the capitalists have disappeared, when there are no classes (i.e., when there is no distinction between the members of society as regards their relation to the social means of production), *only* then "the state . . . ceases to exist," and "*it becomes possible to speak of freedom.*" Only then will a truly complete democracy become possible and be realized, a democracy without any exceptions whatever. And only then will democracy begin to *wither away*, owing to the simple fact that, freed from capitalist slavery, from the untold horrors, savagery, absurdities, and infamies of capitalist exploitation, people will gradually *become accustomed* to observing the elementary rules of social intercourse that have been known for centuries and repeated for thousands of years in all copy-book maxims. They will become accustomed to observing them without force, without coercion, without subordination, *without the special apparatus* for coercion called the state.

The expression "the state *withers away*" is very well chosen, for it indicates both the gradual and the spontaneous nature of the process. Only habit can, and undoubtedly will, have such an effect; for we see around us on millions of occasions how readily people become accustomed to observing the necessary rules of social intercourse when there is no exploitation, when there is nothing that arouses indignation, evokes protest and revolts, and creates the need for *suppression*.

And so in capitalist society we have a democracy that is curtailed, wretched, false, a democracy only for the rich, for the minority. The dictatorship of the proletariat, the period of transition to communism, will for the first time create democracy for the people, for the majority, along with the necessary suppression of the exploiters, of the minority. Communism alone is capable of providing really complete democracy, and the more complete it is, the sooner it will become unnecessary and wither away of its own accord.

In other words, under capitalism we have the state in the proper sense of the word, that is, a special machine for the suppression of one class by another, and, what is more, of the majority by the minority. Naturally, to be successful, such an undertaking as the systematic suppression of the exploited majority by the exploiting minority calls for the utmost ferocity and savagery in the matter of suppressing, it calls for seas of blood, through which mankind is actually wading its way in slavery, serfdom, and wage labor.

Furthermore, during the *transition* from capitalism to communism suppression is *still* necessary, but it is now the suppression of the exploiting minority by the exploited majority. A special apparatus, a special machine for suppression, the "state," is *still* necessary, but this is now a transitional state. It is no longer a state in the proper sense of the word; for the suppression of the minority of exploiters by the majority of the wage slaves of *yesterday* is comparatively so easy, simple, and natural a task that it will entail far less bloodshed than the suppression of the risings of slaves, serfs, or wage-laborers, and it will cost mankind far less. And it is compatible with the extension of democracy to such an overwhelming majority of the population that the need for a *special machine* of suppression will begin to disappear. Naturally, the exploiters are unable to suppress the people without a highly complex machine for performing this task, but *the people* can suppress the exploiters even with a very simple "machine," almost without a "machine," without a special apparatus, by the simple *organization of the armed people* (such as the Soviets of Workers' and Soldiers' Deputies, we would remark, running ahead).

Lastly, only communism makes the state absolutely unnecessary, for there is *nobody* to be suppressed—"nobody" in the sense of a *class*, of a systematic struggle against a definite section of the population. We are not utopians, and do not in the least deny the possibility and inevitability of excesses on the part of *individual persons*, or the need to stop *such* excesses. In the first place, however, no special machine, no special apparatus of suppression, is needed for this; this will be done by the armed people themselves, as simply and as readily as any crowd of civilized people, even in modern society, interferes to put a stop to a scuffle or to prevent a woman from being assaulted. And, secondly, we know that the fundamental social cause of excesses, which consist in the violation of the rules of social intercourse, is the exploitation of the people, their want and their poverty. With the removal of this chief cause, excesses will inevitably begin to "*wither away.*" We do not know how quickly and in what succession, but we do know they will wither away. With their withering away the state will also *wither away*.

Without building utopias, Marx defined more fully what can be defined *now* regarding this future, namely, the difference between the lower and higher places (levels, stages) of communist society.

3. THE FIRST PHASE OF COMMUNIST SOCIETY

In the *Critique of the Gotha Programme*, Marx goes into detail to disprove Lassalle's idea that under socialism the worker will receive the "undiminished" or "full product of his labor." Marx shows that from the whole of the social labor of society there must be deducted a reserve fund, a fund for the expansion of production, a fund for the replacement of the "wear and tear" of machinery, and so on. Then, from the means of consumption must be deducted a fund for administrative expenses, for schools, hospitals, old people's homes, and so on.

Instead of Lassalle's hazy, obscure, general phrase ("the full product of his labor to the worker"), Marx makes a sober estimate of exactly how socialist society will have to manage its affairs. Marx proceeds to make a *concrete* analysis of the conditions of life of a society in which there will be no capitalism, and says: "What we have to deal with here [in analyzing the program of the workers' party] is a communist society, not as it has *developed* on its own foundations, but, on the contrary, just as it *emerges* from capitalist society; which is, therefore, in every respect, economically, morally, and intellectually, still stamped with the birthmarks of the old society from whose womb it comes." It is this communist society, which has just emerged into the light of day out of the womb of capitalism and which is in every respect stamped with the birthmarks of the old society, that Marx terms the "first," or lower, phase of communist society.

The means of production are no longer the private property of individuals. The means of production belong to the whole of society. Every member of society, performing a certain part of the socially-necessary work, receives a certificate from society to the effect that he has done a certain amount of work. And with this certificate he receives from the public store of consumer goods a corresponding quantity of products. After a deduction is made of the amount of labor which goes to the public fund, every worker, therefore, receives from society as much as he has given to it.

"Equality" apparently reigns supreme.

But when Lassalle, having in view such a social order (usually called socialism, but termed by Marx the first phase of communism), says that this is "equitable distribution," that this is "the equal right of all to an equal product of labor," Lassalle is mistaken and Marx exposes the mistake.

"Equal right," says Marx, we certainly do have here; but it is still a "bourgeois right," which, like every right, *implies inequality.* Every right is an application of an *equal* measure to *different* people who in fact are not alike, are not equal to one another. That is why "equal right" is a violation of equality and an injustice. In fact, everyone, having performed as much social labor as another, receives an equal share of the social product (after the above-mentioned deductions).

But people are not alike: one is strong, another is weak; one is married, another is not; one has more children, another has less, and so on. And the conclusion Marx draws is: "With an equal performance of labor, and hence an equal share in the social consumption fund, one will in fact receive more than another, one will be richer than another, and so on. To avoid all these defects, right would have to be unequal rather than equal."

The first phase of communism, therefore, cannot yet provide justice and equality: differences, and unjust differences, in wealth will still persist, but the *exploitation* of man by man will have become impossible because it will be impossible to seize the *means of production*—the factories, machines, land, etc.—and make them private property. In smashing Lassalle's petty-bourgeois, vague phrases about "equality" and "justice" *in general,* Marx shows the *course of develop-ment* of communist society, which is *compelled* to abolish at first *only* the "injustice" of the means of production seized by individuals, and which is *unable* at once to eliminate the other injustice, which consists in the distribution of consumer goods "according to the amount of labor performed" (and not according to needs).

The vulgar economists, including the bourgeois professors and "our" Tugan, constantly reproach the socialists with forgetting the inequality of people and with "dreaming" of eliminating this inequal-ity. Such a reproach, as we see, only proves the extreme ignorance of the bourgeois ideologists.

Marx not only most scrupulously takes account of the inevitable inequality of men, but he also takes into account the fact that the mere conversion of the means of production into the common property of the whole of society (commonly called "socialism") *does not remove* the defects of distribution and the inequality of "bourgeois right," which *continues to prevail* so long as products are divided "according to the amount of labor performed." Continuing, Marx says: "But these defects are inevitable in the first phase of communist society as it is when it has just emerged, after prolonged birth pangs, from capitalist society. Right can never be higher than the economic structure of society and its cultural development conditioned thereby." And so, in the first phase of communist society (usually called socialism) "bourgeois right" is *not* abolished in its entirety, but only in part, only in proportion to the economic revolution so far attained, i.e., only in respect of the means of production. "Bourgeois right" recognizes them as the private property of individuals. Socialism converts them into *common* property. *To that extent*—and to that extent alone—"bourgeois right" disappears.

However, it persists as far as its other part is concerned; it persists in the capacity of regulator (determining factor) in the distribution of products and the allotment of labor among the members of soci-ety. The socialist principle, "He who does not work shall not eat," is *already* realized; the other socialist principle, "An equal amount of products for an equal amount of labor," is also *already* realized. But this is not yet communism, and it does not yet abolish "bourgeois right," which gives unequal individuals, in return for unequal (really unequal) amounts of labor, equal amounts of products.

This is a "defect," says Marx, but it is unavoidable in the first phase of communism; for if we are not to indulge in utopianism, we must not think that having overthrown capitalism people will at once learn to work for society *without any standard of right*. Besides, the abolition of capitalism *does not immediately create* the economic prerequisites for *such* a change.

Now, there is no other standard than that of "bourgeois right." To this extent, therefore, there still remains the need for a state, which, while safeguarding the common ownership of the means of production, would safeguard equality in labor and in the distribution of products.

The state withers away insofar as there are no longer any capitalists, any classes, and, consequently, no *class* can be *suppressed.*

But the state has not yet completely withered away, since there still remains the safeguarding of "bourgeois right," which sanctifies actual inequality. For the state to wither away completely, complete communism is necessary.

4. THE HIGHER PHASE OF COMMUNIST SOCIETY

Marx continues:

> In a higher phase of communist society, after the enslaving subordination of the individual to the division of labor and with it also the antithesis between mental and physical labor has vanished, after labor has become not only a livelihood but life's prime want, after the productive forces have increased with the all-round development of the individual, and all the springs of cooperative wealth flow more abundantly—only then can the narrow horizon of bourgeois right be crossed in its entirety and society inscribe on its banners: From each according to his ability, to each according to his needs!

Only now can we fully appreciate the correctness of Engels's remarks mercilessly ridiculing the absurdity of combining the words "freedom" and "state." So long as the state exists there is no freedom. When there is freedom, there will be no state.

The economic basis for the complete withering away of the state is such a high stage of development of communism at which the antithesis between mental and physical labor disappears, at which there consequently disappears one of the principal sources of modern *social* inequality—a source, moreover, which cannot on any account be removed immediately by the mere conversion of the means of production into public property, by the mere expropriation of the capitalists.

This expropriation will make it *possible* for the productive forces to develop to a tremendous extent. And when we see how incredibly capitalism is already *retarding* this development, when we see how much progress could be achieved on the basis of the level of technique already attained, we are entitled to say with the fullest confidence that the expropriation of the capitalists will inevitably result in an enormous development of the productive forces of human society. But how rapidly this development will proceed, how soon it will reach the point of breaking away from the division of labor, of doing away with the antithesis between mental and physical labor, of transforming labor into "life's prime want"—we do not and *cannot* know.

That is why we are entitled to speak only of the inevitable withering away of the state, emphasizing the protracted nature of this process and its dependence upon the rapidity of development of the *higher phase* of communism, and leaving the question of the time required for, or the concrete forms of, the withering away quite open, because there is *no* material for answering these questions.

The state will be able to wither away completely when society adopts the rule: "From each according to his ability, to each according to his needs," i.e., when people have become so accustomed to observing the fundamental rules of social intercourse and when their labor has become so productive that they will voluntarily work *according to their ability.* "The narrow horizon of bourgeois right," which compels one to calculate with the heartlessness of a Shylock whether one has not worked half an hour more than somebody else, whether one is not getting less pay than somebody else—this narrow horizon will then be crossed. There will then be no need for society, in distributing products, to regulate the quantity to be received by each; each will take freely "according to his needs."

From the bourgeois point of view, it is easy to declare that such a social order is "sheer utopia" and to sneer at the socialists for promising everyone the right to receive from society, without any control over the labor of the individual citizen, any quantity of truffles, cars, pianos, etc. Even to this day, most bourgeois "savants" confine themselves to sneering in this way, thereby betraying both their ignorance and their selfish defense of capitalism.

Ignorance—for it has never entered the head of any socialist to "promise" that the higher phase of the development of communism will arrive; as for the great socialists' *forecast* that it will arrive, it presupposes not the present productivity of labor and *not the present* ordinary run of people, who, like the seminary students in Pomyalovsky's stories, are capable of damaging the stocks of public wealth "just for fun," and of demanding the impossible.

Until the "higher" phase of communism arrives, the socialists demand the *strictest* control by society *and by the state* over the measure of labor and the measure of consumption; but this control must *start* with the expropriation of the capitalists, with the establishment of workers' control over the capitalists, and must be exercised not by a state of bureaucrats, but by a state of *armed workers*.

The selfish defense of capitalism by the bourgeois ideologists (and their hangers-on, like the Tseretelis, Chernovs and Co.) consists in that they *substitute* arguing and talk about the distant future for the vital and burning question of *present-day* politics, namely, the expropriation of the capitalists, the conversion of *all* citizens into workers and other employees of *one* huge "syndicate"—the whole state—and the complete subordination of the entire work of this syndicate to a genuinely democratic state, *the state of the Soviets of Workers' and Soldiers' Deputies.*

In fact, when a learned professor, followed by the philistine, followed in turn by the Tseretelis and Chernovs, talks of wild utopias, of the demagogic promises of the Bolsheviks, of the impossibility of "introducing" socialism, it is the higher stage, or phase, of communism he has in mind, which no one has ever promised or even thought to "introduce," because, generally speaking, it cannot be "introduced."

And this brings us to the question of the scientific distinction between socialism and communism which Engels touched on in his above-quoted argument about the incorrectness of the name "Social-Democrat." Politically, the distinction between the first, or lower, and the higher phase of communism will in time, probably, be tremendous. But it would be ridiculous to recognize this distinction now, under capitalism, and only individual anarchists, perhaps, could invest it with primary importance (if there still are people among the anarchists who have learned nothing from the "Plekhanov" conversion of the Kropotkins, of Grave, Cornelissen and other "stars" of anarchism into social-chauvinists or "anarchotrenchists," as Ghe, one of the few anarchists who have still preserved a sense of honor and a conscience, has put it).

But the scientific distinction between socialism and communism is clear. What is usually called socialism was termed by Marx the "first," or lower, phase of communist society. Insofar as the means of production become *common* property, the word "communism" is also applicable here, providing we do not forget that this is *not* complete communism. The great significance of Marx's explanations is that here, too, he consistently applies materialist dialectics, the theory of development, and regards communism as something which develops *out of* capitalism. Instead of scholastically invented, "concocted" definitions and fruitless disputes over words (What is socialism? What is communism?), Marx gives an analysis of what might be called the stages of the economic maturity of communism.

In its first phase, or first stage, communism *cannot* as yet be fully mature economically and entirely free from traditions or vestiges of capitalism. Hence the interesting phenomenon that communism in its first phase retains "the narrow horizon of *bourgeois* right." Of course, bourgeois right in regard to the distribution of *consumer* goods inevitably presupposes the existence of the *bourgeois state,* for right is nothing without an apparatus capable of *enforcing* the observance of the standards of right.

It follows that under communism there remains for a time not only bourgeois right, but even the bourgeois state, without the bourgeoisie!

This may sound like a paradox or simply a dialectical conundrum of which Marxism is often accused by people who have not taken the slightest trouble to study its extraordinarily profound content.

But in fact, remnants of the old, surviving in the new, confront us in life at every step, both in nature and in society. And Marx did not arbitrarily insert a scrap of "bourgeois" right into communism, but indicated what is economically and politically inevitable in a society emerging *out of the womb* of capitalism.

Democracy is of enormous importance to the working class in its struggle against the capitalists for its emancipation. But democracy is by no means a boundary not to be overstepped; it is only one of the stages on the road from feudalism to capitalism, and from capitalism to communism.

Democracy means equality. The great significance of the proletariat's struggle for equality and of equality as a slogan will be clear if we correctly interpret it as meaning the abolition of _classes_. But democracy means only _formal_ equality. And as soon as equality is achieved for all members of society _in relation_ to ownership of the means of production, that is, equality of labor and wages, humanity will inevitably be confronted with the question of advancing farther, from formal equality to actual equality, i.e., to the operation of the rule "from each according to his ability, to each according to his needs." By what stages, by means of what practical measures humanity will proceed to this supreme aim we do not and cannot know. But it is important to realize how infinitely mendacious is the ordinary bourgeois conception of socialism as something lifeless, rigid, fixed once and for all, whereas in reality _only_ socialism will be the beginning of a rapid, genuine, truly mass forward movement, embracing first the _majority_ and then the whole of the population, in all spheres of public and private life.

Democracy is a form of the state, one of its varieties. Consequently, it, like every state, represents, on the one hand, the organized, systematic use of force against persons; but, on the other hand, it signifies the formal recognition of equality of citizens, the equal right of all to determine the structure of, and to administer, the state. This, in turn, results in the fact that, at a certain stage in the development of democracy, it first welds together the class that wages a revolutionary struggle against capitalism—the proletariat, and enables it to crush, smash to atoms, wipe off the face of the earth the bourgeois, even the republican-bourgeois, state machine, the standing army, the police, and the bureaucracy and to substitute for them a _more_ democratic state machine, but a state machine nevertheless, in the shape of armed workers who proceed to form a militia involving the entire population.

Here "quantity turns into quality": _such_ a degree of democracy implies overstepping the boundaries of bourgeois society and beginning its socialist reorganization. If really _all_ take part in the administration of the state, capitalism cannot retain its hold. The development of capitalism, in turn, creates the *preconditions* that *enable* really "all" to take part in the administration of the state. Some of these preconditions are: universal literacy, which has already been achieved in a number of the most advanced capitalist countries, then the "training and disciplining" of millions of workers by the huge, complex, socialized apparatus of the postal service, railways, big factories, large-scale commerce, banking, etc., etc.

Given these *economic* preconditions, it is quite possible, after the overthrow of the capitalists and the bureaucrats, to proceed immediately, overnight, to replace them in the *control* over production and distribution, in the work of *keeping account* of labor and products, by the armed workers, by the whole of the armed population. (The question of control and accounting should not be confused with the question of the scientifically trained staff of engineers, agronomists, and so on. These gentlemen are working today in obedience to the wishes of the capitalists, and will work even better tomorrow in obedience to the wishes of the armed workers.)

Accounting and control—that is *mainly* what is needed for the "smooth working," for the proper functioning, of the *first phase* of communist society. *All* citizens are transformed into hired employees of the state, which consists of the armed workers. *All* citizens become employees and workers of a *single* country-wide state "syndicate." All that is required is that they should work equally, do their proper share of work, and get equal pay. The accounting and control necessary for this have been *simplified* by capitalism to the utmost and reduced to the extraordinarily simple operations—which any literate person can perform—of supervising and recording, knowledge of the four rules of arithmetic, and issuing appropriate receipts.

When the *majority* of the people begin independently and everywhere to keep such accounts and exercise such control over the capitalists (now coverted into employees) and over the intellectual gentry who preserve their capitalists habits, this control will really become universal, general, and popular; and there will be no getting away from it, there will be "nowhere to go."

The whole of society will have become a single office and a single factory, with equality of labor and pay.

But this "factory" discipline, which the proletariat, after defeating the capitalists, after overthrowing the exploiters, will extend to the whole of society, is by no means our ideal, or our ultimate goal. It is only a necessary *step* for thoroughly cleaning society of all the infamies and abominations of capitalist exploitation, *and for further* progress.

From the moment all members of society, or at least the vast majority, have learned to administer the state *themselves*, have taken this work into their own hands, have organized control over the insignificant capitalist minority, over the gentry who wish to preserve their capitalist habits, and over the workers who have been thoroughly corrupted by capitalism—from this moment the need for government of any kind begins to disappear altogether. The more complete the democracy, the nearer the moment when it becomes unnecessary. The more democratic the "state" which consists of the armed workers, and which is "no longer a state in the proper sense of the word," the more rapidly *every form* of state begins to wither away.

For when *all* have learned to administer and actually do independently administer social production, independently keep accounts, and exercise control over the parasites, the sons of the wealthy, the swindlers and other "guardians of capitalist traditions," the escape from this popular accounting and control will inevitably become so incredibly difficult, such a rare exception, and will probably be accompanied by such swift and severe punishment (for the armed workers are practical men and not sentimental intellectuals, and they will scarcely allow anyone to trifle with them), that the *necessity* of observing the simple, fundamental rules of the community will very soon become a *habit*.

Then the door will be thrown wide open for the transition from the first phase of communist society to its higher phase, and with it to the complete withering away of the state.

QUESTIONS FOR DISCUSSION

Why does Lenin repeatedly state that the communists are "not utopians"?

1. Why does Lenin say that "there is no trace of an attempt on Marx's part to make up a utopia, to indulge in idle guess-work about what cannot be known"? (298)

2. According to Lenin, why did "the utopians" ignore the fact that there must be "a special stage, or a specific phase, of *transition* from capitalism to communism"? (299)

3. Why does Lenin describe Marx as defining the stages of communist society "without building utopias"? (304)

4. Why does Lenin believe that during the transition to communism, "bourgeois right" must be tolerated for a period "if we are not to indulge in utopianism"? (307)

Why does Lenin believe that the state will naturally "wither away" under communism?

1. Why does Lenin believe that once communism is established, the people will *"become accustomed* to observing the elementary rules of social intercourse" and make the state unnecessary? (302)

2. Why does Lenin think that "under capitalism we have the state in the proper sense of the word," but during the transition to communism "it is no longer a state in the proper sense of the word"? (303)

3. Why is Lenin confident that any "excesses" under communism can be dealt with by "the armed people themselves," thus making a state unnecessary? (303, 304)

4. Why does Lenin believe that the withering away of the state will be accomplished once the rule "From each according to his ability, to each according to his needs" is adopted? (308)

FOR FURTHER REFLECTION

1. Does Lenin successfully defend Marx against the charge of utopianism?

2. Are there elements of Lenin's critique of capitalist democracies as embodying "democracy for the rich" that you find persuasive?

3. How do you feel about Lenin's admission that "by what stages, by means of what practical measures humanity will proceed to this supreme aim we do not and cannot know"?

4. Is Lenin's vision of a society of armed workers utopian or dystopian?

We

(selection)

Yevgeny Zamyatin

Record Twenty-Five

The Descent from Heaven
The Greatest Catastrophe in History
The Known—Is Ended

At the beginning all arose, and the Hymn, like a solemn mantle, slowly waved above our heads. Hundreds of tubes of the Musical Tower, and millions of human voices. For a second I forgot everything; I forgot that alarming something at which I-330 had hinted in connection with today's celebration; I think I even forgot about her. At that moment I was the very same little boy who once wept because of a tiny ink stain on his unif, which no one else could see. Even if nobody else sees that I am covered with black, ineffaceable stains, I know it, don't I? I know that there should be no place for a criminal like me among these frank, open faces. What if I should rush forward and shout out everything about myself all at once! The end might follow. Let it happen! At least for a second I would feel myself clear and clean and senseless like that innocent blue sky. . . .

All eyes were directed upward; in the pure morning blue, still moist with the tears of night, a small dark spot appeared. Now it was dark, now bathed in the rays of the sun. It was He, descending to us from the sky, He—the new Jehovah—in an aero, He, as wise and as lovingly cruel as the Jehovah of the ancients. Nearer and nearer He came, and higher toward Him were drawn millions of hearts. Already He saw us. And in my mind with Him I looked over everything from the heights: concentric circles of stands marked with dotted blue lines of unifs—like circles of a spiderweb strewn with microscopic suns (like shining badges). And in the center the wise white spider would soon occupy His place—the Well-Doer clad in white, the Well-Doer who wisely tangled our hands and feet in the salutary net of happiness.

His magnificent descent from the sky was accomplished. The brassy Hymn came to silence; all sat down. At once I perceived that everything was really a very thin spiderweb the threads of which were stretched tense and trembling—and it seemed that in a moment those threads might break and something improbable . . .

I half-rose and looked around, and I met many lovingly worried eyes which passed from one face to another. I saw someone lifting his hand and almost imperceptibly waving his fingers—he was making signs to another. The latter replied with a similar finger sign. And a third. . . . I understood; they were the Guardians. I understood; they were alarmed by something—the spiderweb was stretched and trembling. And within me, as if tuned to the same wave-length, within me there was a corresponding quiver.

On the platform a poet was reciting his pre-electoral ode. I could not hear a single word; I only felt the rhythmic swing of the hexametric pendulum, and with its every motion I felt how nearer and nearer there was approaching some hour set for . . . I continued to turn over face after face like pages, but I could not find the one, the only one, I was seeking, the one I needed to find at once, as soon as possible, for one more swing of the pendulum, and . . .

It was he, certainly it was he! Below, past the main platform, gliding over the sparkling glass, the ear wings flapped by, the running body gave a reflection of a double-curved S-, like a noose which was rolling toward some of the intricate passages among the stands. S-, I-330,—there is some thread between them. I have always felt some thread between them. I don't know yet what that thread is, but someday I shall untangle it. I fixed my gaze on him; he was rushing farther away, behind him that invisible thread. . . . There, he stopped . . . there. . . . I was pierced, twisted together into a knot as if by a lightning-like, many-volted electric discharge; in my row, not more than 40° from me, S- stopped and bowed. I saw I-330, and beside her the smiling, repellent, Negro-lipped R-13.

My first thought was to rush to her and cry, "Why with him? Why did you not want . . .?" But the salutary, invisible spiderweb bound fast my hands and feet; so gritting my teeth, I sat stiff as iron, my gaze fixed upon them. A sharp *physical* pain at my heart. I remember my thought: "If non-physical causes produce physical pain, then it is clear that . . ."

I regret that I did not come to any conclusion. I remember only that something about "heart" flashed through my mind; a purely nonsensical ancient expression, "His heart fell into his boots," passed through my head. My heart sank. The hexameter came to an end. It was about to start. What "It"?

The five-minute pre-election recess established by custom. The custom-established, pre-electional silence. But this time it was not that pious, really prayer-like silence that it usually was. This time it was like the ancient days when the sky, still untamed, would roar from time to time with its "storms." It was like the "lull before the storm" of the ancient days. The air seemed to be made of transparent, vaporized cast iron. You wanted to breathe with your mouth wide open. My hearing, intense to the point of pain, registered from behind a mouse-like, gnawing, worried whisper. Without lifting my eyes I saw those two, I-330 and R-13, side by side, shoulder to shoulder—and on my knees my trembling, foreign, hateful, hairy hands. . . .

Everybody was holding a badge with a clock in his hands. One. . . . Two. . . . Three. . . . Five minutes. From the main platform a cast-iron, slow voice:

"Those in favor shall lift their hands."

If only I dared look straight into his eyes as I always had! If only I could think devotedly: "Here I am, my whole self! Take me!" But now I did not dare. I had to make an effort to raise my hand, as if my joints were rusty.

The whisper of millions of hands. Someone's subdued "Ah," and I felt something was coming, falling heavily, but I could not understand what it was, and I did not have the strength or courage to take a look. . . .

"Those opposed?" . . .

This was always the most magnificent moment of our celebration: all would remain sitting motionless, joyfully bowing their heads under the salutary yoke of that Number of Numbers. But now, to my horror again I heard a rustle—light as a sigh, yet it was even more distinct than the brass tube of the Hymn. Thus the last sigh in a man's life, around him people with their faces pale and with drops of cold sweat upon their foreheads. . . . I lifted my eyes, and . . .

It took one hundredth of a second only; I saw thousands of hands arise "opposed" and fall back. I saw the pale, cross-marked face of I-330 and her lifted hand. Darkness came upon my eyes.

Another hundredth of a second, silence. Quiet. The pulse. Then, as if at the sign of some mad conductor, from all over the stands a rattling, a shouting, a whirlwind of unifs lifted by the rush, the perplexed figures of the Guardians running to and fro. Someone's heels in the air near my eyes, and close to those heels someone's wide-open mouth tearing itself in an inaudible scream. For some reason this picture remains particularly distinct in my memory: thousands of mouths noiselessly yelling as if on the screen of a monstrous cinema. Also, as if on a screen, somewhere below at a distance, for a second, O-90, pressed against the wall in a passage, her lips white, defending her abdomen with her crossed arms. She disappeared as if washed away by a wave, or else I simply forgot her because . . .

This was not on the screen anymore but within me, within my compressed heart, within the rapidly pulsating temples. Over my head, somewhat to the left, R-13 suddenly jumped upon a bench, all sprinkling, red, rabid. In his arms was I-330, pale, her unif torn from shoulder to breast, red blood on white. She held him firmly around the neck, and he with huge leaps from bench to bench, repellent and agile, like a gorilla, was carrying her upward, away.

As if it were in a fire of ancient days, everything became red around me. Only one thing in my head: to jump after them, to catch them. At this moment I cannot explain to myself the source of that strength within me, but like a battering-ram I broke through the crowd, over somebody's shoulders, over a bench, and I was there in a moment and caught R-13 by the collar.

"Don't you dare! Don't you dare, I say! Immediately—"

Fortunately no one could hear my voice, as everyone was shouting and running.

"Who is it? What is the matter? What—" R-13 turned around; his sprinkling lips were trembling. He apparently thought it was one of the Guardians.

"I do not want—I won't allow—Put her down at once!"

But he only sprinkled angrily with his lips, shook his head, and ran on. Then I—I am terribly ashamed to write all this down but I believe I must, so that you, my unknown readers, may make a complete study of my disease—then I hit him over the head with all my might. You understand? I hit him. This I remember distinctly. I remember also a feeling of liberation that followed my action, a feeling of lightness in my whole body.

I-330 slid quickly out of his arms.

"Go away!" she shouted to R-. "Don't you see that he—? Go!"

R-13 showed his white Negro teeth, sprinkled into my face some word, dived down, and disappeared. And I picked up I-330, pressed her firmly to myself, and carried her away.

My heart was beating forcibly. It seemed enormous. And with every beat it would splash out such a thundering, such a hot, such a joyful wave! A flash: "Let them, below there, let them toss and rush and yell and fall; what matter if something has fallen, if something has been shattered to dust? Little matter! Only to remain this way and carry her, carry and carry . . ."

The Same Evening, Twenty-two O'clock

I hold my pen with great difficulty. Such an extraordinary fatigue after all the dizzying events of this morning. Is it possible that the strong, salutary, centuries-old walls of the United State have fallen? Is it possible that we are again without a roof over our heads, back in the wild state of freedom like our remote ancestors? Is it possible that we have lost our Well-Doer? "Opposed!" On the Day of Unanimity— opposed! I am ashamed of *them*, painfully, fearfully ashamed. . . . But who are "they"? And who am I? "They," "We" . . .? Do I know?

I shall continue.

She was sitting where I had brought her, on the uppermost glass bench which was hot from the sun. Her right shoulder and the beginning of the wonderful and incalculable curve were uncovered—an exceedingly thin serpent of blood. She seemed not to be aware of the blood, or that her breast was uncovered. No, I will say rather: she seemed to see all that and seemed to feel that it was essential to her, that if her unif had been buttoned she would have torn it open, she would have . . .

"And tomorrow!" She breathed the words through sparkling white clenched teeth. "Tomorrow, nobody knows what . . . do you understand? Neither I nor anyone else knows; it is unknown! Do you realize what a joy it is? Do you realize that all that was certain has come to an end? Now . . . things will be new, improbable, unforeseen!"

Below the human waves were still foaming, tossing, roaring, but they seemed to be very far away, and to be growing more and more distant. For she was looking at me. She slowly drew me into herself through the narrow golden windows of her pupils. We remained like that, silent, for a long while. And for some reason I recalled how once I had watched some queer yellow pupils through the Green Wall, while above the Wall birds were soaring (or was this another time?).

"Listen, if nothing particular happens tomorrow, I shall take you there; do you understand?"

No, I did not understand, but I nodded in silence. I was dissolved, I became infinitesimal, a geometrical point . . .

After all, there is some logic—a peculiar logic of today—in this state of being a point. A point has more unknowns than any other entity. If a point should start to move, it might become thousands of curves, or hundreds of solids.

I was afraid to budge. What might I have become if I had moved? It seemed to me that everybody, like myself, was afraid now of even the most minute of motions.

At this moment, for instance, as I sit and write, everyone is sitting hidden in his glass cell, expecting something. I do not hear the buzzing of the elevators, usual at this hour, or laughter, or steps; from time to time Numbers pass in couples through the hall, whispering, on tiptoe . . .

What will happen tomorrow? What will become of me tomorrow?

Record Twenty-Six

The World Does Exist
Rash
Forty-one Degrees Centigrade

Morning. Through the ceiling the sky is, as usual, firm, round, red-cheeked. I think I should have been less surprised had I found above some extraordinary quadrangular sun, or people clad in many-colored dresses made of the skins of animals, or opaque walls of stone. Then the world, *our world*, does exist still? Or is it only inertia? Is the generator already switched out, while the armature is still roaring and revolving; two more revolutions, or three, and at the fourth it will die away?

Are you familiar with that strange state in which you wake up in the middle of the night, when you open your eyes into the darkness, and then suddenly feel you are lost in the dark; you quickly, quickly begin to feel around, seeking in the Journal of the United State; quickly, quickly—I found this:

"The celebration of the Day of Unanimity, long awaited by all, took place yesterday. The same Well-Doer who so often has proved his unshakable wisdom was unanimously re-elected for the forty-eighth time. The celebration was clouded by a little confusion, created by the enemies of happiness, who by their action naturally lost the right to be the bricks for the foundation of the renovated United State. It is clear to everyone that to take their votes into account would mean to consider as a part of a magnificent, heroic symphony the accidental cough of a sick person who happened to be in the concert hall."

Oh, great Sage! Is it really true that despite everything we are saved? What objection, indeed, can one find to this most crystalline syllogism? And further on a few more lines:

"Today at twelve o'clock a joint meeting of the Administrative Bureau, Medical Bureau, and Bureau of Guardians will take place. An important State decree is to be expected momentarily."

No, the Walls still stand erect. Here they are! I can feel them. And that strange feeling of being lost somewhere, of not knowing where I am—that feeling is gone. I am no longer surprised to see the sky blue and the sun round and all the Numbers going to work as usual. . . .

I walked along the avenue with a particularly firm, resounding step. It seemed to me that everyone else walked exactly like me. But at the crossing, on turning the corner, I noticed people strangely shying away, going around the corner of a building sidewise, as if a pipe had burst in the wall, as if cold water were spurting like a fountain on the sidewalk and it was impossible to cross it.

Another five or ten steps and I, too, felt a spurt of cold water that struck me and threw me from the sidewalk; at a height of approximately two meters a quadrangular piece of paper was pasted to the wall, and on that sheet of paper, unintelligible, poisonously green letters:

MEPHI

And under the paper—an S-like curved back and wing ears shaking with anger or emotion. With right arm lifted as high as possible, his left arm hopelessly stretched out backward like a hurt wing, he was trying to jump high enough to reach the paper and tear it off, but he was unable to do so. He was a fraction of an inch too short.

Probably every one of the passers-by had the same thought: "If I go to help him, I, only one of the many, will he not think that I am guilty of something and that I am therefore anxious to . . ."

I must confess I had that thought. But remembering how many times he had proved my real Guardian Angel and how often he had saved me, I stepped toward him and with courage and warm assurance I stretched out my hand and tore off the sheet. S- turned around. The little drills sank quickly into me to the bottom and found something there. Then he lifted his left brow, and winked toward the wall where "Mephi" had been hanging a minute ago. The tail of his little smile even twinkled with a certain pleasure, which greatly surprised me. But why should I be surprised? A doctor always prefers a temperature of 40°C. and a rash to the slow, languid rise of the temperature during the incubation period of a disease; it enables him to determine the character of the disease. Today "Mephi" broke out on the walls like a rash. I understood his smile.

In the passage to the underground railway, under our feet on the clean glass of the steps, again a white sheet: "Mephi." And also on the walls of the tunnel, and on the benches, and on the mirror of the car (apparently pasted on in haste as some were hanging on a slant). Everywhere, the same white, gruesome rash.

I must confess that the exact meaning of that smile became clear to me only after many days which were overfilled with the strangest and most unexpected events.

The roaring of the wheels, distinct in the general silence, seemed to be the noise of infected streams of blood. Some Number was inadvertently touched on the shoulder, and he started so that a package of papers fell out of his hands. To my left another Number was reading a paper, his eyes fixed always on the same line; the paper perceptibly trembled in his hands. I felt that everywhere, in the wheels, in the hands, in the newspapers, even in the eyelashes, the pulse was becoming more and more rapid, and I thought it probable that today when I-330 and I found ourselves *there*, the temperature would rise to 39°C., 40°, perhaps 41° and . . .

At the docks—the same silence filled with the buzzing of an invisible propeller. The lathes were silent as if brooding. Only the cranes were moving almost inaudibly as if on tiptoe, gliding, bending over, picking up with their tentacles the lumps of frozen air and loading the tanks of the *Integral*. We are already preparing the *Integral* for a trial flight.

"Well, shall we have her up in a week?" This was my question addressed to the Second Builder. His face is like porcelain, painted with sweet blue and tender little pink flowers (eyes and lips), but today those little flowers looked faded and washed out. We were counting aloud when suddenly I broke off in the midst of a word and stopped, my mouth wide open; above the cupola, above the blue lump lifted by the crane, there was a scarcely noticeable small white square. I felt my whole body trembling—perhaps with laughter. Yes! I *myself heard* my own laughter. (Did you ever hear your own laughter?)

"No, listen," I said. "Imagine you are in an ancient airplane. The altimeter shows 5,000 meters. A wing breaks; you are dashing down like . . . And on the way you calculate: 'Tomorrow from twelve to two . . . from two to six . . . and dinner at five!' Would it not be absurd?"

The little blue flowers began to move and bulge out. What if I were made of glass and he could have seen what was going on within me at that moment? If he knew that some three or four hours later . . .

Record Twenty-Seven

No Headings. It Is Impossible!

I was alone in the endless corridors. In those same corridors . . . A mute, concrete sky. Water was dripping somewhere upon a stone. The familiar, heavy, opaque door—and the subdued noise from behind it.

She said she would come out at sixteen sharp. It was already five minutes, then ten, then fifteen past sixteen. No one appeared. For a second I was my former self, horrified at the thought that the door might open.

"Five minutes more, and if she does not come out . . ."

Water was dripping somewhere upon a stone. No one about. With melancholy pleasure I felt: "Saved," and slowly I turned and walked back along the corridor. The trembling dots of the small lamps on the ceiling became dimmer and dimmer. Suddenly a quick rattle of a door behind me. Quick steps, softly echoing from the ceiling and the walls. It was she, light as a bird, panting somewhat from running.

"I knew you would be here, you would come! I knew you—you . . ."

The spears of her eyelashes moved apart to let me in and . . . How can I describe what effect that ancient, absurd, and wonderful rite has upon me when her lips touch mine? Can I find a formula to express that whirlwind which sweeps out of my soul everything, everything save her? Yes, yes, from my *soul*. You may laugh at me if you will.

She made an effort to raise her eyelids, and her slow words, too, came with an effort:

"No. Now we must go."

The door opened. Old, worn steps. An unbearably multicolored noise, whistling and light. . . .

Twenty-four hours have passed since then and everything seems to have settled in me, yet it is most difficult for me to find words for even an approximate description. . . . It is as though a bomb had exploded in my head. . . . Open mouths, wings, shouts, leaves, words, stones, all these one after another in a heap. . . .

I remember my first thought was: "Fast—back!" For it was clear to me that while I was waiting there in the corridors, *they* somehow had blasted and destroyed the Green Wall, and from behind it everything rushed in and splashed over our city which until then had been kept clean of that lower world. I must have said something of this sort to I-330. She laughed.

"No, we have simply come out *beyond the Green Wall*."

Then I opened my eyes, and close to me, actually, I saw those very things which until then not a single living Number had ever seen except depreciated a thousand times, dimmed and hazy through the cloudy glass of the Wall.

The sun—it was no longer our light evenly diffused over the mirror surface of the pavements; it seemed an accumulation of living fragments, of incessantly oscillating, dizzy spots which blinded the eyes. And the trees! Like candles rising into the very sky, or like spiders that squatted upon the earth, supported by their clumsy paws, or like mute green fountains. And all this was moving, jumping, rustling. Under my feet some strange little ball was crawling. . . . I stood as though rooted to the ground. I was unable to take a step because under my foot there was not an even plane, but (imagine!) something disgustingly soft, yielding, living, springy, green! . . .

I was dazed; I was strangled—yes, strangled; it is the best word to express my state. I stood holding fast with both hands to a swinging branch.

"It is nothing. It is all right. It is natural, the first time. It will pass. Courage!"

At I-330's side, bouncing dizzily on a green net, someone's thinnest profile, cut out of paper. No, not "someone's." I recognized him. I remembered. It was the doctor. I understood everything very clearly. I realized that they both caught me beneath the arms and laughingly dragged me forward. My legs twisted and glided. . . . Terrible noise, cawing, stumps, yelling, branches, tree trunks, wings, leaves, whistling. . . .

The trees drew apart. A bright clearing. In the clearing, people, or perhaps, to be more exact, *beings.* Now comes the most difficult part to describe, for *this* was beyond any bounds of probability. It is clear to me now why I-330 was stubbornly silent about it before; I would not have believed it, would not have believed even her. It is even possible that tomorrow I shall not believe myself, shall not believe my own description in these pages.

In the clearing, around a naked, skull-like rock, a noisy crowd of three or four hundred . . . people. Well, let's call them people. I find it difficult to coin new words. Just as on the stands you recognize in the general accumulation of faces only those which are familiar to you, so at first I recognized only our grayish-blue unifs. But one second later and I saw distinctly and clearly among the unifs dark, red, golden, black, brown, and white humans—apparently they were humans. None of them had any clothes on, and their bodies were covered with short, glistening hair, like that which may be seen on the stuffed horse in the Prehistoric Museum. But their females had faces exactly, yes, exactly, like the faces of our women: tender, rosy, and not overgrown with hair. Also their breasts were free of hair, firm breasts of wonderful geometrical form. As to the males, only a part of their faces were free from hair, like our ancestors', and the organs of reproduction were similar to ours.

All this was so unbelievable, so unexpected, that I stood there quietly (I assert positively that I stood quietly) and looked around. Like a scale: overload one side sufficiently and then you may gently put on the other as much as you will; the arrow will not move.

Suddenly I felt alone. I-330 was no longer with me. I don't know how or where she disappeared. Around me were only *those*, with their hair glistening like silk in the sunlight. I caught someone's warm, strong, dark shoulder.

"Listen, please, in the name of the Well-Doer, could you tell me where she went? A while, a minute ago, she . . ."

Long-haired, austere eyebrows turned to me.

"Sh . . . sh . . . silence!" He made a sign with his head toward the center of the clearing where there stood the yellow skull-like stone.

There above the heads of all I saw her. The sun beat straight into my eyes, and because of that she seemed coal-black, standing out on the blue cloth of the sky—a coal-black silhouette on a blue background. A little higher the clouds were floating. And it seemed that not the clouds but the rock itself, and she herself upon that rock, and the crowd and the clearing—all were silently floating like a ship, and the earth was light and glided away from under the feet. . . .

"Brothers!" (It was she.) "Brothers, you all know that there inside the Wall, in the City, they are building the *Integral*. And you know also that the day has come for us to destroy that Wall and all other walls, so that the green wind may blow over all the earth, from end to end. But the *Integral* is going to take these walls up, up into the heights, to the thousands of other worlds which every evening whisper to us with their lights through the black leaves of night . . ."

Waves and foam and wind were beating the rock:

"Down with the *Integral*! Down!"

"No, brothers, not 'down.' The *Integral* must be ours. And it *shall* be ours. On the day when it first sets sail into the sky *we* shall be on board. For the Builder of the *Integral* is with us. He left the walls, he came with me here in order to be with us. Long live the Builder!"

A second—and I was somewhere above everything. Under me: heads, heads, heads, wide-open, yelling mouths, arms rising and falling. . . . There was something strange and intoxicating in it all. I felt myself *above everybody*; I was, I, a separate world; I ceased to be the usual item; I became unity. . . .

Again I was below, near the rock, my body happy, shaken, and rumpled, as after an embrace of love. Sunlight, voices, and from above—the smiles of I-330. A golden-haired woman, her whole body silky-golden and diffusing an odor of different herbs, was nearby. She held a cup, apparently made of wood. She drank a little from it with her red lips, and then offered the cup to me. I closed my eyes and eagerly drank the sweet, cold, prickly sparks, pouring them down on the fire which burned within me.

Soon afterward my blood and the whole world began to circulate a thousand times faster; the earth seemed to be flying, light as dawn. And within me everything was simple, light, and clear. Only then I noticed on the rock the familiar, enormous letters: M E P H I, and for some reason the inscription seemed to me *necessary*. It seemed to be a simple thread binding everything together. A rather rough picture hewn in the rock—this, too, seemed comprehensible; it represented a youth with wings and a transparent body and, in the place ordinarily occupied by the heart, a blinding, red, blazing coal. Again I understood that coal—or no, I *felt* it as I felt without hearing every word of I-330's (she continued to speak from above, from the rock); and I felt that all of them breathed one breath, and that they were all ready to fly somewhere like the birds over the Wall.

From behind, from the confusion of breathing bodies, a loud voice: "But this is folly!"

It seems to me it was I—yes, I am certain it was I who then jumped on the rock; from there I saw the sun, the heads, a green sea on a blue background, and I cried:

"Yes, yes, precisely. All must become insane; we must become insane as soon as possible! We must: I know it."

I-330 was at my side. Her smile—two dark lines from the angles of her mouth directed upward. . . . And within me a blazing coal. It was momentary, light, a little painful, beautiful. . . . And later, only stray fragments that remained sticking in me. . . .

. . . Very low and slowly a bird was moving. I saw it was living, like me. It was turning its head now to the right and then to the left like a human being, and its round black eyes drilled themselves into me. . . .

. . . Then: a human back glistening with fur the color of ancient ivory; a mosquito crawling on that back, a mosquito with tiny transparent wings. The back twitched to chase the mosquito away; it twitched again. . . .

. . . And yet another thing: a shadow from the leaves, a woven, net-like shadow. Some humans lay in that shadow, chewing something, something similar to the legendary food of the ancients, a long yellow fruit and a piece of something dark. They put some of it in my hand, and it seemed strange to me for I did not know whether I might eat it or not. . . .

. . . And again: a crowd, heads, legs, arms, mouths, faces appearing for a second and disappearing like bursting bubbles. For a second (or perhaps it was only a hallucination?) the transparent, flying wing ears appeared. . . .

With all my might I pressed the hand of I-330. She turned to me.

"What is the matter?"

"He is here! I thought, I—"

"Who?"

"S-, a second ago, in the crowd."

The ends of the thin, coal-black brows moved to the temples—a smile like a sharp triangle. I could not see clearly why she smiled. How could she smile?

"But you understand, I-330, don't you, you understand what it means if he, or one of them, is here?"

"You are funny! How could it ever enter the heads of those within the Wall that we are here? Remember; take yourself. Did you ever think it was possible? They are busy hunting us *there*—let them! You are delirious!"

Her smile was light and cheerful and I, too, was smiling; the earth was drunken, cheerful, light, floating. . . .

Record Twenty-Eight

Both of Them
Entropy and Energy
The Opaque Part of the Body

If your world is similar to the world of the ancients, then you may eas-ily imagine that one day you suddenly come upon a sixth or a seventh continent, upon some Atlantis, and you find there unheard-of cities, labyrinths, people flying through the air without the aid of wings or aeros, stones lifted into the air by the power of a gaze—in brief, imagine that you see things that cannot come to your mind even if you suffer from dream sickness. That is how I feel now. For you must understand that no one has ever gone beyond the Green Wall since the Two Hundred Years' War, as I have already told you.

I know it is my duty to you, my unknown friends, to give more details about that unsuspected, strange world which has opened to me since yesterday. But for the time being I am unable to return to that subject. Everything is so novel, so novel it is like a rainstorm, and I am not big enough to embrace it all. I spread out the folds of my unif, my palms—and yet pailfuls splash past me and only drops can reach these pages. . . .

At first I heard behind me, behind the door, a loud voice. I recog-nized her voice, the voice of I-330, tense, metallic—and another one, almost inflexible, like a wooden ruler, the voice of U-. Then the door burst open with a crack and both of them shot into the room. *Shot* is the right word.

I-330 put her hand on the back of my armchair and smiled over her shoulder, but only with her teeth, at U-. I should not care to stand before such a smile.

"Listen," she said to me, "this woman seems to have made it her business to guard you from me like a little child. Is it with your permission?"

"But he *is* a child. Yes! That is why he does not notice that you . . . that it is only in order . . . That all this is only a foul game! Yes! And it is my duty . . ."

For a second (in the mirror) the broken, trembling line of brows. I leaped, controlling with difficulty the other self within me, the one with the hairy fists. With difficulty, pushing every word through my teeth, I cried straight into her face, into her very gills:

"Get out of here at once! Out! At once!"

The gills swelled at first into brick-red lumps, then fell and became gray. She opened her mouth to say something, but without a word she slammed it shut and went out.

I threw myself toward I-330.

"Never, never will I forgive myself! She dared! You . . . But you don't think, do you, that you, that she . . . This is all because she wants to register on me, but I . . ."

"Fortunately she will not have time for that now. Besides, even a thousand like her . . . I don't care . . . I know you will not believe that thousand, but only me. For after all that happened yesterday, I am all yours, all, to the very end, as you wanted it. I am in your hands; you can now at any moment . . ."

"What, 'at any moment'?" (But immediately I understood what. The blood rushed to my ears and cheeks.) "Don't speak about that, you must never speak about that! The *other* I, my former self . . . but now . . ."

"How do I know? Man is like a novel: up to the last page one does not know what the end will be. It would not be worth reading otherwise."

She was stroking my head. I could not see her face, but I could tell by her voice that she was looking somewhere far into the distance; she had hooked herself on to that cloud which was floating silently, slowly, no one knows where to.

Suddenly she pushed me away with her hand, firmly but tenderly.

"Listen. I came to tell you that perhaps we are now . . . our last days . . . You know, don't you, that all Auditoriums are to be closed after tonight?"

"Closed?"

"Yes. I passed by and saw that in all Auditoriums preparations are going on: tables, medics all in white . . ."

"But what does it all mean?"

"I don't know. Nobody knows as yet. That's the worst of it. I feel only that the current is on, the spark is jumping, and if not today, then tomorrow. . . . Yet perhaps they will not have time. . . . "

It has been a long while since I ceased to understand who *they* are and who *we* are. I do not understand what *I* want; do I want them to have or not to have enough time? One thing is clear to me: I-330 is now on the very edge, on the very edge, and in one second more . . .

"But it is folly," I said. "You, versus the United State! It's the same as if you were to cover the muzzle of a gun with your hands and expect that way to prevent the shot. . . . It is absolute folly!"

A smile.

" 'We must all go insane—as soon as possible go insane.' It was yesterday, do you remember?"

Yes, she was right; I had even written it down. Consequently, it really had taken place. In silence I looked into her face. At that moment the dark cross was especially distinct.

"I-, dear, before it is too late . . . If you want . . . I'll leave everything, I'll forget everything, and we'll go there beyond the Wall, to *them.* . . . I do not even know who they are. . . . "

She shook her head. Through the dark windows of her eyes I saw within her a flaming oven, sparks, tongues of flame, and above them a heap of dry wood. It was clear to me that it was too late, my words could be of no avail.

She stood up. She would soon leave. Perhaps these were the last days, or the last minutes. . . . I grasped her hand.

"No, stay a little while longer . . . for the sake . . . for the sake . . ."

She slowly lifted my hand toward the light, my hairy paw which I detest. I wanted to withdraw it, but she held it tightly.

"Your hand . . . You undoubtedly don't know, and very few do know, that women from here occasionally used to fall in love with *them.* Probably there are in you a few drops of that blood of the sun and the woods. Perhaps that is why I . . ."

Silence. It was so strange that because of that silence, because of an emptiness, because of a nothing, my heart should beat so wildly. I cried:

"Ah, you shall not go yet! You shall not go until you tell me about *them,* for you love . . . them, and I don't even know who they are, nor where they come from."

"Where are they? The half we have lost. H_2 and O, two halves, but in order to get water—H_2O, creeks, seas, waterfalls, storms—those two halves must be united."

I distinctly remember every movement of hers. I remember she picked up a glass triangle from my table, and while talking she pressed its sharp edge against her check; a white scar would appear, then it would fill again and become pink and disappear. And it is strange that I cannot remember her words, especially the beginning of the story. I remember only different images and colors. At first, I remember, she told me about the Two Hundred Years' War. Red color. . . . On the green of the grass, on the dark clay, on the pale blue of the snow—everywhere red ditches that would not become dry. Then, yellow; yellow grass burned by the sun, yellow, naked wild men and wild dogs side by side near swollen cadavers of dogs or perhaps of men. All this certainly beyond the Walls, for the City was already the victor, and it already possessed our present-day petroleum food. And at night . . . down from the sky . . . heavy black folds. The folds would swing over the woods, the villages—blackish-red, slow columns of smoke. A dull moaning; endless strings of people driven into the City to be saved by force and to be whipped into happiness.

". . . You knew almost all this."

"Yes, almost."

"But you did not know, and only a few did, that a small part of them remained together and stayed to live beyond the Wall. Being naked, they went into the woods. They learned there from the trees, beasts, birds, flowers, and sun. Hair soon grew over their bodies, but under that hair they preserved their warm red blood. With you it was worse; numbers covered your bodies; numbers crawled over you like lice. One ought to strip you of everything, and naked you ought to be driven into the woods. You ought to learn how to tremble with fear, with joy, with wild anger, with cold; you should pray to fire! And we Mephi, we want . . ."

"Wait a minute! 'Mephi,' what does it mean?"

"Mephi? It is from Mephisto. You remember, there on the rock, the figure of the youth? Or, no. I shall explain it to you in your own language, and you will understand better. There are two forces in the world, entropy and energy. One leads into blessed quietude, to happy equilibrium, the other to the destruction of equilibrium, to torturingly perpetual motion. Our, or rather your ancestors, the Christians, worshiped entropy like a God. But we are not Christians, we . . ."

At that moment a slight whisper was suddenly heard, a knock at the door, and in rushed that flattened man with the forehead low over his eyes, who several times had brought me notes from I-330. He ran straight to us, stopped, panting like an air pump, and could say not a word, as he must have been running at top speed.

"But tell me! What has happened?" I-330 grasped him by the hand.

"They are coming here," panted the air pump, "with guards. . . . And with them that what's-his-name, the hunchback . . ."

"S-?"

"Yes. They are in the house by this time. They'll soon be here. Quick, quick!"

"Nonsense, we have time!" I-330 was laughing, cheerful sparks in her eyes. It was either absurd, senseless courage, or else there was something I did not understand.

"I-, dear, for the sake of the Well-Doer! You must understand that this . . ."

"For the sake of the Well-Doer!" The sharp, triangle smile.

"Well . . . well, for my sake, I implore you!"

"Oh, yes, I wanted to talk to you about some other matters. . . . Well, never mind. . . . We'll talk about them tomorrow."

And cheerfully (yes, cheerfully) she nodded to me; the other came out for a second from under his forehead's awning and nodded also. I was alone.

Quick! To my desk! I opened this manuscript and took up my pen so that they should find me at this work, which is for the benefit of the United State. Suddenly I felt every hair on my head living, separated, moving. "What if they should read even one page of these most recently written?"

Motionless I sat at the table, but everything around me seemed to be moving, as if the less than microscopic movements of the atoms had suddenly been magnified millions of times; I saw the walls trembling, my pen trembling, and the letters swinging and fusing together. "To hide them! But where?" Glass all around. "To burn them?" But they would notice the fire through the corridor and in the neighboring room. Besides, I felt unable, I felt too weak, to destroy this torturing and perhaps dearest piece of my own self. . . .

Voices from a distance (from the corridor), and steps. I had time only to snatch a handful of pages and put them under me and then, as if soldered to the armchair—every atom of which was quivering—I remained sitting, while the floor under my feet rolled like the deck of a ship, up and down. . . .

All shrunk together and hidden under the awning of my own forehead, like that messenger, I watched them stealthily; they were going from room to room, beginning at the right end of the corridor. Nearer . . . nearer. . . . I saw that some sat in their rooms, torpid like me; others would jump up and open their doors wide—lucky ones! If only I, too, could . . .

"The Well-Doer is the most perfect fumigation humanity needs; consequently, no peristalsis in the organism of the United State could . . ." I was writing this nonsense, pressing my trembling pen hard, and lower and lower my head bent over the table, and within me some sort of crazy forge . . . With my back I was listening . . . and I heard the click of the doorknob. . . . A current of fresh air. . . . My armchair was dancing a mad dance. . . . Only then, and even then with difficulty, I tore myself away from the page and turned my head in the direction of the newcomers (how difficult it is to play a foul game!). In front of all was S-, morose, silent, his eyes swiftly drilling deep shafts within me, within my armchair, and within the pages which were twitching in my hands. Then for a second—familiar, everyday faces at the door; one of them separated itself from the rest with its bulging, pinkish-brown gills. . . .

At once I recalled everything that had happened in the same room half an hour ago, and it was clear to me that they would presently . . .

All my being was shriveling and pulsating in that fortunately opaque part of my body with which I was covering the manuscript. U- came up to S-, gently plucked his sleeve, and said in a low voice:

"This is D-503, the builder of the *Integral*. You have probably heard of him. He is always like that, at his desk—does not spare himself at all!"

. . . And I thought . . . What a dear, wonderful woman! . . .

S- slid up to me, bent over my shoulder toward the table. I covered the lines I had written with my elbow, but he shouted severely:

"Show us at once what you have there, please!"

Dying with shame, I held out the sheet of paper. He read it over, and I noticed a tiny smile jump out of his eyes, scamper down his face, and, slightly wagging its tail, perch upon the right angle of his mouth. . . .

"Somewhat ambiguous, yet. . . . Well, you may continue; we shall not disturb you any further."

He went splashing toward the door as if in a ditch of water. And with every step of his I felt coming back to me my legs, my arms, my fingers—my soul again distributed itself evenly throughout my whole body; I breathed . . . .

The last thing: U- lingered in my room to come back to me and say right in my ear, in a whisper: "It is lucky for you that I . . ."

I did not understand. What did she mean by that? The same evening I learned that they had led away three Numbers, although nobody speaks aloud about it, or about anything that happened. This ostensible silence is due to the educational influence of the Guardians who are ever present among us. Conversations deal chiefly with the quick fall of the barometer and the forthcoming change in the weather.

QUESTIONS FOR DISCUSSION

At the end of this excerpt, how does D-503 feel about the rebellion being discovered and repressed?

1. How does D-503 feel about the "wild state of freedom" that may result if society has lost its Well-Doer? (321)

2. During the Mephi assembly, why does D-503 shout, "All must become insane; we must become insane as soon as possible! We must: I know it"? (329)

3. After going beyond the Green Wall, why does D-503 feel that "it has been a long while since I ceased to understand who *they* are and who *we* are"? (333)

4. Why is D-503 "dying with shame" when S- demands to see what he is writing at the desk? (337)

Why does D-503 go with I-330 beyond the Green Wall?

1. During the Day of Unanimity, why does D-503 want to look at the Well-Doer and think "Here I am, my whole self! Take me!" but does not dare to do so? (319)

2. While counting aloud with the Second Builder, why does D-503 laugh and say, "Yes! I *myself heard* my own laughter"? (325)

3. When D-503 goes beyond the wall, why is his first thought that the city has been contaminated by the "lower world"? (326)

4. After the Mephi embrace D-503 as the Builder, why does everything seem "simple, light, and clear" to him? (329)

FOR FURTHER REFLECTION

1. Why are some people willing to mount a rebellion against injustice even when that rebellion seems doomed to failure?

2. Is it possible to form a society in which there is no "they" that "we" are defined against?

3. What elements of the social organization of *We* do you recognize in today's society?

4. To what extent do attitudes many find offensive today, such as the reference to a character as being "repellent, Negro-lipped," undermine the enduring value of a text?

Unrest in the Soul

The twentieth century saw the rise of dystopian writing, envisioning future states both repressive and encroaching. Authors often focused on the perceived threats of technology, consumerism, and environmental calamity, imagining a restrictive future with little individual freedom. And yet, even amid the most dire predictions of humanity's future, many authors found space for defiance, escape, and recovery from oppressive conditions. Authors have imagined numerous routes out of dystopia, sometimes through the restoration of a previous order that is perceived as somehow more "natural," or through the hope that a new society will arise to take the place of a destroyed civilization. Hope endures, in a variety of forms, throughout many dystopian tales.

The short story "The Machine Stops," by **E. M. Forster** (1879–1970), appears to be years ahead of its time. Published in 1909, it prefigures a world of global communications uncannily similar to today's digital age. Against the futuristic technical developments imagined in the story, Forster highlights the isolated existence of people, his characters living beneath the ground in individual cells. Is his vision of a technologically driven society one that resonates with today's digital users? Does the existence of those living outside Forster's technological realm have echoes and implications in our society?

Pulitzer Prize–winning author **Jennifer Egan** (1962–), in her short story "Black Box" (2012), takes the interaction of humanity and technology a step further, exploring how the human body itself might become a vessel for data storage. Initially published as a series of tweets released over ten days, Egan's story poses difficult questions about communication, ethics, and truth in a dystopian near-future. How does the means of publication interact with the story's theme of technology and individual response? Is the reader more or less complicit when encountering the narrative through Twitter?

George Saunders (1958–), in his short story "Jon" (2006), also depicts a futuristic world where human relationships and interaction have been eroded, this time in favor of commercial interests. Teenagers are isolated and housed in camp-like facilities where they assess commercials and evaluate consumer goods. But Saunders's teenage characters are drawn to the world outside, even at great personal cost. They cannot easily ignore the allure of personal relationships and free will. What does the overarching corporate interference of these facilities say about commercialism in our world? Do the detrimental effects of leaving such a facility invalidate the freedom achieved?

In her brief imagining of a planet's historical trajectory, "Time Capsule Found on the Dead Planet" (2009), **Margaret Atwood** (1939–) posits the hope that future readers will encounter the text and its description of decline. She charts the demise of a willfully destroyed planet, but there remains a vestige of humanity that seeks longevity and wants its story to be heard in the future. Is the time capsule created in order that others might learn from it, and perhaps follow a different path? Is there something innately human in this possibly futile gesture? And is this effort an element of all utopian and dystopian writing? The excerpt from *Silent Spring* (1962), by the biologist **Rachel Carson** (1907–1964), complements Atwood's selection. In this excerpt, Carson sounds an alarm and raises a fundamental question that resonates with many utopian plans: how can we be assured that an attempted solution to a manifest social and environmental problem will not bring "a train of disaster in its wake."

Spanning a range of issues, the selections here all touch on dystopian concepts while gesturing toward possible redemption and the restoration of a healthier society. Is a function of dystopian writing then to exhort readers to change, or is there something more dubiously pleasurable in reading of decline?

The Machine Stops

E. M. Forster

THE AIRSHIP

I magine, if you can, a small room, hexagonal in shape, like the cell of a bee. It is lighted neither by window nor by lamp, yet it is filled with a soft radiance. There are no apertures for ventilation, yet the air is fresh. There are no musical instruments, and yet, at the moment that my meditation opens, this room is throbbing with melodious sounds. An armchair is in the centre, by its side a reading desk—that is all the furniture. And in the armchair there sits a swaddled lump of flesh—a woman, about five feet high, with a face as white as a fungus. It is to her that the little room belongs.

An electric bell rang.

The woman touched a switch and the music was silent.

"I suppose I must see who it is," she thought, and set her chair in motion. The chair, like the music, was worked by machinery, and it rolled her to the other side of the room, where the bell still rang importunately.

"Who is it?" she called. Her voice was irritable, for she had been interrupted often since the music began. She knew several thousand people; in certain directions human intercourse had advanced enormously.

But when she listened into the receiver, her white face wrinkled into smiles, and she said:

"Very well. Let us talk, I will isolate myself. I do not expect anything important will happen for the next five minutes—for I can give you fully five minutes, Kuno. Then I must deliver my lecture on 'Music during the Australian Period.'"

She touched the isolation knob, so that no one else could speak to her. Then she touched the lighting apparatus, and the little room was plunged into darkness.

"Be quick!" She called, her irritation returning. "Be quick, Kuno; here I am in the dark wasting my time."

But it was fully fifteen seconds before the round plate that she held in her hands began to glow. A faint blue light shot across it, darkening to purple, and presently she could see the image of her son, who lived on the other side of the earth, and he could see her.

"Kuno, how slow you are."

He smiled gravely.

"I really believe you enjoy dawdling."

"I have called you before, mother, but you were always busy or isolated. I have something particular to say."

"What is it, dearest boy? Be quick. Why could you not send it by pneumatic post?"

"Because I prefer saying such a thing. I want—"

"Well?"

"I want you to come and see me."

Vashti watched his face in the blue plate.

"But I can see you!" she exclaimed. "What more do you want?"

"I want to see you not through the Machine," said Kuno. "I want to speak to you not through the wearisome Machine."

"Oh, hush!" said his mother, vaguely shocked. "You mustn't say anything against the Machine."

"Why not?"

"One mustn't."

"You talk as if a god had made the Machine," cried the other. "I believe that you pray to it when you are unhappy. Men made it, do not forget that. Great men, but men. The Machine is much, but it is not everything. I see something like you in this plate, but I do not see you. I hear something like you through this telephone, but I do not hear you. That is why I want you to come. Come and stop with me. Pay me a visit, so that we can meet face to face, and talk about the hopes that are in my mind."

She replied that she could scarcely spare the time for a visit.

"The airship barely takes two days to fly between me and you."

"I dislike airships."

"Why?"

"I dislike seeing the horrible brown earth, and the sea, and the stars when it is dark. I get no ideas in an airship."

"I do not get them anywhere else."

"What kind of ideas can the air give you?"

He paused for an instant.

"Do you not know four big stars that form an oblong, and three stars close together in the middle of the oblong, and hanging from these stars, three other stars?"

"No, I do not. I dislike the stars. But did they give you an idea? How interesting; tell me."

"I had an idea that they were like a man."

"I do not understand."

"The four big stars are the man's shoulders and his knees. The three stars in the middle are like the belts that men wore once, and the three stars hanging are like a sword."

"A sword?"

"Men carried swords about with them, to kill animals and other men."

"It does not strike me as a very good idea, but it is certainly original. When did it come to you first?"

"In the airship—" He broke off, and she fancied that he looked sad. She could not be sure, for the Machine did not transmit *nuances* of expression. It only gave a general idea of people—an idea that was good enough for all practical purposes, Vashti thought. The imponderable bloom, declared by a discredited philosophy to be the actual essence of intercourse, was rightly ignored by the Machine, just as the imponderable bloom of the grape was ignored by the manufacturers of artificial fruit. Something "good enough" had long since been accepted by our race.

"The truth is," he continued, "that I want to see these stars again. They are curious stars. I want to see them not from the airship, but from the surface of the earth, as our ancestors did, thousands of years ago. I want to visit the surface of the earth."

She was shocked again.

"Mother, you must come, if only to explain to me what is the harm of visiting the surface of the earth."

"No harm," she replied, controlling herself. "But no advantage. The surface of the earth is only dust and mud, no life remains on it, and you would need a respirator, or the cold of the outer air would kill you. One dies immediately in the outer air."

"I know; of course I shall take all precautions."

"And besides—"

"Well?"

She considered, and chose her words with care. Her son had a queer temper, and she wished to dissuade him from the expedition.

"It is contrary to the spirit of the age," she asserted.

"Do you mean by that, contrary to the Machine?"

"In a sense, but—"

His image is the blue plate faded.

"Kuno!"

He had isolated himself.

For a moment Vashti felt lonely.

Then she generated the light, and the sight of her room, flooded with radiance and studded with electric buttons, revived her. There were buttons and switches everywhere—buttons to call for food, for music, for clothing. There was the hot-bath button, by pressure of which a basin of (imitation) marble rose out of the floor, filled to the brim with a warm deodorised liquid. There was the cold-bath button. There was the button that produced literature. And there were of course the buttons by which she communicated with her friends. The room, though it contained nothing, was in touch with all that she cared for in the world.

Vashti's next move was to turn off the isolation switch, and all the accumulations of the last three minutes burst upon her. The room was filled with the noise of bells, and speaking tubes. What was the new food like? Could she recommend it? Had she had any ideas lately? Might one tell her one's own ideas? Would she make an engagement to visit the public nurseries at an early date?—say this day month.

To most of these questions she replied with irritation—a growing quality in that accelerated age. She said that the new food was horrible. That she could not visit the public nurseries through press of engagements. That she had no ideas of her own but had just been told one—that four stars and three in the middle were like a man: she doubted there was much in it. Then she switched off her correspondents, for it was time to deliver her lecture on Australian music.

The clumsy system of public gatherings had been long since abandoned; neither Vashti nor her audience stirred from their rooms. Seated in her armchair she spoke, while they in their armchairs heard her, fairly well, and saw her, fairly well. She opened with a humorous account of music in the pre-Mongolian epoch, and went on to describe the great outburst of song that followed the Chinese conquest. Remote and primeval as were the methods of I-San-So and the Brisbane school, she yet felt (she said) that study of them might repay the musician of today: they had freshness; they had, above all, ideas.

Her lecture, which lasted ten minutes, was well received, and at its conclusion she and many of her audience listened to a lecture on the sea; there were ideas to be got from the sea; the speaker had donned a respirator and visited it lately. Then she fed, talked to many friends, had a bath, talked again, and summoned her bed.

The bed was not to her liking. It was too large, and she had a feeling for a small bed. Complaint was useless, for beds were of the same dimension all over the world, and to have had an alternative size would have involved vast alterations in the Machine. Vashti isolated herself—it was necessary, for neither day nor night existed under the ground—and reviewed all that had happened since she had summoned the bed last. Ideas? Scarcely any. Events—was Kuno's invitation an event?

By her side, on the little reading desk, was a survival from the ages of litter—one book. This was the Book of the Machine. In it were instructions against every possible contingency. If she was hot or cold or dyspeptic or at a loss for a word, she went to the book, and it told her which button to press. The Central Committee published it. In accordance with a growing habit, it was richly bound.

Sitting up in the bed, she took it reverently in her hands. She glanced round the glowing room as if someone might be watching her. Then, half ashamed, half joyful, she murmured "O Machine! O Machine!" and raised the volume to her lips. Thrice she kissed it, thrice inclined her head, thrice she felt the delirium of acquiescence. Her ritual performed, she turned to page 1367, which gave the times of the departure of the airships from the island in the Southern Hemisphere, under whose soil she lived, to the island in the Northern Hemisphere, whereunder lived her son.

She thought, "I have not the time."

She made the room dark and slept; she awoke and made the room light; she ate and exchanged ideas with her friends, and listened to music and attended lectures; she made the room dark and slept. Above her, beneath her, and around her, the Machine hummed eternally; she did not notice the noise, for she had been born with it in her ears. The earth, carrying her, hummed as it sped through silence, turning her now to the invisible sun, now to the invisible stars. She awoke and made the room light.

"Kuno!"

"I will not talk to you," he answered, "until you come."

"Have you been on the surface of the earth since we spoke last?"

His image faded.

Again she consulted the book. She became very nervous and lay back in her chair palpitating. Think of her as without teeth or hair. Presently she directed the chair to the wall, and pressed an unfamiliar button. The wall swung apart slowly. Through the opening she saw a tunnel that curved slightly, so that its goal was not visible. Should she go to see her son, here was the beginning of the journey.

Of course she knew all about the communication system. There was nothing mysterious in it. She would summon a car and it would fly with her down the tunnel until it reached the lift that communicated with the airship station: the system had been in use for many, many years, long before the universal establishment of the Machine. And of course she had studied the civilisation that had immediately preceded her own—the civilisation that had mistaken the functions of the system, and had used it for bringing people to things, instead of for bringing things to people. Those funny old days, when men went for change of air instead of changing the air in their rooms! And yet—she was frightened of the tunnel: she had not seen it since her last child was born. It curved—but not quite as she remembered; it was brilliant—but not quite as brilliant as a lecturer had suggested. Vashti was seized with the terrors of direct experience. She shrank back into the room, and the wall closed up again. "Kuno," she said, "I cannot come to see you. I am not well."

Immediately an enormous apparatus fell onto her out of the ceiling, a thermometer was automatically inserted between her lips, a stethoscope was automatically laid upon her heart. She lay powerless. Cool pads soothed her forehead. Kuno had telegraphed to her doctor.

So the human passions still blundered up and down in the Machine. Vashti drank the medicine that the doctor projected into her mouth, and the machinery retired into the ceiling. The voice of Kuno was heard asking how she felt.

"Better." Then with irritation: "But why do you not come to me instead?"

"Because I cannot leave this place."

"Why?"

"Because, any moment, something tremendous may happen."

"Have you been on the surface of the earth yet?"

"Not yet."

"Then what is it?"

"I will not tell you through the Machine."

She resumed her life.

But she thought of Kuno as a baby, his birth, his removal to the public nurseries, her one visit to him there, his visits to her—visits which stopped when the Machine had assigned him a room on the other side of the earth. "Parents, duties of," said the book of the Machine, "cease at the moment of birth. P.422327483." True, but there was something special about Kuno—indeed there had been something special about all her children—and, after all, she must brave the journey if he desired it. And "something tremendous might happen." What did that mean? The nonsense of a youthful man, no doubt, but she must go. Again she pressed the unfamiliar button, again the wall swung back, and she saw the tunnel that curved out of sight. Clasping the Book, she rose, tottered onto the platform, and summoned the car. Her room closed behind her: the journey to the Northern Hemisphere had begun.

Of course it was perfectly easy. The car approached and in it she found armchairs exactly like her own. When she signalled, it stopped, and she tottered into the lift. One other passenger was in the lift, the first fellow creature she had seen face to face for months. Few travelled in these days, for, thanks to the advance of science, the earth was exactly alike all over. Rapid intercourse, from which the previous civilisation had hoped so much, had ended by defeating itself. What was the good of going to Pekin when it was just like Shrewsbury? Why return to Shrewsbury when it would be just like Pekin? Men seldom moved their bodies; all unrest was concentrated in the soul.

The airship service was a relic from the former age. It was kept up, because it was easier to keep it up than to stop it or to diminish it, but it now far exceeded the wants of the population. Vessel after vessel would rise from the vomitories of Rye or of Christchurch (I use the antique names), would sail into the crowded sky, and would draw up at the wharves of the south—empty. So nicely adjusted was the system, so independent of meteorology, that the sky, whether calm or cloudy, resembled a vast kaleidoscope whereon the same patterns periodically recurred. The ship on which Vashti sailed started now at sunset, now at dawn. But always, as it passed above Rheims, it would neighbour the ship that served between Helsingfors and the Brazils, and, every third time it surmounted the Alps, the fleet of Palermo would cross its track behind. Night and day, wind and storm, tide and earthquake, impeded man no longer. He had harnessed Leviathan. All the old literature, with its praise of Nature, and its fear of Nature, rang false as the prattle of a child.

Yet as Vashti saw the vast flank of the ship, stained with exposure to the outer air, her horror of direct experience returned. It was not quite like the airship in the cinematophote. For one thing it smelt—not strongly or unpleasantly, but it did smell, and with her eyes shut she should have known that a new thing was close to her. Then she had to walk to it from the lift, had to submit to glances from the other passengers. The man in front dropped his Book—no great matter, but it disquieted them all. In the rooms, if the Book was dropped, the floor raised it mechanically, but the gangway to the airship was not so prepared, and the sacred volume lay motionless. They stopped—the thing was unforeseen—and the man, instead of picking up his property, felt the muscles of his arm to see how they had failed him. Then someone actually said with direct utterance: "We shall be late"—and they trooped on board, Vashti treading on the pages as she did so.

Inside, her anxiety increased. The arrangements were old fashioned and rough. There was even a female attendant, to whom she would have to announce her wants during the voyage. Of course a revolving platform ran the length of the boat, but she was expected to walk from it to her cabin. Some cabins were better than others, and she did not get the best. She thought the attendant had been unfair, and spasms of rage shook her. The glass valves had closed, she could not go back. She saw, at the end of the vestibule, the lift in which she had ascended going quietly up and down, empty. Beneath those corridors of shining tiles were rooms, tier below tier, reaching far into the earth, and in each room there sat a human being, eating, or sleeping, or producing ideas. And buried deep in the hive was her own room. Vashti was afraid.

"O Machine! O Machine!" she murmured, and caressed her Book, and was comforted.

Then the sides of the vestibule seemed to melt together, as do the passages that we see in dreams, the lift vanished, the Book that had been dropped slid to the left and vanished, polished tiles rushed by like a stream of water, there was a slight jar, and the airship, issuing from its tunnel, soared above the waters of a tropical ocean.

It was night. For a moment she saw the coast of Sumatra edged by the phosphorescence of waves, and crowned by lighthouses, still sending forth their disregarded beams. These also vanished, and only the stars distracted her. They were not motionless, but swayed to and fro above her head, thronging out of one skylight into another, as if the universe and not the airship was careening. And, as often happens on clear nights, they seemed now to be in perspective, now on a plane; now piled tier beyond tier into the infinite heavens, now concealing infinity, a roof limiting forever the visions of men. In either case they seemed intolerable. "Are we to travel in the dark?" called the passengers angrily, and the attendant, who had been careless, generated the light, and pulled down the blinds of pliable metal. When the airships had been built, the desire to look direct at things still lingered in the world. Hence the extraordinary number of skylights and windows, and the proportionate discomfort to those who were civilised and refined. Even in Vashti's cabin one star peeped through a flaw in the blind, and after a few hours' uneasy slumber, she was disturbed by an unfamiliar glow, which was the dawn.

Quick as the ship had sped westward, the earth had rolled eastward quicker still, and had dragged back Vashti and her companions
towards the sun. Science could prolong the night, but only for a little,
and those high hopes of neutralising the earth's diurnal revolution had
passed, together with hopes that were possibly higher. To "keep pace
with the sun," or even to outstrip it, had been the aim of the civilisation preceding this. Racing aeroplanes had been built for the purpose,
capable of enormous speed, and steered by the greatest intellects of
the epoch. Round the globe they went, round and round, westward,
westward, round and round, amidst humanity's applause. In vain.
The globe went eastward quicker still, horrible accidents occurred,
and the Committee of the Machine, at the time rising into prominence, declared the pursuit illegal, unmechanical, and punishable by
Homelessness.

Of Homelessness more will be said later.

Doubtless the Committee was right. Yet the attempt to "defeat the
sun" aroused the last common interest that our race experienced about
the heavenly bodies, or indeed about anything. It was the last time
that men were compacted by thinking of a power outside the world.
The sun had conquered, yet it was the end of his spiritual dominion.
Dawn, midday, twilight, the zodiacal path, touched neither men's lives
nor their hearts, and science retreated into the ground, to concentrate
herself upon problems that she was certain of solving.

So when Vashti found her cabin invaded by a rosy finger of light,
she was annoyed, and tried to adjust the blind. But the blind flew
up altogether, and she saw through the skylight small pink clouds,
swaying against a background of blue, and as the sun crept higher, its
radiance entered direct, brimming down the wall, like a golden sea.
It rose and fell with the airship's motion, just as waves rise and fall,
but it advanced steadily, as a tide advances. Unless she was careful, it
would strike her face. A spasm of horror shook her and she rang for the
attendant. The attendant too was horrified, but she could do nothing;
it was not her place to mend the blind. She could only suggest that the
lady should change her cabin, which she accordingly prepared to do.

People were almost exactly alike all over the world, but the attendant of the airship, perhaps owing to her exceptional duties, had
grown a little out of the common. She had often to address passengers

with direct speech, and this had given her a certain roughness and originality of manner. When Vashti swerved away from the sunbeams with a cry, she behaved barbarically—she put out her hand to steady her.

"How dare you!" exclaimed the passenger. "You forget yourself!"

The woman was confused, and apologised for not having let her fall. People never touched one another. The custom had become obsolete, owing to the Machine.

"Where are we now?" asked Vashti haughtily.

"We are over Asia," said the attendant, anxious to be polite.

"Asia?"

"You must excuse my common way of speaking. I have got into the habit of calling places over which I pass by their unmechanical names."

"Oh, I remember Asia. The Mongols came from it."

"Beneath us, in the open air, stood a city that was once called Simla."

"Have you ever heard of the Mongols and of the Brisbane school?"

"No."

"Brisbane also stood in the open air."

"Those mountains to the right—let me show you them." She pushed back a metal blind. The main chain of the Himalayas was revealed. "They were once called the Roof of the World, those mountains."

"What a foolish name!"

"You must remember that, before the dawn of civilisation, they seemed to be an impenetrable wall that touched the stars. It was supposed that no one but the gods could exist above their summits. How we have advanced, thanks to the Machine!"

"How we have advanced, thanks to the Machine!" said Vashti.

"How we have advanced, thanks to the Machine!" echoed the passenger who had dropped his Book the night before, and who was standing in the passage.

"And that white stuff in the cracks?—what is it?"

"I have forgotten its name."

"Cover the window, please. These mountains give me no ideas."

The northern aspect of the Himalayas was in deep shadow: on the Indian slope the sun had just prevailed. The forests had been destroyed during the literature epoch for the purpose of making newspaper pulp, but the snows were awakening to their morning glory, and clouds still hung on the breasts of Kinchinjunga. In the plain were seen the ruins of cities, with diminished rivers creeping by their walls, and by the sides of these were sometimes the signs of vomitories, marking the cities of today. Over the whole prospect airships rushed, crossing the intercrossing with incredible *aplomb*, and rising nonchalantly when they desired to escape the perturbations of the lower atmosphere and to traverse the Roof of the World.

"We have indeed advanced, thanks to the Machine," repeated the attendant, and hid the Himalayas behind a metal blind.

The day dragged wearily forward. The passengers sat each in his cabin, avoiding one another with an almost physical repulsion and longing to be once more under the surface of the earth. There were eight or ten of them, mostly young males, sent out from the public nurseries to inhabit the rooms of those who had died in various parts of the earth. The man who had dropped his Book was on the homeward journey. He had been sent to Sumatra for the purpose of propagating the race. Vashti alone was travelling by her private will.

At midday she took a second glance at the earth. The airship was crossing another range of mountains, but she could see little, owing to clouds. Masses of black rock hovered below her, and merged indistinctly into grey. Their shapes were fantastic; one of them resembled a prostrate man.

"No ideas here," murmured Vashti, and hid the Caucasus behind a metal blind.

In the evening she looked again. They were crossing a golden sea, in which lay many small islands and one peninsula.

She repeated, "No ideas here," and hid Greece behind a metal blind.

THE MENDING APPARATUS

By a vestibule, by a lift, by a tubular railway, by a platform, by a sliding door—by reversing all the steps of her departure did Vashti arrive at her son's room, which exactly resembled her own. She might well declare that the visit was superfluous. The buttons, the knobs, the reading desk with the Book, the temperature, the atmosphere, the illumination—all were exactly the same. And if Kuno himself, flesh of her flesh, stood close beside her at last, what profit was there in that? She was too well bred to shake him by the hand.

Averting her eyes, she spoke as follows:

"Here I am. I have had the most terrible journey and greatly retarded the development of my soul. It is not worth it, Kuno, it is not worth it. My time is too precious. The sunlight almost touched me, and I have met with the rudest people. I can only stop a few minutes. Say what you want to say, and then I must return."

"I have been threatened with Homelessness," said Kuno.

She looked at him now.

"I have been threatened with Homelessness, and I could not tell you such a thing through the Machine."

Homelessness means death. The victim is exposed to the air, which kills him.

"I have been outside since I spoke to you last. The tremendous thing has happened, and they have discovered me."

"But why shouldn't you go outside?" she exclaimed. "It is perfectly legal, perfectly mechanical, to visit the surface of the earth. I have lately been to a lecture on the sea; there is no objection to that; one simply summons a respirator and gets an Egression permit. It is not the kind of thing that spiritually minded people do, and I begged you not to do it, but there is no legal objection to it."

"I did not get an Egression permit."

"Then how did you get out?"

"I found out a way of my own."

The phrase conveyed no meaning to her, and he had to repeat it.

"A way of your own?" she whispered. "But that would be wrong."

"Why?"

The question shocked her beyond measure.

"You are beginning to worship the Machine," he said coldly. "You think it irreligious of me to have found out a way of my own. It was just what the Committee thought, when they threatened me with Homelessness."

At this she grew angry. "I worship nothing!" she cried. "I am most advanced. I don't think you irreligious, for there is no such thing as religion left. All the fear and the superstition that existed once have been destroyed by the Machine. I only meant that to find out a way of your own was—Besides, there is no new way out."

"So it is always supposed."

"Except through the vomitories, for which one must have an Egression permit, it is impossible to get out. The Book says so."

"Well, the Book's wrong, for I have been out on my feet."

For Kuno was possessed of a certain physical strength.

By these days it was a demerit to be muscular. Each infant was examined at birth, and all who promised undue strength were destroyed. Humanitarians may protest, but it would have been no true kindness to let an athlete live; he would never have been happy in that state of life to which the Machine had called him; he would have yearned for trees to climb, rivers to bathe in, meadows and hills against which he might measure his body. Man must be adapted to his surroundings, must he not? In the dawn of the world our weakly must be exposed on Mount Taygetus, in its twilight our strong will suffer euthanasia, that the Machine may progress, that the Machine may progress, that the Machine may progress eternally.

"You know that we have lost the sense of space. We say 'space is annihilated,' but we have annihilated not space, but the sense thereof. We have lost a part of ourselves. I determined to recover it, and I began by walking up and down the platform of the railway outside my room. Up and down, until I was tired, and so did recapture the meaning of 'Near' and 'Far.' 'Near' is a place to which I can get quickly *on my feet*, not a place to which the train or the airship will take me quickly. 'Far' is a place to which I cannot get quickly on my feet; the vomitory is 'far,' though I could be there in thirty-eight seconds by summoning the train. Man is the measure. That was my first lesson. Man's feet are the measure for distance, his hands are the measure for ownership, his body is the measure for all that is lovable and desirable and strong. Then I went further: it was then that I called to you for the first time, and you would not come.

"This city, as you know, is built deep beneath the surface of the earth, with only the vomitories protruding. Having paced the platform outside my own room, I took the lift to the next platform and paced that also, and so with each in turn, until I came to the topmost, above which begins the earth. All the platforms were exactly alike, and all that I gained by visiting them was to develop my sense of space and my muscles. I think I should have been content with this—it is not a little thing—but as I walked and brooded, it occurred to me that our cities had been built in the days when men still breathed the outer air, and that there had been ventilation shafts for the workmen. I could think of nothing but these ventilation shafts. Had they been destroyed by all the food tubes and medicine tubes and music tubes that the Machine has evolved lately? Or did traces of them remain? One thing was certain. If I came upon them anywhere, it would be in the railway tunnels of the topmost story. Everywhere else, all space was accounted for.

"I am telling my story quickly, but don't think that I was not a coward or that your answers never depressed me. It is not the proper thing, it is not mechanical, it is not decent to walk along a railway tunnel. I did not fear that I might tread upon a live rail and be killed. I feared something far more intangible—doing what was not contemplated by the Machine. Then I said to myself, 'Man is the measure,' and I went, and after many visits I found an opening.

"The tunnels, of course, were lighted. Everything is light, artificial light; darkness is the exception. So when I saw a black gap in the tiles, I knew that it was an exception, and rejoiced. I put in my arm—I could put in no more at first—and waved it round and round in ecstasy. I loosened another tile, and put in my head, and shouted into the darkness: 'I am coming, I shall do it yet,' and my voice reverberated down endless passages. I seemed to hear the spirits of those dead workmen who had returned each evening to the starlight and to their wives, and all the generations who had lived in the open air called back to me, 'You will do it yet, you are coming.'"

He paused, and, absurd as he was, his last words moved her. For Kuno had lately asked to be a father, and his request had been refused by the Committee. His was not a type that the Machine desired to hand on.

"Then a train passed. It brushed by me, but I thrust my head and arms into the hole. I had done enough for one day, so I crawled back to the platform, went down in the lift, and summoned my bed. Ah, what dreams! And again I called you, and again you refused."

She shook her head and said:

"Don't. Don't talk of these terrible things. You make me miserable. You are throwing civilisation away."

"But I had got back the sense of space and a man cannot rest then. I determined to get in at the hole and climb the shaft. And so I exercised my arms. Day after day I went through ridiculous movements, until my flesh ached, and I could hang by my hands and hold the pillow of my bed outstretched for many minutes. Then I summoned a respirator, and started.

"It was easy at first. The mortar had somehow rotted, and I soon pushed some more tiles in, and clambered after them into the darkness, and the spirits of the dead comforted me. I don't know what I mean by that. I just say what I felt. I felt, for the first time, that a protest had been lodged against corruption, and that even as the dead were comforting me, so I was comforting the unborn. I felt that humanity existed, and that it existed without clothes. How can I possibly explain this? It was naked, humanity seemed naked, and all these tubes and buttons and machineries neither came into the world with us, nor will they follow us out, nor do they matter supremely while we are here. Had I been strong, I would have torn off every garment I had, and gone out into the outer air unswaddled. But this is not for me, nor perhaps for my generation. I climbed with my respirator and my hygienic clothes and my dietetic tabloids! Better thus than not at all.

"There was a ladder, made of some primeval metal. The light from the railway fell upon its lowest rungs, and I saw that it led straight upwards out of the rubble at the bottom of the shaft. Perhaps our ancestors ran up and down it a dozen times daily, in their building. As I climbed, the rough edges cut through my gloves so that my hands bled. The light helped me for a little, and then came darkness and, worse still, silence which pierced my ears like a sword. The Machine hums! Did you know that? Its hum penetrates our blood, and may even guide our thoughts. Who knows! I was getting beyond its power. Then I thought: 'This silence means that I am doing wrong.' But I heard voices in the silence, and again they strengthened me." He laughed. "I had need of them. The next moment I cracked my head against something."

She sighed.

"I had reached one of those pneumatic stoppers that defend us from the outer air. You may have noticed them on the airship. Pitch dark, my feet on the rungs of an invisible ladder, my hands cut; I cannot explain how I lived through this part, but the voices still comforted me, and I felt for fastenings. The stopper, I suppose, was about eight feet across. I passed my hand over it as far as I could reach. It was perfectly smooth. I felt it almost to the centre. Not quite to the centre, for my arm was too short. Then the voice said: 'Jump. It is worth it. There may be a handle in the centre, and you may catch hold of it and so come to us your own way. And if there is no handle, so that you may fall and are dashed to pieces—it is still worth it: you will still come to us your own way.' So I jumped. There was a handle, and—"

He paused. Tears gathered in his mother's eyes. She knew that he was fated. If he did not die today he would die tomorrow. There was not room for such a person in the world. And with her pity disgust mingled. She was ashamed at having borne such a son, she who had always been so respectable and so full of ideas. Was he really the little boy to whom she had taught the use of his stops and buttons, and to whom she had given his first lessons in the Book? The very hair that disfigured his lip showed that he was reverting to some savage type. On atavism the Machine can have no mercy.

"There was a handle, and I did catch it. I hung tranced over the darkness and heard the hum of these workings as the last whisper in a dying dream. All the things I had cared about and all the people I had spoken to through tubes appeared infinitely little. Meanwhile the handle revolved. My weight had set something in motion and I span slowly, and then—

"I cannot describe it. I was lying with my face to the sunshine. Blood poured from my nose and ears and I heard a tremendous roaring. The stopper, with me clinging to it, had simply been blown out of the earth, and the air that we make down here was escaping through the vent into the air above. It burst up like a fountain. I crawled back to it—for the upper air hurts—and, as it were, I took great sips from the edge. My respirator had flown goodness knows where, my clothes were torn. I just lay with my lips close to the hole, and I sipped until the bleeding stopped. You can imagine nothing so curious. This hollow in the grass—I will speak of it in a minute—the sun shining into it, not brilliantly but through marbled clouds—the peace, the nonchalance, the sense of space, and, brushing my cheek, the roaring fountain of our artificial air! Soon I spied my respirator, bobbing up and down in the current high above my head, and higher still were many airships. But no one ever looks out of airships, and in my case they could not have picked me up. There I was, stranded. The sun shone a little way down the shaft, and revealed the topmost rung of the ladder, but it was hopeless trying to reach it. I should either have been tossed up again by the escape, or else have fallen in, and died. I could only lie on the grass, sipping and sipping, and from time to time glancing around me.

"I knew that I was in Wessex, for I had taken care to go to a lecture on the subject before starting. Wessex lies above the room in which we are talking now. It was once an important state. Its kings held all the southern coast from the Andredswald to Cornwall, while the Wansdyke protected them on the north, running over the high ground. The lecturer was only concerned with the rise of Wessex, so I do not know how long it remained an international power, nor would the knowledge have assisted me. To tell the truth I could do nothing but laugh, during this part. There was I, with a pneumatic stopper by my side and a respirator bobbing over my head, imprisoned, all three of us, in a grass-grown hollow that was edged with fern."

Then he grew grave again.

"Lucky for me that it was a hollow. For the air began to fall back into it and to fill it as water fills a bowl. I could crawl about. Presently I stood. I breathed a mixture, in which the air that hurts predominated whenever I tried to climb the sides. This was not so bad. I had not lost my tabloids and remained ridiculously cheerful, and as for the Machine, I forgot about it altogether. My one aim now was to get to the top, where the ferns were, and to view whatever objects lay beyond.

"I rushed the slope. The new air was still too bitter for me and I came rolling back, after a momentary vision of something grey. The sun grew very feeble, and I remembered that he was in Scorpio—I had been to a lecture on that too. If the sun is in Scorpio and you are in Wessex, it means that you must be as quick as you can, or it will get too dark. (This is the first bit of useful information I have ever got from a lecture, and I expect it will be the last.) It made me try frantically to breathe the new air, and to advance as far as I dared out of my pond. The hollow filled so slowly. At times I thought that the fountain played with less vigour. My respirator seemed to dance nearer the earth; the roar was decreasing."

He broke off.

"I don't think this is interesting you. The rest will interest you even less. There are no ideas in it, and I wish that I had not troubled you to come. We are too different, mother."

She told him to continue.

"It was evening before I climbed the bank. The sun had very nearly slipped out of the sky by this time, and I could not get a good view. You, who have just crossed the Roof of the World, will not want to hear an account of the little hills that I saw—low colourless hills. But to me they were living and the turf that covered them was a skin, under which their muscles rippled, and I felt that those hills had called with incalculable force to men in the past, and that men had loved them. Now they sleep—perhaps forever. They commune with humanity in dreams. Happy the man, happy the woman, who awakes the hills of Wessex. For though they sleep, they will never die."

His voice rose passionately.

"Cannot you see, cannot all your lecturers see, that it is we who are dying, and that down here the only thing that really lives is the Machine? We created the Machine, to do our will, but we cannot make it do our will now. It has robbed us of the sense of space and of the sense of touch, it has blurred every human relation and narrowed down love to a carnal act, it has paralysed our bodies and our wills, and now it compels us to worship it. The Machine develops—but not on our lines. The Machine proceeds—but not to our goal. We only exist as the blood corpuscles that course through its arteries, and if it could work without us, it would let us die. Oh, I have no remedy—or, at least, only one—to tell men again and again that I have seen the hills of Wessex as Ælfrid saw them when he overthrew the Danes.

"So the sun set. I forgot to mention that a belt of mist lay between my hill and other hills, and that it was the colour of pearl."

He broke off for the second time.

"Go on," said his mother wearily.

He shook his head.

"Go on. Nothing that you say can distress me now. I am hardened."

"I had meant to tell you the rest, but I cannot: I know that I cannot: goodbye."

Vashti stood irresolute. All her nerves were tingling with his blasphemies. But she was also inquisitive.

"This is unfair," she complained. "You have called me across the world to hear your story, and hear it I will. Tell me—as briefly as possible, for this is a disastrous waste of time—tell me how you returned to civilisation."

"Oh—that!" he said, starting. "You would like to hear about civilisation. Certainly. Had I got to where my respirator fell down?"

"No—but I understand everything now. You put on your respirator, and managed to walk along the surface of the earth to a vomitory, and there your conduct was reported to the Central Committee."

"By no means."

He passed his hand over his forehead, as if dispelling some strong impression. Then, resuming his narrative, he warmed to it again.

"My respirator fell about sunset. I had mentioned that the fountain seemed feebler, had I not?"

"Yes."

"About sunset, it let the respirator fall. As I said, I had entirely forgotten about the Machine, and I paid no great attention at the time, being occupied with other things. I had my pool of air, into which I could dip when the outer keenness became intolerable, and which would possibly remain for days, provided that no wind sprang up to disperse it. Not until it was too late did I realize what the stoppage of the escape implied. You see—the gap in the tunnel had been mended; the Mending Apparatus; the Mending Apparatus, was after me.

"One other warning I had, but I neglected it. The sky at night was clearer than it had been in the day, and the moon, which was about half the sky behind the sun, shone into the dell at moments quite brightly. I was in my usual place—on the boundary between the two atmospheres—when I thought I saw something dark move across the bottom of the dell, and vanish into the shaft. In my folly, I ran down. I bent over and listened, and I thought I heard a faint scraping noise in the depths.

"At this—but it was too late—I took alarm. I determined to put on my respirator and to walk right out of the dell. But my respirator had gone. I knew exactly where it had fallen—between the stopper and the aperture—and I could even feel the mark that it had made in the turf. It had gone, and I realized that something evil was at work, and I had better escape to the other air, and, if I must die, die running toward the cloud that had been the colour of a pearl. I never started. Out of the shaft—it is too horrible. A worm, a long white worm, had crawled out of the shaft and was gliding over the moonlit grass.

"I screamed. I did everything that I should not have done, I stamped upon the creature instead of flying from it, and it at once curled round the ankle. Then we fought. The worm let me run all over the dell, but edged up my leg as I ran. 'Help!' I cried. (That part is too awful. It belongs to the part that you will never know.) 'Help!' I cried. (Why cannot we suffer in silence?) 'Help!' I cried. Then my feet were wound together, I fell, I was dragged away from the dear ferns and the living hills, and past the great metal stopper (I can tell you this part), and I thought it might save me again if I caught hold of the handle. It also was enwrapped, it also. Oh, the whole dell was full of the things. They were searching it in all directions, they were denuding it, and the white snouts of others peeped out of the hole, ready if needed. Everything that could be moved they brought—brushwood, bundles of fern, everything, and down we all went intertwined into hell. The last things that I saw, ere the stopper closed after us, were certain stars, and I felt that a man of my sort lived in the sky. For I did fight, I fought till the very end, and it was only my head hitting against the ladder that quieted me. I woke up in this room. The worms had vanished. I was surrounded by artificial air, artificial light, artificial peace, and my friends were calling to me down speaking tubes to know whether I had come across any new ideas lately."

Here his story ended. Discussion of it was impossible, and Vashti turned to go.

"It will end in Homelessness," she said quietly.

"I wish it would," retorted Kuno.

"The Machine has been most merciful."

"I prefer the mercy of God."

"By that superstitious phrase, do you mean that you could live in the outer air?"

"Yes."

"Have you ever seen, round the vomitories, the bones of those who were extruded after the Great Rebellion?"

"Yes."

"They were left where they perished for our edification. A few crawled away, but they perished, too—who can doubt it? And so with the Homeless of our own day. The surface of the earth supports life no longer."

"Indeed."

"Ferns and a little grass may survive, but all higher forms have perished. Has any airship detected them?"

"No."

"Has any lecturer dealt with them?"

"No."

"Then why this obstinacy?"

"Because I have seen them," he exploded.

"Seen *what*?"

"Because I have seen her in the twilight—because she came to my help when I called—because she, too, was entangled by the worms, and, luckier than I, was killed by one of them piercing her throat."

He was mad. Vashti departed, nor, in the troubles that followed, did she ever see his face again.

THE HOMELESS

During the years that followed Kuno's escapade, two important developments took place in the Machine. On the surface they were revolutionary, but in either case men's minds had been prepared beforehand, and they did but express tendencies that were latent already.

The first of these was the abolition of respirators.

Advanced thinkers, like Vashti, had always held it foolish to visit the surface of the earth. Airships might be necessary, but what was the good of going out for mere curiosity and crawling along for a mile or two in a terrestrial motor? The habit was vulgar and perhaps faintly improper: it was unproductive of ideas, and had no connection with the habits that really mattered. So respirators were abolished, and with them, of course, the terrestrial motors, and except for a few lecturers, who complained that they were debarred access to their subject matter, the development was accepted quietly. Those who still wanted to know what the earth was like had after all only to listen to some gramophone, or to look into some cinematophote. And even the lecturers acquiesced when they found that a lecture on the sea was nonetheless stimulating when compiled out of other lectures that had already been delivered on the same subject. "Beware of first-hand ideas!" exclaimed one of the most advanced of them. "First-hand ideas do not really exist. They are but the physical impressions produced by love and fear, and on this gross foundation who could erect a philosophy? Let your ideas be second-hand, and if possible tenth-hand, for then they will be far removed from that disturbing element—direct observation. Do not learn anything about this subject of mine—the French Revolution. Learn instead what I think that Enicharmon thought Urizen thought Gutch thought Ho-Yung thought Chi-Bo-Sing thought Lafcadio Hearn thought Carlyle thought Mirabeau said about the French Revolution. Through the medium of these eight great minds, the blood that was shed at Paris and the windows that were broken at Versailles will be clarified to an idea which you may employ most profitably in your daily lives. But be sure that the intermediates are many and varied, for in history one authority exists to counteract another. Urizen must counteract the scepticism of Ho-Yung and Enicharmon, I must myself counteract the impetuosity of Gutch. You who listen to me are in a better position to judge about the French Revolution than I am. Your descendants will be even in a better position than you, for they will learn what you think I think, and yet another intermediate will be added to the chain. And in time"—his voice rose—"there will come a generation that has got beyond facts, beyond impressions, a generation absolutely colourless, a generation

> 'seraphically free
> From taint of personality,'

which will see the French Revolution not as it happened, nor as they would like it to have happened, but as it would have happened, had it taken place in the days of the Machine."

Tremendous applause greeted this lecture, which did but voice a feeling already latent in the minds of men—a feeling that terrestrial facts must be ignored, and that the abolition of respirators was a positive gain. It was even suggested that airships should be abolished too. This was not done, because airships had somehow worked themselves into the Machine's system. But year by year they were used less, and mentioned less by thoughtful men.

The second great development was the reestablishment of religion.

This, too, had been voiced in the celebrated lecture. No one could mistake the reverent tone in which the peroration had concluded, and it awakened a responsive echo in the heart of each. Those who had long worshipped silently, now began to talk. They described the strange feeling of peace that came over them when they handled the Book of the Machine, the pleasure that it was to repeat certain numerals out of it, however little meaning those numerals conveyed to the outward ear, the ecstasy of touching a button, however unimportant, or of ringing an electric bell, however superfluously.

"The Machine," they exclaimed, "feeds us and clothes us and houses us; through it we speak to one another, through it we see one another, in it we have our being. The Machine is the friend of ideas and the enemy of superstition: the Machine is omnipotent, eternal; blessed is the Machine." And before long this allocution was printed on the first page of the Book, and in subsequent editions the ritual swelled into a complicated system of praise and prayer. The word "religion" was sedulously avoided, and in theory the Machine was still the creation and the implement of man. But in practice all, save a few retrogrades, worshipped it as divine. Nor was it worshipped in unity. One believer would be chiefly impressed by the blue optic plates, through which he saw other believers; another by the Mending Apparatus, which sinful Kuno had compared to worms; another by the lifts, another by the Book. And each would pray to this or to that, and ask it to intercede for him with the Machine as a whole. Persecution—that also was present. It did not break out, for reasons that will be set forward shortly. But it was latent, and all who did not accept the minimum known as "undenominational Mechanism" lived in danger of Homelessness, which means death, as we know.

To attribute these two great developments to the Central Committee is to take a very narrow view of civilisation. The Central Committee announced the developments, it is true, but they were no more the cause of them than were the kings of the imperialistic period the cause of war. Rather did they yield to some invincible pressure, which came no one knew whither, and which, when gratified, was succeeded by some new pressure equally invincible. To such a state of affairs it is convenient to give the name of progress. No one confessed the Machine was out of hand. Year by year it was served with increased efficiency and decreased intelligence. The better a man knew his own duties upon it, the less he understood the duties of his neighbour, and in all the world there was not one who understood the monster as a whole. Those master brains had perished. They had left full directions, it is true, and their successors had each of them mastered a portion of those directions. But Humanity, in its desire for comfort, had overreached itself. It had exploited the riches of nature too far. Quietly and complacently, it was sinking into decadence, and progress had come to mean the progress of the Machine.

As for Vashti, her life went peacefully forward until the final disaster. She made her room dark and slept; she awoke and made the room light. She lectured and attended lectures. She exchanged ideas with her innumerable friends and believed she was growing more spiritual. At times a friend was granted Euthanasia, and left his or her room for the homelessness that is beyond all human conception. Vashti did not much mind. After an unsuccessful lecture, she would sometimes ask for Euthanasia herself. But the death rate was not permitted to exceed the birth rate, and the Machine had hitherto refused it to her.

The troubles began quietly, long before she was conscious of them.

One day she was astonished at receiving a message from her son. They never communicated, having nothing in common, and she had only heard indirectly that he was still alive, and had been transferred from the Northern Hemisphere, where he had behaved so mischievously, to the Southern—indeed, to a room not far from her own.

"Does he want me to visit him?" she thought. "Never again, never. And I have not the time."

No, it was madness of another kind.

He refused to visualize his face upon the blue plate, and speaking out of the darkness with solemnity said:

"The Machine stops."

"What do you say?"

"The Machine is stopping, I know it, I know the signs."

She burst into a peal of laughter. He heard her and was angry, and they spoke no more.

"Can you imagine anything more absurd?" she cried to a friend. "A man who was my son believes that the Machine is stopping. It would be impious if it was not mad."

"The Machine is stopping?" her friend replied. "What does that mean? The phrase conveys nothing to me."

"Nor to me."

"He does not refer, I suppose, to the trouble there has been lately with the music?"

"Oh no, of course not. Let us talk about music."

"Have you complained to the authorities?"

"Yes, and they say it wants mending, and referred me to the Committee of the Mending Apparatus. I complained of those curious gasping sighs that disfigure the symphonies of the Brisbane school. They sound like someone in pain. The Committee of the Mending Apparatus say that it shall be remedied shortly."

Obscurely worried, she resumed her life. For one thing, the defect in the music irritated her. For another thing, she could not forget Kuno's speech. If he had known that the music was out of repair—he could not know it, for he detested music—if he had known that it was wrong, "the Machine stops" was exactly the venomous sort of remark he would have made. Of course he had made it as a venture, but the coincidence annoyed her, and she spoke with some petulance to the Committee of the Mending Apparatus.

They replied, as before, that the defect would be set right shortly.

"Shortly! At once!" she retorted. "Why should I be worried by imperfect music? Things are always put right at once. If you do not mend it at once, I shall complain to the Central Committee."

"No personal complaints are received by the Central Committee," the Committee of the Mending Apparatus replied.

"Through whom am I to make my complaint, then?"

"Through us."

"I complain then."

"Your complaint shall be forwarded in its turn."

"Have others complained?"

This question was unmechanical, and the Committee of the Mending Apparatus refused to answer it.

"It is too bad!" she exclaimed to another of her friends. "There never was such an unfortunate woman as myself. I can never be sure of my music now. It gets worse and worse each time I summon it."

"I too have my troubles," the friend replied. "Sometimes my ideas are interrupted by a slight jarring noise."

"What is it?"

"I do not know whether it is inside my head, or inside the wall."

"Complain, in either case."

"I have complained, and my complaint will be forwarded in its turn to the Central Committee."

Time passed, and they resented the defects no longer. The defects had not been remedied, but the human tissues in that latter day had become so subservient, that they readily adapted themselves to every caprice of the Machine. The sigh at the crisis of the Brisbane symphony no longer irritated Vashti; she accepted it as part of the melody. The jarring noise, whether in the head or in the wall, was no longer resented by her friend. And so with the mouldy artificial fruit, so with the bathwater that began to stink, so with the defective rhymes that the poetry machine had taken to emit. All were bitterly complained of at first, and then acquiesced in and forgotten. Things went from bad to worse unchallenged.

It was otherwise with the failure of the sleeping apparatus. That was a more serious stoppage. There came a day when over the whole world—in Sumatra, in Wessex, in the innumerable cities of Courland and Brazil—the beds, when summoned by their tired owners, failed to appear. It may seem a ludicrous matter, but from it we may date the collapse of humanity. The Committee responsible for the failure was assailed by complainants, whom it referred, as usual, to the Committee of the Mending Apparatus, who in its turn assured them that their complaints would be forwarded to the Central Committee. But the discontent grew, for mankind was not yet sufficiently adaptable to do without sleeping.

"Someone is meddling with the Machine—" they began.

"Someone is trying to make himself king, to reintroduce the personal element."

"Punish that man with Homelessness."

"To the rescue! Avenge the Machine! Avenge the Machine!"

"War! Kill the man!"

But the Committee of the Mending Apparatus now came forward, and allayed the panic with well-chosen words. It confessed that the Mending Apparatus was itself in need of repair.

The effect of this frank confession was admirable.

"Of course," said a famous lecturer—he of the French Revolution, who gilded each new decay with splendour—"of course we shall not press our complaints now. The Mending Apparatus has treated us so well in the past that we all sympathize with it, and will wait patiently for its recovery. In its own good time it will resume its duties. Meanwhile let us do without our beds, our tabloids, our other little wants. Such, I feel sure, would be the wish of the Machine."

Thousands of miles away his audience applauded. The Machine still linked them. Under the seas, beneath the roots of the mountains, ran the wires through which they saw and heard, the enormous eyes and ears that were their heritage, and the hum of many workings clothed their thoughts in one garment of subserviency. Only the old and the sick remained ungrateful, for it was rumoured that Euthanasia, too, was out of order, and that pain had reappeared among men.

It became difficult to read. A blight entered the atmosphere and dulled its luminosity. At times Vashti could scarcely see across her room. The air, too, was foul. Loud were the complaints, impotent the remedies, heroic the tone of the lecturer as he cried: "Courage, courage! What matter so long as the Machine goes on? To it the darkness and the light are one." And though things improved again after a time, the old brilliancy was never recaptured, and humanity never recovered from its entrance into twilight. There was an hysterical talk of "measures," of "provisional dictatorship," and the inhabitants of Sumatra were asked to familiarize themselves with the workings of the central power station, the said power station being situated in France. But for the most part panic reigned, and men spent their strength praying to their Books, tangible proofs of the Machine's omnipotence. There were gradations of terror—at times came rumours of hope—the Mending Apparatus was almost mended—the enemies of the Machine had been got under—new "nerve centres" were evolving which would do the work even more magnificently than before. But there came a day when, without the slightest warning, without any previous hint of feebleness, the entire communication system broke down, all over the world, and the world, as they understood it, ended.

Vashti was lecturing at the time and her earlier remarks had been punctuated with applause. As she proceeded the audience became silent, and at the conclusion there was no sound. Somewhat displeased, she called to a friend who was a specialist in sympathy. No sound: doubtless the friend was sleeping. And so with the next friend whom she tried to summon, and so with the next, until she remembered Kuno's cryptic remark, "The Machine stops."

The phrase still conveyed nothing. If Eternity was stopping it would of course be set going shortly.

For example, there was still a little light and air—the atmosphere had improved a few hours previously. There was still the Book, and while there was the Book there was security.

Then she broke down, for with the cessation of activity came an unexpected terror—silence.

She had never known silence, and the coming of it nearly killed her—it did kill many thousands of people outright. Ever since her birth she had been surrounded by the steady hum. It was to the ear what artificial air was to the lungs, and agonizing pains shot across her head. And scarcely knowing what she did, she stumbled forward and pressed the unfamiliar button, the one that opened the door of her cell.

Now the door of the cell worked on a simple hinge of its own. It was not connected with the central power station, dying far away in France. It opened, rousing immoderate hopes in Vashti, for she thought that the Machine had been mended. It opened, and she saw the dim tunnel that curved far away toward freedom. One look, and then she shrank back. For the tunnel was full of people—she was almost the last in that city to have taken alarm.

People at any time repelled her, and these were nightmares from her worst dreams. People were crawling about, people were screaming, whimpering, gasping for breath, touching each other, vanishing in the dark, and ever and anon being pushed off the platform onto the live rail. Some were fighting round the electric bells, trying to summon trains which could not be summoned. Others were yelling for Euthanasia or for respirators, or blaspheming the Machine. Others stood at the doors of their cells fearing, like herself, either to stop in them or to leave them. And behind all the uproar was silence—the silence which is the voice of the earth and of the generations who have gone.

No—it was worse than solitude. She closed the door again and sat down to wait for the end. The disintegration went on, accompanied by horrible cracks and rumbling. The valves that restrained the Medical Apparatus must have been weakened, for it ruptured and hung hideously from the ceiling. The floor heaved and fell and flung her from the chair. A tube oozed toward her serpent fashion. And at last the final horror approached—light began to ebb, and she knew that civilisation's long day was closing.

She whirled around, praying to be saved from this, at any rate, kissing the Book, pressing button after button. The uproar outside was increasing, and even penetrated the wall. Slowly the brilliancy of her cell was dimmed, the reflections faded from the metal switches. Now she could not see the reading stand, now not the Book, though she held it in her hand. Light followed the flight of sound, air was following light, and the original void returned to the cavern from which it had so long been excluded. Vashti continued to whirl, like the devotees of an earlier religion, screaming, praying, striking at the buttons with bleeding hands.

It was thus that she opened her prison and escaped—escaped in the spirit: at least so it seems to me, ere my meditation closes. That she escapes in the body—I cannot perceive that. She struck, by chance, the switch that released the door, and the rush of foul air on her skin, the loud throbbing whispers in her ears, told her that she was facing the tunnel again, and that tremendous platform on which she had seen men fighting. They were not fighting now. Only the whispers remained, and the little whimpering groans. They were dying by hundreds out in the dark.

She burst into tears.

Tears answered her.

They wept for humanity, those two, not for themselves. They could not bear that this should be the end. Ere silence was completed their hearts were opened, and they knew what had been important on the earth. Man, the flower of all flesh, the noblest of all creatures visible, man who had once made god in his image, and had mirrored his strength on the constellations, beautiful naked man was dying, strangled in the garments that he had woven. Century after century had he toiled, and here was his reward. Truly the garment had seemed heavenly at first, shot with colours of culture, sewn with the threads of self-denial. And heavenly it had been so long as it was a garment and no more, so long as man could shed it at will and live by the essence that is his soul, and the essence, equally divine, that is his body. The sin against the body—it was for that they wept in chief; the centuries of wrong against the muscles and the nerves, and those five portals by which we can alone apprehend—glozing it over with talk of evolution, until the body was white pap, the home of ideas as colourless, last sloshy stirrings of a spirit that had grasped the stars.

"Where are you?" she sobbed.

His voice in the darkness said, "Here."

"Is there any hope, Kuno?"

"None for us."

"Where are you?"

She crawled towards him over the bodies of the dead. His blood spurted over her hands.

"Quicker," he gasped, "I am dying—but we touch, we talk, not through the Machine."

He kissed her.

"We have come back to our own. We die, but we have recaptured life, as it was in Wessex, when Ælfrid overthrew the Danes. We know what they know outside, they who dwelt in the cloud that is the colour of a pearl."

"But, Kuno, is it true? Are there still men on the surface of the earth? Is this—this tunnel, this poisoned darkness—really not the end?"

He replied:

"I have seen them, spoken to them, loved them. They are hiding in the mist and the ferns until our civilisation stops. Today they are the Homeless—tomorrow—"

"Oh, tomorrow—some fool will start the Machine again, tomorrow."

"Never," said Kuno, "never. Humanity has learnt its lesson."

As he spoke, the whole city was broken like a honeycomb. An airship had sailed in through the vomitory into a ruined wharf. It crashed downwards, exploding as it went, rending gallery after gallery with its wings of steel. For a moment they saw the nations of the dead, and, before they joined them, scraps of the untainted sky.

QUESTIONS FOR DISCUSSION

According to the story, is it inevitable that the Machine grows "out of hand"? (369)

1. Why must the strong be killed so "that the Machine may progress, that the Machine may progress, that the Machine may progress eternally"? (358)

2. Why do people readily accept the abolition of respirators and the reestablishment of religion?

3. When the Central Committee is yielding to "invincible pressure," why is it "convenient" to call it progress? (369)

4. At what point in the story has society decisively "overreached itself"? (369)

At the end of the story, why does Kuno tell Vashti, "Humanity has learnt its lesson"? (376)

1. Why does Vashti finally take the airship to visit Kuno, despite "her horror of direct experience"? (352)

2. What does Kuno mean when he says, "Man is the measure"? (358)

3. Why does Vashti feel both pity and disgust when Kuno tells her about his explorations in the outer world?

4. Just before they die, why does Vashti tell Kuno that "some fool will start the Machine again"? (375)

FOR FURTHER REFLECTION

1. What do we mean when we speak of being controlled by technology, rather than controlling it? In what ways might control over technology be possible?

2. Should the widespread consequences of technology developed and proliferated by the workings of open market economies be regulated by public policy?

3. How does digital communications technology work to bring people closer? How does it work to separate them?

4. How would you define "the spirit" of our own age? How does it compare to the spirit of Vashti's and Kuno's age?

Black Box

Jennifer Egan

1

People rarely look the way you expect them to, even when you've seen pictures.

The first thirty seconds in a person's presence are the most important.

If you're having trouble perceiving and projecting, focus on projecting.

Necessary ingredients for a successful projection: giggles; bare legs; shyness.

The goal is to be both irresistible and invisible.

When you succeed, a certain sharpness will go out of his eyes.

2

Some powerful men actually call their beauties "Beauty."

Counter to reputation, there is a deep camaraderie among beauties.

If your Designated Mate is widely feared, the beauties at the house party where you've gone undercover to meet him will be especially kind.

Kindness feels good, even when it's based on a false notion of your identity and purpose.

3

Posing as a beauty means not reading what you would like to read on a rocky shore in the South of France.

Sunlight on bare skin can be as nourishing as food.

Even a powerful man will be briefly self-conscious when he first disrobes to his bathing suit.

It is technically impossible for a man to look better in a Speedo than in swim trunks.

If you love someone with dark skin, white skin looks drained of something vital.

4

When you know that a person is violent and ruthless, you will see violent ruthlessness in such basic things as his swim stroke.

"What are you doing?" from your Designated Mate amid choppy waves after he has followed you into the sea may or may not betray suspicion.

Your reply—"Swimming"—may or may not be perceived as sarcasm.

"Shall we swim together toward those rocks?" may or may not be a question.

"All that way?" will, if spoken correctly, sound ingenuous.

"We'll have privacy there" may sound unexpectedly ominous.

5

A hundred feet of blue-black Mediterranean will allow you ample time to deliver a strong self-lecture.

At such moments, it may be useful to explicitly recall your training:

"You will be infiltrating the lives of criminals.

"You will be in constant danger.

"Some of you will not survive, but those who do will be heroes.

"A few of you will save lives and even change the course of history.

"We ask of you an impossible combination of traits: ironclad scruples and a willingness to violate them;

"An abiding love for your country and a willingness to consort with individuals who are working actively to destroy it;

"The instincts and intuition of experts, and the blank records and true freshness of ingénues.

"You will each perform this service only once, after which you will return to your lives.

"We cannot promise that your lives will be exactly the same when you go back to them."

6

Eagerness and pliability can be expressed even in the way you climb from the sea onto chalky yellow rocks.

"You're a very fast swimmer," uttered by a man who is still submerged, may not be intended as praise.

Giggling is sometimes better than answering.

"You are a lovely girl" may be meant straightforwardly.

Ditto "I want to fuck you now."

"Well? What do you think about that?" suggests a preference for direct verbal responses over giggling.

"I like it" must be uttered with enough gusto to compensate for a lack of declarative color.

"You don't sound sure" indicates insufficient gusto.

"I'm *not* sure" is acceptable only when followed, coyly, with "You'll have to convince me."

Throwing back your head and closing your eyes allows you to give the appearance of sexual readiness while concealing revulsion.

7

Being alone with a violent and ruthless man, surrounded by water, can make the shore seem very far away.

You may feel solidarity, at such a time, with the beauties just visible there in their bright bikinis.

You may appreciate, at such a time, why you aren't being paid for this work.

Your voluntary service is the highest form of patriotism.

Remind yourself that you aren't being paid when he climbs out of the water and lumbers toward you.

Remind yourself that you aren't being paid when he leads you behind a boulder and pulls you onto his lap.

The Dissociation Technique is like a parachute—you must pull the cord at the correct time.

Too soon, and you may hinder your ability to function at a crucial moment;

Too late, and you will be lodged too deeply inside the action to wriggle free.

You will be tempted to pull the cord when he surrounds you with arms whose bulky strength reminds you, fleetingly, of your husband's.

You will be tempted to pull it when you feel him start to move against you from below.

You will be tempted to pull it when his smell envelops you: metallic, like a warm hand clutching pennies.

The directive "Relax" suggests that your discomfort is palpable.

"No one can see us" suggests that your discomfort has been understood as fear of physical exposure.

"Relax, relax," uttered in rhythmic, throaty tones, suggests that your discomfort is not unwelcome.

8

Begin the Dissociation Technique only when physical violation is imminent.

Close your eyes and slowly count backward from ten.

With each number, imagine yourself rising out of your body and moving one step farther away from it.

By eight, you should be hovering just outside your skin.

By five, you should be floating a foot or two above your body, feeling only vague anxiety over what is about to happen to it.

By three, you should feel fully detached from your physical self.

By two, your body should be able to act and react without your participation.

By one, your mind should drift so free that you lose track of what is happening below.

White clouds spin and curl.

A blue sky is as depthless as the sea.

The sound of waves against rocks existed millennia before there were creatures who could hear it.

Spurs and gashes of stone narrate a violence that the earth itself has long forgotten.

Your mind will rejoin your body when it is safe to do so.

9

Return to your body carefully, as if you were reentering your home after a hurricane.

Resist the impulse to reconstruct what has just happened.

Focus instead on gauging your Designated Mate's reaction to the new intimacy between you.

In some men, intimacy will prompt a more callous, indifferent attitude.

In others, intimacy may awaken problematic curiosity about you.

"Where did you learn to swim like that?," uttered lazily, while supine, with two fingers in your hair, indicates curiosity.

Tell the truth without precision.

"I grew up near a lake" is both true and vague.

"Where was the lake?" conveys dissatisfaction with your vagueness.

"Columbia County, New York" suggests precision while avoiding it.

"Manhattan?" betrays unfamiliarity with the geography of New York State.

Never contradict your Designated Mate.

"Where did *you* grow up?," asked of a man who has just asked you the same thing, is known as "mirroring."

Mirror your Designated Mate's attitudes, interests, desires, and tastes.

Your goal is to become part of his atmosphere: a source of comfort and ease.

Only then will he drop his guard when you are near.

Only then will he have significant conversations within your earshot.

Only then will he leave his possessions in a porous and unattended state.

Only then can you begin to gather information systematically.

10

"Come. Let's go back," uttered brusquely, suggests that your Designated Mate has no more wish to talk about himself than you do.

Avoid the temptation to analyze his moods and whims.

Salt water has a cleansing effect.

11

You will see knowledge of your new intimacy with your Designated Mate in the eyes of every beauty on shore.

"We saved lunch for you" may or may not be an allusion to the reason for your absence.

Cold fish is unappealing, even when served in a good lemon sauce.

Be friendly to other beauties, but not solicitous.

When you are in conversation with a beauty, it is essential that you be perceived as no more or less than she is.

Be truthful about every aspect of your life except marriage (if any).

If married, say that you and your spouse have divorced, to give an impression of unfettered freedom.

"Oh, that's sad!" suggests that the beauty you're chatting with would like to marry.

12

If your Designated Mate abruptly veers toward the villa, follow him.

Taking his hand and smiling congenially can create a sense of low-key accompaniment.

An abstracted smile in return, as if he'd forgotten who you are, may be a sign of pressing concerns.

The concerns of your Designated Mate are your concerns.

The room assigned to a powerful man will be more lavish than the one you slept in while awaiting his arrival.

Never look for hidden cameras: the fact that you're looking will give you away.

Determine whether your Designated Mate seeks physical intimacy; if not, feign the wish for a nap.

Your pretense of sleep will allow him to feel that he is alone.

Curling up under bedclothes, even those belonging to an enemy subject, may be soothing.

You're more likely to hear his handset vibrate if your eyes are closed.

13

A door sliding open signals his wish to take the call on the balcony.

Your Designated Mate's important conversations will take place outdoors.

If you are within earshot of his conversation, record it.

Since beauties carry neither pocketbooks nor timepieces, you cannot credibly transport recording devices.

A microphone has been implanted just beyond the first turn of your right ear canal.

Activate the microphone by pressing the triangle of cartilage across your ear opening.

You will hear a faint whine as recording begins.

In extreme quiet, or to a person whose head is adjacent to yours, this whine may be audible.

Should the whine be detected, swat your ear as if to deflect a mosquito, hitting the on/off cartilage to deactivate the mike.

You need not identify or comprehend the language your subject is using.

Your job is proximity; if you are near your Designated Mate, recording his private speech, you are succeeding.

Profanity sounds the same in every language.

An angry subject will guard his words less carefully.

14

If your subject is angry, you may leave your camouflage position and move as close to him as possible to improve recording quality.

You may feel afraid as you do this.

Your pounding heartbeat will not be recorded.

If your Designated Mate is standing on a balcony, hover in the doorway just behind him.

If he pivots and discovers you, pretend that you were on the verge of approaching him.

Anger usually trumps suspicion.

If your subject brushes past you and storms out of the room, slamming the door, you have eluded detection.

15

If your Designated Mate leaves your company a second time, don't follow him again.

Deactivate your ear mike and resume your "nap."

A moment of repose may be a good time to reassure your loved ones.

Nuanced communication is too easily monitored by the enemy.

Your Subcutaneous Pulse System issues pings so generic that detection would reveal neither source nor intent.

A button is embedded behind the inside ligament of your right knee (if right-handed).

Depress twice to indicate to loved ones that you are well and thinking of them.

You may send this signal only once each day.

A continuous depression of the button indicates an emergency.

You will debate, each day, the best time to send your signal.

You will reflect on the fact that your husband, coming from a culture of tribal allegiance, understands and applauds your patriotism.

You will reflect on the enclosed and joyful life that the two of you have shared since graduate school.

You will reflect on the fact that America is your husband's chosen country, and that he loves it.

You will reflect on the fact that your husband's rise to prominence would have been unimaginable in any other nation.

You will reflect on your joint conviction that your service had to be undertaken before you had children.

You will reflect on the fact that you are thirty-three, and have spent your professional life fomenting musical trends.

You will reflect on the fact that you must return home the same person you were when you left.

You will reflect on the fact that you've been guaranteed you will *not* be the same person.

You will reflect on the fact that you had stopped being that person even before leaving.

You will reflect on the fact that too much reflection is pointless.

You will reflect on the fact that these "instructions" are becoming less and less instructive.

Your Field Instructions, stored in a chip beneath your hairline, will serve as both a mission log and a guide for others undertaking this work.

Pressing your left thumb (if right-handed) against your left middle fingertip begins recording.

For clearest results, mentally speak the thought, as if talking to yourself.

Always filter your observations and experience through the lens of their didactic value.

Your training is ongoing; you must learn from each step you take.

When your mission is complete, you may view the results of the download before adding your Field Instructions to your mission file.

Where stray or personal thoughts have intruded, you may delete them.

16

Pretend sleep can lead to actual sleep.

Sleep is restorative in almost every circumstance.

The sound of showering likely indicates the return of your Designated Mate.

As a beauty, you will be expected to return to your room and change clothes often; a fresh appearance at mealtimes is essential.

The goal is to be a lovely, innocuous, evolving surprise.

A crisp white sundress against tanned skin is widely viewed as attractive.

Avoid overbright colors; they are attention-seeking and hinder camouflage.

White is not, technically speaking, a bright color.

White is, nevertheless, bright.

Gold spike-heeled sandals may compromise your ability to run or jump, but they look good on tanned feet.

Thirty-three is still young enough to register as "young."

Registering as "young" is especially welcome to those who may not register as "young" much longer.

If your Designated Mate leads you to dinner with an arm at your waist, assume that your attire change was successful.

17

When men begin serious talk, beauties are left to themselves.

"How long have you been divorced?" suggests the wish to resume a prior conversation.

"A few months," when untrue, should be uttered without eye contact.

"What was he like, your husband?" may be answered honestly.

"From Africa. Kenya" will satisfy your wish to talk about your husband.

"Black?," with eyebrows raised, may indicate racism.

"Yes. Black," in measured tones, should deliver a gentle reprimand.

"How black?" suggests that it did not.

"Very black" is somewhat less gentle, especially when accompanied by a pointed stare.

"Nice" hints at personal experience.

"Yes. It is nice" contradicts one's alleged divorce. "Was nice" is a reasonable correction.

"But not nice enough?," with laughter, indicates friendly intimacy. Especially when followed by "Or too nice!"

18

House-party hosts are universally eager to make guests eat.

For most beauties, the lure of food is a hazard; as a beauty of limited tenure, you may eat what you want.

Squab can be consumed by ripping the bird apart with your hands and sucking the meat from the bones.

A stunned expression reveals that your host expected the use of utensils.

A host who caters to violent guests will understand implicitly the need for discretion.

The adjacency of your host's chair to your own may presage a confidence.

If your job is to appear simple-minded, a confidence may mean that you have failed.

Everyone should brush his teeth before dinner.

Turning your ear toward your host's mouth will prevent you from having to smell the breath coming from it.

Ears must be kept clean at all times.

If your host warns you that your Designated Mate may pose an immediate danger to you, assume that your Designated Mate has left the room.

19

Going to the restroom is the most efficient means of self-jettisoning.

Never betray urgency, not even in an empty hallway.

If you have no idea in which direction your Designated Mate has gone, hold still.

If you find yourself hovering beside a pair of glass doors, you may open them and step outside.

Nights in the South of France are a strange, dark, piercing blue.

A bright moon can astonish, no matter how many times you have seen it.

If you were a child who loved the moon, looking at the moon will forever remind you of childhood.

Fatherless girls may invest the moon with a certain paternal promise.

Everyone has a father.

A vague story like "Your father died before you were born" may satisfy a curious child for an unlikely number of years.

The truth of your paternity, discovered in adulthood, will make the lie seem retroactively ludicrous.

Publicists occasionally have flings with their movie-star clients.

Discovering that you are a movie star's daughter is not necessarily a comfort.

It is especially not a comfort when the star in question has seven other children from three different marriages.

Discovering that you are a movie star's daughter may prompt you to watch upward of sixty movies, dating from the beginning of his career.

You may think, watching said movies, You don't know about me, but I am here.

You may think, watching said movies, I'm invisible to you, but I am here.

A sudden reconfiguration of your past can change the fit and feel of your adulthood.

It may cleave you, irreparably, from the mother whose single goal has been your happiness.

If your husband has transformed greatly in his own life, he will understand your transformation.

Avoid excessive self-reflection; your job is to look out, not in.

20

"There you are," whispered from behind by your Designated Mate, suggests that he has been looking for you.

Holding still can sometimes prove more effective than actively searching.

"Come," uttered softly, may communicate a renewed wish for intimate contact.

The moon's calm face can make you feel, in advance, that you are understood and forgiven.

The sea is audible against the rocks well before you see it.

Even at night, the Mediterranean is more blue than black.

If you wish to avoid physical intimacy, the sight of a speedboat will bring relief, despite the myriad new problems it presents.

If no words are exchanged between your Designated Mate and the speedboat's captain, their meeting was likely prearranged.

A man known for his cruelty may still show great care in guiding his beauty into a rocking speedboat.

He may interpret her hesitation to board as a fear of falling in.

Resist the impulse to ask where you are going.

Try, when anxious, to summon up a goofy giggle.

Locate your Personal Calming Source and use it.

If your Personal Calming Source is the moon, be grateful that it is dark and that the moon is especially bright.

Reflect on the many reasons you can't yet die:

You need to see your husband.

You need to have children.

You need to tell the movie star that he has an eighth child, and that she is a hero.

21

The moon may appear to move, but really it is you who are moving.

At high velocity, a speedboat slams along the tops of waves.

Fear and excitement are sometimes indistinguishable.

When the captain of a boat adjusts his course in response to commands from your Designated Mate, he may not know where he is taking you.

If your Designated Mate keeps looking up, he's probably using the stars for navigation.

The Mediterranean is vast enough to have once seemed infinite.

A beauty should require no more context than the presence of her Designated Mate.

A beauty must appear to enjoy any journey he initiates.

Simulate said enjoyment by putting an affectionate arm around him and nestling your head close to his.

A beauty whose head is aligned with her Designated Mate's can share in his navigation and thus calculate the route.

At night, far from shore, stars pulse with a strength that is impossible to conceive of in the proximity of light.

Your whereabouts will never be a mystery; you will be visible at all times as a dot of light on the screens of those watching over you.

You are one of hundreds, each a potential hero.

Technology has afforded ordinary people a chance to glow in the cosmos of human achievement.

Your lack of espionage and language training is what makes your record clean and neutral.

You are an ordinary person undertaking an extraordinary task.

You need not be remarkable for your credentials or skill sets, only for your bravery and equilibrium.

Knowing that you are one of hundreds shouldn't feel belittling.

In the new heroism, the goal is to merge with something larger than yourself.

In the new heroism, the goal is to throw off generations of self-involvement.

In the new heroism, the goal is to renounce the American fixation with being seen and recognized.

In the new heroism, the goal is to dig beneath your shiny persona.

You'll be surprised by what lies under it: a rich, deep crawl space of possibilities.

Some liken this discovery to a dream in which a familiar home acquires new wings and rooms.

The power of individual magnetism is nothing against the power of combined selfless effort.

You may accomplish astonishing personal feats, but citizen agents rarely seek individual credit.

They liken the need for personal glory to cigarette addiction: a habit that feels life-sustaining even as it kills you.

Childish attention-seeking is usually satisfied at the expense of real power.

An enemy of the state could not have connived a better way to declaw and distract us.

Now our notorious narcissism is our camouflage.

22

After a juddering ride of several hours, you may not notice at first that the boat is approaching a shore.

A single lighted structure stands out strongly on a deserted coastline.

Silence after a roaring motor is a sound of its own.

The speedboat's immediate departure signals that you won't be making a return trip anytime soon.

Knowing your latitude and longitude is not the same as knowing where you are.

A new remote and unfamiliar place can make the prior remote and unfamiliar place seem like home.

Imagining yourself as a dot of light on a screen is oddly reassuring.

Because your husband is a visionary in the realm of national security, he occasionally has access to that screen.

If it calms you to imagine your husband tracking your dot of light, then imagine it.

Do not, however, close your eyes while ascending a rocky path in darkness.

At Latitude X, Longitude Y, the flora is dry and crumbles under your feet.

A voice overhead suggests that your arrival was expected and observed.

An empty shore is not necessarily unpatrolled.

The best patrols are imperceptible.

23

A formal handshake between your new host and your Designated Mate implies that this is their first meeting.

A formal handshake followed by a complex and stylized hand gesture implies a shared allegiance.

So does the immediate use of a language you don't recognize.

In certain rich, powerful men, physical slightness will seem a source of strength.

The failure of your new host to acknowledge you may indicate that women do not register in his field of vision.

Being invisible means that you won't be closely watched.

Your job is to be forgotten yet still present.

A white, sparkling villa amid so much scrabbly darkness will appear mirage-like.

A man to whom women are invisible may still have many beauties in his domain.

These neglected beauties will vie for his scant attention.

Among neglected beauties, there is often an alpha beauty who assumes leadership.

As you enter the house, her cool scrutiny will ripple through the other beauties and surround you.

The sensation will remind you of going as a child with your mother to visit families with two parents and multiple children.

At first, the knot of unfamiliar kids would seem impenetrable.

You would wish, keenly, that you had a sibling who could be your ally.

Feeling at the mercy of those around you prompted a seismic internal response.

The will to dominate was deeper than yourself.

You were never childish, even as a child.

Your unchildishness is something your husband has always loved in you.

Once the new children were under your control, it was crushing to leave their midst.

24

A small table and chairs carved into a spindly clifftop promontory are doubtless designed for private conversation.

If your Designated Mate brings you with him to this place, it may mean that he feels less than perfectly at ease with your new host.

When your new host dismisses his own alpha beauty, important business may be under way.

An alpha beauty will not tolerate her own exclusion if another beauty is included.

If your new host makes a motion of dismissal at you, look to your Designated Mate.

Take orders from no one but your Designated Mate.

If your Designated Mate keeps an arm around you in the face of your new host's dismissal, you have become the object of a power play.

If your new host moves close to your face and speaks directly into it, he is likely testing your ignorance of his language.

If your Designated Mate stiffens beside you, your new host's words are probably offensive.

When you become an object of contention, try to neutralize the conflict.

A giggle and a look of incomprehension are a beauty's most reliable tools.

If the men relax into their chairs, neutralization has been successful.

Your new host has insulted you and, by extension, your Designated Mate.

Your Designated Mate has prevailed in his claim that you're too harmless to bother sending away.

Congratulate yourself on preserving your adjacency and activate your ear mike.

25

In the presence of business conversation, project an utter lack of interest or curiosity.

Notice where you are at all times.

On a high, narrow promontory at Latitude X, Longitude Y, the ocean and heavens shimmer in all directions.

There will be moments in your mission, perhaps very few, when you'll sense the imminence of critical information.

It may come in the form of a rush of joy.

This joy may arise from your discovery that the moon, hard and radiant, is still aloft.

It may arise from the knowledge that, when your task is complete, you will return to the husband you adore.

It may arise from the extremity of the natural beauty around you, and the recognition that you are alive in this moment.

It may arise from your knowledge that you have accomplished every goal you've set for yourself since childhood.

It may arise from the knowledge that at long last you've found a goal worthy of your considerable energies.

It may arise from the knowledge that, by accomplishing this goal, you'll have helped to perpetuate American life as you know it.

A wave of joy can make it difficult to sit still.

Beware of internal states—positive or negative—that obscure what is happening around you.

When two subjects begin making sketches, concrete planning may have commenced.

The camera implanted in your left eye is operated by pressing your left tear duct.

In poor light, a flash may be activated by pressing the outside tip of your left eyebrow.

When using the flash, always cover your non-camera eye to shield it from temporary blindness occasioned by the flash.

Never deploy flash photography in the presence of other people.

26

Springing from your seat with a gasp and peering toward the house will focus the attention of others in that direction.

Having heard something inaudible to others puts you in an immediate position of authority.

"What? What did you hear?," uttered close to your face by your Designated Mate, means that your diversion was successful.

Wait until their eagerness to know verges on anger, evidenced by the shaking of your shoulders.

Then tell them, faintly, "I heard screaming."

Men with a history of violence live in fear of retribution.

Your new host will be the first to depart in the direction of alleged screaming.

Your Designated Mate's glance toward the dock, far below, may reveal that his interests are not fully aligned with your new host's.

His attention to his handset may portend that your diversion has run amok, undermining the transaction you meant to capture.

Among the violent, there is always a plan for escape.

27

It is reasonable to hope that a backlit screen will distract its user from a camera flash at some slight distance.

Move close to the sketches you wish to photograph, allowing them to fill your field of vision.

Hold very still.

A flash is far more dramatic in total darkness.

An epithet in another language, followed by "What the fuck was that?," means you overestimated your Designated Mate's handset absorption.

A bright, throbbing total blindness means that you neglected to cover your non-camera eye.

Distance yourself from agency in the flash by crying out, truthfully, "I can't see!"

It is hard to safely navigate a clifftop promontory at high speed while blind.

It is hard to defer said navigation when your Designated Mate is forcefully yanking your hand.

A distant buzz presages an approaching speedboat.

Cooler air and a downward slope indicate that you are now below the cliff's edge.

Trying to negotiate a crumbling wooded path in a state of blindness (and heels) will soon lead to tripping and collapsing.

Receding downhill footfalls indicate that you've overtaxed your limited value to your Designated Mate.

A sense of helpless disorientation may prevent you from doing much more than sitting there in the dirt.

28

Variegation in the textures around you is a first sign that your temporary blindness has begun to fade.

Temporary blindness sharpens one's appreciation for not being blind.

In the aftermath of blindness, the accretion of objects around you may have an almost sensual quality.

A boat departing at high speed will send a vibration trembling up through the soil.

The knowledge that you are alone, without your Designated Mate, will settle upon you slowly and coldly.

Each new phase of aloneness reveals that you were previously less alone than you thought.

This more profound isolation may register, at first, as paralysis.

If it soothes you to lie back in the dirt, then lie back.

The moon shines everywhere.

The moon can seem as expressive as a face.

Human beings are fiercely, primordially resilient.

In uneasy times, draw on the resilience you carry inside you.

Recall that the mythical feats you loved to read about as a child are puny beside the accomplishments of human beings on earth.

29

The presence of another person can be sensed, even when not directly perceived.

The discovery of another person at close range, when you thought you were alone, may occasion fear.

Leaping from a supine into a standing posture will induce a head rush.

"I see you. Come out" must be uttered calmly, from the Readiness Position.

If you show fear, make sure that it isn't the fear you actually feel.

When you've expected a man, the appearance of a woman may be shocking.

Despite all that you know and are, you may experience that shock as a relief.

"Why are you here?," uttered by your new host's alpha beauty, is likely hostile.

Respond to abstract questions on the most literal level: "He left without me."

"Bastard," muttered bitterly, suggests familiarity with the phenomenon of being left behind.

Sympathy from an unexpected source can prompt a swell of emotion.

Measure the potential liability of shedding tears before you let them fall.

The perfumed arm of a beauty may pour strength and hope directly into your skin.

30

A lavish clifftop villa may look even more mirage-like on a second approach.

Sustaining an atmosphere of luxury in a remote place requires an enormous amount of money.

So does coordinated violence.

Your job is to follow money to its source.

A powerful man whose associate has fled the premises after a false alarm is unlikely to be cheerful.

The reappearance of the vanished associate's stranded beauty will likely startle him.

Astonishment is satisfying to witness on any face.

"Where the fuck did he go?" is remarkably easy to decipher, even in a language you don't recognize.

A shrug is comprehensible to everyone.

An alpha beauty's complete indifference to the consternation of her mate may mean that he's easily moved to consternation.

It may also mean that he's not her mate.

As a beauty, you will sometimes be expected to change hands.

Generally, you will pass from the hands of a less powerful man to those of a more powerful man.

Greater proximity to the source of money and control is progress.

Your job is identical regardless of whose hands you are in.

If your vulnerability and helplessness have drawn the interest of an enemy subject, accentuate them.

Scraped and dirty legs may accentuate your vulnerability to the point of disgust.

They might get you a hot shower, though.

31

Homes of the violent rich have excellent first-aid cabinets.

If, after tending to your scrapes, you are shown to a bathing area with a stone-encrusted waterfall, assume you won't be alone for long.

The fact that a man has ignored and then insulted you does not mean that he won't want to fuck you.

Slim, powerful men often move with catlike swiftness.

Begin your countdown early—as he lowers himself into the tub.

By the time he seizes your arm, you should be at five.

By the time your forehead is jammed against a rock, you should perceive your body only vaguely, from above.

32

If you feel, on returning to your body, that much time has passed, don't dwell on how much.

If your limbs are sore and your forehead scraped and raw, don't dwell on why.

When you emerge from a warm, churning bath where you've spent an indeterminate period of time, expect to feel shaky and weak.

Remind yourself that you are receiving no payment, in currency or kind, for this or any act you have engaged in.

These acts are forms of sacrifice.

An abundance of diaphanous bathrobes suggests that the occupants of this bathroom are often female.

A soiled and tattered white sundress can seem oddly precious when it's all you have.

Keep with you the things that matter—you won't come back for them later.

The stationing of a male attendant outside the bathroom means that you haven't been forgotten.

If he shows you to a tiny room containing a very large bed, your utility to your new host may not have been exhausted.

A tray containing a meat pie, grapes, and a pitcher of water suggests that visits such as yours are routine.

At times, you may wish to avoid the moon.

At times, the moon may appear like a surveillance device, tracking your movements.

The ability to sleep in stressful conditions is essential to this work.

Sleep whenever you can safely do so.

33

Your abrupt awakening may feel like a reaction to a sound.

In moments of extreme solitude, you may believe you've heard your name.

We reassure ourselves by summoning, in our dreams, those we love and miss.

Having awakened to find them absent, we may be left with a sense of having spoken with them.

Even the most secure houses achieve, in deep night, a state of relative unconsciousness.

A beauty in a diaphanous lavender bathrobe can go anywhere, as long as she appears to be delivering herself to someone.

34

A universal principle of home construction makes it possible to guess which door will lead to the master bedroom.

Linen closets, with doors closed, can resemble master bedrooms.

So can bathrooms.

Bare feet are virtually soundless on a stone floor.

Even a slim, catlike man may snore.

When trespassing in a sleeping man's bedroom, go straight to his bed, as if you were seeking him out.

An alpha beauty who has appeared to have no tie to your new host may turn out to be his intimate, after all.

Their sleeping entanglement may contradict everything you have witnessed between them.

A small crib near the bed may indicate the presence of a baby.

Avoid indulging your own amazement; it wastes time.

Master bedrooms in lavish homes often divide into "his" and "hers" areas.

A beauty's closet is unmistakable, like a quiver of bright arrows.

The closet of a slight, catlike man will usually be compact.

Having penetrated a man's personal space, immediately seek out his Sweet Spot.

The Sweet Spot is where he empties his pockets at the end of the day and stores the essentials he needs to begin the next.

The Sweet Spot of a secretive, catlike man will most often be inside a cupboard or a drawer.

When you find it, consider using a Data Surge to capture the contents of his handset.

A Data Surge must be deployed with extreme caution, and only if you feel confident of an exceptional yield.

The quantity of information captured will require an enormous amount of manpower to tease apart.

Its transmission will register on any monitoring device.

We can guarantee its effectiveness only once.

35

Reach between your right fourth and pinky toes (if right-handed) and remove the Data Plug from your Universal Port.

Attached to the plug is a cable with a connection pin at one end for insertion into the handset's data port.

Sit on the floor, away from sharp surfaces, and brace your back against a wall.

A red ribbon has been tucked inside your Universal Port; enclose this in one of your palms.

Spread apart your toes and gently reinsert the plug, now fused to your subject's handset, into your Universal Port.

You will feel the surge as the data flood your body.

The surge may contain feeling, memory, heat, cold, longing, pain, even joy.

Although the data are alien, the memories dislodged will be your own:

Peeling an orange for your husband in bed on a Sunday, sunlight splashing the sheets;

The smoky earthen smell of the fur of your childhood cat;

The flavor of the peppermints your mother kept for you inside her desk.

The impact of a Data Surge may prompt unconsciousness or short-term memory loss.

The purpose of the red ribbon is to orient you; if you awaken to find yourself clutching one, look to your foot.

When your body is quiet, unplug the handset and return it to its original location.

36

A Data Surge leaves a ringing in your ears that may obscure the sound of another person's arrival.

A face that brought you relief once may trigger relief a second time.

When an alpha beauty accosts you at high volume in an unfamiliar language, it may mean she's too sleepy to remember who you are.

It may also mean she's calling someone else.

Beauty status will not excuse, for another beauty, your appearance where you are not supposed to be.

Should you be perceived as an enemy, prepare to defend yourself at the first sign of physical encroachment.

Your new host lunging at you, shouting, "What the fuck are you doing?," constitutes physical encroachment.

Thrust your elbow upward into the tender socket underneath his jaw, sending him backward onto the floor.

The wails of a newborn will lure its mother away from almost anything, including the physical travails of her mate.

A man disabled by an elbow blow will have little reaction to infant cries.

37

At the revelation of martial-arts expertise, a man who has perceived you as merely a beauty will recalculate your identity and purpose.

Watch his eyes: he'll be measuring the distance to his nearest firearm.

An immediate exit is advisable.

A slim, catlike man may well rebound before a hasty exit can be made.

Obstructing the path of a violent man to his firearm will nearly always result in another encroachment.

Kicking him in the foreneck, even barefoot, will temporarily occlude his windpipe.

The alpha beauty of a violent man will know where his firearm is kept, and how to use it.

A woman holding a gun and a baby no longer qualifies as a beauty.

No beauty is really a beauty.

Disabling a gun holder is likely to hurt the baby she is holding, too.

When self-preservation requires that you harm the innocent, we can provide no more than guidelines.

As Americans, we value human rights above all else and cannot sanction their violation.

When someone threatens *our* human rights, however, a wider leeway becomes necessary.

Follow your instincts while bearing in mind that we must, and will, hew to our principles.

A woman holding a thrashing baby in one arm may have trouble aiming a firearm with the other.

Bullets do actually whistle in an enclosed space.

If a person has shot at you and missed, incapacitate her before she can fire again.

We are most reluctant to hurt those who remind us of ourselves.

38

A lag time exists between getting shot and knowing that you have been shot.

Assuming there is no artery involvement, wounds to the upper limbs are preferable.

Bony, tendony body parts bleed less, but are harder to reconstruct if shattered.

The right shoulder is a bony, tendony part.

When shots have been fired in a powerful man's home, you have minutes, if not seconds, before the arrival of security.

Your physical person is our Black Box; without it, we have no record of what has happened on your mission.

It is imperative that you remove yourself from enemy possession.

When you find yourself cornered and outnumbered, you may unleash, as a last resort, your Primal Roar.

The Primal Roar is the human equivalent of an explosion, a sound that combines screaming, shrieking, and howling.

The Roar must be accompanied by facial contortions and frenetic body movement, suggesting a feral, unhinged state.

The Primal Roar must transform you from a beauty into a monster.

The goal is to horrify your opponent, the way trusted figures, turned evil, are horrifying in movies and in nightmares.

Deploy your camera flash repeatedly while Roaring.

When approached by a howling, spasmodic, flashing monster, most women holding newborns will step aside.

Discontinue Roaring the instant you're free from immediate danger.

Those stampeding to the aid of a powerful man will barely notice a disheveled beauty they pass in a hallway.

If you're lucky, this will buy you time to flee his house.

Resume your beauty role while running: smooth your hair and cover your bleeding wound with the sundress scrunched in your pocket.

The fact that you can't hear alarms doesn't mean you haven't set them off.

39

After violence in a closed room, cool night air will have a clarifying effect.

Get to the bottom of a hill any way you can, including sliding and rolling.

In residences of the violent rich, there will be at least one guard at each port of egress.

In deep night, if you are extremely lucky (and quiet), that guard will be asleep.

Assume, as well as you can, the air of a beauty larkishly gamboling.

If running barefoot onto a dock transports you back to your childhood, pain may be making you hallucinate.

Lying with girlfriends on a still-warm dock in upstate New York, watching shooting stars, is a sensation you remember after many years.

Hindsight creates the illusion that your life has led you inevitably to the present moment.

It's easier to believe in a foregone conclusion than to accept that our lives are governed by chance.

Showing up for a robotics course by accident, because of a classroom mix-up, is chance.

Finding an empty seat beside a boy with very dark skin and beautiful hands is chance.

When someone has become essential to you, you will marvel that you could have lain on a warm dock and not have known him yet.

Expect reimmersion in your old life to be difficult.

Experience leaves a mark, regardless of the reasons and principles behind it.

What our citizen agents most often require is simply for time to pass.

Our counselors are available around the clock for the first two weeks of your reimmersion and during business hours thereafter.

We ask that you allow our Therapeutic Agents, rather than those in the general population, to address your needs.

Secrecy is the basis of what we do, and we require your extreme discretion.

40

Even preternatural swimming strength cannot propel you across a blue-black sea.

Staring with yearning ferocity from the end of a dock cannot propel you across a blue-black sea.

When your body has been granted exceptional powers, it is jarring to encounter a gulf between your desires and your abilities.

For millennia, engineers have empowered human beings to accomplish mythical feats.

Your husband is an engineer.

Children raised among wild animals learn to detect irregular movements in their landscape.

That particular awareness, coupled with scientific genius, has made your husband a national-security hero.

Intimacy with another human can allow you to scrutinize your surroundings as he would.

Along a rocky, moonlit shore, the irregular movement is the one that is lurching in time with the water beneath an overhang of brush.

A speedboat has most likely been hidden by your new host as a means of emergency escape.

The key will be inside it.

41

Slither between branches and board the boat; untie it and lower its motor into the water.

Be grateful for the lakes in upstate New York where you learned to pilot motorboats.

Fluff up your hair with your functional arm and essay a wide, carefree smile.

A smile is like a shield; it freezes your face into a mask of muscle that you can hide behind.

A smile is like a door that is both open and closed.

Turn the key and gun the motor once before aiming into the blue-black sea and jamming the accelerator.

Wave and giggle loudly at the stunned, sleepy guard.

Steer in a zigzag motion until you are out of gunshot range.

42

The exultation of escape will be followed almost immediately by a crushing onslaught of pain.

The house, its occupants, even the gunshots will seem like phantoms beside this clanging immediacy.

If the pain makes thought impossible, concentrate solely on navigation.

Only in specific Geographic Hotspots can we intervene.

While navigating toward a Hotspot, indicate an emergency by pressing the button behind your knee for sixty continuous seconds.

You must remain conscious.

If it helps, imagine yourself in the arms of your husband.

If it helps, imagine yourself in your apartment, where his grandfather's hunting knife is displayed inside a Plexiglas box.

If it helps, imagine harvesting the small tomatoes you grow on your fire escape in summer.

If it helps, imagine that the contents of the Data Surge will help thwart an attack in which thousands of American lives would have been lost.

Even without enhancements, you can pilot a boat in a semiconscious state.

Human beings are superhuman.

Let the moon and the stars direct you.

43

When you reach the approximate location of a Hotspot, cut the engine.

You will be in total darkness, in total silence.

If you wish, you may lie down at the bottom of the boat.

The fact that you feel like you're dying doesn't mean that you will die.

Remember that, should you die, your body will yield a crucial trove of information.

Remember that, should you die, your Field Instructions will provide a record of your mission and lessons for those who follow.

Remember that, should you die, you will have triumphed merely by delivering your physical person into our hands.

The boat's movement on the sea will remind you of a cradle.

You'll recall your mother rocking you in her arms when you were a baby.

You'll recall that she has always loved you fiercely and entirely.

You'll discover that you have forgiven her.

You'll understand that she concealed your paternity out of faith that her own inexhaustible love would be enough.

The wish to tell your mother that you forgive her is yet another reason you must make it home alive.

You will not be able to wait, but you will have to wait.

We can't tell you in advance what direction relief will come from.

We can only reassure you that we have never yet failed to recover a citizen agent, dead or alive, who managed to reach a Hotspot.

44

Hotspots are not hot.

Even a warm night turns frigid at the bottom of a wet boat.

The stars are always there, scattered and blinking.

Looking up at the sky from below can feel like floating, suspended, and looking down.

The universe will seem to hang beneath you in its milky glittering mystery.

Only when you notice a woman like yourself, crumpled and bleeding at the bottom of a boat, will you realize what has happened.

You've deployed the Dissociation Technique wihout meaning to.

There is no harm in this.

Released from pain, you can waft free in the night sky.

Released from pain, you can enact the fantasy of flying that you nurtured as a child.

Keep your body in view at all times; if your mind loses track of your body, it may be hard—even impossible—to reunite the two.

As you waft free in the night sky, you may notice a steady rhythmic churning in the gusting wind.

Helicopter noise is inherently menacing.

A helicopter without lights is like a mixture of bat, bird, and monstrous insect.

Resist the urge to flee this apparition; it has come to save you.

45

Know that in returning to your body you are consenting to be racked, once again, by physical pain.

Know that in returning to your body you are consenting to undertake a jarring reimmersion into an altered life.

Some citizen agents have chosen not to return.

They have left their bodies behind, and now they shimmer sublimely in the heavens.

In the new heroism, the goal is to transcend individual life, with its petty pains and loves, in favor of the dazzling collective.

You may picture the pulsing stars as the heroic spirits of former agent beauties.

You may imagine Heaven as a vast screen crowded with their dots of light.

46

If you wish to return to your body, it is essential that you reach it before the helicopter does.

If it helps, count backward.

By eight, you should be close enough to see your bare and dirty feet.

By five, you should be close enough to see the bloody dress wrapped around your shoulder.

By three, you should be close enough to see the dimples you were praised for as a child.

By two, you should hear the shallow bleating of your breath.

47

Having returned to your body, witness the chopper's slow, throbbing descent.

It may appear to be the instrument of a purely mechanical realm.

It may look as if it had come to wipe you out.

It may be hard to believe that there are human beings inside it.

You won't know for sure until you see them crouching above you, their faces taut with hope, ready to jump.

QUESTIONS FOR DISCUSSION

Why does Egan envision a future where women's bodies are recorders of data?

1. Why does the manual state, "Now our notorious narcissism is our camouflage"? (395)

2. Why does the manual emphasize that "these acts are forms of sacrifice," rather than work that the agents are paid for? (404)

3. Why does the manual state that "no beauty is really a beauty"? (408)

4. Why might some citizen agents choose "not to return"? (416)

How does the story's "new heroism," where "the goal is to transcend individual life, with its petty pains and loves, in favor of the dazzling collective," comment on our society today? (416)

1. Why does the manual tell agents that "kindness feels good, even when it's based on a false notion of your identity and purpose"? (379)

2. Why are agents required to possess an "impossible combination of traits: ironclad scruples and a willingness to violate them"? (381)

3. Why are agents instructed that they "need not identify or comprehend the language" used by a subject? (386)

4. What distinction is Egan making between "human rights" in general and "*our* human rights"? (409)

FOR FURTHER REFLECTION

1. Why does the manual point out that the instructions are "becoming less and less instructive"? Why is the advice given in such specific terms as to seem to describe a single series of events?

2. How might the advice to agents to "always filter your observations and experience through the lens of their didactic value. / Your training is ongoing; you must learn from each step you take" extend to the process of reading Egan's story?

3. Does knowing that "Black Box" was initially published as a series of tweets make it more, or less, effective as a story?

4. What are the consequences of suppressing individual sentiment for the common good?

Jon

George Saunders

Back in the time of which I am speaking, due to our Coordinators had mandated us, we had all seen that educational video of *It's Yours to Do With What You Like!* in which teens like ourselfs speak on the healthy benefits of getting off by oneself and doing what one feels like in terms of self-touching, which what we learned from that video was, there is nothing wrong with self-touching, because love is a mystery but the mechanics of love need not be, so go off alone, see what is up, with you and your relation to your own gonads, and the main thing is, just have fun, feeling no shame!

And then nightfall would fall and our facility would fill with the sounds of quiet fast breathing from inside our Privacy Tarps as we all experimented per the techniques taught us in *It's Yours to Do With What You Like!* and what do you suspect, you had better make sure that that little gap between the main wall and the wall that slides out to make your Gender Areas is like really really small.

Which, guess what, it wasn't.

That is all what I am saying.

Also all what I am saying is, who could blame Josh for noting that little gap and squeezing through it snakelike in just his Old Navy boxers that Old Navy gave us to wear for gratis, plus who could blame Ruthie for leaving her Velcro knowingly un-Velcroed? Which soon all the rest of us heard them doing what the rest of us so badly wanted to be doing, only we, being more mindful of the rules than them, just laid there doing the self-stuff from the video, listening to Ruth and Josh really doing it for real, which believe me, even that was pretty fun.

And when Josh came back next morning so happy he was crying, that was a further blow to our morality, because why did our Coordinators not catch him on their supposedly nighttime monitors? In all of our hearts was the thought of, okay, we thought you said no boy-and-girl stuff, and yet here is Josh, with his Old Navy boxers in his hand and a hickey on his waist, and none of you guys is even saying boo?

Because I for one wanted to do right, I did not want to sneak through that gap, I wanted to wed someone when old enough (I will soon tell who) and relocate to the appropriate facility in terms of demographics, namely Young Marrieds, such as Scranton, PA, or Mobile, AL, and then along comes Josh doing Ruthie with imperity, and no one is punished, and soon the miracle of birth results and all our Coordinators, even Mr. Delacourt, are bringing Baby Amber stuffed animals? At which point every cell or chromosome or whatever it was in my gonads that had been holding their breaths was suddenly like, Dude, slide through that gap no matter how bad it hurts, squat outside Carolyn's Privacy Tarp whispering, Carolyn, it's me, please un-Velcro your Privacy opening!

Then came the final straw that broke the back of my saying no to my gonads, which was I dreamed I was that black dude on MTV's *Hot and Spicy Christmas* (around like Location Indicator 34412, if you want to check it out) and Carolyn was the oiled-up white chick, and we were trying to earn the Island Vacation by miming through the ten Hot 'n' Nasty Positions before the end of "We Three Kings," only then, sadly, during Her On Top, Thumb In Mouth, her Elf Cap fell off, and as the Loser Buzzer sounded she bent low to me, saying, Oh, Jon, I wish we did not have to do this for fake in front of hundreds of kids on Spring Break doing the wave but instead could do it for real with just each other in private.

And then she kissed me with a kiss I can only describe as melting.

So imagine that is you, you are a healthy young dude who has been self-practicing all these months, and you wake from that dream of a hot chick giving you a melting kiss, and that same hot chick is laying or lying just on the other side of the sliding wall, and meanwhile in the very next Privacy Tarp is that sleeping dude Josh, who a few weeks before, a baby was born to the girl he had recently did it with, and nothing bad happened, except now Mr. Slippen sometimes let them sleep in.

What would you do?

Well, you would do what I did, you would, you would slip through, and when Carolyn un-Velcroed that Velcro wearing her blue Guess kimono, whispering, Oh my God, I thought you'd never ask, that would be the most romantic thing you had ever underwent.

And though I had many times seen LI 34321 for Honey Grahams, where the stream of milk and the stream of honey enjoin to make that river of sweet-tasting goodness, I did not know that, upon making love, one person may become like the milk and the other like the honey, and soon they cannot even remember who started out the milk and who the honey, they just become one fluid, this like honey/milk combo.

Well, that is what happened to us.

Which is why soon I had to go to Mr. Slippen hat in hand and say, Sir, Baby Amber will be having a little playmate if that is okay with you, to which he just rolled his eyes and crushed the plastic cup in his hand and threw it at my chest, saying, What are we running in here, Randy, a freaking playschool?

Then he said, Well, Christ, what am I supposed to do, lose two valuable team members because of this silliness? All right all right, how soon will Baby Amber be out of that crib or do I have to order your kid a whole new one?

Which I was so happy, because soon I would be a father and would not even lose my job.

A few days later, like how it was with Ruthie and Josh, Mr. Delacourt's brother the minister came in and married us, and afterward barbecue beef was catered, and we danced at our window while outside pink and purple balloons were released, and all the other kids were like, Rock on you guys, have a nice baby and all!

It was the best day of our lifes thus far for sure.

But I guess it is true what they say at LI 11006 about life throwing us not only curves and sliders but sometimes even worse, as Dodger pitcher Hector Jones throws from behind his back a grand piano for Allstate, because soon here came that incident with Baby Amber, which made everybody just loony.

Which that incident was, Baby Amber died.

Sometimes it was just nice and gave one a fresh springtime feeling to sit in the much-coveted window seat, finalizing one's Summary while gazing out at our foliage strip, which sometimes slinking through it would be a cat from Rustic Village Apartments, looking so cute that one wished to pet or even smell it, with wishful petting being the feeling I was undergoing on the sad day of which I am telling, such as even giving the cat a tuna chunk and a sip of my Diet Coke! If cats even like soda. That I do not know.

And then Baby Amber toddled by, making this funny noise in her throat of not being very happy, and upon reaching the Snack Cart she like seized up and tumped over, giving off this sort of shriek.

At first we all just looked at her, like going, Baby Amber, if that is some sort of new game, we do not exactly get it, plus come on, we have a lot of Assessments to get through this morning, such as a First-Taste Session for Diet Ginger-Coke, plus a very critical First View of Dean Witter's Preliminary Clip Reel for their campaign of "Whose Ass Are You Kicking Today?"

But then she did not get up.

We dropped our Summaries and raced to the Observation Window and began pounding, due to we loved her so much, her being the first baby we had ever witnessed living day after day, and soon the paramedics came and took her away, with one of them saying, Jesus, how stupid are you kids, anyway, this baby is burning up, she is like 107 with meningitis!

And maybe we were stupid, but also, I would like to see them paramedics do that many Assessments and still act smart, as we had a lot of stress on our plate at that time.

So next morning there was Carolyn all freaked out with her little baby belly, watching Amber's crib being dismantled by Physical Plant, who wiped all facility surfaces with Handi Wipes in case the meningitis was viral, and there was the rest of us, just like thrashing around the place kicking things down, going like, This sucks, this is totally fucked up!

Looking back, I commend Mr. Slippen for what he did next, which was he said, Christ, folks, all our hearts are broken, it is not just yours, do you or do you not think I have Observed this baby from the time she was born, do you or do you not think that I too feel like kicking things down while shouting, This sucks, this is totally fucked up? Only what would that accomplish, would that bring Baby Amber back? I am at a loss, in terms of how can we best support Ruth and Josh in this sad tragic time, is it via feeling blue and cranky, or via feeling refreshed and hopeful and thus better able to respond to their needs?

So that was a non-brainer, and we all voted to accept Mr. Slippen's Facility Morale Initiative, and soon were getting our Aurabon® twice a day instead of once, plus it seemed like better stuff, and I for one had never felt so glad or stress-free, and my Assessments became very nuanced, and I spent many hours doing and enjoying them and then redoing and reenjoying them, and it was during this period that we won the McDorland Prize for Excellence in Assessing in the Midwest Region in our demographic category of White Teens.

The only one who failed to become gladder was Carolyn, who due to her condition of pregnant could not join us at the place in the wall where we hooked in for our Aurabon.® And now whenever the rest of us hooked in she would come over and say such negative things as, Wake up and smell the coffee, you feel bad because a baby died, how about honoring that by continuing to feel bad, which is only natural, because a goddam baby died, you guys?

At night in our shared double Privacy Tarp in Conference Room 11, which our Coordinators had gave us so we would feel more married, I would be like, Honey look, your attitude only sucks because you can't hook in, once baby comes all will be fine, due to you'll be able to hook in again, right? But she always blew me off, like she would say she was thinking of never hooking in again and why was I always pushing her to hook in and she just didn't know who to trust anymore, and one night when the baby kicked she said to her abdomen, Don't worry angel, Mommy is going to get you Out.

Which my feeling was: Out? Hello? My feeling was: Hold on, I like what I have achieved, and when I thought of descending Out to somewhere with no hope of meeting luminaries such as actress Lily Farrell-Garesh or Mark Belay, chairperson of Thatscool.com, descending Out to, say, some lumberyard, like at LI 77656 for Midol, merely piling lumber as cars rushed past, cars with no luminaries inside, only plain regular people who did not know me from Adam, who, upon seeing me, saw just some mere guy stacking lumber having such humdrum thoughts as thinking, Hey, I wonder what's for lunch, duh—I got a cold flat feeling in my gut, because I did not want to undergo it.

Plus furthermore (and I said this to Carolyn) what will it be like for us when all has been taken from us? Of what will we speak of? I do not want to only speak of my love in grunts! If I wish to compare my love to a love I have previous knowledge of, I do not want to stand there in the wind casting about for my metaphor! If I want to say like, Carolyn, remember that RE/MAX one where as the redhead kid falls asleep holding that Teddy bear rescued from the trash, the bear comes alive and winks, and the announcer goes, Home is the place where you find yourself suddenly no longer longing for home (LI 34451)—if I want to say to Carolyn, Carolyn, LI 34451, check it out, that is how I feel about you—well, then, I want to say it! I want to possess all the articulate I can, because otherwise there we will be, in non-designer clothes, no longer even on TrendSetters & TasteMakers gum cards with our photos on them, and I will turn to her and say, Honey, uh, honey, there is a certain feeling but I cannot name it and cannot cite a precedent-type feeling, but trust me, dearest, wow, do I ever feel it for you right now. And what will that be like, that stupid standing there, just a man and a woman and the wind, and nobody knowing what nobody is meaning?

Just then the baby kicked my hand, which at that time was on Carolyn's stomach.

And Carolyn was like, You are either with me or agin me.

Which was so funny, because she was proving my point! Because you are either with me or agin me is what the Lysol bottle at LI 12009 says to the scrubbing sponge as they approach the grease stain together, which is making at them a threatening fist while wearing a sort of Mexican bandolera!

When I pointed this out, she removed my hand from her belly.

I love you, I said.

Prove it, she said.

So next day Carolyn and I came up to Mr. Slippen and said, Please, Mr. Slippen, we hereby Request that you supply us with the appropriate Exit Paperwork.

To which Mr. Slippen said, Guys, folks, tell me this is a joke by you on me.

And Carolyn said softly, because she had always liked Mr. Slippen, who had taught her to ride a bike when small in the Fitness Area, It's no joke.

And Slippen said, Holy smokes, you guys are possessed of the fruits of the labors of hundreds of thousands of talented passionate men and women, some of whom are now gone from us, they poured forth these visions in the prime of their lives, reacting spontaneously to the beauty and energy of the world around them, which is why these stories and images are such an unforgettable testimony to who we are as a nation! And you have it all within you! I can only imagine how thrilling that must be. And now, to give it all up? For what? Carolyn, for what?

And Carolyn said, Mr. Slippen, I did not see you raising your babies in such a confined environment.

And Slippen said, Carolyn, that is so, but also please note that neither I nor my kids have ever been on TrendSetters & TasteMakers gum cards and believe me, I have heard a few earfuls vis-à-vis that, as in: Dad, you could've got us In but no, and now, Dad, I am merely another ophthalmologist among millions of ophthalmologists. And please do not think that is not something that a father sometimes struggles with, in terms of coulda shoulda woulda.

And Carolyn said, Jon, you know what, he is not even really listening to us.

And Slippen said, Randy, since when is your name Jon?

Because by the way my name is really Jon. Randy is just what my mother put on the form the day I was Accepted, although tell the truth I do not know why.

But in my dimmest mind I can very clear recall her voice calling me Jon in my possibly baby days.

It is one thing to see all this stuff in your head, Carolyn said. But altogether different to be Out in it, I would expect.

And I could see that she was softening into a like daughter role, as if wanting him to tell her what to do, and up came LI 27493 (Prudential Life), where, with Dad enstroked in the hospital bed, Daughter asks should she marry the guy who though poor has a good heart, and we see the guy working with inner-city kids via spray-painting a swing set, and Dad says, Sweetie the heart must lead you. And then later here is Dad all better in a tux, and Daughter hugging the poor but good dude while sneaking a wink at Dad, who raises his glass and points at the groom's shoe, where there is this little smudge of swing-set paint.

I cannot comment as to that, Slippen said. Everyone is different. Nobody can know someone else's experiences.

Larry, no offense but you are talking shit, Carolyn said. We deserve better than that from you.

And Slippen looked to be softening, and I remembered when he would sneak all of us kids in doughnuts, doughnuts we did not even need to Assess but could simply eat with joy with jelly on our face before returning to our Focused Purposeful Play with toys we would Assess by coloring in on a sheet of paper either a smiling duck if the toy was fun or a scowling duck if the toy bit.

And Slippen said, Look, Carolyn, you are two very fortunate people, even chosen people. A huge investment was made in you, which I would argue you have a certain responsibility to repay, not to mention, with a baby on the way, there is the question of security, security for your future that I—

Uncle, please, Carolyn said, which was her trumpet cart, because when she was small he had let her call him that and now she sometimes still did when the moment was right, such as at Christmas Eve when all of our feelings was high.

Jesus, Slippen said. Look, you two can do what you want, clearly. I cannot stop you kids, but golly I wish I could. All that is required is the required pre-Exit visit to the Lerner Center, which as you know you must take before I can give you the necessary Exit Paperwork. When would you like to take or make that visit?

Now, Carolyn said.

Gosh, Carolyn, when did you become such a pistol? Mr. Slippen said, and called for the minivan.

The Lerner Center, even when reached via blackened-window mini-van, is a trip that will really blow one's mind, due to all the new sights and sounds one experiences, such as carpet on floor is different from carpet on facility floor, such as smoke smell from the minivan ashtrays, whereas we are a No Smoking facility, not to mention, wow, when we were led in blindfolded for our own protection, so many new smells shot forth from these like sidewalkside blooms or whatever that Carolyn and I were literally bumping into each other like swooning.

Inside they took our blindfolds off, and, yes, it looked and smelled exactly like our facility, and like every facility across the land, via the PervaScent® system, except in other facilities across the land a lady in blue scrubs does not come up to you with crossed eyes, sloshing around a cup of lemonade, saying in this drunk voice like, *A barn is more than a barn it is a memory of a time when you were cared for by a national chain of caregivers who bring you the best of life with a selfless evening in Monterey when the stars are low you can be thankful to your Amorino Co broker!*

And then she burst into tears and held her lemonade so crooked it was like spilling on the Foosball table. I had no idea what Location Indicator or Indicators she was even at, and when I asked, she didn't seem to know what I meant by Location Indicator, and was like, *Oh I just don't know anymore what is going on with me or why I would expose that tenderest part of my baby to the roughest part of the forest where the going gets rough, which is not the accomplishment of any one man but an entire team of dreamers who dream the same dreams you dream in the best interests of that most important system of all, your family!*

Then this Lerner Center dude came over and led her away, and she slammed her hand down so hard on the Foosball table that the little goalie cracked and his head flew over by us, and someone said, Good one, Doreen, now there's no Foosball.

At which time luckily it was time for our Individual Consultation.

Who we got was this Mid-Ager from Akron, OH, who, when I asked my first question off my Question Card they gave us, which was, What is it like in terms of pain, he said, There is no pain except once I poked myself in my hole with a coffee stirrer and Jesus that smarted, but otherwise you can't really even feel it.

So I was glad to hear it, although not so glad when he showed us where he had poked his hole with the stirrer, because I am famous as a wimp among my peers in terms of gore, and he had opted not to use DermaFill® and you could see right in. And, wow, there is something about observing up close a raw bloody hole at the base of somebody's hair that really gets one thinking. And though he said, in Question No. 2, that his hole did not present him any special challenges in terms of daily maintenance, looking into that hole, I was like, Dude, how does that give you no challenges, it is like somebody blew off a firecracker inside your freaking neck!

And when Carolyn said Question No. 3, which was, How do you now find your thought processes, his brow darkened and he said, Well, to be frank, though quite advanced, having been here three years, there are, if you will, places where things used to be when I went looking for them, brainwise, but now, when I go there, nothing is there, it is like I have the shelving but not the cans of corn, if you get my drift. For example, looking at you, young lady, I know enough to say you are pretty, but when I direct my brain to a certain place, to find there a more vivid way of saying you are pretty, watch this, some words will come out, which I, please excuse me, oh dammit—

Then his voice changed to this announcer voice and he was like, *These women know that for many generations entrenched deep in this ancient forest is a secret known by coffee growers since the dawn of time man has wanted one thing which is to watch golf in peace will surely follow once knowledge is dispersed via the World Book is a super bridge across the many miles the phone card can close the gap!*

And his eyes were crossing and he was sputtering, which would have been funny if we did not know that soon our eyes would be the crossing eyes and out of our mouths would the sputter be flying.

Then he got up and fled from the room, hitting himself hard in the face.

And I said to Carolyn, Well, that about does it for me.

And I waited for her to say that about did it for her, but she only sat there looking conflicted with her hand on her belly.

Out in the Common Room, I took her in my arms and said, Honey, I do not really think we have it all that bad, why not just go home and love each other and our baby when he or she comes, and make the best of all the blessings what we have been given?

And her head was tilted down in this way that seemed to be saying, Yes, sweetie, my God, you were right all along.

But then a bad decisive thing happened, which was this old lady came hobbling over and said, Dear, you must wait until Year Two to truly know, some do not thrive but others do, I am Year Two, and do you know what? When I see a bug now, I truly see a bug, when I see a paint chip I am truly seeing that paint chip, there is no distraction and it is so sweet, nothing in one's field of vision but what one opts to put there via moving one's eyes, and also do you hear how well I am speaking?

Out in the minivan I said, Well, I am decided, and Carolyn said, Well, I am too. And then there was this long dead silence, because I knew and she knew that what we had both decided was not the same decision, not at all, that old crony had somehow rung her bell!

And I said, How do you know what she said is even true?

And she said, I just know.

That night in our double Privacy Tarp, Carolyn nudged me awake and said, Jon, doesn't it make sense to make our mistakes in the direction of giving our kid the best possible chance at a beautiful life?

And I was like, Chick, please take a look in the Fridge, where there is every type of food that must be kept cold, take a look on top of the Fridge, where there is every type of snack, take a look in our Group Closet, which is packed with gratis designer wear such as Baby Gap and even Baby Ann Taylor, whereas what kind of beautiful life are you proposing, with a Fridge that is empty both inside and on top, and the three of us going around all sloppenly, because I don't know about you but my skill set is pretty limited in terms of what do I know how to do, and if you go into the Fashion Module for Baby Ann Taylor and click with your blinking eyes on Pricing Info you will find that they are not just giving that shit away.

And she said, Oh, Jon, you break my heart, that night when you came to my Tarp you were like a lion taking what he wanted but now you are like some bunny wiffling his nose in fright.

Well, that wasn't nice, and I told her that wasn't nice, and she said, Jesus, don't whine, you are whining like a bunny, and I said I would rather be a bunny than a rag, and she said maybe I better go sleep somewhere else.

So I went out to Boys and slept on the floor, it being too late to check out a Privacy Tarp.

And I was pissed/sad, because no dude likes to think of himself as a rabbit, because once your girl thinks of you as a rabbit, how will she ever again think of you as a lion? And all of the sudden I felt very much like starting over with someone who would always think of me as a lion and never as a rabbit, and who really got it about how lucky we were.

Laying there in Boys, I did what I always did when confused, which was call up my Memory Loop of my mom, where she is baking a pie with her red hair up in a bun, and as always she paused in her rolling and said, Oh, my little man, I love you so much, which is why I did the most difficult thing of all, which was part with you, my darling, so that you could use your exceptional intelligence to do that most holy of things, help other people. Stay where you are, do not get distracted, have a content and productive life, and I will be happy too.

Blinking on End, I was like, Thanks, Mom, you have always been there for me, I really wish I could have met you in person before you died.

In the morning Slippen woke me by giving me the light shock on the foot bottom which was sometimes useful to help us arise if we had to arise early and were in need of assistance, and said to please accompany him, as we had a bit of a sticky wicket in our purview.

Waiting in Conference Room 6 were Mr. Dove and Mr. Andrews and Mr. Delacourt himself, and at the end of the table Carolyn, looking small, with both hands on her pile of Exit Paperwork and her hair in braids, which I had always found cute, her being like that milkmaid for Swiss Rain Chocolate (LI 10003), who suddenly throws away her pail and grows sexy via taking out her braids, and as some fat farm ladies line up by a silo and also take out their braids to look sexy their thin husbands look dubious and run for the forest.

Randy, Mr. Dove said, Carolyn here has evinced a desire to Exit. What we would like to know is, being married, do you have that same desire?

And I looked at Carolyn like, You are jumping to some conclusion because of one little fight, when it was you who called me the rabbit first, which is the only reason I called you rag?

It's not because of last night, Jon, Carolyn said.

Randy, I sense some doubt? Mr. Dove said.

And I had to admit that some doubt was being felt by me, because it seemed more than ever like she was some sort of malcontentish girl who would never be happy no matter how good things were.

Maybe you kids would like some additional time, Mr. Andrews said. Some time to talk it over and be really sure.

I don't need any additional time, Carolyn said.

And I said, You're going no matter what? No matter what I do?

And she said, Jon, I want you to come with me so bad, but, yes, I'm going.

And Mr. Dove said, Wait a minute, who is Jon?

And Mr. Andrews said, Randy is Jon, it is apparently some sort of pet name between them.

And Slippen said to us, Look, guys, I have been married for nearly thirty years and it has been my experience that, when in doubt, take a breath. Err on the side of being together. Maybe, Carolyn, the thing to do is, I mean, your Paperwork is complete, we will hold on to it, and maybe Randy, as a concession to Carolyn, you could complete your Paperwork, and we'll hold on to it for you, and when you both decide the time is right, all you have to do is say the word and we will—

I'm going today, Carolyn said. As soon as possible.

And Mr. Dove looked at me and said, Jon, Randy, whoever, are you prepared to go today?

And I said no. Because what is her rush, I was feeling, why is she looking so frantic with furrowed anxious brow like that Claymation chicken at LI 98473 who says the sky is falling the sky is falling and turns out it is only a Dodge Ramcharger, which crushes her from on high and one arm of hers or wing sticks out with a sign that says March Madness Daze?

And Slippen said, Guys, guys, I find this a great pity. You are terrific together. A real love match.

Carolyn was crying now and said, I am so sorry, but if I wait I might change my mind, which I know in my heart would be wrong.

And she thrust her Exit Paperwork across at Slippen.

Then Dove and Andrews and Delacourt began moving with great speed, as if working directly from some sort of corporate manual, which actually they were, Mr. Dove had some photocopied sheets, and reading from the sheets, he asked was there anyone with whom she wished to have a fond last private conversation, and she said, Well, duh, and we were both left briefly alone.

She took a deep breath while looking at me all tender and said, Oh Gadzooks. Which that broke my heart, Gadzooks being what we sometimes said at nice privacy moments in our Privacy Tarp when overwhelmed by our good luck in terms of our respective bodies looking so hot and appropriate, Gadzooks being from LI 38492 for Zookers Gum, where the guy blows a bubble so Zookified it ingests a whole city and the city goes floating up to Mars.

At this point her tears were streaming down and mine also, because up until then I thought we had been so happy.

Jon, please, she said.

I just can't, I said.

And that was true.

So we sat there quiet with her hands against my hands like Colonel Sanders and his wife at LI 87345, where he is in jail for refusing to give up the recipe for KFC Haitian MiniBreasts, and then Carolyn said, I didn't mean that thing about the rabbit, and I scrinkled up my nose rabbitlike to make her laugh.

But apparently in the corporate manual there is a time limit on fond last private conversations, because in came Kyle and Blake from Security, and Carolyn kissed me hard, like trying to memorize my mouth, and whispered, Someday come find us.

Then they took her away, or she took them away rather, because she was so far in front that they had to like run to keep up as she clomped loudly away in her Kenneth Cole boots, which by the way

they did not let her keep those, because that night, selecting my paja-
mas, I found them back in the Group Closet.

Night after night after that I would lay or lie alone in our Privacy Tarp,
which now held only her nail clippers and her former stuffed dog Lefty,
and during the days Slippen let me spend many unbillable hours in
the much-coveted window seat, just scanning some images or multi-
scanning some images, and around me would be the other facility
Boys and Girls, all Assessing, all smiling, because we were still on the
twice-a-day Aurabon®, and thinking of Carolyn in those blue scrubs,
alone in the Lerner Center, I would apply for additional Aurabon® via
filling out a Work-Affecting Mood-Problem Notification, which Slippen
would always approve, being as he felt so bad for me.

And the Aurabon® would make things better, as Aurabon® always
makes things better, although soon what I found was, when you are
hooking in like eight or nine times a day, you are always so happy,
and yet it is a kind of happy like chewing on tinfoil, and once you are
living for that sort of happy, you soon cannot be happy enough, even
when you are very very happy and are even near tears due to the
beauty of the round metal hooks used to hang your facility curtains,
you feel this intense wish to be even happier, so you tear yourself
away from the beautiful curtain hooks and with shaking happy hands
fill out another Work-Affecting Mood-Problem Notification, and then,
because nothing in your facility is beautiful enough to look at with
your new level of happiness, you sit in the much-coveted window seat
and start lendelling in this crazy uncontrolled way, calling up, say,
the Nike one with the Hanging Gardens of Babylon (LI 89736), and
though it is beautiful, it is not beautiful enough, so you scatter around
some Delicate Secrets lingerie models from LI 22314, and hang fat Dole
oranges and bananas in the trees (LI 76765), and add like a sky full of
bright stars from LI 74638 for Crest, and from the Smell Palate supplied
by the antiallergen Capaviv® you fill the air with jasmine and myrrh,
but still that is not beautiful enough, so you blink on End and fill out
another Work-Affecting Mood-Problem Notification, until finally one
day Mr. Dove comes over and says, Randy, Jon, whatever you are calling yourself these days—a couple of items. First, it seems to us that

you are in some private space not helpful to you, and so we are cutting back your Aurabon® to twice a day like the other folks, and please do not sit in that window seat anymore, it is hereby forbidden to you, and plus we are going to put you on some additional Project Teams, since it is our view that idle hands are the devil's work area. Also, since you are only one person, it is not fair, we feel, for you to have a whole double Privacy Tarp to yourself, you must, it seems to us, rejoin your fellow Boys in Boys.

So that night I went back with Rudy and Lance and Jason and the others, and they were nice, as they are always nice, and via No. 10 cable Jason shared with me some Still Photos from last year's Christmas party, of Carolyn hugging me from behind with her cute face appearing beneath my armpit, which made me remember how after the party in our Privacy Tarp we played a certain game, which it is none of your beeswax who I was in that game and who she was, only believe me, that was a memorable night, with us watching the snow fall from the much-coveted window seat, in which we sat snuggling around midnight, when we had left our Tarp to take a break for air, and also we were both sort of sore.

Which made it all that much more messed up and sad to be sleeping once again alone in Boys.

When the sliding wall came out to make our Gender Areas, I noticed they had fixed it so nobody could slide through anymore, via five metal rods. All we could do was, by putting our mouths to the former gap, say good night to the Girls, who all said good night back from their respective Privacy Tarps in this sort of muffled way.

But I did not do that, as I had nobody over there I wished to say good night to, they all being like merely sisters to me, and that was all.

So that was the saddest time of my life thus far for sure.

Then one day we were all laying or lying on our stomachs playing Hungarian Headchopper for GameBoy, a new proposed one where you are this dude with a scythe in your mother's garden, only what your mother grows is heads, when suddenly a shadow was cast over my game by Mr. Slippen, which freaked up my display, and I harvested three unripe heads, but the reason Slippen was casting his shadow was, he had got a letter for me, from Carolyn!

And I was so nervous opening it, and even more nervous after opening it, because inside were these weird like marks I could not read, like someone had hooked a pen to the back leg of a bird and said, Run little bird, run around this page and I will mail it for you. And the parts I could read were bumming me out even worse, such as she had wrote all sloppenly, *Jon a abbot is a cove, a glen, it is something with prayerful guys all the livelong day in silence as they move around they are sure of one thing which is the long-term stability of a product we not only stand behind we run behind since what is wrong with taking a chance even if that chance has horns and hoofs and it is just you and your worst fear in front of ten thousand screaming supporters of your last chance to be the very best you can be?*

And then thank God it started again looking like the pen on the foot of the running bird.

I thought of how hot and smart she had looked when doing a crossword with sunglasses on her head in Hilfiger cutoffs, I thought of her that first night in her Privacy Tarp, naked except for her La Perla panties in the light that came from the Exit sign through the thin blue Privacy Tarp, so her flat tummy and not-flat breasts and flirty smile were all blue, and then all of the sudden I felt like the biggest jerk in the world, because why had I let her go? It was like I was all of the sudden waking up! She was mine and I was hers, she was so thin and cute, and now she was at the Lerner Center all alone? Shaking and scared with a bloody hole in her neck and our baby in her belly, hanging out with all those other scared shaking people with bloody holes in their necks, only none of them knew her and loved her like I did? I had done such a dumb-shit thing to her, all the time thinking it was sound reasoning, because isn't that how it is with our heads, when we are in them it always makes sense, but then later, when you look back, we sometimes are like, I am acting like a total dumb-ass!

Then Brad came up and was like, Dude, time to hook in.

And I was like, Please Brad, do not bother me with that shit at this time.

And I went to get Slippen, only he was at lunch, so I went to get Dove and said, Sir, I hereby Request my appropriate Exit Paperwork.

And he said, Randy, please, you're scaring me, don't act rash, have a look out the window.

I had a look, and tell the truth it did not look that good, such as the Rustic Village Apartments, out of which every morning these bummed-out-looking guys in the plainest non-designer clothes ever would trudge out and get in their junky cars. And was someone joyfully kissing them goodbye, like saying when you come home tonight you will get a big treat, which is me? No, the person who should have been kissing them with joy was yelling, or smoking, or yelling while smoking, and when the dudes came home they would sit on their stoops with heads in hand, as if all day long at work someone had been pounding them with clubs on their heads, saying they were jerks.

Then Mr. Dove said, Randy, Randy, why would a talented young person like yourself wish to surrender his influence in the world and become just another lowing cattle in the crowd, don't you know how much people out there look up to you and depend on you?

And that was true. Because sometimes kids from Rustic Village would come over and stand in our lava rocks with our TrendSetters & TasteMakers gum cards upheld, pressing them to our window, and when we would wave to them or strike the pose we were posing on our gum cards, they would race back all happy to their crappy apartments, probably to tell their moms they had seen the real actual us, which was probably like the high point of their weeks.

But still, when I thought of those birdlike markings of Carolyn's letter, I don't know, something just popped, I felt I was at a distinct tilt, and I blurted out, No, no, just please bring me the freaking Paperwork, I am Requesting, and I thought when I Requested you had to do it!

And Dove said sadly, We do, Randy, when you Request, we have to do it.

Dove called the other Coordinators over and said, Larry, your little pal here has just Requested his Paperwork.

And Slippen said, I'll be damned.

What a waste, Delacourt said. This is one super kid.

One of our best, Andrews said.

Which was true, with me five times winning the Cooperative Spirit Award and once even the Denny O'Malley Prize, Denny O'Malley being this Assessor in Chicago, IL, struck down at age ten, who died with a smile on his face of leukemia.

Say what you will, it takes courage, Slippen said. Going after one's wife and all.

Yes and no, Delacourt said. If you, Larry, fall off a roof, does it help me to go tumbling after you?

But I am not your wife, Slippen said. Pregnant wife.

Wife or no, pregnant or no, Delacourt said. What we then have are two folks not feeling so good in terms of that pavement rushing up. No one is helped. Two are crushed. In effect three are crushed.

Baby makes three, Andrews said.

Baby does make three, said Delacourt.

Although anything is possible, Slippen said. You know, the two of them together, the three of them, maybe they could make a go of it—

Larry, whose side are you on? Dove said.

I am on all sides, Slippen said.

You see this thing from various perspectives, Andrews said.

Anyway, this is academic, Delacourt said. He has Requested his Paperwork and we must provide it.

His poor mother, Dove said. The sacrifices she made, and now this.

Oh, please, Slippen said. His mother.

Larry, sorry, did you say something? Dove said.

Which mother did he get? Slippen said.

Larry, please go to that Taste-and-Rate in Conference Room 6, Delacourt said. See how they are doing with those CheezWands.

Which mother did we give him? Slippen said. The redhead baking the pie? The blonde in the garden?

Larry, honestly, Dove said. Are you freaking out?

The brunette at prayer? Slippen said. Who, putting down her prayer book, says, as they all say: Stay where you are, do not get distracted, have a content and productive life, and I will be happy too?

Larry has been working too hard, Andrews said.

Plus taking prescription pills not prescribed to him, Delacourt said.

I have just had it with all of this, Slippen said and stomped off to the Observation Room.

Ha, that Larry! Dove said. He did not even know your mom, Randy.

Only we did, Andrews said.

Very nice lady, Delacourt said.

Made terrific pies, Dove said.

And I was like, Do you guys think I am that stupid, I know something is up, because how did Slippen know my mom's exact words said to me on my private Memory Loop?

Then there was this long silence.

And Delacourt said, Randy, when you were a child, you thought as a child. Do you know that one?

And I did know that one, it being LI 88643 for Trojan Ribbed.

Well, you are not a child anymore, he said. You are a man. A man in the middle of making a huge mistake.

We had hoped it would not come to this, Dove said.

Please accompany us to the Facility Cinema, Delacourt said.

Which that was a room off of Dining, with a big-screen plasma TV and Pottery Barn leather couch and a deluxe Orville Redenbacher Corn Magician.

Up on the big screen came this old-fashioned-looking film of a plain young girl with stringy hair, smoking a cigarette in a house that looked pretty bad.

And this guy unseen on the video said, Okay, tell us precisely why, in your own words.

And the girl said, Oh, I dunno, due to my relation with the dad, I got less than great baby interest?

Okay, said the unseen voice. And the money is not part?

Well, sure, yeah, I can always use money, she said.

But it is not the prime reason? the voice said. It being required that it not be the prime reason, but rather the prime reason might be, for example, your desire for a better life for your child?

Okay, she said.

Then they pulled back and you could see bashed-out windows with cardboard in them and the counters covered with dirty dishes and in the yard a car up on blocks.

And you have no objections to the terms and conditions? the voice said. Which you have read in their entirety?

It's all fine, the girl said.

Have you read it? the voice said.

I read in it, she said. Okay, okay, I read it cover to freaking cover.

And the name change you have no objection to? the voice said.

Okay, she said. Although why Randy?

And the No-Visit Clause you also have no objection to? the voice said.

Fine, she said, and took a big drag.

Then Dove tapped on the wall twice and the movie Paused.

Do you know who that lady is, Randy? he said.

No, I said.

Do you know that lady is your mom? he said.

No, I said.

Well, that lady is your mom, Randy, he said. We are sorry you had to learn it in this manner.

And I was like, Very funny, that is not my mom, my mom is pretty, with red hair in a bun.

Randy, we admit it, Delacourt said. We gave some of you stylized mothers, in your Memory Loops, for your own good, not wanting you to feel bad about who your real mothers were. But in this time of crisis we must give you the straight skinny. That is your real mother, Randy, that is your real former house, that is where you would have been raised, had your mother not answered our ad all those years ago, that is who you are. So much in us is hardwired! You cannot fight fate without some significant help from an intervening entity, such as us, such as our resources, which we have poured into you in good faith all these years. You are a prince, we have made you a prince. Please do not descend back into the muck.

Please reconsider, Randy, Dove said. Sleep on it.

Will you? Delacourt said. Will you at least think about it?

Tell the truth, that thing with my mom had freaked me out, it was like my foundation had fallen away, like at LI 83743 for Advil, where the guy's foundation of his house falls away and he thunks his head on the floor of Hell and thus needs a Advil, which the Devil has some but won't give him any.

So I said I would think about it.

As he left, Dove unhit Pause, and I had time to note many things on that video, such as that lady's teeth were not good, such as my chin and hers were similar, such as she referred to our dog as Shit Machine, which what kind of name is that for a dog, such as at one point they zoomed in on this little baby sitting on the floor in just a diaper, all dirty and looking sort of dumb, and I could see very plain it was me.

Just before Dinner, Dove came back in.

Randy, your Paperwork, per your Request, he said. Do you still want it?

I don't know, I said. I'm not sure.

You are making me very happy, Dove said.

And he sent in Tony from Catering with this intense Dinner of steak *au poivre* and our usual cheese tray with Alsatian olives, and a milkshake in my monogrammed cup, and while I watched *Sunset Terror Home* on the big screen, always a favorite, Bedtime passed and nobody came and got me, them letting me stay up as late as I wanted.

Later that night in my Privacy Tarp I was wakened by someone crawling in, which, hitting my Abercrombie & Fitch night-light, I saw it was Slippen.

Randy, I am so sorry for my part in all of this, he whispered. I just want to say you are a great kid and always have been since Day One and in truth I at times have felt you were more of a son than my own personal sons, and likewise with Carolyn, who was the daughter I never had.

Well I did not know what to say to that, it being so personal and all, plus he was like laying or lying practically right on top of me and I could smell wine on his breath. We had always learned in Religion that if something is making you uncomfortable you should just say it, so I just said it, I said, Sir, this is making me uncomfortable.

You know what is making me uncomfortable? he said. You farting around in here while poor Carolyn sits in the Lerner Center all alone, big as a house, scared to death. Randy, one only has one heart, and when that heart is breaking via thinking of what is in store for poor Carolyn, one can hardly be blamed for stepping in, can one? Can one? Randy, do you trust me?

He had always been good to me, having taught me so much, like how to hit a Wiffle and how to do a pushup, and once he even brought in this trough and taught me and Ed and Josh to fish, and how fun was that, all of us laughing and feeling around on the floor for the fish we kept dropping during those moments of involuntary blindness that would occur as various fish-related LIs flashed in our heads, like the talking whale for Stouffer's FishMeals (LI 38322), like the fish and loafs Jesus makes at LI 83722 and then that one dude goes, Lord, this bread is dry, can you not summon up some ButterSub?

I do trust you, I said.

Then come on, he said, and crawled out of my Privacy Tarp.

We crossed the Common Area and went past Catering, which I had never been that far before, and soon were standing in front of this door labeled Caution Do Not Open Without Facility Personnel Accompaniment.

Randy, do you know what is behind this door? Slippen said.

No, I said.

Take a look, he said.

And smiling a smile like that mother on Christmas morning at LI 98732 for Madpets.com, who throws off that tablecloth to reveal a real horse in their living room chewing on the rug, Slippen threw open that door.

Looking out, I saw no walls and no rug and no ceiling, only lawn and flowers, and above that a wide black sky with stars, which all of that made me a little dizzy, there being no glass between me and it.

Then Slippen very gently pushed me Out.

And I don't know, it is one thing to look out a window, but when you are Out, actually Out, that is something very powerful, and how embarrassing was that, because I could not help it, I went down flat on my gut, checking out those flowers, and the feeling of the one I chose was like the silk on that Hermès jacket I could never seem to get Reserved because Vance was always hogging it, except the flower was even better, it being very smooth and built in like layers? With the outside layer being yellow, and inside that a white thing like a bell, and inside the white bell-like thing were fifteen (I counted) smaller bell-like red things, and inside each red thing was an even smaller orange two-dingly-thing combo.

Which I was like, Dude, who thought this shit up? And though I knew very well from Religion it was God, still I had never thought so high of God as I did just then, seeing the kind of stuff He could do when He put His or Her mind to it.

Also amazing was, laying there on my gut, I was able to observe very slowly some grass, on a blade basis! And what I found was, each blade is its total own blade, they are not all exact copies as I had always thought when looking at the Rustic Village Apartments lawn from the much-coveted window seat. No, each blade had a special design of up-and-down lines on it, plus some blades were wider than others, and some were yellow, with some even having little holes that I guessed had been put there via bugs chewing them?

By now as you know I am sometimes a kidder, with Humor always ranked by my peers as one of my Principal Positives on my Yearly Evaluation, but being totally serious? If I live one million years I will never forget all the beautiful things I saw and experienced in that kick-ass outside yard.

Isn't it something? Slippen said. But look, stand up, here is something even better.

And I stood up, and here came this bland person in blue scrubs, and my first thought was, Ouch, why not accentuate that killer bone structure with some makeup, and also what is up with that dull flat hair, did you never hear of Bumble & Bumble Plasma Volumizer?

And then she said my name.

Not my name of Randy but my real name of Jon.

Which is how I first got the shock of going, Oh my God, this poor washed-out gal is my Carolyn.

And wow was her belly ever bigger.

Then she touched my face very tender and said, *The suspense of waiting is over and this year's Taurus far exceeds expectations already high in this humble farming community.*

And I was like, Carolyn?

And she was like, *The beauty of a reunion by the sea of this mother and son will not soon again be parted and all one can say is amen and open another bag of chips, which by spreading on a thin cream on the face strips away the harsh effect of the destructive years.*

Then she hugged me, which is when I saw the gaping hole in her neck where her gargadisk had formerly been.

But tell you the truth, even with a DermaFilled® neckhole and nada makeup and huge baby belly, still she looked so pretty, like someone had put a light inside her and switched it on.

But I guess it is true what they say at LI 23005, life is full of ironic surprises, where that lady in a bikini puts on sunscreen and then there is this nuclear war and she takes a sip of her drink only she has been like burned to a crisp, because all that time Out not one LI had come up, as if my mind was stymied or holding its breath, but now all of the sudden here came all these LIs of Flowers, due to I had seen those real-life flowers, such as big talking daisies for Polaroid (LI 10119), such as that kid who drops a jar of applesauce but his anal mom totally melts when he hands her a sunflower (LI 22365), such as the big word PFIZER that as you pan closer is made of roses (LI 88753), such as LI 73486, where as you fly over wildflowers to a Acura Legend on a cliff the announcer goes, Everyone is entitled to their own individual promised land.

And I blinked on Pause but it did not Pause, and blinked on End but it did not End.

Then up came LIs of Grass, due to I had seen that lawn, such as an old guy sprinkling grass seed while repetitively checking out his neighbor girl who is sunbathing, and then in spring he only has grass in that one spot (LI 11121), such as LI 76567, with a sweeping lawn leading up to a mansion for Grey Poupon, such as (LI 00391) these grass blades screaming in terror as this lawnmower approaches but then when they see it is a Toro they put on little party hats.

Randy, can you hear me? Slippen said. Do you see Carolyn? She has been waiting out here an hour. During that hour she has been going where she wants, looking at whatever she likes. See what she is doing now? Simply enjoying the night.

And that was true. Between flinches and blinks on End I could dimly persee her sitting cross-legged near me, not flinching, not blinking, just looking pretty in the moonlight with a look on her face of deep concern for me.

Randy, this could all be yours, Slippen was saying. This world, this girl!

And then I must have passed out.

Because when I came to I was sitting inside that door marked Caution Do Not Open Without Facility Personnel Accompaniment, with my Paperwork in my lap and all my Coordinators standing around me.

Randy, Dove said. Larry Slippen here claims that you wish to Exit. Is this the case? Did you in fact Request your Paperwork, then thrust it at him?

Okay, I said. Yes.

So they rushed me to Removals, where this nurse named Vivian was like, Welcome, please step behind that screen and strip off, then put these on.

Which I did, I dropped my Calvin Klein khakis and socks and removed my Country Road shirt as well as my Old Navy boxers, and put on the dreaded blue scrubs.

Best of luck, Randy, Slippen said, leaning in the door. You'll be in my prayers.

Out out out, Vivian said.

Then she gave me this Patient Permission Form, which the first question was, Is patient aware of risk of significantly reduced postoperative brain function?

And I wrote, Yes.

And then it said, Does patient authorize Dr. Edward Kenton to perform all procedures associated with a complete gargadisk removal, including but not limited to e-wire severance, scar-tissue removal, forceful Kinney Maneuver (if necessary to fully disengage gargadisk), suturing, and postoperative cleansing using the Foreman Vacuum Device, should adequate cleaning not be achievable via traditional methods?

And I wrote, Yes.

I have been here since Wednesday, due to Dr. Kenton is at a wedding.

I want to thank Vivian for all this paper, and Mr. Slippen for being the father I never had, and Carolyn for not giving up on me, and Dr. Kenton, assuming he does not screw it up.

(Ha ha, you know what, Dr. Kenton, I am just messing with you, even if you do screw it up, I know you tried your best. Only please do not screw it up, ha ha ha!)

Last night they let Carolyn send me a fax from the Lerner Center, and it said, I may not look my best or be the smartest apple on the applecart, but believe me, in time I will again bake those ninety-two pies.

And I faxed back, However you are is fine with me, I will see you soon, look for me, I will be the one with the ripped-up neck, smacking himself in the head!

No matter what, she faxed, at least we will now have a life, that life dreamed of by so many, living in freedom with all joys and all fears, let it begin, I say, the balloon of our excitement will go up up up, to that land which is the land of true living, we will not be denied!

I love you, I wrote.

Love you too, she wrote.

Which I thought that was pretty good, it being so simple and all, and it gave me hope.

Because maybe we can do it.

Maybe we can come to be normal, and sit on our porch at night, the porch of our own house, like at LI 87326, where the mom knits and the dad plays guitar and the little kid works very industrious with his Speak & Spell, and when we talk, it will make total sense, and when we look at the stars and moon, if choosing to do that, we will not think of LI 44387, where the moon frowns down at this dude due to he is hiding in his barn eating Rebel CornBells instead of proclaiming his SnackLove aloud, we will not think of LI 09383, where this stork flies through some crying stars who are crying due to the baby who is getting born is the future Mountain Dew Guy, we will not think of that alien at LI 33081 descending from the sky going, Just what is this thing called a Cinnabon?

In terms of what we will think of, I do not know. When I think of what we will think of, I draw this like total blank and get scared, so scared my Peripheral Area flares up green, like when I have drank too much soda, but tell the truth I am curious, I think I am ready to try.

QUESTIONS FOR DISCUSSION

Why does Saunders create a world where some people live out their lives in market research facilities and departure requires hazardous surgery?

1. Why is Jon unable to imagine speaking his feelings without referring to advertisements? Why does he say, "I want to possess all the articulate I can"? (424)

2. Why does Saunders have Jon attribute a biblical quotation— "when you were a child, you thought as a child"—to an advertisement? (438)

3. Why is the process of gargadisk removal and its potential consequences described in such graphic detail?

4. Why does Carolyn consistently call the main character Jon instead of Randy?

When Dove asks Jon if he thrust his Exit Paperwork at Slippen, why does Jon first say "okay" and then "yes"? (443)

1. Why does Jon initially request his Exit Paperwork after reading Carolyn's letter?

2. When Delacourt and Andrews ask Slippen whose side he is on, why does Slippen say, "I am on all sides"? (437)

3. Why does Slippen push Jon out of the facility and arrange for Carolyn to meet him outside?

4. Why does Jon feel "ready to try" life outside the facility despite the possible complications of gargadisk removal? (445)

FOR FURTHER REFLECTION

1. Do you think advertising reflects existing social reality, or does it create that reality?

2. Why are brand names so important to many people?

3. Do you agree with Delacourt's statement that "so much in us is hardwired! You cannot fight fate without some significant help from an intervening entity"?

4. Do you think the vision of the future described in "Jon" is within the bounds of possibility?

Time Capsule Found on the Dead Planet

Margaret Atwood

1. In the first age, we created gods. We carved them out of wood; there was still such a thing as wood, then. We forged them from shining metals and painted them on temple walls. They were gods of many kinds, and goddesses as well. Sometimes they were cruel and drank our blood, but also they gave us rain and sunshine, favourable winds, good harvests, fertile animals, many children. A million birds flew over us then, a million fish swam in our seas.

Our gods had horns on their heads, or moons, or sealy fins, or the beaks of eagles. We called them All-Knowing, we called them Shining One. We knew we were not orphans. We smelled the earth and rolled in it; its juices ran down our chins.

2. In the second age, we created money. This money was also made of shining metals. It had two faces: on one side was a severed head, that of a king or some other noteworthy person; on the other face was something else, something that would give us comfort: a bird, a fish, a fur-bearing animal. This was all that remained of our former gods. The money was small in size, and each of us would carry some of it with him every day, as close to the skin as possible. We could not eat this money, wear it, or burn it for warmth; but as if by magic it could be changed into such things. The money was mysterious, and we were in awe of it. If you had enough of it, it was said, you would be able to fly.

3. In the third age, money became a god. It was all-powerful, and out of control. It began to talk. It began to create on its own. It created feasts and famines, songs of joy, lamentations. It created greed and hunger, which were its two faces. Towers of glass rose at its name, were destroyed and rose again. It began to eat things. It ate whole forests, croplands, and the lives of children. It ate armies, ships, and cities. No one could stop it. To have it was a sign of grace.

4. In the fourth age, we created deserts. Our deserts were of several kinds, but they had one thing in common: nothing grew there. Some were made of cement, some were made of various poisons, some of baked earth. We made these deserts from the desire for more money and from despair at the lack of it. Wars, plagues, and famines visited us, but we did not stop in our industrious creation of deserts. At last all wells were poisoned, all rivers ran with filth, all seas were dead; there was no land left to grow food.

Some of our wise men turned to the contemplation of deserts. A stone in the sand in the setting sun could be very beautiful, they said. Deserts were tidy, because there were no weeds in them, nothing that crawled. Stay in the desert long enough, and you could apprehend the absolute. The number zero was holy.

5. You who have come here from some distant world, to this dry lake-shore and this cairn, and to this cylinder of brass, in which on the last day of all our recorded days I place our final words:

Pray for us, who once, too, thought we could fly.

Silent Spring
(selection)

Rachel Carson

A Fable for Tomorrow

There was once a town in the heart of America where all life seemed to live in harmony with its surroundings. The town lay in the midst of a checkerboard of prosperous farms, with fields of grain and hillsides of orchards where, in spring, white clouds of bloom drifted above the green fields. In autumn, oak and maple and birch set up a blaze of color that flamed and flickered across a backdrop of pines. Then foxes barked in the hills and deer silently crossed the fields, half hidden in the mists of the fall mornings.

Along the roads, laurel, viburnum and alder, great ferns and wild-flowers delighted the traveler's eye through much of the year. Even in winter the roadsides were places of beauty, where countless birds came to feed on the berries and on the seedheads of the dried weeds rising above the snow. The countryside was, in fact, famous for the abundance and variety of its bird life, and when the flood of migrants was pouring through in spring and fall, people traveled from great distances to observe them. Others came to fish the streams, which flowed clear and cold out of the hills and contained shady pools where trout lay. So it had been from the days many years ago when the first settlers raised their houses, sank their wells, and built their barns.

Then a strange blight crept over the area and everything began to change. Some evil spell had settled on the community: mysterious maladies swept the flocks of chickens; the cattle and sheep sickened and died. Everywhere was a shadow of death. The farmers spoke of much illness among their families. In the town the doctors had become more and more puzzled by new kinds of sickness appearing among their patients. There had been several sudden and unexplained deaths, not only among adults but even among children, who would be stricken suddenly while at play and die within a few hours.

There was a strange stillness. The birds, for example—where had they gone? Many people spoke of them, puzzled and disturbed. The feeding stations in the backyards were deserted. The few birds seen anywhere were moribund; they trembled violently and could not fly. It was a spring without voices. On the mornings that had once throbbed with the dawn chorus of robins, catbirds, doves, jays, wrens, and scores of other bird voices there was now no sound; only silence lay over the fields and woods and marsh.

On the farms the hens brooded, but no chicks hatched. The farmers complained that they were unable to raise any pigs—the litters were small and the young survived only a few days. The apple trees were coming into bloom but no bees droned among the blossoms, so there was no pollination and there would be no fruit.

The roadsides, once so attractive, were now lined with browned and withered vegetation as though swept by fire. These, too, were silent, deserted by all living things. Even the streams were now lifeless. Anglers no longer visited them, for all the fish had died.

In the gutters under the eaves and between the shingles of the roofs, a white granular powder still showed a few patches; some weeks before it had fallen like snow upon the roofs and the lawns, the fields and streams.

No witchcraft, no enemy action had silenced the rebirth of new life in this stricken world. The people had done it themselves.

This town does not actually exist, but it might easily have a thousand counterparts in America or elsewhere in the world. I know of no community that has experienced all the misfortunes I describe. Yet every one of these disasters has actually happened somewhere, and many real communities have already suffered a substantial number of them. A grim specter has crept upon us almost unnoticed, and this imagined tragedy may easily become a stark reality we all shall know.

What has already silenced the voices of spring in countless towns in America? This book is an attempt to explain.

The Obligation to Endure

The history of life on earth has been a history of interaction between living things and their surroundings. To a large extent, the physical form and the habits of the earth's vegetation and its animal life have been molded by the environment. Considering the whole span of earthly time, the opposite effect, in which life actually modifies its surroundings, has been relatively slight. Only within the moment of time represented by the present century has one species—man—acquired significant power to alter the nature of his world.

During the past quarter century this power has not only increased to one of disturbing magnitude but it has changed in character. The most alarming of all man's assaults upon the environment is the contamination of air, earth, rivers, and sea with dangerous and even lethal materials. This pollution is for the most part irrecoverable; the chain of evil it initiates not only in the world that must support life but in living tissues is for the most part irreversible. In this now universal contamination of the environment, chemicals are the sinister and little-recognized partners of radiation in changing the very nature of the world—the very nature of its life. Strontium 90, released through nuclear explosions into the air, comes to earth in rain or drifts down as fallout, lodges in soil, enters into the grass or corn or wheat grown there, and in time takes up its abode in the bones of a human being, there to remain until his death. Similarly, chemicals sprayed on croplands or forests or gardens lie long in soil, entering into living organisms, passing from one to another in a chain of poisoning and death. Or they pass mysteriously by underground streams until they emerge and, through the alchemy of air and sunlight, combine into new forms that kill vegetation, sicken cattle, and work unknown harm on those who drink from once pure wells. As Albert Schweitzer has said, "Man can hardly even recognize the devils of his own creation."

It took hundreds of millions of years to produce the life that now inhabits the earth—eons of time in which that developing and evolving and diversifying life reached a state of adjustment and balance with its surroundings. The environment, rigorously shaping and directing the life it supported, contained elements that were hostile as well as supporting. Certain rocks gave out dangerous radiation; even within the light of the sun, from which all life draws its energy, there were short-wave radiations with power to injure. Given time—time not in years but in millennia—life adjusts, and a balance has been reached. For time is the essential ingredient; but in the modern world there is no time.

The rapidity of change and the speed with which new situations are created follow the impetuous and heedless pace of man rather than the deliberate pace of nature. Radiation is no longer merely the background radiation of rocks, the bombardment of cosmic rays, the ultraviolet of the sun that have existed before there was any life on earth; radiation is now the unnatural creation of man's tampering with the atom. The chemicals to which life is asked to make its adjustment are no longer merely the calcium and silica and copper and all the rest of the minerals washed out of the rocks and carried in rivers to the sea; they are the synthetic creations of man's inventive mind, brewed in his laboratories, and having no counterparts in nature.

To adjust to these chemicals would require time on the scale that is nature's; it would require not merely the years of a man's life but the life of generations. And even this, were it by some miracle possible, would be futile, for the new chemicals come from our laboratories in an endless stream; almost five hundred annually find their way into actual use in the United States alone. The figure is staggering and its implications are not easily grasped—500 new chemicals to which the bodies of men and animals are required somehow to adapt each year, chemicals totally outside the limits of biologic experience.

Among them are many that are used in man's war against nature. Since the mid-1940s over 200 basic chemicals have been created for use in killing insects, weeds, rodents, and other organisms described in the modern vernacular as "pests"; and they are sold under several thousand different brand names.

These sprays, dusts, and aerosols are now applied almost universally to farms, gardens, forests, and homes—nonselective chemicals that have the power to kill every insect, the "good" and the "bad," to still the song of birds and the leaping of fish in the streams, to coat the leaves with a deadly film, and to linger on in soil—all this though the intended target may be only a few weeds or insects. Can anyone believe it is possible to lay down such a barrage of poisons on the surface of the earth without making it unfit for all life? They should not be called "insecticides," but "biocides."

The whole process of spraying seems caught up in an endless spiral. Since DDT was released for civilian use, a process of escalation has been going on in which ever more toxic materials must be found. This has happened because insects, in a triumphant vindication of Darwin's principle of the survival of the fittest, have evolved super races immune to the particular insecticide used, hence a deadlier one has always to be developed—and then a deadlier one than that. It has happened also because, for reasons to be described later, destructive insects often undergo a "flareback," or resurgence, after spraying, in numbers greater than before. Thus the chemical war is never won, and all life is caught in its violent crossfire.

Along with the possibility of the extinction of mankind by nuclear war, the central problem of our age has therefore become the contamination of man's total environment with such substances of incredible potential for harm—substances that accumulate in the tissues of plants and animals and even penetrate the germ cells to shatter or alter the very material of heredity upon which the shape of the future depends.

Some would-be architects of our future look toward a time when it will be possible to alter the human germ plasm by design. But we may easily be doing so now by inadvertence, for many chemicals, like radiation, bring about gene mutations. It is ironic to think that man might determine his own future by something so seemingly trivial as the choice of an insect spray.

All this has been risked—for what? Future historians may well be amazed by our distorted sense of proportion. How could intelligent beings seek to control a few unwanted species by a method that contaminated the entire environment and brought the threat of disease and death even to their own kind? Yet this is precisely what we have done. We have done it, moreover, for reasons that collapse the moment we examine them. We are told that the enormous and expanding use of pesticides is necessary to maintain farm production. Yet is our real problem not one of *overproduction*? Our farms, despite measures to remove acreages from production and to pay farmers *not* to produce, have yielded such a staggering excess of crops that the American taxpayer in 1962 is paying out more than one billion dollars a year as the total carrying cost of the surplus-food storage program. And is the situation helped when one branch of the Agriculture Department tries to reduce production while another states, as it did in 1958, "It is believed generally that reduction of crop acreages under provisions of the Soil Bank will stimulate interest in use of chemicals to obtain maximum production on the land retained in crops."

All this is not to say there is no insect problem and no need of control. I am saying, rather, that control must be geared to realities, not to mythical situations, and that the methods employed must be such that they do not destroy us along with the insects.

The problem whose attempted solution has brought such a train of disaster in its wake is an accompaniment of our modern way of life. Long before the age of man, insects inhabited the earth—a group of extraordinarily varied and adaptable beings. Over the course of time since man's advent, a small percentage of the more than half a million species of insects have come into conflict with human welfare in two principal ways: as competitors for the food supply and as carriers of human disease.

Disease-carrying insects become important where human beings are crowded together, especially under conditions where sanitation is poor, as in time of natural disaster or war or in situations of extreme poverty and deprivation. Then control of some sort becomes necessary. It is a sobering fact, however, as we shall presently see, that the method of massive chemical control has had only limited success, and also threatens to worsen the very conditions it is intended to curb.

Under primitive agricultural conditions the farmer had few insect problems. These arose with the intensification of agriculture—the devotion of immense acreages to a single crop. Such a system set the stage for explosive increases in specific insect populations. Single-crop farming does not take advantage of the principles by which nature works; it is agriculture as an engineer might conceive it to be. Nature has introduced great variety into the landscape, but man has displayed a passion for simplifying it. Thus he undoes the built-in checks and balances by which nature holds the species within bounds. One important natural check is a limit on the amount of suitable habitat for each species. Obviously then, an insect that lives on wheat can build up its population to much higher levels on a farm devoted to wheat than on one in which wheat is intermingled with other crops to which the insect is not adapted.

The same thing happens in other situations. A generation or more ago, the towns of large areas of the United States lined their streets with the noble elm tree. Now the beauty they hopefully created is threatened with complete destruction as disease sweeps through the elms, carried by a beetle that would have only limited chance to build up large populations and to spread from tree to tree if the elms were only occasional trees in a richly diversified planting.

Another factor in the modern insect problem is one that must be viewed against a background of geologic and human history: the spreading of thousands of different kinds of organisms from their native homes to invade new territories. This worldwide migration has been studied and graphically described by the British ecologist Charles Elton in his recent book *The Ecology of Invasions*. During the Cretaceous Period, some hundred million years ago, flooding seas cut many land bridges between continents, and living things found themselves confined in what Elton calls "colossal separate nature reserves." There, isolated from others of their kind, they developed many new species. When some of the land masses were joined again, about 15 million years ago, these species began to move out into new territories—a movement that is not only still in progress but is now receiving considerable assistance from man.

The importation of plants is the primary agent in the modern spread of species, for animals have almost invariably gone along with the plants, quarantine being a comparatively recent and not completely effective innovation. The United States Office of Plant Introduction alone has introduced almost 200,000 species and varieties of plants from all over the world. Nearly half of the 180 or so major insect enemies of plants in the United States are accidental imports from abroad, and most of them have come as hitchhikers on plants.

In new territory, out of reach of the restraining hand of the natural enemies that kept down its numbers in its native land, an invading plant or animal is able to become enormously abundant. Thus it is no accident that our most troublesome insects are introduced species.

These invasions, both the naturally occurring and those dependent on human assistance, are likely to continue indefinitely. Quarantine and massive chemical campaigns are only extremely expensive ways of buying time. We are faced, according to Dr. Elton, "with a life-and-death need not just to find new technological means of suppressing this plant or that animal"; instead we need the basic knowledge of animal populations and their relations to their surroundings that will "promote an even balance and damp down the explosive power of outbreaks and new invasions."

Much of the necessary knowledge is now available but we do not use it. We train ecologists in our universities and even employ them in our governmental agencies but we seldom take their advice. We allow the chemical death rain to fall as though there were no alternative, whereas in fact there are many, and our ingenuity could soon discover many more if given opportunity.

Have we fallen into a mesmerized state that makes us accept as inevitable that which is inferior or detrimental, as though having lost the will or the vision to demand that which is good? Such thinking, in the words of the ecologist Paul Shepard, "idealizes life with only its head out of water, inches above the limits of toleration of the corruption of its own environment. . . . Why should we tolerate a diet of weak poisons, a home in insipid surroundings, a circle of acquaintances who are not quite our enemies, the noise of motors with just enough relief to prevent insanity? Who would want to live in a world which is just not quite fatal?"

Yet such a world is pressed upon us. The crusade to create a chemically sterile, insect-free world seems to have engendered a fanatic zeal on the part of many specialists and most of the so-called control agencies. On every hand there is evidence that those engaged in

spraying operations exercise a ruthless power. "The regulatory ento-
mologists . . . function as prosecutor, judge and jury, tax assessor and
collector and sheriff to enforce their own orders," said Connecticut
entomologist Neely Turner. The most flagrant abuses go unchecked in
both state and federal agencies.

It is not my contention that chemical insecticides must never be
used. I do contend that we have put poisonous and biologically potent
chemicals indiscriminately into the hands of persons largely or wholly
ignorant of their potentials for harm. We have subjected enormous
numbers of people to contact with these poisons, without their consent and often without their knowledge. If the Bill of Rights contains
no guarantee that a citizen shall be secure against lethal poisons distributed either by private individuals or by public officials, it is surely
only because our forefathers, despite their considerable wisdom and
foresight, could conceive of no such problem.

I contend, furthermore, that we have allowed these chemicals to
be used with little or no advance investigation of their effect on soil,
water, wildlife, and man himself. Future generations are unlikely to
condone our lack of prudent concern for the integrity of the natural
world that supports all life.

There is still very limited awareness of the nature of the threat.
This is an era of specialists, each of whom sees his own problem and
is unaware of or intolerant of the larger frame into which it fits. It is
also an era dominated by industry, in which the right to make a dollar
at whatever cost is seldom challenged. When the public protests, confronted with some obvious evidence of damaging results of pesticide
applications, it is fed little tranquilizing pills of half-truth. We urgently
need an end to these false assurances, to the sugarcoating of unpalatable facts. It is the public that is being asked to assume the risks that
the insect controllers calculate. The public must decide whether it
wishes to continue on the present road, and it can do so only when in
full possession of the facts. In the words of Jean Rostand, "The obligation to endure gives us the right to know."

QUESTIONS FOR DISCUSSION

In Atwood's piece, is there any indication that the course of history the writer outlines could have been reversed or changed?

1. How did the subjects of this piece know they "were not orphans"? (449)

2. Why does the writer speak of deserts as creations, and not as a consequence?

3. Why was the number zero "holy"? (450)

4. What are the similarities between the "we" in the first four sections and the "you" in the last section?

What does Carson mean when she writes that "in the modern world there is no time"? (454)

1. Why are the citizens in the fable unaware that they are the ones who have damaged the environment? Why does Carson then go on to argue that humans are conscious of the damage we are doing but choose to ignore it?

2. Who are the "would-be architects of our future"? (455)

3. How does Carson suggest we use the "necessary knowledge" that is available to solve the environmental problems she outlines? (458)

4. According to Carson, what are humans enduring and why is it an obligation?

FOR FURTHER REFLECTION

1. Do the problems suggested by Atwood's piece lend themselves to the same kinds of solutions that Carson points to?

2. In which of Atwood's "ages" might the citizens of Carson's "A Fable for Tomorrow" exist?

3. Can a utopia ever be achieved by making changes to an existing society, or is it necessary for citizens to start from scratch?

4. Could the problems arising from humanity's actions be anticipated more in the world described by Atwood or by Carson?

Acknowledgments

All possible care has been taken to trace ownership and secure permission for each selection in this anthology. The Great Books Foundation wishes to thank the following authors, publishers, and representatives for permission to reproduce copyrighted material:

The Ones Who Walk Away from Omelas, from THE WIND'S TWELVE QUARTERS, by Ursula K. Le Guin. Copyright © 1973 by Ursula K. Le Guin. Reproduced by permission of Curtis Brown, Ltd.

Selection from UTOPIA, by Thomas More, translated with an introduction by Paul Turner. Copyright © 1961, 2003 by Paul Turner. Reproduced by permission of Penguin Books Ltd.

Utopia, from POEMS NEW AND COLLECTED 1957–1997, by Wislawa Szymborska, translated by Stanislaw Baranczak and Clare Cavanagh. Copyright © 1976 by the Wislawa Szymborska Foundation. English translation copyright © 1998 by Houghton Mifflin Harcourt Publishing Company. Reproduced by permission of Houghton Mifflin Harcourt Publishing Company.

Selection from ILIAD, by Homer, translated by Stanley Lombardo. Copyright © 1997 by Hackett Publishing Company, Inc. Reproduced by permission of Hackett Publishing Company, Inc.

The Shield of Achilles, from W. H. AUDEN COLLECTED POEMS, by W. H. Auden. Copyright © 1952, 1955 by W. H. Auden, renewed 1980 by the Estate of W. H. Auden. Print edition reproduced by permission of Random House LLC. Ebook edition reproduced by permission of Curtis Brown, Ltd.

Selection from A PARADISE BUILT IN HELL, by Rebecca Solnit. Copyright © 2009 by Rebecca Solnit. Reproduced by permission of Penguin Group (USA) LLC.

Time, by Riichi Yokomitsu, from MODERN JAPANESE LITERATURE. Copyright © 1956 by Grove Press. Reproduced by permission of Grove/Atlantic, Inc.

On the Cannibals, from THE COMPLETE ESSAYS, by Michel de Montaigne, translated with an introduction and notes by M. A. Screech. Translation copyright © 1987, 1991 by M. A. Screech. Reproduced by permission of Penguin Books Ltd.

The Dream of a Ridiculous Man, from THE BEST SHORT STORIES OF DOSTOEVSKY, by Fyodor Dostoevsky, translated by David Magarshack. Copyright © 2001 by Random House. Reproduced by permission of Random House LLC.

Selection from MENCIUS, by Mencius, translated with an introduction by D. C. Lau. Copyright © 1970 by D. C. Lau. Reproduced by permission of Penguin Classics.

Selection from THE POLITICS, by Aristotle, translated by T. A. Sinclair. Copyright © 1962 by the Estate of T. A. Sinclair. Revised translation copyright © 1981 by Trevor J. Saunders. Reproduced by permission of Penguin Books Ltd.

A Framework for Utopia, from ANARCHY, STATE, AND UTOPIA, by Robert Nozick. Copyright © 1974 by Basic Books, Inc. Reproduced by permission of Basic Books, Inc., a member of the Perseus Books Group.

The Economic Basis of the Withering Away of the State, from THE LENIN ANTHOLOGY, by Vladimir Lenin, edited by Robert C. Tucker. Copyright © 1975 by W. W. Norton & Company, Inc. Reproduced by permission of W. W. Norton & Company, Inc.

Selection from WE, by Yevgeny Zamyatin, translated by Gregory Zilboorg. Copyright © 1924 by E. P. Dutton & Co., Inc., copyright renewed 1952 by Gregory Zilboorg. Reproduced by permission of Dutton, a division of Penguin Group (USA) LLC.

The Machine Stops, from THE ETERNAL MOMENT AND OTHER STORIES, by E. M. Forster. Copyright © 1928 by Houghton Mifflin Harcourt Publishing Company, renewed 1956 by E. M. Forster. Print edition reproduced by permission of Houghton Mifflin Harcourt Publishing Company. Ebook edition reproduced by permission of The Society of Authors as the Literary Representative of the Estate of E. M. Forster.

Black Box, by Jennifer Egan. Copyright © 2012 by Jennifer Egan. Reproduced by permission of the author. All rights reserved.

Jon, from IN PERSUASION NATION: STORIES, by George Saunders. Copyright © 2006 by George Saunders. Reproduced by permission of Riverhead Books, an imprint of Penguin Group (USA) LLC.

Time Capsule from the Dead Planet, from IN OTHER WORLDS: SF AND THE HUMAN IMAGINATION, by Margaret Atwood. Copyright © 2011 by O. W. Toad Ltd. Reproduced by permission of Nan A. Talese, a division of Random House LLC.

Selection from SILENT SPRING, by Rachel Carson. Copyright © 1962 by Rachel L. Carson, renewed 1990 by Roger Christie. Print edition reproduced by permission of Houghton Mifflin Harcourt Publishing Company. Ebook edition reproduced by permission of Frances Collin, Trustee.

About the cover
The cover image shows a ventilation stack from the Unité d'Habitation (completed in 1952) in Marseille, France. This residential development was designed by modernist architect and urban planner Le Corbusier, and aimed to offer a new, modern way of living in the postwar world.